TEARS OF RAGE

Part Three:

ARMS OF THE STORM

A Novel By:
M Todd Gallowglas

M Todd Gallowglas

9 8 7 6 5 4 3 2 1 0

Other books by M Todd Gallowglas:

TEARS OF RAGE
First Chosen
Once We Were Like Wolves
Judge of Dooms
A Rise of Lesser Gods*

Jaludin's Road

Halloween Jack and the Devil's Gate
Halloween Jack and the Curse of Frost
Halloween Jack and the Red Emperor

The Dragon Bone Flute
Legacy of the Dragon Bone Flute
Legend of the Dragon Bone Flute

Spellpunk*

*Forthcoming

Arms of the Storm

For Robert and Mathew,
Thanks for giving me some of my best stories.

Acknowledgements

Here we go again into one of the hardest parts of writing a book.

First and foremost, I have to thank my wife, Robin. She's largely the reason why I gathered up the courage to dive into the Darwinian jungle of the self-publishing food chain. She keeps me going even when the writing gets tough, especially with this volume, which I wouldn't have finished without her pointing to my writing space and telling me, "Suck it up, go sit down, and write me a novel."

Damon Stone, for being there at the very beginning of this writing thing I started so many years ago.

My beta readers: Penny, Ash, and Christopher. You guys really made the book better.

My editor, Durelle, for pointing out the very little things.

I spend a lot of my time writing outside of the house. Thanks to Josie, Simon, Henry, and all the staff at De'Vere's Pub for the smiles, encouragement, and giving me the perfect place to launch a writing career. Also, thanks to all the wonderful coffee pushers at my local Starbucks in Lincoln, CA for keeping me caffeinated.

Ed Litfin and Alyxx Duggins for the spectacular cover work.

The Genre Underground guys: Christopher "Arbiter Codex" Kellen, A. E. "Brood of Bones" Marling, Robert "Hero Always Wins" Eaton, Dave "Stalker Squadron" Meek, and M.D. "Allmother's Fire" Kenning. (Yes, those are shameless plugs.)

James Rollins, Steven Erikson, Ian C. Esslemont, Brandon Sanderson, Robin Hobb, Jennifer Brozek, and David Brinn for the kind words and support (whether they knew they were giving it or not) for a lowly Indie writer like me.

Sean Greathorn for the title, and for introducing me to some of the great works of fantasy that helped shape me as a writer.

Finally, my father and mother, who supported my imagination in too many ways to count over the years, for making it okay to dream the big dreams.

Dramatis Personæ

The Morigahnti

- Julianna Taraen – The Lord Morigahn, High Priest of Grandfather Shadow. Duchess and last member of the Taraen family.
- Parshyval Thaedus – A baron and Morigahnti Fist captain. Called "Parsh" by those close to him.
- Korrin Sontam – A Morigahnti in Parsh's Fist.
- Nathan Sontam – Korrin's brother, also of Parsh's Fist.
- Wyndolen Sontam – Nathan's wife, called Wynd, also of Parsh's Fist.
- Aurell Palment – A Morigahnti of Parsh's Fist.
- Sandré Collaen – Prince of House Aesin and a Morigahnti Fist captain.
- Alerick Thaedus – A Count. Son to the late Allifar Thaedus. A Morigahnti of Sandré's Fist.
- Charise Garieth – A viscountess. Julianna's childhood friend.
- Karstyn Agostan – A lord and Morigahnti of Sandré's Fist.
- Haden – Captain of the *Stormrider*.
- Aniya Dashette – A Morigahnti serving as a protector to Josephine Adryck.

The Vara

- Dyrk – Commander of the Vara of Koma City.
- Paedrik Sardon – Dyrk's second in command.
- Staephyn Rool – A sergeant of the Johki City Vara.
- Kaenyth Rool – A Vara of Johki City. Staephyn's Nephew.
- Rayce Rool – A Vara of Johki City. Staephyn's Nephew. Kaenyth's Cousin.
- Gabryl Raesu – A minor noble.
- Coltaenan Tuada – Called "Colt." A baronet.

The Komati

- Sylvie Raelle – A countess, prisoner of the Brotherhood of the Night, lover to Carmine D'Mario.
- Colette – Julianna's maid, prisoner of the Brotherhood of the Night.
- Faelin vara'Traejyn – A bastard wanderer. Named by Grandfather Shadow to protect Julianna.
- Damian Adryck – Known also as Zephyr. A smuggler and fugitive of Kingdom Justice.

- Xander Rosha – Damian's half-brother. Volunteer of the Draqon Armies of the Kingdom of the Sun.
- Josephine Adryck – An aging noble lady.
- Donal Bastian – An innkeeper in Johki City.
- Tarshiva Bastian – Donal Bastian's daughter.
- Gareth – A smuggler and gun runner.
- Tade – A street tough.
- Layla – A servant in the Governor's Palace.
- Alyxandros Vivaen – Julianna's uncle. Follower of Yrgaeshkil.

Kingdom of the Sun

- Octavio Salvatore – Kingdom Governor of Koma.
- Portia Salvatore – Octavio's wife.
- Hardin Thorinson – Adept of Old Uncle Night.
- Carmine D'Mario – Half-blood noble of House Floraen and Komati blood.
- Rosella Andres – A High Blood of House Floraen. Cousin to both Carmine and the Sun King.
- Syr Graegyr Vaesna – Adept of Grandfather Shadow. Engaged to Rosella.
- Luciano Salvatore – House Floraen Inquisitor.
- Sabina Maedoc – An Adept of House Aernacht.
- Don Gianni D'Mario yp Caenacht – An Adept of House Aernacht
- Jorgen – A Nightbrother
- Brynn – A Nightbrother
- Kraetor Ilsaen – A High Blood of House Kaesiak. First Adept of Grandfather Shadow.
- Czenzi – Kraetor's Apprentice.
- Tamaz Aegotha – An Adept of Grandfather Shadow.
- Lancyl Maedoc – An Adept of Mother Earth.
- Larayne – A servant in the Governor's Palace.
- Flirt – A human woman assigned to the White Draqon Garrison of Koma City.

Others

- Razka – A Stormseeker.
- Thyr – A Stormcrow.
- Raze – A Stormcrow.
- Kysh – A Stormcrow.
- Black Claw – A White Draqon, in command of the Koma City Garrison.
- Barrier – A White Draqon.

- ➤ Smiles – A White Draqon, in Command of the Honor Guard of the Governor's Palace in Koma City.
- ➤ Plague – A White Draqon.
- ➤ Fury – A White Draqon.
- ➤ Kavala
- ➤ Maxian, sometimes called Smoke.

Celestials and Infernals

- ➤ Grandfather Shadow – Known also as Galad'Ysoysa. A Greater God.
- ➤ Yrgaeshkil – The Mother of Daemyns, Goddess of Lies.
- ➤ Kahddria – Goddess of Wind.
- ➤ Skaethak – Goddess of Winter.
- ➤ Muriel the Destroyer – Saent of Yrgaeshkil.
- ➤ Saent Julian the Courageous – A Saent of Grandfather Shadow.
- ➤ Saent Khellan – A Saent of Grandfather Shadow.
- ➤ Taelan'sha'Naeporishn – A Daemyn.
- ➤ Nae'Toran'borlahisth – A Daemyn.

PROLOGUE

I stood on a hill, looking out over the forest.
It felt like the morning after a grand celebration,
the celebration of winter's first storm.
I was a guest who had
stayed the night
and woke only to find my host absent.

Other guests woke around me
and together,
we marveled at the mess we had all made in our host's home.

I found a note.
"I'll not return for some time.
Please
clean and care for my house until I do."
The five of us had not been able to agree
on how best to celebrate,
is it any wonder we could not agree
on how best to clean?
I fear the mess we make trying to tidy this place
will be even greater.
- Julian Adryck, after the Battle of Ykthae Wood

As time went on, I missed Grandfather Shadow less than I missed the counsel of those
who had been Lord Morigahn before me. – The final recorded words of Saent
Julian the Courageous.

Just over a thousand years after the Battle of Ykthae Wood and the signing of the Ykthae Accord, Saent Julian the Courageous walked the streets of a town in the mortal world. Johki was one of three towns that had grown on the banks where the River Thaedus joined the larger River Aesin. Johki was the second largest of these three towns, having grown into a prosperous trading center since Julian had last been here. Then, it had been a fishing village of only a handful of huts and one larger building that might have been called a public house, certainly not anything close to an inn.

Before coming to the physical realm in search of the renegade Saent, Julian had studied Johki through the Well of Knowledge. He refused to make the rush into action as both Kaeldyr and Khellan had. Kaeldyr had already paid for his hastiness. Time would tell with Khellan, but if this was how Grandfather Shadow's newest Saent was going to behave, well, Grandfather Shadow was not known for tolerating foolishness.

As Julian studied and watched the people of Johki, many of the citizenry had noticed the appearance of an old man with his ever-present dog. The old man wore dusty clothes that had seen better days, and his hair and beard were wild and unkempt. His eyes were dark and brooding, so much so, that those who looked into them for longer than a moment quickly averted their gaze and hurried about their business. The dog also did not appear as mangy as it had at first, and many people thought that it might have wolf blood deep in its ancestry. A few souls had noticed a murder of crows coming to the old man at least once a day. The birds would stay for only a few moments, but the people who saw this would swear by all the lesser gods that the old man spoke to them as a father would to his children when he expected them to perform unpleasant chores.

A few of the people, children mostly, who watched the old man and his dog enough to see them in the moments when something changed – usually at dawn, dusk, or noon – saw the old man become tall with a cloak of living shadows about him. Watching him in those moments drew something deep within their hearts that they had never known was there, something called for them to stand straighter and to be proud of their heritage for the first time in their lives. When this happened, the dog became a wolf which seemed as large as a small pony. It looked as wild and untamed as an autumn storm.

As Julian sought his quarry, he happened across this old man and the dog. Julian and the old man nodded to each other, as old friends might after a long absence, perhaps due to some wrongdoing by one or the other. They passed, Saent Julian and the old man and his dog, and they did not spare a word for each other. That nod was enough. And while Julian's world began to shift back into balance for the first time in a millennium, old memories flooded back, first with a poem, and then the events that came with the poem, being forced to come to terms with…

13

...the Greater Gods were gone.

Julian Adryck sat next to a fire that did nothing to warm the chill spreading through him. In the camp around him, forty-nine Morigahnti – the last forty-nine – prayed in low voices. With the absence of Grandfather Shadow from the world, the quiet, whispered chorus of Galad'laman brought Julian a little comfort, but he knew it would be short-lived.

He stood and turned his back to the fire.

Ykthae Wood stretched out below the rise where the Morigahnti camped. Five of the six Greater Gods had signed the King of Order's Ykthae Accord, and now those gods were gone, trapped away from the world. Julian wondered what Grandfather Shadow thought of seeing the world through his high priest's eyes. How had Grandmother Dream managed to avoid capture?

Footsteps crunched in the dying grass behind Julian.

"I bring a message, Lord Morigahn." It was Ilsaen, one of the last remaining Fist captains. "The high priests of the other gods wish to join together for solidarity."

Julian had been expecting this from at least one of the captains. Stormcrows had brought him the news of messengers from the other gods' high priests about banding together. For a short time, Julian had considered meeting with those other high priests, but he rejected the idea. Now more than ever, the Morigahnti needed to remain steadfast.

"No," Julian replied.

"But, Lord Mor—"

"No." Julian paused, considering if he should add any sort of explanation. Ilsaen deserved something more that simple refusal. "We Morigahnti have always been alone in our struggles. We will survive as we are. We will not cower and scrape to the others just because the future looks grim. For us, the future has always looked grim."

"But we've always had Grandfather Shadow with us," Ilsaen said. "With the others banding together, the Morigahnti are in even greater peril."

"We will survive," Julian said.

"How can you be sure?"

Julian faced Ilsaen. Worry lines creased the Fist captain's forehead, and his frown was nearly a pout. Julian tried not to blame the man; they'd all lost so many friends and family in this war, everyone was grasping at any sliver of hope.

Julian took his brother Morigahnti by the shoulders and pulled him close, so that their foreheads touched.

"My faith makes me sure," Julian said. "We may be the last Morigahnti, but we are the last because we are the strongest. Grandfather Shadow is not gone; he is merely trapped, waiting for someone to come who will call him from his prison with the same faith we hold in our hearts now. It is our duty to preserve that faith, without polluting it with alliances with the other religions. They will surely seek to dilute our conviction in an attempt to ensure their deity is freed first."

"Yes, Lord Morigahn." Ilsaen pulled from Julian's grasp and returned to the camp.

Julian let a slow breath out through pursed lips as Ilsaen retreated.

"You should prepare to lose that one," three female voices said next to Julian.

As high priest to Grandfather Shadow, he'd grown accustomed to these sudden visitations from all manner of Eldar. He faced the trio of young women, or at least the three ladies who appeared as young women — most of the Eldar could mold their appearance to suit their whim. He looked them over, one after the other, studying their faces. Bright blue eyes looked back at him, partially hidden behind dark hair. One wore a robe that had gone from fashion centuries ago — Julian only knew of it from statues in the Morigahnti Citadel. The second wore a dress that any noble lady might wear to court: velvet with silk trim. The third wore a strange garment, a dress unlike any he'd ever seen; it cinched her waist in tight and flared out from her hips and made it seem as if she was floating. After a few moments he understood.

"Good evening, Dream," Julian said, offering a polite bow.

The goddess's relationship with his own god had been a tricky, tenuous thing, and Julian had taken care anytime she was about or when Grandfather Shadow spoke of her.

"We are not Dream," one lady said.

"Dream is a Greater Eldar," another said.

"And would have been forced to sign the Ykthae Accord," the third said.

Together, they said, "We are Hope, Imagination, and Necessity. And we have a gift for you."

Julian found it interesting that he'd never seen these lesser Eldar, hadn't even heard of them at any point in the war, and yet, here they stood, each one claiming one of Grandmother Dream's Dominions. Julian decided against commenting on that.

"Forgive me if I am leery of accepting gifts from any Eldar today," Julian said.

"These have no attachments or obligations," they said. "They are to ensure, when the time comes, the Morigahnti are prepared to take back what is theirs."

"Very well," Julian said. *He didn't trust them, but also couldn't afford to offend an Eldar, even a lesser, when Grandfather Shadow was not available to protect him.* "What are the gifts?"

They each held out a ceramic jug.

The lady in the ancient dress said, "Saltpeter."

The lady in the familiar dress said, "Charcoal."

The lady in the strange dress said, "Sulfur."

"And what am I supposed to do with these?" *Julian asked as a he took the gifts.*

"Study."

"Experiment."

"But carefully."

"Yes," *they all said together.* "Very carefully."

And with that, the three Eldar who used to be Grandmother Dream were gone.

Julian gently put the bowls aside and went back to staring down at Ykthae Wood.

Had it only been a week ago that the fighting here had begun? So much had changed in that time. Could the world recover?

As he watched the sun set behind the trees, Julian saw a group of seven riders heading away from the Morigahnti camp and toward the camps of the other Greater Gods. Again, footsteps crunched in the dying grass behind Julian, only this time much more hurried.

"Lord Morigahn, Ilsaen Kaesiak has…" Julian held up his hand, quieting the messenger.

"I know," Julian replied. "I see them."

"What shall we do?"

"Nothing. We are all feeling lost and confused. Ilsaen and his Fist must make their own way in the world now. Perhaps, one day, they will find their way back to us, but we cannot force them. We cannot afford to fight amongst ourselves."

Julian turned his back on Ykthae Wood and the seven Morigahnti who felt they had a better chance throwing in with the other survivors than they did with their own kind. Was this the new shape of the world? He wished he could seek the counsel of Saent Kaeldyr, but that privilege was lost to him as well.

"Spread the news to break camp," Julian said. "I want to be rid of this place. We must take this news to the Emperor."

He looked down at the three gifts from Hope, Imagination, and Necessity. What could he possibly do with saltpeter, charcoal, and sulfur?

So much had changed that day, in so many ways. How far had the Morigahnti come, and how far they had fallen, all because of that little gift?

Pushing old memories from his mind, Julian found his quarry right where he expected the fool to be. Like a moth to the flame, Khellan hadn't been able to resist the lure of his heart. Even without having met the current Lord Morigahn – Julian's chest swelled at the thought she'd been named for him – he could have told Khellan that she was no longer the girl he had fallen in love with.

Saent Khellan, the only Lord Morigahn risen to Saenthood yet to be granted a word, leaned against a wall between a bakery and haberdasher. He stared across the street at a three-story inn. The building had been constructed before the Kingdom of the Sun had conquered Koma, back when most buildings could serve as a defensible position in addition to their primary function. Bastian's Inn was actually three buildings attached to each other, forming three sides of a square: the inn portion on the east, the Bastian residences on the north, and the stables to the west. The south remained open in these times. Before the Kingdom conquered Koma, the inn would have had a wall that could have been wheeled from the stables, closing the inn yard in as a staging area or a killing field.

The surrounding neighborhood was more modern, having grown as Johki had grown: simple buildings serving only a single function. The buildings in this neighborhood stood apart from each other, allowing any attacking enemy easy movement. An idiotic thing, especially considering this neighborhood stood on the area's highest point. Julian would have made the citizens build a wall around this neighborhood for a secondary fallback position. On the other side of the coin, Johki didn't have a primary wall.

Julian walked up behind Saent Khellan, making no attempt at stealth. Grandfather Shadow's newest Saent hadn't even twitched at Julian's approach. Instead, Khellan continued staring at Bastian's Inn. From this vantage point, he could see through the southern opening to the inn yard to the large window of the second floor master suite. Even from this distance, Julian saw a young woman standing at the window.

"You should not be here," Julian said, as he stepped next to Khellan.

Khellan jumped, but recovered quickly. "Where else should I be?"

"You should be in Grandfather's hall, waiting for him to call."

Khellan drew in a deep breath and let it out before he faced Julian. "Why should I wait on his whim?" Khellan demanded. "He has not given me a word yet. I bore the title of Lord Morigahn, just as the rest of you. I led the Morigahnti. Why does he mock me and spurn me like this? I should bear the word "the Sentinel," not that commoner, that bastard who let us all believe he was dead."

"It is not our place to question Grandfather Shadow," Julian said. "You may find doing so unpleasant. Now, return with me before he decides to notice you."

"He's off looking after his precious *Galad Setseman'Vuori aen Keisari* and *Tsumari'osa*, neither of whom worship or serve him. He should be watching over the one who does."

"And what would you have him do?" a deep voice asked.

Julian and Khellan turned. The man and his dog stood there, regarding both Saents. Julian gave a respectful bow. Khellan stood stiff and glared at the old man.

"Explain what he plans to do about the Morigahnti who come to challenge the Lord Morigahn," Khellan demanded.

"Nothing," the old man answered. "If she cannot lead them through her own merits, then I chose wrong."

"And if they kill her?"

"She will die, and I will choose again," the old man replied. "And then you two will be reunited, though, I suspect the experience will be much different than you hope it will."

"Julianna and I love each other," Khellan said. "Nothing, not even death can break that bond."

"Perhaps," Julian said, unable to keep quiet any longer. "But you are young as a man, and even younger as a Saent. Neither the mortal nor the celestial realms conform nicely to the certainty of youth."

Khellan did not acknowledge Julian, instead he continued interrogating the old man. "And you will not assist her at all?"

The old man looked down at the dog. "Isn't it touching how this one is so dedicated to his love?"

The canine snorted.

Julian wondered at the game being playing here.

The old man stood taller, allowing his divinity to seep into his guise. Shadows lengthened toward him, and thunder rolled behind his voice when he spoke. "I will not aid her with the Morigahnti. If the mood strikes, I might aid her with outside threats, but only if she asks. But you need not concern yourself with her for the time being. I have decided upon your name, and I have a duty for you."

"In truth?" Khellan asked.

"In Truth," Grandfather Shadow replied. "Skaethak, join me."

In the span of three heartbeats, the air around them cooled. A young woman with pale skin and dark hair stepped out of nowhere. She wore a shimmering dress of snowflakes and icicles.

"Skaethak, goddess of winter," Grandfather Shadow said. "This is my newest Saent, Khellan, whom I have named *the Unworthy*. He will assist you in the task I have set for you. If he displeases you, you may send him back to my hall or end him, whichever is more convenient."

Skaethak smirked as she dropped into a curtsy.

Khellan the Unworthy opened his mouth, no doubt to protest this, but no words escaped his lips.

"Silly child," Grandfather Shadow said. "I will only hear the voice of those followers I consider worthy. Now be off."

"Yes," Skaethak said, frost forming in the air as she spoke. "Let us be away and about our task."

She reached up, took Khellan by the ear, and pulled him away with her. When they were gone, Grandfather Shadow returned to the guise of being just an old man again.

"I had forgotten how hard you are," Julian said.

"The world is hard," the old man said. "As it has been since my brothers forced the first human to choose between light and dark."

"And you have no responsibility in perpetuating this?" the dog asked.

"Of course I do," the old man replied. "But that is because there must be more to the world than light and dark, night and day. If humanity truly desired to exist in one extreme or the other, then the world would have no need of me. Saent Kaeldyr proved that some actually wish freedom from the extremes my brothers press down upon the world."

"And what of Julianna?" the dog asked. "Does she share Saent Kaeldyr's view? Did she come seeking your help as he did?"

Julian considered joining this conversation but thought better of it. Grandfather Shadow had named him "the Courageous" not "the Foolish."

The old man chuckled. "You think Julianna had no choice?"

"I do," the wolf replied.

"I gave her a choice. She accepted through her own free will."

"But she did not fully realize the ramifications of that choice."

"Neither did Saent Kaeldyr when he accepted my offer all those centuries ago, nor you when you broke away from your brethren and entered my service, nor *Ahmyr'Shuol* and *Tzizma'Uthra* when they shattered the world and created me. The King of Order did not realize the ramifications of placing my siblings and me into our prisons. The Truth is that no being, mortal, celestial, or infernal, can grasp how their choices, no matter how well planned, will affect the entirety of existence.

"By the time the sun rises and sets again, Julianna will have proven her worth as the Lord Morigahn, or she will be dead, all depending on the choices she, the Morigahnti, and their enemies make."

Grandfather Shadow faced Julian. "Are any of my other Saents planning any idiocy that I should know of?"

"If they are, I am unaware," Julian replied.

"Well, that is something at least. However, I would prefer certainty in this matter. Return to my hall, use the Well of Knowledge, and ensure they are not," Grandfather Shadow said. "One Saent Khellan the Unworthy is an irritation. Seven such as he could be disastrous."

"Yes, Grandfather," Julian bowed. "Where shall I seek you if I have news?"

"Either here or Koma City," Grandfather Shadow replied. "This night isn't important just for the Lord Morigahn; Xander Rosha and Damian Adryck also have important choices to make."

BASTIAN'S INN

Leadership granted rather than earned, even if granted by a god, is a precarious throne at best. – Maxian Taraen

As Lord Morigahn, I take up the task of recording my thoughts into this book, and already many Morigahnti claim that my writings and teachings shall be second only to Kaeldyr the Gray. I cannot speak to the truth of this, as each Morigahnti must judge the teachings of each Lord Morigahn for himself. Let me begin by giving the qualities I believe all Morigahnti leaders should possess, some of these come from my understanding of the Laws of Shadow, some from my understanding of my own observations.

Lead from the front, but do not rush headlong into the fray.

Create a vision for your followers, but do not make it impossible to believe.

Understand and trust in the strength of cooperation and teamwork, but do not discount the worth of the individual.

Take risks when necessary, but do not be an idiot.

Everyone has lessons to teach you, but do not forget to heed your own council.

Prepare for battle every day, but do not forget the world requires peace as well.

Balance your emotions. Followers respect passion, but too much can lead to poor strategies.

We will see as time goes on how well I live up to my own meditations on leadership.

From *The Tome of Shadows*
Saent Julian the Courageous

ONE

Julianna held the mirror up. She had been able to stomach seeing her reflection without breaking the mirror for three days. Each time she looked at herself, no matter the angle, the scar looked the same, as if a river of blood were ready to pour from it at any moment. Even though nearly a fortnight had passed since Grandfather Shadow marked her face with a heated blade, the wound showed no sign of healing.

The Lord Morigahn's mark was part of her now, just as it had been a part of Khellan. Thinking of him brought a sad smile to her lips. His scar *had* healed and made him look dashing. Julianna had finally come to terms with the mark, and while the wound would mar her until the day she died, it did not completely diminish her beauty. It might never become as charming on her as it might on a man, especially if it did not heal; however, she could see how she could use that as an advantage.

A week had passed since Julianna and Faelin had arrived at Bastian's Inn. Nathan and Wynd had arrived the next day, followed by Aurell and Parsh the day after that. They'd heard no word from Korrin. During their stay, Julianna remained mostly in her room studying the *Galad'parma*. She had learned so much about the Morigahnti. It made her head swim to think that all the old legends were true, and that she led the Morigahnti.

She laughed, though there was no humor in the sound. She had spoken with a Greater God, fought Daemyn Hounds, called upon the power of miracle to fight her enemies, and still she questioned all the whispered legends of the Morigahnti warrior-priests.

Someone knocked on the door. Julianna pulled her eyes away from her reflection.

"Who is it?" Julianna called.

"It's Donal Bastian," the innkeeper's muffled voice came from the other side of the door.

"A moment," Julianna replied.

Julianna took the *Galad'fana* and wrapped it around her head, hiding all of her face except her eyes. This *Galad'fana* was cool against her skin, being some sort of woven metal rather than cloth.

Everyone at the inn thought she was a spoiled noble girl having an affair with a minstrel – learning Faelin could play the flute and mandolin had come as quite a surprise to her. As it was, she and Faelin saw no reason to dissuade such thinking. When Parsh arrived, he agreed that having Faelin and Julianna play the part of forbidden lovers was the best way for them to stay hidden in plain sight. The tarnished side of this coin meant they had to share the room at night, and that's when the dream still came. Some nights were worse than others, but she had yet to make it through the night without waking at least twice, and while Faelin tried to comfort her, some nights Julianna wanted to be alone with her pain.

"Come in," Julianna called.

The door opened. Donal Bastian, a short, wiry man with a wild mane of sandy brown hair, entered balancing a tray on one hand and holding a pitcher and goblet in the other. The tray carried bread, half a game hen, and two bowls, one of stew and one of sweet peaches and fall apples covered in cinnamon. As he crossed the room, the stout cudgel that he always had hooked on his belt swung back and forth. When they'd first arrived, Faelin had asked about the weapon. Bastian answered, beaming with pride, *Never had problems with ruffians at my inn, and I mean to keep it that way.* He placed the meal on the table. "Is there anything else, my lady?"

"That will be sufficient, Master Bastian."

"Shall I open the window, my lady? I know it's late in the day, but it opens to the courtyard. It's pleasant outside now that the storm has passed, and people are enjoying the afternoon. I know you prefer solitude, but fresh air might raise your spirits."

"Yes," Julianna said. "That would be fine."

Bastian opened the double windows, and a fresh breeze flowed through the room pushing out the stuffy air from the last few days. Laughter did float up from the courtyard below. It sounded as though quite a crowd had gathered down there.

"Thank you, Master Bastian," Julianna said, and before the innkeeper could make another offer of assistance. "That will be all."

"Yes, my lady." Bastian bowed and backed toward the door.

As he retreated, Julianna said, "Thank you for every kindness, Master Bastian. We will be traveling on soon and no longer be a bother."

"Don't think yourself a bother, my lady. I appreciate your custom, and Master Faelin's playing and stories bring even more. Since he's been here, my business has doubled. I don't ever take payment for your meals, only for the space of your room and the stabling of your horses. You are more than welcome to stay as long as you wish."

"Again, thank you," Julianna said.

With a final bow, Donal Bastian left her room.

While Bastian's regular patrons might believe the story of Julianna and Faelin, Julianna suspected the innkeeper did not. He never pried, and never tried to sneak answers out of her with flattery or slippery words. Though he wore the guise of a simpleton, Julianna found him a shrewd and observant man, one who stayed out of business that was no concern of his own.

Julianna went to the window.

It was late enough that the sun already hid behind the building's west side and cast everything into light shadows. Nathan stood in the courtyard with a throwing knife in hand. Wynd and the innkeeper's daughter, Tarshiva, leaned against the stable wall, each holding a brace of knives. Faelin and Aurell sat on a bench and watched the game.

Nathan took aim at a small target on the other side of the inn yard. Then, with a flick of his wrist, Nathan sent the knife end over end toward the target. It hit just to the left of the center. The target held the traditional gray center of Koma rather than the yellow center common in the Kingdom of the Sun.

Nathan stepped aside and Wynd took his place. She threw her knife with less care, and it hit further from the center than her husband's did. Wynd's lips formed a sneer. She hit the bullseye more often than Nathan, but lost more money than he did because her aim was less consistent.

Now that the two Morigahnti had thrown, Tarshiva, or Tar as most people around the inn called her, stepped forward. She possessed an ample bosom and shapely hips, accentuated by the bodice that she kept cinched tight, making her popular with Bastian's customers. The first night Aurell arrived at the inn, the stout Morigahnti girl had attempted a bit of posturing with the attractive innkeeper's daughter. That posturing ended when they all saw Tar's skill with the knives.

Tar's wrist flicked three times in rapid succession. Three knives appeared in the target's bullseye.

With the contest decided, coins changed hands between Nathan, Wynd, and Tar.

Julianna couldn't help but smile. She suspected Master Bastian's cudgel was only part of the reason for the peaceful nature of the inn. Each day the innkeeper's daughter won more money than she lost throwing knives against the Morigahnti. Only Nathan and Wynd would play against her now.

As the three knife-throwers retrieved their weapons, Julianna glanced at Faelin who looked back at her. Faelin nodded. Aurell also looked up, saw Julianna, stood, and bowed. When Nathan and Wynd realized what had happened, they turned to the window and bowed as well. Julianna inclined her head, as Faelin had instructed her, and the Morigahnti straightened. Tar did not bow, but not out of disrespect. Innkeepers and their staff dealt with nobility so frequently that it was impractical for them to bow every time they saw someone. Tradition held that each day, inn workers gave one deep bow to show their respect, and then conducted their business as usual.

Julianna returned to the table. Sitting, she removed the veil from her face and poked at the game hen with a fork. She ate by habit alone. Hunger still did not come to her, but Julianna tried to eat every time Bastian brought food. Not even the power of Grandfather Shadow could sustain her without nourishment of some kind.

Swallowing another mouthful of food, Julianna heard a commotion coming from the inn yard. The sound of cantering hooves came closer and closer, coming to a halt inside the courtyard.

"Korrin!" Nathan yelled from below her window.

"Parsh!" Korrin's voice rang out. "Where is he?"

"He's off on an errand," Aurell said, as Julianna went to the window.

Korrin, tall and lanky as his brother Nathan, sat in his saddle. The horse was covered in foamy sweat.

"What news do you bring?" Julianna called down.

Everyone looked up at her.

"Great news, my lady," Korrin replied, affecting as much of a bow as he could as he walked his horse in circles so it could cool slowly. "Prince Sandré Collaen is behind me, coming from the docks. He has a ship docked here and will be here in moments."

Julianna recalled once meeting Prince Sandré Collaen, the first seat of House Aesin, when she was very young, back when her parents were alive. In her memory, Sandré Collaen seemed old. How ancient had he become by now?

She wrapped the Lord Morigahn's *Galad'fana*, her *Galad'fana*, around her head, buckled her rapier to her waist, and headed out toward the courtyard.

TWO

The darkened room came into focus as Carmine's vision returned to his own eyes. He maintained a steady breath as the vertigo faded. During the battle of Shadybrook, he thought that he'd mastered bringing his awareness back to his body from the Nightbat. Now, he'd shortened the time to a mere few breaths. Concentrating, he brought his right hand up to his left ear and tugged his earlobe. The longer he remained sharing the experience of being a Nightbat, the more difficult it was to control his body when he returned. Sure that he wouldn't spill all over himself, Carmine reached for a tankard of small beer and swallowed several healthy gulps. Remaining in the Nightbat's experience for long periods was also thirsty work.

After quenching his thirst and taking several tentative steps to make certain he wouldn't fall over from vertigo, Carmine dashed down the stairs of the house the Nightbrothers used to spy on the Morigahnti. He and Hardin had arrived in Johki three days ago and had located the Morigahnti a day later. In order to better observe the Morigahnti, the Brotherhood had taken over a house facing Bastian's Inn. Carmine had commanded the Brotherhood to send the original occupants of this house to Old Uncle Night's embrace. Hardin had concealed the Brotherhood's presence from the Morigahnti by judicious use of Old Uncle Night's Dominion of Lies and Aunt Moon's Dominion of Luck.

"Send a runner if they attempt to leave," Carmine ordered as he raced past two of the Brothers and out the back door.

"Yes, Adept Carmine," the Nightbrothers said.

Once in the alley behind the house, two of his Red Draqons dropped in behind him and matched his pace. With the two divinely altered wariors of the Kingdom of the Sun walking behind him, Carmine strode tall and proud through Johki's streets. The Komati commoners were quick to move from his path. While Carmine enjoyed the reaction, he couldn't take too much pleasure in it; they were still in Johki after all, when they should have been done with this business with Julianna and the Morigahnti back in Shadybrook.

Had they been in any Kingdom protectorate other than Koma, and had they been facing any enemies besides the Morigahnti, Hardin and Carmine would have simply led their remaining Nightbrothers and Red Draqons to attack and be done with it. However, the Morigahnti had proven resourceful and quick to counterattack, even when they were taken by surprise. Carmine and Hardin had also noticed quite a few Adepts in Johki. Some of those Adepts might catch the Brotherhood's scent on the wind, and that would rouse an entirely new hornet's nest. So rather than a direct assault, Carmine had observed the Morigahnti over the last two days. Just this morning, he and Hardin had devised a strategy to divide and destroy the Morigahnti. Only now, one of Julianna's followers had announced the arrival of Prince Sandré Collaen. While it couldn't be confirmed until the prince arrived, Carmine would wager heavy coin that he was Morigahnti, and would likely bring at least two more Fists with him. With only six Nightbrothers and three Reds remaining after the battle of Shadybrook, Carmine and Hardin didn't stand a chance against those numbers.

"Carmine?" somebody called in the singsong accent of House Aernacht, so that his name came out sounding like Cor-moin. "Carmine D'Mario?"

Carmine stopped, hoping he wouldn't have to have his Red Draqon escort kill someone. Meeting the wrong person now could throw everything into disarray. He groaned as he recognized his cousin, Gianni D'Mario yp Caenacht, or more accurately now, Adept Gianni of House Aernacht. Gods and goddesses, the mixed Floraen and Aernacht names sounded ridiculous.

"Earth and stone!" Gianni's mouth broke into a wide grin. He had inherited his dark hair and dusky skin from his father, but his green eyes were a gift from his Aernacht mother. "How long has it been? Six months? A year?"

Not long enough, Carmine thought as they embraced and kissed each other's cheeks. Every time Gianni came into his sight, Carmine struggled against the urge to strangle his cousin, and not just because a House had accepted him as an Adept. "Almost a year."

Gianni looked like a fool in his House Aernacht Adept's garb. Of all of the Adepts' orders in the Kingdom, House Aernacht was the only one that demanded its Adepts not only wear the mantle of Mother Earth, they also required their Adepts to wear the traditional garb. Even now Gianni wore the *laenya*, the knee length shirt with full sleeves that hung almost to the ground, *aeinar*, a short coat with open sleeves that hung to the waist, and the *cochaellan*, the plaid cape with its bits of animal sewn into the inside: horn, bone, hoof, claw, and tooth. Supposedly, each of those things represented one of the heavy moralistic parables Aernacht Adepts used for teaching the lessons of their goddess.

"What brings you to Johki, cousin?" Gianni asked.

"The House leaders are still upset at my father's choice of a bride," Carmine said. He had to end this conversation quickly without being rude to his Adept cousin. "To punish me for *his* lack of judgment, I've been attached to Adept Hardin of House Swaenmarch. He's got us traveling all over Koma collecting every kind of gemstone he can find to see how they compare to gemstones of other lands. I think he has it in his mind to go to Heidenmarch next."

Gianni gave Carmine a sympathetic look. "If you do head down to Heidenmarch, let me know. I'll speak to my mistress about enchanting something to help protect you."

"Thank you," Carmine said. "If we're still in Johki when Adept Hardin chooses to head to Heidenmarch, I'll try and find an excuse to come see you."

"Do," Gianni said. "I'd hate to hear that some disaster had come upon a cousin of mine when I could have done something to prevent it. As for me, I don't know exactly why I'm here. About two months ago, the Singer of Life called my mistress for an audience. When my mistress returned, she commanded me to pack for an extended journey and we came to Koma. She's so secretive. Sometimes I wonder if she's not really a Kaesiak Adept trying to infiltrate our House. The only thing I know about our task is that we're looking for someone, but I don't know who."

"Well, best of luck finding whoever it is," Carmine said. "I would love to stay and chat the afternoon away, cousin, but Adept Hardin is one of those Swaenmarch Adepts who has lived past their prime, and he can't quite live out his passions the way he used to. If you grasp my meaning?"

"I understand quite well," Gianni said. "He's doubly jealous because you've likely got all the pretty inn girls hanging on you every time you come to a new town."

"Not really. He keeps me too busy for that, but I'm fairly certain that's how he sees it, anyway."

"Well then, I'll pray for Mother Earth to deliver you away from your Swaenmarch master and return you to your family."

"My thanks, Adept Gianni." Carmine gave Gianni a deep bow and forced his expression to remain smooth. The last thing Carmine wanted was a blessing from the goddess of life.

"Oh stop that, cousin." Gianni pulled Carmine into a deep embrace.

They kissed cheeks again, and muttering more apologies, Carmine fled. He hurried back to the other house that he and Hardin had appropriated after coming to Johki. The way Carmine's luck was going today, there was no telling who else might be in this town waiting to waylay him.

When Carmine came around the corner to what the Nightbrothers had begun referring to as Hardin's House — the house across the street from Bastian's Inn had become Carmine's House — Carmine saw a squad of Reds standing at attention. Before Carmine could alter his path, one of the Reds saluted him. It was the tallest of the squad, easily two heads taller than Carmine and half-a-head taller than either of the Reds escorting him, and the thing had a mane of tiny braids, one for each battle it had survived.

"Marquis Carmine D'Mario," the Red's voice was more than half a growl. "You are expected inside."

Carmine's mouth and throat became even drier than they had after his awareness returned from the Nightbat.

THREE

When Julianna reached the inn yard, six people stood in a circle around Faelin and Korrin, and four people stood blocking Nathan, Wynd, and Aurell outside the circle. Each of the newcomers wore a *Galad'fana* around their necks like scarves.

Two people stood facing Faelin and Korrin. One was a man, the *Galad'fana* pulled across his face obscuring his features. He was so thin that he might disappear if he stepped behind Nathan or Korrin. The other was a young woman, slightly older than Julianna, and did not have her face covered. Julianna paused midstride as she recognized her cousin through marriage, Charise Garieth. Charise was a tiny wisp with fair skin and hair, unlike the dark coloring of most Komati, though her eyes were a deep brown. Julianna blinked at seeing a *Galad'fana* draped across her cousin's shoulders.

Shaking off the hesitation, Julianna strode up to the circle and placed her hand on the shoulder of the first Morigahnti in her way. He was only a bit taller than Julianna and jerked away from her hand. He turned, jaw clenched as he looked her over, gaze settling on her face. His cheeks tightened, and he cocked his head to the side for a moment, as if studying her. After a moment, his jaw went slack and his whole face widened in shock.

"Stand aside." Julianna kept her voice soft, yet firm. She wanted the presence of her scar to speak for her more than her voice — at least for now.

The Morigahnti tried to nod, bow, and step out of the way at the same time. This caused him to bump into the man next to him. That man turned.

He opened his mouth to say something, but when he took in the sight of Julianna's face, he also moved aside.

By this time, others had noticed her, and a murmur passed through the assembled Morigahnti. The arguing in the center died when Julianna stepped through the Morigahnti to join Charise and the other man in the center.

"Where is Parsh?" Julianna asked.

"Lord Morigahn." Korrin bowed. "This is Prince Syr Sandré Aesin'Collaen and Viscountess Charise Kaeski'Garieth. Prince Sandré, may I—?"

"You are not answering the question I asked you." Julianna cut Korrin off. "Where is Parsh?"

"He is running errands," Nathan answered.

"Parsh spends much of his time running errands," Julianna said. "It is good that he keeps himself busy." Julianna sighed. "Now, that we've determined that Parsh isn't here, will someone explain to me what is going on?"

"Julianna?" Charise's mouth hung open for a moment, and then she snapped it shut. Her eyes glanced from side to side.

Julianna realized that she stood at the crossroads of another important choice. How would she relate to this woman who was once her friend?

"*Ji* Charise," Julianna replied. "*Muta nyt mina myos aen Morigahnti'uljas.*"

Julianna forced herself to breathe normally while she waited for Charise's response. They had been playmates once, and Julianna had always followed where the older girl had led. The last time they'd spoken, Charise threaded their conversations with talk of Koma freedom while Julianna had spoken of a handsome young noble with a dashing scar down his face.

"Yes, Lord Morigahn." Charise bowed. "Forgive my outburst. It will not happen again."

"No forgiveness is needed. We haven't seen each other in months, and I am not what you expected." Then Julianna pulled Charise out of her bow. "And the Morigahnti are not to bow to me any longer. I expect to be saluted as any other Morigahnti leader."

Charise looked deeply into Julianna's eyes. Julianna met her gaze without flinching or smiling. Finally, Charise nodded and saluted.

"This little slip of a girl is the Lord Morigahn?" Sandré asked. "She will lead us to greater doom than that young hothead, Khellan."

Julianna kept her face still. "This *little slip of a girl* is the first chosen of *Galad'Ysoysa*, as was that *young hothead*. Have care with your words, Prince Collaen, or you may offend."

"How do we know that you are *Morigahn'uljas*?" Sandré demanded. "Anyone can put a cut across their face."

This had come sooner than Julianna would have liked – one of the Morigahnti challenging her claim. Any misspoken word here could cause her downfall, if not death. Grandfather Shadow would not intervene on her behalf. A Lord Morigahn who could not bring the Morigahnti to follow was of no use to the God of Shadows.

Julianna reached up and pulled the *Galad'jana* from Sandré's face. With the cloth gone, he looked like a pit fighting dog at the tail end of a glorious career. Small scars crossed his face, and his lips were drawn into a thin line. He reached for Julianna with no more grace than any number of drunkards who groped for her at balls and parties. She ducked underneath his reach as easily as she avoided those other noblemen who underestimated her, and stepped to the side. This threw Sandré off-balance. Julianna reached out and pushed his shoulder, hard. Sandré sprawled to the ground. Knowing her success came only from surprise, Julianna drew her rapier as Sandré began to rise. When he reached his knees, Julianna placed the tip of the sword at his neck.

"From what I've read," Julianna said in an even tone, "most of my predecessors would have killed you for that. I am not by my nature a bloodthirsty woman, but I am learning that I must be hard. So now you have me in a bind, Prince Syr Sandré Aesin'Collaen. Do I do kill you and be seen as too hard? Or shall I spare you and be seen as too soft? What would you do in my place?"

They stared at each other for a long while. If he chose to live, Julianna would have to watch him closely. Part of her wanted to slide her blade though his throat and end the matter altogether, but she'd already offered the choice and couldn't change that now, at least not if she wanted to retain any respect from those she asked to follow her.

"I would spare a captain of such distinction," Sandré said, "in hopes that he would learn from his errors, but surely I would have him watched."

"Your words carry wisdom, Your Highness." Julianna removed the rapier from his neck, "I will follow your advice. Korrin."

Korrin stepped forward, "Yes, Lord Morigahn?"

"In the absence of your Fist captain, I command you to set one of your Morigahnti to watch this man," Julianna said. "Report any suspicious behaveior to me immediately. If his watcher witnesses anything outright treasonous or seditious, kill him."

Korrin saluted. "Your will is my action, Lord Morigahn."

"Stand with me, Sandré," Julianna said, extending her hand. "We are on our way for me to undergo the trials. If I do not succeed, I will let you kill me without protest."

"Fair enough," Sandré said, standing without her help.

"Now," Julianna asked, once the prince stood and dusted himself off, "what is the problem here?"

"It's Faelin," Korrin said.

"Why?"

"He claims I'm not Branton Traejyn's son," Faelin replied.

31

"You cannot be Faelin vara'Traejyn," Sandré said. "All the Traejyns died when the Whites and Reds attacked. I was there just before the battle and saw the man you're impersonating. Everyone who stayed was slain."

"I remember that, Prince Sandré," Faelin said. "And I remember hearing you tell my father and grandfather that they should kill me. I was sent away just before the battle began because it wasn't my place to fight beside the nobles of my family."

"Then where have you been all this time?" Charise asked.

"Studying with the Taekuri," Faelin replied. That confession caused a few murmurs to spread through the surrounding Morigahnti.

"Who are the Taekuri? Julianna asked.

"A secretive order of scholars that swears allegiance to no one," Sandré said.

"I thought they were a martial brotherhood," Charise said.

"There are many roles within the Taekuri," Faelin replied. "Just as there are many roles within the Morigahnti, or were at one time."

"And what brings the bastard son back to Koma?" Sandré asked.

"The will of *Galad'Ysoysa*," Julianna said. "Faelin found me just after *Galad'Ysoysa* marked me. If not for him, you would not stand before *aen Morigahn'uljas*."

"But he is not Morigahnti," Sandré said. "He should have at least followed his forefathers' path. If not before his family's death, then after."

"I honor them by keeping all that my father and grandfather taught me alive," Faelin said. "Perhaps some Morigahnti need to learn that there is more than one way to worship Grandfather Shadow."

At that, Charise's mouth dropped open again, and the right side of Sandré's face twitched. Even without looking around, Julianna sensed the tension Faelin's comment had raised. She had to quell this hostility before others were swept up by it.

"Enough! The third law states, *The Morigahnti succeed together as a greater whole*. Let us fight the Kingdom, not each other."

Sandré and Charise nodded and went to their men, but not before Faelin and Sandré eyed each other like territorial wolves.

Korrin said in a tone just above a whisper. "Prince Sandré is well loved among the Morigahnti."

"Grandfather Shadow set me to the task of leading the Morigahnti to greatness once again. I can't do that if I have to keep watching over my shoulder every time a Fist captain gets riled up because I'm not what he expected."

"Yes, Lord Morigahn."

Korrin saluted, and walked over to Aurell. They spoke for a moment, and then Aurell went over to stand behind Sandré.

When Sandré noticed Aurell, he gave the stocky girl an annoyed glance and then went back to commanding his Fist. Aurell shrugged, nodded to a few of the other Morigahnti, and watched Sandré with a bored expression.

"Wynd," Julianna said. "I want you to keep an eye on the Bastians. They have treated us well, and I don't want the Morigahnti harassing them or taking advantage of the hospitality that they have shown."

"Yes, Lord Morigahn," Wynd said, saluted, and went inside.

"Lord Morigahn," Faelin said. "This might not be the best time, but remember that not all Morigahnti are as true as the laws dictate."

"What do you mean?" Julianna asked.

"Old Uncle Night is a cunning seducer," Faelin said. "And if someone, anyone, is told the right lies, they can be led to do anything."

With that, Faelin turned on his heel and went inside as Sandré returned.

"Why do you suffer him, Lord Morigahn?" Sandré asked, returning from his men with Charise and Korrin right behind him.

"Because, even with a country full of Morigahnti, Grandfather Shadow sent Faelin to protect me," Julianna answered. There was more she wanted to say, but it would have made her sound like a simpering fool and possibly given someone an indirect means of hurting her.

"My dear friend," Charise said. "I can see that you are fond of him, but you should send him away now that you have true Morigahnti to protect you."

"My dear Charise," Julianna smiled without any warmth. "I would not dream of turning away the man *Galad'Ysoysa* chose to protect me. Were it not for him, I would not be alive now for the Morigahnti to protect. I will also not turn away any Komati who will swear to me, whether they are Morigahnti or not. Grandfather Shadow watches over all the Komati, not just the Morigahnti. In the past, the Morigahnti forgot that, and it led to the Kingdom conquering our lands. I will not make the same mistake."

"As you say, Lord Morigahn, but many of the other Komati have stood with the Kingdom against us for a long time. The Morigahnti remember this, and may not want to fight with them."

"For good or for ill," Julianna said, "I mean to change things for the Morigahnti and for Koma."

"Change is not always a good thing," Charise said.

"True, not always," Julianna replied. "But without change, Saent Kaeldyr would have never discovered Grandfather Shadow, and Koma would not exist. Change is coming. Prepare for it."

Sandré Collaen drew in breath and licked his lips. He seemed about to say something, but then closed his mouth into a tight line.

"If you have something to say, Your Highness," Julianna said, "I would hear it."

"I have nothing to say," Sandré replied.

"I am aware that you don't like me," Julianna said. "If your reputation is even remotely accurate of the man behind that reputation, I would be a fool not to seek your council, regardless of our feelings for each other."

"Very well," Sandré said. "I just pray you don't fracture the Morigahnti more than we already are."

"See there," Julianna said, "we actually agree on something. It's not much, but a start. Perhaps we can find more common ground at some point. For now, I must retire and pray to *Galad'Ysoysa* for guidance. I will see the both of you in the morning. We leave then."

FOUR

Kaenyth leaned against a lamppost and watched over the street traffic with only half interest. Even this late, the scent of bread and pastries wafted out of the bakery behind him. Like the passersby in the street, Kaenyth was only barely aware of this. Rather than maintain his attention where it should have been, he kept shifting his gaze to Bastian's Inn.

"Kaenyth?" Rayce asked from the other side of the lamppost.

"Rayce?" Kaenyth replied, hoping the question would be quick to answer. If that nobleman and his entourage settled into their rooms before the sun sank too low for decent light, Tarshiva and the other guests might start another game of knife throwing.

As if summoned by his thoughts, Tarshiva came into view, making a wide circle around the nobleman's entourage. Kaenyth pulled his hood from his shoulders over his head. He left his face open, wanting to make it easier for the innkeeper's daughter to see he wore that particular gray garment. He also stood straighter and scanned the crowd moving past him as if he were patrolling the east end docks and not High Hill.

"Well?" Rayce asked.

"Well what?" Kaenyth replied.

"I asked a question," Rayce sighed. "But you were too busy pining for her. Best you let go of those fancies. She's devoted to her father and that inn. There's no room for you in there."

"We'll see," Kaenyth said. "Just repeat the bloody question and get back to watching the crowds."

"Like we'll see any crime here before sundown."

"Could be pickpockets and cut purses."

"Bah. Not this high up, even the boldest of them know better. They'd stick out like I would at court."

"Just ask the question," Kaenyth said.

"Fine." Rayce cleared his throat, as he usually did when embarking on what he referred to as discourse of the intellect. "We've been part of the

Vara nearly a year now, and I still can't figure out why they call us *the Vara*. I heard the word means *false*, which I suppose that's why they put that at the beginning of a bastard's surname, but why call us that since there ain't anything false about us?"

Kaenyth drew in a breath and rubbed his chin as he always did to humor Rayce's fantasy of the discourse of the intellect. As it was, he actually did have to consider this for a moment. Occasionally, not often but once in a while, Rayce did pose something that Kaenyth had to think about from several different angles. This was one of the reasons Kaenyth indulged all the other simple and downright foolish questions his cousin asked.

"Well," Kaenyth said after a moment. "I've heard the same rumor. Hadn't thought about it much, but you're the one who does the questioning. If pressed for an answer," which he would be if he didn't answer Rayce's question quickly and succinctly, "I'd say the name comes from the Kingdom High Blood. They probably started calling us that because we can't even come close to the protection the Draqons offer. So, essentially we'd be the Vara'Draqons, but we aren't even worthy of that much honor."

"Huh," Rayce muttered. "That's a much safer explanation than I thought of."

"And you best keep that other explanation to yourself," a gruff voice said behind them.

Kaenyth jumped. Before shame could rise too high in him, he registered that Rayce had jumped as well, and he'd even shrieked a little.

They both turned. Their Uncle Staephyn stared at them from under the edge of his hood of gray wool that almost matched the mustache that grew heavy on his upper lip. That was the only hair their uncle grew on his head – cheeks, chin, and scalp were all bare, and had been ever since Kaenyth could remember. Both Kaenyth and Rayce had joined the Vara to follow Uncle Staephyn's footsteps, hoping to make him proud. He'd helped raise both young men since their fathers had died before either of them had reached their second by seventh birthday.

Uncle Staephyn put a hand on Rayce's shoulder. "Keep that thought locked tight in your mind, and don't even whisper it to yourself in the deepest night when you're sure you're alone." He faced Kaenyth. "You're a smart lad, and I'm sure you're already piecing it together. You do the same as your cousin. No good at all will ever come from speaking those realizations. Bad enough to think them."

Rayce shuffled. "You make it sound as if we can't keep our thoughts secret."

"Does seem like that's what I'm saying," Uncle Staephyn replied. "Now lads, there's been a change in our schedule tonight. We aren't watching over High Hill tonight. I want you to head over to Tavern Row; find a table at the

Seven Mountains… No… Crows' Court… Yes. Get a table at the Crows' Court, in the back corner away from both the bar and the fireplace."

"But our duty?" Rayce started.

Uncle Staephyn silenced him by raising a single finger. "Your duty tonight is to stay out of trouble, and alive, so that you can reach into the duty bucket and get lucky enough to draw the tiles for High Hill another day. Don't ask questions lads – just listen to your uncle. There's trouble brewing here. If the gods and goddesses smile on us, it'll move on before it truly makes itself known. If it doesn't, not a single prayer we can make to any deity will do us a bit of good. Now go and get a table. I'm going to gather the other lads patrolling High Hill."

"But—" Rayce started.

Uncle Staephyn raised his finger again. "Don't ask. Don't argue. Don't question. Just do. I'll buy the drinks and bear the brunt of the captain's anger should it come to that."

"Let's go," Kaenyth said.

He grabbed his cousin by the arm and pulled him toward Crows' Court. It was a fine tavern, with some very pretty servers – not as pretty as Tarshiva, but well enough to look on. If luck truly smiled on them, Rayce would drink enough to bolster his courage and try to flirt with one of the serving girls. That might be enough entertainment to draw Kaenyth's mind from Tar, at least for a while.

"What do you—?"

Kaenyth silenced his cousin by smacking him in the back of the head; he hadn't mastered Uncle Staephyn's finger trick yet.

"You're so good at following orders except when it comes to your mouth. We got told not to ask, so bloody well don't ask. Something's got to be bad if he's having us stand off our watch – something worse than the grain riots. He was right about those, too. Tonight, we keep our mouths closed and our ears and eyes open, do what he says when he says to do it, and pray to the gods and goddesses, especially Sister Wind, that whatever this is passes us without notice."

For one of the few times in his life, Rayce managed to keep control of his curiosity. "Free drinks for the evening sounds very nice. Maybe at a table toward the back of Crows' Court."

The cousins nodded and continued walking away from Bastian's Inn.

Kaenyth couldn't help but glance back over his shoulder, hoping for one final look at Tarshiva. The gods only knew when he was going to be lucky enough to draw the duty tile for High Hill again. He didn't see Tarshiva, but he did see the tall lanky man she'd been throwing knives with. That man now had one of those dark gray scarves that everyone in the nobleman's entourage had been wearing, and it was wrapped around his neck. The man placed his hand on the hilt of his rapier, made eye contact with Kaenyth, and nodded, as if to say, *wise choice to move on.*

"Yes," Kaenyth said, taking his eyes away from Bastian's Inn. "Free drinks sounds splendid."

FIVE

A cold sweat rolled between Carmine's shoulder blades as he walked past the Reds and into the house. In the front room, Hardin sat with a man wearing the mantle of an Adept of House Kaesiak and a lady of House Floraen. He didn't recognize the Kaesiak Adept, but the Floraen was yet another relative. However, unlike Gianni, Contessa Rosella Andres served Old Uncle Night. Her presence was almost welcome. While she wasn't a halfblood like Carmine, she had not been allowed to train as an Adept of All Father Sun for political reasons.

"Ah, Carmine," Hardin said. "I was just telling Rosella and Graegyr about the potion you developed allowing you to control Draqons."

"Good morning, dear cousin," Rosella said. "I think it's marvelous what you've done."

As always, her dark eyes smiled and her brown hair fell from her head in perfectly curled ringlets. She stood up and offered Carmine her right hand. He kissed the knuckle above her second finger, then they kissed each other on both cheeks.

"Thank you for the kind words, cousin," Carmine replied.

"Might you have enough for another squad?" the Kaesiak Adept asked, his voice coming out as a scratched whisper from behind his mask. Like all Kaesiak Adepts, Graegyr wore a mask, though unlike many of House Kaesiak whose masks were tokens at best, his mask covered every part of his face except his eyes.

"Carmine, allow me to introduce my fiancé, Adept Syr Graegyr Vaesna of the Order of Doom," Rosella said. "His father is Prince Gaeriok Vaesna, and his mother is Patrizia Salvatore. Our marriage will help the bonds of our Houses when the Zenith changes."

"Your acquaintance is my pleasure," Carmine said. "I have enough to make sure your squad will obey after learning our true loyalties."

"The privilege is mine," Graegyr said, the very edges of his eyes turning upward. "And I will consider myself indebted to you, if you can get those creatures outside to follow me as a Night Adept rather than a Shadow Adept."

"It will be done, Syr Graegyr," Carmine said, offering a polite bow.

"These two are going to help us with our Morigahnti problem," Hardin said. "Aside from the squad of Draqons Graegyr brings, thirty Brothers follow Rosella."

"That's good," Carmine replied. "Because another two Morigahnti Fists are joining Julianna today."

"Julianna?" Graegyr asked.

"The Lord Morigahn," Carmine replied. "I know her from before she gained the title. It is difficult for me to think of her in such terms."

"Her?" Rosella's face tightened, revealing her shock. "The Lord Morigahn is a woman?"

Carmine and Hardin nodded.

"Interesting," Graegyr said.

"Why?" Hardin asked.

"To our knowledge," Graegyr said, "no woman has ever held the title of Lord Morigahn. I wonder what this means for the future of the Morigahnti."

"It does not matter what this means," Rosella snapped. "Once the Brotherhood solidifies its hold on the Zenith, we will eradicate every faction of heretics in every Kingdom province."

"That might well happen with the Shining Knights of Heidenmarch and other more vocal heretical groups," Hardin said. "But the Morigahnti are like the wasting sickness. You can amputate the limb with festering skin, however, by that time it has spread beneath the surface and the only way to kill the sickness is to burn the body. I fear the world will never be free of the Morigahnti."

"But—" Rosella started.

"He is right, my love," Graegyr said. "The Morigahnti will always be, and we want it that way. How many times has the Brotherhood used the Morigahnti and groups like them to mask our own activities? Why do you think that we have such a strong presence in Koma?"

"Fellow Night Adepts," Carmine said, "we could discuss this well into the night while allowing the Morigahnti to either fortify their position or flee the city, or we could formulate some strategy for attacking them."

"An excellent thought," Graegyr said. "I think first we should see to the Reds."

"Very well," Carmine said. "If you will follow me, I have the potion upstairs. It will probably be better if you gave it to them."

For a moment, Graegyr sat and stared out from behind his mask. Carmine bit down on the inside of his cheek. Gods and goddesses, he wanted to know what that man was thinking.

"You are correct," Graegyr said at last. "Lead the way."

Carmine bit the other cheek to keep from heaving a relieved sigh. As he went up the stairs, he heard Graegyr's heavy boots pounding behind him.

When they were alone upstairs, Graegyr faced Carmine. "You seemed eager to get me alone."

"I was," Carmine replied.

As he rummaged through his pack, someone knocked on the door. Carmine paused and considered.

"Come in, Sylvie," Carmine said.

The door opened, and Sylvie entered the room. She had changed out of the sitting dress she'd been wearing earlier and now wore the carefully crafted outfit they'd constructed to deceive their target.

"Oh, pardon, Adept Carmine," Sylvie said, dropping into a curtsy, "I didn't know you had a guest."

Carmine glanced at Graegyr. Even though the mask hid most of the Kaesiak Adept's features, his gaze was noticeably drifting toward Sylvie's neckline. Being so young and slight, the dark-haired beauty did not have an ample bosom; however, her bodice and chemise had been arranged to tease men's imaginations, to make them wonder if Sylvie's breasts were everything the low neckline and uplifting bodice promised.

"May I introduce Countess Sylvie Raelle of House Tsieskas," Carmine said. "Countess, this is Adept Syr Graegyr Vaesna of the Order of Doom."

"It is my very good pleasure to meet you, Adept Syr Graegyr," Sylvie lowered her curtsy. "And again, I apologize for my interruption."

"No need to apologize, my dear," Graegyr said. "And rise." Graegyr glanced at Carmine. "I have a feeling that the two of you don't stand so much on ceremony and propriety in this room."

Sylvie blushed just a slight shade of pink and looked away. What a beautiful little liar she was, having learned well Carmine's lessons about containing and channeling her emotions.

Sylvie rose. "Thank you, Syr Adept."

Graegyr kept his attention lingering on her a moment longer before he faced Carmine.

"How much does she know?' Graegyr asked.

"She knows as much as any initiate Nightbrother," Carmine replied.

"Interesting," Graegyr said. "I believed that all Komati secretly harbored the hope that the Morigahnti would rise and reclaim their right to worship Grandfather Shadow. Is this not the truth in your heart, Countess Sylvie Raelle?"

"Syr Adept, until a few short weeks ago, I was content to send my prayers to the lesser gods. Several of my sister's friends worshipped above their stations, and because of that, my sister is dead. At first I blamed the Brotherhood, but then I learned that the fault lies with my countrymen. If they wish to raise themselves to be worthy of worshipping one of the five, then they should have dedicated themselves to proving their loyalty to the Sun King and being raised to the High Blood."

"The Sun King?" Graegyr's question held a dangerous air.

"Yes, Syr Adept. As flawed as it is, they wish to worship Grandfather Shadow. I desire to prove myself to the First Adept of Old Uncle Night once the Brotherhood achieves the Zenyth, and be named High Blood by him. Then I will help Adept Carmine hunt down the traitors and blasphemers. They deserve nothing less than the Rite of Undoing."

"And if the Night King does not find her worthy?" Graegyr asked Carmine.

"Then she has failed," Carmine said.

"Very well." Graegyr nodded. "It will be interesting to watch and see how this plays out."

"Indeed," Carmine said. "As for now, Sylvie must go meet with one of the Morigahnti – their captain. We've been laying this trap for him for several days. If she is late, it will raise his suspicions."

"And how have you baited this Morigahnti captain?" Graegyr asked.

"One hears all sorts of things about men at Court when one is looking to better herself with a profitable marriage," Sylvie said. "For example, a certain count who will not allow his younger brother to come to court because his younger brother, a baron, has an appreciation for young ladies and isn't terribly discerning about gaining their affections. This baron was found with two of my mother's servants during a visit to court."

"When Sylvie told me of this scandal, I knew we could make use of it somehow," Carmine said. "Sylvie herself offered to play the part of a young lady just looking for a little extra coin to help feed her family."

"Brilliant," Graegyr said. "I understand what the First Adept sees in you, even if that idiot Swaenmarch he's shackled you to does not."

"Sylvie," Carmine said, "take Jorgen and two other Nightbrothers to watch you, on the chance something goes wrong."

"Two of the Brothers that came with Rosella and myself," Graegyr said. "We need the Brothers to mingle together, and our men are fresher."

"Yes, Syr Adept," Sylvie said, and gave her wonderfully alluring curtsy again.

"Don't worry, my sweet," Carmine said. "We'll be there in time to make sure we take him before he can do anything to you."

When Sylvie left, Graegyr said, "That's quite a young lady. Are you sure you'll be able to handle her once she becomes High Blood in her own right?"

"No," Carmine replied, "but that's part of what makes her so enticing."

"Indeed, and well said. Now, let us return to the reason you brought me up here."

Carmine returned to his pack. After a few moments of rummaging at the bottom, he found the mask he had taken from Vycktor Ilsaen. Carmine held the mask out to Graegyr and pointed to the symbol he'd found inside. "Do you know what this means?"

Graegyr studied the symbol for a moment. "That is the symbol of the Mother of Lies. I would expect you to know that."

"I *do* know that. I'm wondering what this symbol is doing on the inside of a Kaesiak Adept's mask?"

"Ah. As to that, I have no idea. I haven't even heard the whisper of a rumor that members of my family had demeaned themselves by pledging to a *lesser* god. Have you told anyone else about this?"

"No." Again, Carmine wished he could see the Kaesiak's face to better judge his reaction. "I've been waiting to speak with a Brother from your House before bringing this to anyone else's attention."

"Perhaps once we finish with these Morigahnti, we will have to investigate these High Blood who have blasphemed themselves and thinned their blood."

Carmine nodded. For the first time since the First Adept had sent him out with Hardin, Carmine felt he had an ally, even if he was Kaesiak.

SIX

Faelin sat in the corner of the inn yard, observing the Morigahnti. Sandré's Fist moved around the yard like kings in their own palaces. They pushed past the other Morigahnti and made it clear that anyone who was not Morigahnti was not welcome. On four separate occasions, a customer entered the yard, and each time, three men of Sandré's Fist blocked their way. They laughed and joked with each other but became quiet and sullen whenever anyone outside their numbers came near. Even the members of the other two Fists received some of this treatment, though to a lesser extent. While Sandré's Fist wasn't outright belligerent to the other Morigahnti, they made it obvious who owed deference to whom.

Nathan left a conversation with two of Sandré's Morigahnti with all the quiet fury of a storm cloud on the horizon. Four steps away, he heaved a deep breath, saw Faelin, changed direction, and sat down next to him.

"Shades, I hate the Collaen Morigahnti sometimes," Nathan snarled between clenched teeth. "There's been no one to keep them in check ever since we lost House Eras to the Kingdom. Someday there will be a reckoning for their betrayal."

"Do you seek to pass judgment?" Faelin asked.

"Oh, no," Nathan replied. "I will happily leave that honor and duty to *aen Tsumari'osa.*"

"That may be a long way off," Faelin said, as he recalled his friend Damian running into the night after the fighting at Shadybrook. *Hide among your sultans and nomad lords across the sea. Koma is no place for you right now.*

They sat in silence. He thought about Damian, smiling at fond memories and shaking his head at the audacious schemes Damian would convince them all were good ideas. If the gods smiled on Damian, Faelin was unlikely to see him again. On the other side of the coin, if the gods did not smile on Damian, the same would likely be true. He quietly thanked Grandfather Shadow for giving him one last happy moment with his friend. This brought to mind other friends that he would never see again: Khellan Dubhan and Allifar Thaedus, among many others.

Then Faelin remembered another person who was absent, yet should not be.

"Where is Parsh, really?" Faelin asked. "What errands keep him away from the inn so much? If he were here, Prince Sandré's arrival might have gone a little more smoothly."

"No it wouldn't," Nathan said.

Faelin looked at Nathan, seeking further explanation.

The Morigahnti shrugged.

"If there is a rift in the Morigahnti," Faelin said, "now would be a good time to decide where your loyalties lie."

Nathan returned Faelin's unblinking stare. He shrugged again.

"I call her Lord Morigahn. Not Julianna. Not Duchess Taraen. Even in my own thoughts, I call her Lord Morigahn. Thyr has called her Lord Morigahn, and that is enough for me."

"So, explain about Parsh."

Nathan took in a deep breath, held it for a moment, and let it out slowly. He scratched his forehead, right at the edge of his hairline, and then ran his hand through his hair. Finally, he sighed and spoke in a low tone, barely above a whisper. "Parsh believes Sandré has the longest shadow in Koma. Support for or against Prince Sandré Collaen was the longest running and most heated argument between Parsh and Count Allifar. I won't bore you with the details, but even standing next to the Lord Morigahn, Parsh would have at the very least remained silent rather than oppose Prince Sandré. Speaking of this, why does His Highness show you so much hostility?"

Faelin considered how much of his past he should reveal. He weighed it in his mind and realized that Nathan had just shared a dangerous confidence of his own. "Prince Sandré and my father were friends. My father's wife was Sandré's sister. My acceptance into the Traejyn family always struck the Collaen family as an affront to their honor. Sandré took it especially hard, and because he wouldn't confront my father about it for political reasons, he vented his frustrations on me."

"Why does he think you are not yourself?"

"He's being an idiot," Faelin answered. "What he said was true, he saw me with my family just before the battle. I wanted to fight, but then Sandré convinced them I wasn't worthy. They sent me away just before the Draqons attacked. He knows who I am, but he likely believes that my presence might gain sympathy and loyalty for the Lord Morigahn from those who were friendly to my family. If he can discredit me, then he robs the Lord Morigahn of that advantage."

"He may not need to work overly hard to convince anyone," Nathan said. "It will be hard for most Morigahnti to accept that Grandfather Shadow sent you, and not a true Morigahnti, to protect the Lord Morigahn."

"I know," Faelin replied. "But perhaps it is because I am not Morigahnti that Grandfather Shadow sent me."

"What do you mean?"

"I think somebody betrayed Khellan. One of his supposed friends was an Adept of the Brotherhood of the Night, but someone had to let that Adept know who Khellan was."

"No Morigahnti would betray the Lord Morigahn." Nathan's voice grew hard.

Faelin considered his next words carefully. "Think of how long the Kingdom has existed. In all of those centuries, the four Great Houses have been trying to eradicate the Brotherhood of the Night. They have never succeeded, and the Brotherhood maintains enough power to assume the Zenith every few centuries. That means Old Uncle Night has a continuous flow of followers from the High Blood of all the Great Houses. How do they hide so well, especially considering the Adepts of Kaesiak and Floraen have powers granted by their gods to pierce through any secret or lie?"

Nathan nodded. "Except for those who follow the God of Lies."

"When truth and knowledge die, only lies remain," Faelin said.

"I still can't believe one of our own might betray a Lord Morigahn."

"Someone betrayed the Traejyns," Faelin said. "That's the only way the Kingdom could have discovered them. Like Allifar's family, the Traejyns and their servants followed the old ways. It had to be someone from the outside, but close enough to know the family's secret.

"Then there was Khellan. How did the Brotherhood happen upon him? They had more than enough men and Daemyn hounds to fight Khellan and his friends."

"Do you have any suspicions?" Nathan asked.

"No," Faelin said. "I don't know enough Morigahnti, much less who might have known my family and Khellan. Also, it might be more than one person. Who knows how fully the Morigahnti have been infiltrated or corrupted?"

Nathan scanned the Morigahnti milling about the inn yard. "That is a chilling thought."

"It is," Faelin said.

Faelin had to consider that any Morigahnti might be a danger to Julianna. If this idea circulated through their ranks, many would see him as a threat. Since Faelin was not Morigahnti, they would have no qualms about killing him. Julianna hadn't ordered any of them not to harm him. Even if she did, some doubted her claim and might try to kill him anyway.

"You never answered my question," Faelin said. "Where is Parsh?"

"He's found a whore that he likes," Nathan replied as if it were the most natural thing in the world. "Shadow willing, he'll be back soon."

SEVEN

Julianna looked up from the *Galad'parma* when someone knocked on the door.

She wrapped her *Galad'fana* around her face, just to be safe, and called, "Enter."

The door opened, and Nathan put just his head in.

"Lord Morigahn," he said, "a man wishes to speak with you. He wears the leathers and mask of a Dosahan, though I think he is Komati. He said you would know him."

Julianna allowed herself a smile beneath the shadow veil concealing her face. She had been wondering when she would see this man again.

"I know this man, and he has done me a service," Julianna said. "Show him in."

Nathan opened the door all the way. The strange man still wore his unpainted leathers, including the mask, which was really just a panel of leather, that covered his face, including mouth and eyes.

"Thank you, Nathan. See that we're not disturbed."

Nathan nodded and closed the door after Smoke entered. Julianna lowered her *Galad'fana*.

"Good evening," she said, and gestured to the chair on the other side of the table. "Please sit. May I offer you some tea?"

"Thank you." Smoke sat. From the way he lowered himself into the chair, Julianna wondered how long it had been since the man had actually sat in one. "But I must decline the tea. I would have to show my face, and my…"

"…identity is a precious and dangerous coin," Julianna said. "How close was I?"

"Fairly," Smoke replied. "Not exactly as I would have put it, but closer than not. You've changed much since our last conversation."

"The world and circumstances have forced me to change," Julianna replied. "The last time we spoke, I was still coming to terms with my situation, and in some ways I still am. I was also too quick to lie to myself. I'm attempting to change that."

Smoke nodded. "You've discovered more wisdom than most people born to noble title ever will."

"They have a luxury I can't afford," Julianna said. She took a sip of tea, giving Smoke time to fill the silence. When he did not, Julianna asked, "What do you want?"

"Since you have learned my first lesson, accepting truths that you don't actually want to hear, I've come to teach you the other side of that coin. Being brave enough to tell people what they don't want to hear, especially when they have the power to make life unpleasant for you."

"I believe I already know that lesson," Julianna said.

"Oh, really?" Smoke replied, and even though Julianna could not see his face, she sensed the smile his mask hid. "In that case, you have the perfect opportunity to prove it. Sandré Collaen approaches, I'm fairly certain that you'll have to tell him something he doesn't want to hear."

Julianna sighed as she heard voices raised outside her door. She stood, walked across the room, and opened the door.

Sandré Collaen stood there, finger waving under Nathan's nose. Aurell leaned against the wall on the other side of the hall.

"Thank you, Nathan, for observing my wishes," Julianna said, then turned to Sandré. "Prince Collaen, won't you come in?"

Sandré sniffed and pushed past her into the room.

Aurell stood stiffly and started after Sandré, hand on the hilt of her rapier. She and Nathan looked as if they were about to draw rapiers and cut Sandré down from behind. Julianna raised her hand to calm them. Her guard looked at her questioningly.

"I'll be fine," Julianna said.

Nathan saluted and returned to watching the hall. Aurell hesitated for a moment longer. She set her shoulders and craned her neck to look past Julianna, eyeing Sandré with no small amount of suspicion. Julianna caught Aurell's attention and nodded. Aurell sighed, saluted, and leaned back against the wall.

When Julianna shut the door and turned back to the room, she wasn't at all surprised to find Smoke no longer there.

"Please sit," Julianna said, as she returned to her chair. She remained standing, waiting for him to accept her invitation. "May I offer you some tea?"

"I prefer to stand, Your Grace," Sandré replied, "and no tea."

Julianna sat and looked at Sandré for a long moment. Sandré returned this inspection with a sneer.

"So it's to be like that?" Julianna asked

"Like what?" Sandré retorted.

45

"All titles and honorifics? Prince this. Duchess that."

"You are a duchess of House Kolmonen, are you not?" Sandré asked. "I am a Prince of House Aesin. And as you have asked, yes, it is to be like that, Your Grace. I believe you should be referring to me as *Your Highness.*"

Julianna took a long sip of tea. Coming to Smoke's lesson had been faster than she had anticipated.

"Very well then, Your Highness," Julianna said. "What would you have of me?"

"I know that many believe you to be the Lord Morigahn, and I am willing to entertain this façade until such time that the trials kill you, ending this farce, at least in public. In private, Duchess Taraen, I expect you to follow the proper order of precedence. Do you understand?"

Julianna took another drink of tea, and considered how to respond.

"Anything else," she asked, and added after a noticeable pause, "Your Highness?"

"Yes. We should be away from this place. Now. You've been here too long already. The Brotherhood of the Night or the Floraen Inquisitors may already know where you are. Remaining only increases their chances of taking you. I have a river craft in the harbor. Every man aboard follows the old ways and is prepared to fight our enemies to the death."

And every man aboard is undoubtedly loyal to you. Julianna kept that suspicion to herself. Instead she replied, "Such concern for someone you do not believe is the Lord Morigahn."

"My concern is for the Morigahnti following you. Your actions and choices affect them as well, as well as what your death may do to the morale and spirit of the Morigahnti as a whole."

The dead of Shadybrook came unbidden into Julianna's mind. The memory of Mistress Dressel lying in her own blood would haunt Julianna for the rest of her life.

Julianna stood. "I understand the expectation, Your Highness. I also understand that you have no idea how aware I am that my choices and actions affect others. I understand also that you should steel yourself for disappointment if you believe that you can come in here and bully me about."

Julianna rounded the table and walked right up to Sandré Collaen, less than two hand spans separating them.

"Look at my scar," Julianna said.

Sandré tried to step away from her, but Julianna grabbed his shoulder. She expected him to pull away, but he had a slight, frail frame, and so she held him in place. Perhaps he was also too shocked to fight.

"Look how it does not heal."

Sandré's face flushed, and his lips pulled back in a feral snarl. "I will not be mocked in this way by a fraud." He shoved her away from him. Despite his frail form, Sandré Collaen possessed surprising strength.

Julianna stumbled back and gave a curtsy so perfect in its formality that Aunt Maerie would have beamed with pride. "Congratulations, Your Highness. You have discovered me."

Sandré blinked at her several times. Her formality and the admission of his accusation seemed to take him by surprise. She stood and spoke to him plainly.

"Prince Collaen, look at the scar. Do you think I inflict this on myself every day, that I put my mother's knife in a fire until it glows red, and then use it to cut my face time and time again, every day, just to draw the Morigahnti into my subterfuge?"

Julianna returned to her chair and poured herself a fresh cup of tea.

"I do not intend to mock you, Prince Sandré." Julianna took a sip of the tea. "You are too great a man, and I am not that foolish a woman; however, on the other side of that coin, I will not be denied my place as Shadow's voice on earth."

She drank again, letting him take in her words.

"I am the Lord Morigahn, Prince Sandré. You may not believe this, but the Morigahnti you found with me do believe. We have fought together, lost good and loyal friends together. In all likelihood, they have spoken with the Morigahnti who arrived with you. I would wager some of them believe already."

She sipped her tea without removing her eyes from his.

"We will be at the trials soon enough, and if you are correct, I will die, and you can turn my death to whatever advantage you wish. Until then, we should work together as best we can, or we may very well pit Morigahnti against Morigahnti."

Sandré drew in a slow breath and released it. "Very well, but that means we should be away before the Brotherhood of the Night is upon us. At least to my river boat *The Stormrider*."

Julianna set her teacup down and looked out the window to the last vestiges of fading daylight. She had no intention of bowing to his suggestion.

"I've been the Lord Morigahn only a short time, but I've learned much since *Galad'Ysoysa* cut this scar on my face. It will take us at least an hour to properly prepare to leave, and that's *if* Baron Parshyval Thaedus returns from his *errand* by then. If the Brotherhood of the Night has discovered us, then fleeing now, during the *night* when they are at their strongest and have the advantage, would be foolish. No. It would be stupid. We've taken precautions in case of attack, Your Highness. We will leave at dawn. We will discuss our plans for leaving Johki. I'll see you in the morning."

"We still must discuss this *Taekuri* bastard you have serving you."

"Take care, Prince Sandré," Julianna kept her voice perfectly even, "Faelin vara'Traejyn was chosen by Grandfather Shadow to guide and protect me. He has been at my side from nearly the time Grandfather Shadow marked me as *aen Morigahn'uljas*. Do not broach this subject with me again. Ever again. All other matters can wait for the morning."

Sandré opened his mouth to say something, but Julianna cut him off. "I said, *in the morning.*"

With that, Julianna reopened the *Galad'parma* and gave the appearance of looking over a page from the writings of Saent Kyllian the Cunning. When she heard the door open, then close, Julianna looked up to ensure that Sandré Collaen had actually left her suite. Seeing him gone, Julianna ruffled through the *Galad'parma* to the writings of Saent Julian the Courageous. Her namesake had had issues with several of his Fist captains. Perhaps Julianna could learn to deal with Sandré Collaen from those tales. That's what she would focus on until Smoke returned.

EIGHT

Carmine smiled as his vision returned to his own eyes. Hardin and Rosella looked as if they were children sitting at the Festival of Sweets waiting for the bags to fall.

"They are staying the night," Carmine said, "for fear that moving now will be too great a risk." He decided to keep the knowledge of Faelin training with the Taekuri to himself. That might prove precious coin in a future bargain, and he wouldn't spend it lightly.

"Excellent," Hardin said. "Between four Adepts, more than a full squad of Reds, and our remaining Bothers, victory is nearly guaranteed."

"I wonder," Graegyr said. "Did you also think that at Shadybrook?"

Hardin's face tightened and darkened to a deep red.

Carmine bit hard into his lip, almost to the point of drawing blood, to keep from laughing. Rosella snickered, but then, she was a full Adept of Old Uncle Night. Her relation to the First Adept even put her status slightly above that of both Hardin and Graegyr.

"Shadybrook was a disaster because of those two Adepts serving lesser gods." Hardin spoke in a high-pitched whine. "Had we been able to act as true Brothers of the Night, the Lord Morigahn would be dead or carrying a Daemyn child inside her by now."

Rosella's snickering stopped. "Well, she's neither," her tone was flat and cool, "and now we have to rectify that." She turned to Carmine and her voice softened. "And thanks to my cousin, we know we have all night to take them. Excellent work."

"Thank you," Carmine said.

"Adepts?" came a voice from the door. It was one of the Nightbrothers who followed Rosella and Graegyr. "I apologize for the interruption, but two of the Reds seem to be resisting Adept Carmine's potion."

"Deal with your mess," Hardin snapped. "Then let us be on our way."

Carmine hurried out the door and heard Rosella say, "Really, Hardin, must you be so harsh with him?"

That gave Carmine a smile. He had little love for many of his relatives on either side of his family, but Rosella had always been kind.

Outside, two of the Reds stood back to back over the corpse of one of the Nightbrothers. They moved in a slow circle keeping their weapons moving to dissuade the Reds that surrounded them from coming too close. Carmine couldn't determine which Brother they had killed – the front half of his head, including his face, had been sliced off.

Carmine drew on the Dominion of Fear and focused on the two Reds in the center. "*Tzizma shu moth Dragon roos.*"

The two Reds in the center of the circle froze.

"Kill them."

With the two rebellious Reds paralyzed by fear, the loyal Reds made short work of them. Carmine didn't bother to watch, though normally he would have. Instead, he pondered why those two Reds had resisted the potion. Once they dealt with the Morigahnti, he would have to study this.

"Dispose of the bodies," Carmine said, "then return. We're hunting Morigahnti tonight."

The Reds hurried to carry out his command, and Carmine smiled. He had allies now, and soon Julianna would be his.

NINE

Watching the disgusting old man – he was something like thirty, *and* only a baron – approach and not spit in his face was one of the most difficult things Sylvie had ever done. He swaggered toward her, hand on the hilt of his rapier and a rakish smile on his lips, as if she would ever have had anything to do with him if killing him wasn't part of Carmine's plan. He was *old*, and more than that, he was only a baron.

"Parsh, my darling," Sylvie said. "I expected you long ago."

When he reached her, the traitor swept her into his arms. He was strong, especially considering his age, in his late thirties at least. And that strength was about the only thing he could claim to his credit.

"I'm sorry, sweetling," Parsh replied. "I was detained by the lady I serve. But I'm here now, and I brought good coin."

"You should pay double for making me wait," Sylvie said, whispering into his ear. Then she pouted. "I missed you."

"If you can do all the things you claim, and make me feel the way you promised, I'll pay you triple."

"In that case, I'll make you beg me to take quadruple," Sylvie said, and squirmed out of his grip.

Sylvie took him by the hand and led him into an alley, up a flight of rickety stairs, and into a shabby, one-room flat with only a sink, stove, table, and bed for furnishings. There were no chairs. Only two wooden boxes sat next to the table. She led Parsh to the edge of the bed and pushed him over. Then, as his eyes soaked in the sight of her, she undressed. She made it a slow process, teasing him with every ribbon she tugged and every unfastened button. He sat up and reached for her, but she put her hand on his forehead and pushed him back down.

"No touching." She waved a stern finger at him. "Yet."

When Sylvie was naked, she turned around several times, letting him see every part of her. She ran her hands over all the places she knew he wanted to explore. It was just another way to stall. Before he could get too impatient with her, she walked over and knelt between his legs. To keep from vomiting, she imagined it was Carmine she knelt before rather than this ancient creature.

As she fumbled with his belt and drawstring of his pants, she thanked all the lesser gods that many whores refused to kiss their clients on the mouth. She'd learned that eavesdropping on her father and his friends at her parents' last dinner party.

When she had Parsh's pants down around his ankles, she recalled the first time she'd given herself to Carmine. He made her mind and body melt with the things he'd done to her with his fingers, tongue, and manhood. His stamina amazed her, as did his desire to please her as much as she pleased him. As they continued pleasing each other, Sylvie found herself craving his touch more and more. Now they shared each other at least once a day.

Parsh moaned as she fondled him. She would have to use her mouth soon, but not yet. Sunset was close, but not that close, and that was how long she needed to distract him. He might have too much power during twilight. They needed to strike at him after night fell, transforming most of the shadows into true darkness.

"Why are you going so slowly?" Parsh asked between gasps.

"You have somewhere you'd rather be?" Sylvie asked.

"No."

"Good." She put her mouth right next to him so he could feel her breath as she spoke. Carmine loved that. "Now shut up while I convince you to pay me more by seven."

To further remove her mind from the task at hand, Sylvie thought of the talks she had with Carmine while she rode behind him. She had ridden in the wagon the first day, but after that she rode on his horse, holding onto his well-muscled torso, and Carmine explained more about the Brotherhood of the Night. They were a necessary part of Kingdom politics, just as Old Uncle Night was a necessary part of the celestial order.

"What was that?" Parsh asked, sitting bolt upright.

Sylvie had heard it too – a creak on the stairs outside. She looked out the room's single window. Darkness had not quite fallen outside. She only needed to keep the traitor distracted a few more moments, and then Carmine could come in and finish him.

She lowered her face into his lap, taking him into her mouth. He gasped. A moment later, white and black spots flashed in her eyes when Parsh slapped her. Sylvie pulled back, shaking her head to clear the pain. Parsh pushed her away with such force that she stumbled across the room and fell.

Rather than pull his pants up, Parsh snatched his gray scarf and wrapped it around his head, hiding all but his eyes.

"*Kraeston kansa aen thanya'haeth!*" Parsh shouted, and pushed his hands toward the door.

Sylvie struggled to breathe as all the air in the room blasted away from Parsh with the force of a gale and ripped the wall containing the door to shreds. As the debris flew across the alley and smashed into the next building, the wind also carried two Red Draqons cartwheeling through the air. They crashed into the opposite wall with a sickening crunch. Their broken bodies fell to the cobblestones below.

Moments later, air rushed back into the room and Sylvie gasped for it, trying to suck it in as a man dying of thirst might ravage a goblet of water.

Parsh pulled his pants up and tied the drawstrings as he moved. He kicked his rapier into his hand as he ran to the edge of the floor.

Even sobbing on the floor, Sylvie did her best to be still. The last thing she wanted to do was call attention to herself and remind him that she was part of this attempt to end his life.

"*Galad y stiva rus mina!*" Parsh shouted.

He stepped into the air, and a plane of darkness rose to meet his feet. As he ran, that solid darkness rose ahead of him all the way to the rooftop across the alley. Moments later, Parsh disappeared across the rooftops.

Still gasping and sobbing, Sylvie spat several times, trying to get the taste of the traitor out of her mouth. The nausea she felt was only partially due to that. Adept Hardin would blame this on her. In her secret heart, she prayed to Old Uncle Night that Carmine wouldn't believe the lies Adept Hardin would tell him and be disappointed with her.

TEN

Carmine ground his teeth together while watching the scene through his Nightbat's eyes. The Draqons had climbed the stairs with all the stealth of a pair of pregnant cows. It was no wonder the Morigahnti heard them and was able to escape. For a moment, Carmine considered pushing a knife into Hardin's eye, but stayed his hand. Not because of any loyalty, but because he didn't know who Rosella would side with. She and Carmine were cousins by blood, but Hardin ranked high in the Brotherhood. Rosella might choose religion over blood – especially since she was unaware of Carmine's close ties to the First Adept. Guessing Graegyr's alliance was no great feat of intellect. Carmine had no doubt the Kaesiak would side with Rosella.

If only Hardin had waited, their plan would have worked and they could pick the Morigahnti off one by one. Now, because of House Swaenmarch's damned impatience, they were going to have to fight another battle, and this time the Morigahnti knew they were coming. It had also taken him the better part of two days to convince Sylvie to act the part of a whore. There was no telling how much damage this had done to his attempts to train her.

Hardin made eye contact with the Nightbat. "Take the Brothers, and the Draqons, and kill them all."

"Yes, Adept Hardin," Carmine said.

He would obey – for now. However, he wouldn't save Julianna for the Daemyn. Carmine knew a special ritual that he planned to use as he watched the life fade from her eyes. He would send her soul to the Realm of the Godless Dead.

ELEVEN

Dice rolled, and four of the six Vara sitting around the table cried out: three in excitement, one in a groan of defeat. Kaenyth couldn't quite sympathize with Rayce for rolling six. Tarshiva and all those strangers at Bastian's Inn plagued Kaenyth's mind. Granted, Tar and her father ran an inn; strangers were a part of that business. But so many at once? And why did they seem more like soldiers than household guards and servants?

Copper coins rattled on the table. Kaenyth added his penny to the pile. He hadn't even heard what game they were playing. Dice rolled. More cheers and groans echoed from their little corner of Crows' Court. Again, Kaenyth Rool didn't follow the outcome; he hardly noticed when someone else pushed two coins in front of him.

"I'm out for this game," Kaenyth said, stood up, and wove his way through the crowd to the bar. "Stout," he said before the tavern keeper opened his mouth to ask what Kaenyth wanted, "The thickest, strongest stout you have."

Less than a minute later, the tavern keeper placed a new mug in front of Kaenyth.

"Heavy drinking," Uncle Staephyn said, pushing up to the bar next to Kaenyth.

"It's that kind of night," Kaenyth replied.

"You've got the look of a man with a woman on his mind," Staephyn said. "Your father had the same look when he was worried about your mother."

Kaenyth took a long draw off his stout and held it in his mouth for a long moment, ten heartbeats worth, before swallowing. He exhaled to make sure not to inhale the lingering traces of the brew into his lungs. He missed his father, the man who'd taught him the secrets to drinking like a proper man. Thinking of seeing his father heading off to what would be later known as the battle of Kyrtigaen Pass, Kaenyth took another drink. As he swallowed, everything came together, the strangers acting like soldiers, Kyrtigaen Pass, and Uncle's insistence that they not stand their posts.

"It's *them* isn't it?" Kaenyth asked.

"You're a smart lad," Uncle Staephyn said. "Smarter than your cousin and most of the other Vara recruits. You learn when it's a good time to use those smarts and when it's a better time not to, I'll be calling you Sir one day."

Kaenyth looked to the door. "I have to—"

"Do nothing," Uncle Staephyn said. "She's beyond your help. Just pray to the proper gods and goddesses that *they* move on without incident. We're in a city, so odds might favor us, but it's all in the gods' hands. If things are going to go bad, there isn't a damn and bloody thing we can do about it."

"Yes, Uncle." Kaenyth took another drink.

"That's to be your last," Uncle Staephyn said. "We still have to report in at the end of our watch, and you'd best not have any lingering on your breath."

"I've got a ginger root in my purse," Kaenyth said.

It was one of the first lessons any recruits learned. Businesses liked to offer the Vara who patrolled their neighborhoods a friendly drink. While it was rude to decline such offers, it was also against regulations to drink while on duty. Ginger root became a patrolling Vara's best friend.

"Well enough then," Uncle Staephyn said. "Now, let's be back to our dicing."

Kaenyth took up his mug and followed his uncle back to the table.

The dicing continued, and Kaenyth did his best to push Tarshiva, his father, and *them* out of his mind. The stout and his friends' excitement helped. A short while later, his head spinning just a bit from his nearly gone drink, the Crows' Court became very quiet.

"Keep your eyes and faces plain, lads," Uncle Staephyn said. "I'll speak for us all. Keep your eyes down and maybe we'll be fine."

Kaenyth did as he was told and kept his eyes steady on his drink until Rayce sitting next to him muttered, "Damn and bloody damn." Then he couldn't help it. Kaenyth looked to the door. All the stout and ale he'd had that evening threatened to come back up.

The golden sun emblazoned on the silver breast plate caught Kaenyth's eye first. His breath caught in his throat. He blinked, and he managed to take in the golden cloak. *I'm looking at an Inquisitor*, his mind whispered through the haze brought on by the stout. And while that thought terrified Kaenyth, he also couldn't help but notice that golden cloak was not nearly as pure as he'd imagined it would be. Mud and dirt stained the cloak's edges. After a moment of staring, Kaenyth managed to pull his gaze from the breastplate and cloak to take in the man, that House Floraen Inquisitor of All Father Sun. His graying hair and dark eyes suggested he might be well into his forties; however, Staephyn's mind also whispered that he'd heard rumors that an Inquisitor often aged more quickly than other men.

The Inquisitor's gaze swept across the tavern: once, twice, and a third time. It settled on the table where the Vara had been dicing and drinking and trying to avoid trouble. Nodding, though Kaenyth wasn't sure if the Inquisitor was nodding to himself or the Vara, the Inquisitor made his way through the Crows' Court. He wove through the crowd with a grace that only men used to fighting for their lives seemed to possess. When Rayce and Kaenyth's class of recruits had been truly admitted to the Vara, Commander Dyrk had come up from Koma City. He walked in much the same way.

When the Inquisitor stepped up to the Vara's table, Uncle Staephyn met his gaze with a smooth expression.

"How may I serve the Sun King?" Uncle Staephyn asked.

"I am Inquisitor Don Luciano Salvatore of House Floraen, Order of the Dawn," the Inquisitor announced. "You are Sergeant Rool." That was not a question.

"I am," Uncle Staephyn replied.

"I would know why you and your men are not at your assigned watch."

Kaenyth and all of the Vara watched Uncle Staephyn carefully. Their sergeant couldn't very well lie, not to an Inquisitor.

"Lord Inquisitor." Staephyn took a deep breath and let it out slowly. He tapped the tabletop with his finger. "To be true, my two brothers fought at Kyrtigaen Pass. They were common men, and only serving their lord's orders, not traitors but men in fear for their wives, sons, and daughters. I know enough to know Morigahnti when I see them. We are simple watchmen and have no means to capture such as them. I brought my boys here to keep them out of trouble."

Inquisitor Luciano stared at Uncle Staephyn for a long moment. As the two men stared at each other, Kaenyth's throat grew dry. He really wanted to take a drink but dared not call any attention to himself. Rayce and the others started to fidget in their seats.

Finally, the Inquisitor broke the silence with, *"Kun vaen ovat kuten makae-sti."*

Staephyn blinked several times, and his head tilted a bit to the left. Kaenyth recalled hearing something like those words before, a long time ago, but he couldn't place where.

"I know those words," Staephyn said, "though none of the lads do. Punish me if you wish, but leave them be. They are the Sun King's good and loyal subjects."

"And how do you feel about those words, Sergeant Rool?" Inquisitor Luciano asked.

"They can be damned for all I bloody care. I miss my brothers."

The Inquisitor nodded. "I'd heard that you could be counted on. It seems loyal subjects to the Crown are in short supply these days. I need you to help me arrest someone: a woman at an inn not too far from here. I understand and appreciate your wisdom in wanting to stay clear of the Morigahnti. Know that standing with me, you have my protection and the protection of the Sun King...and likely his gratitude as well."

"We are the Sun King's subjects," Uncle Staephyn said, standing.

Kaenyth couldn't help but stare at his uncle for fear the man had gone mad. They weren't traitors by any means, but this display of false loyalty? Uncle Staephyn caught the look and fixed Kaenyth a stern stare in return. It was only a moment, but Kaenyth read the expression plain as if his uncle had spoken, "We have no choice but to obey and pray the gods and goddesses take pity on us."

Inquisitor Luciano stepped away from the table. Staephyn stood and the rest of the Vara recruits did likewise. They followed the Inquisitor out of the Crows' Court. Uncle Staephyn bade them slow to let the Inquisitor get a ways ahead of them.

"Keep your wits about you lads," Uncle Staephyn said. "Don't do anything stupid, and if it gets ugly, don't be a hero. Try to get somewhere safe and quiet. Oh, and pray. Pray like you've never prayed before. Maybe if we do, one of the gods or goddesses will hear you and some of us might survive this bloody mess."

SIDES OF A COIN

The creators called Koma City
the eighth mountain
when they completed their work and
saw it rising from the fog
supported on the islands
in the swamp
where the seven great rivers meet the great eastern sea.

A marvel unparalleled,
Built in a forgotten mix of technology and miracle,
The monument remains
Towering, reminding the world of Komati drive and ingenuity.

Huge stone pillars, like the hands of the gods themselves,
Support the levels of this city.
Levels
And neighborhoods
Span whole islands,
Where some people live out their lives traveling the spiral staircases and bridges
between the islands
Without ever placing their feet upon the ground.

Shrouded in fog.
Lit by lanterns throughout the city,
The Kingdom, ever failing, strives to maintain its laws.
Criminals, driven by greed and patriotism,
worm their way through the waterways, hidden passages, and darkened corners
as they did when the Morigahnti ruled, as they do as the Kingdom High Blood
rule,
as they shall do when Grandfather Shadow comes to rule again.

It is how the God of Balance would have it.
For he understands that opposition grants validity.
Balance
Opposition
These two mingle in perfect unison
Testing and pushing the Komati
Who call the Eighth Mountain home.
-          Kaelvinos

ONE

Damian Adryck crouched in an alley, ears straining for any sound of pursuit. Anyone who spent any amount of time in the lower levels of Koma City trained their ears well. Biting his lower lip, he forced his breathing to steady as he listened. The same fog and darkness that hid him also concealed his pursuers. His sides burned from outrunning the Wraiths, a gang of street toughs who ran in the Dockside and Warehouse districts of Koma City. Damian hadn't known the Wraiths controlled this territory, nor did he know this sale was supposed to be with the Wraiths.

"Damn you, Gareth!" Damian spat, then silenced himself. Any sound might give him away.

The fence was a fool. When Damian and Gareth met the Wraiths instead of their intended client – a disgruntled Komati baron who was likely being tortured by a House Floraen Inquisitor – Gareth tried to deal with the Wraiths instead. Before Damian could stop him, the gods-be-damned idiot had taken out the two-shot pistols. The Wraiths were one of the few gangs in Koma that swore fealty to one of the four Great Houses of the Kingdom of the Sun, and anyone who knew enough to listen to whispers on street corners could learn that – the Wraiths seemed to revel in it. If Gareth actually knew the streets half as well as he had claimed, he would still be alive.

By this time, White Draqons must have joined in the hunt. Now Damian had to focus on surviving the night, and he only had his clothes, a knife, a handful of coins, and three loaded firearms. He had some supplies hidden away, but that was on the other side of the city, too far to reach safely and get out of the city before sunlight rose and the Floraen Inquisitor would seek him through the aid of All Father Sun.

Someone coughed just outside of Damian's vision. He jumped, and then forced himself to calm down. No Wraith would make that kind of noise just before an attack. After Damian's heart slowed to normal, he edged forward. In the dim light cast by the far off gas lamps, he saw a large man fast asleep, cradling a bottle as if it were a lover.

The man's loose and baggy pants flowed free at the cuff, not bunched up at the ankles like current Komati fashion, and they only went down to the middle of his calf. His shoes had no laces and could be slipped on and off easily. His jacket was short with tight fitting sleeves, not long and loose like Damian's. Then, looking even closer, Damian saw pockets in the man's trousers and no purse at his belt. A sailor. Even though the jacket was tight on the sailor, he was easily twice Damian's size so that shouldn't be a problem.

Damian allowed himself the luxury of a smile as he gripped his scattergun with both hands. It was shorter than a long-gun, only coming up to his hip if he placed the butt on the ground. But it did have a good weight and was better for bludgeoning than the two-shot pistols in his belt. The scattergun's butt came down on the sailor's head, ensuring that he wouldn't wake while Damian stole his clothes. If Damian didn't rob him, someone else would, and they'd be less polite about it.

Shedding his coat, Damian turned the garment into a pack by folding it and tying the sleeves together. He slipped his boots off and put them in the pack. Next, Damian stripped the sailor of his coat and pants. As suspected, the sailor's coat was huge on Damian's slender frame, and that pleased him just fine. Damian stuffed his makeshift pack down the back of his new coat, giving himself the appearance of being a hunchback. For a moment, Damian considered taking the sailor's shoes, but then he rejected the thought. Anyone trying to find him by sound might ignore bare feet slapping the cobblestones. After all, who in their right mind would take their shoes off while running for their life? Damian pulled the sailors pants on over his own and then poured the last dregs of wine around his mouth and over his chest. He took some grime from the alley and rubbed it into his blond hair. Without a mirror, he couldn't see how well the disguise worked, but it was better than nothing. He concealed both two-shot pistols, but the scattergun was another matter entirely. He might be able to trade it for passage across the sea or sell the thing once he reached the Lands of Endless Summer. Discarding the weapon was out of the question. So Damian decided to use it as a cane. He prayed the fog obscured the firearm enough to actually fool any observers.

Turning to leave, Damian stopped. He examined his few remaining coins, shook out a few silver sevens, and shoved them into the sailor's under-britches. It was more than enough for him to buy some better-fitting clothes and have some left over for more wine.

When Damian hobbled out of the alley, the fog had cleared a bit and he studied his surroundings. Just on the other side of the street was Otto's butcher shop. Next to it was the Old Maids' Bakery, run by a trio of old women who nobody in Koma City seemed to remember ever being young. That meant he stood in between the seamstress's shop and the candlemaker's.

Damian smiled.

He was near the edge of Low Market, only a few blocks from a bridge leading to the Bazaar. There he could lose his hunters on the island of foreign tents and stalls, cross another bridge to the High Market, and then it was just a dance and a jig back to the Warrens. He might even be there within the hour. Once in the Warrens, Damian could disappear into one of his dens. After a few days the search would die down, and he could quietly slip out of the city without arousing any suspicions.

"Kahddria," Damian prayed under his breath, "if you are listening, for the aid I gave you, please let me make it. If I do, I'll consider our account balanced."

He wanted to imagine that the wind picked up ever so slightly, but he knew that was even more foolish than Gareth trying to sell the guns to the Wraiths. Then again, enlisting the goddess's aid might not be his wisest choice either.

The blocks passed by in agonizing slowness. Every few steps, he heard a sound or someone stepped from out of the fog. Forcing himself not to react took all of Damian's concentration. He was just a drunk hunchback on his way home from the public house, too blind by drink to care about strange noises in the night. Thankfully, each time it turned out to be nothing more than the normal sounds of dockside denizens. Soon, but not soon enough, only one block lay between Damian and escape. He fought the urge to quicken his pace. If he did anything but stumble like a drunkard, someone would take notice. If that someone were a Wraith, he would never finish his journey.

With less than a block to go, a firm grip fell on Damian's shoulder.

TWO

Walking through the dense fog that permeated the lower levels of Koma City, Xander Rosha approached the stronghold of the White Draqons. When he got close enough to see the structure – it was much more than a mere building, it was a giant shadow looming against the lights from the city's upper levels – Xander stopped. He dropped the bag that carried his clothes and few other belongings onto the cobblestone street. Cocking his head to one side, he considered this place he would call home until he proved his loyalty to the Kingdom or he died in service.

Xander had already served for two years with the Red Draqons. His blond hair had grown long in that time, and it was pulled back into nine braids, one for each of the battles he'd fought in. None of those battles had proven his loyalty, and neither had saving the life of his High Blood patron who had sponsored his rise from the Reds to the Whites. Xander was one of the few humans to ever be admitted to that elite group, and the only Komati.

Sighing, Xander picked up his bag and started for the fortress. As he approached, the building seemed to grow larger and larger and Xander felt smaller and smaller. When he stepped up to the gates and fell under the gaze of the two White Draqon sentries there, Xander found himself biting his cheek in order to focus his courage.

Both looked closer to their pure dragon ancestors than most of the Red Draqons Xander had known. Even in the gloom of the fog, Xander could see distinct scales on their faces. Their jaws jutted forward, and they had pronounced fangs and claws. Xander tried to count the braids spilling down over their shoulders, but they each had too many. Each of those braids represented a time when they saved a High Blood's life or had taken a wound protecting a High Blood.

The sentries looked him up and down with their solid white eyes. One of them snorted through its flattened nose.

The Draqons considered all humans beneath them, save for Kingdom High Blood and Adepts. However, their scorn for him was special. Each and every White Draqon in Koma, if not the entire Kingdom of the Sun, would know him. With his stepfather and brother's crimes, the Adryck family had been declared traitors to the Sun Crown. Being married into the Adryck family, his mother was also suspect. Only by enlisting in the Draqons had Xander kept them from being stripped of their titles and possibly executed. His presence had not set well with the Red Draqons he had served with. The Whites would probably like it even less.

Xander announced himself. "I am Xander Rosha."

At one time, Xander's introduction took longer with his titles and honorifics. Now he had none.

"Did the Reds give you a name?" one of the Whites asked.

"Yes," Xander said. "Some called me Quest, most called me Hopeless."

"What was your full name?" the other White asked.

"Wasting-His-Time-on-a-Hopeless-Quest," Xander replied.

Both Draqons snorted at that.

"That won't do for you here," the first White said. "If you were Hopeless, the High Blood wouldn't have sent you here. We are the strongest White garrison of any Kingdom protectorate. The commander has decided that you are Hatchling until you earn a proper name."

Xander clenched his teeth together. Picking fights this early would not do him any good. He would have to choose his battles very carefully, and make tactical retreats from any that were brought to him.

Damn you, Vincent, Xander cursed his stepfather, and not for not the first time. *And damn you, Damian, for taking the guns.*

"We received news of your coming more than a week ago," the other White challenged. "Why are you arriving only now?"

"I was given leave to visit my mother, the Princess Josephine Adryck of House Eras," Xander said. "I haven't seen her since becoming a Red. I have the papers right here, signed by Kraetor Ilsaen, First Adept of Grandfather Shadow and High Blood of House Kaesiak. He is my patron. The hour of my arrival is because the ship bringing me downriver from my mother's estates was delayed."

Xander pulled from his satchel the documents granting him leave and handed them over. The Whites examined the papers. One grunted, but could say nothing to refute it. All Draqon breeds were bound to obey any High Blood or Adept, who were bound to obey the First Adept and Highest Blood of their House. Only the Sun King or the High Seat of a House could override an order given by the First Adept.

"Follow me, Hatchling," the first White said, and led Xander into the fortress.

A small courtyard of perhaps forty paces by forty paces opened up on the other side of the gates. Even at this late hour, more than a dozen Whites practiced their fighting skills. Seven pairs of Whites faced each other with large practice swords made from wooden slats bound together with leather cords. An eighth pair grappled in the corner, each attempting to push the other to its knees.

All activity stopped when Xander entered. Each White tensed and growled, as if ready to pounce.

Again, Xander ground his teeth. One Draqon he could fight well enough to give a strong showing for himself. He'd bested many Reds, but then Reds weren't bred for wits. They were bred for numbers to overwhelm the enemy on the battlefield. Whites faced assassins and other threats that demanded a bit more flexibility and creativity in their thinking. Xander feared a very quick dismissal from the Whites – by way of his own funeral.

THREE

The hand that gripped Damian's shoulder spun him around and slammed him into the side of a building. If not for the clothes creating a hump on his back, he would have lost his wind. As it was, the arm carrying the scattergun was pinned so that Damian couldn't bring the weapon to bear.

Although only one man held Damian to the wall, he heard others laughing in the fog. Even through the makeup, Damian recognized Tade, leader of the Wraiths. All the Wraiths painted their faces white, except for the black circles around their eyes. Tade used his left hand to pin Damian to the wall. The Wraith leader's right hand held a long dagger.

"This was a merry little chase you led us on," Tade said. Then with a mocking smile, he asked, "What do you have to say for yourself?"

For a moment, Damian considered begging for his life, but he knew it would do no good. No matter what he did, they were either going to kill him or give him over to the White Draqons. He almost remained silent when something deep within him stirred. It was the part that cried to go on when logic said stand down and give up.

Damian looked Tade in the eye. "I'm sorry."

"You're sorry?" Tade asked

"Yes. I'm sorry that I didn't kill you earlier."

Tade blinked in confusion for a moment before his mouth split into a wide grin. He let out a laugh from deep within his belly. Others in the fog joined him.

"Now that's what I like!" Tade said over his shoulder to the other Wraiths. "A man who's not afraid to laugh just before he dies."

That met with more laughter. Damian suppressed the urge to chuckle to himself, but not to join their humor at his expense. As usual, Damian shared a private jest with himself. When Tade turned to speak to his men, he eased the pressure on Damian just enough for him to free the scattergun.

"Old Uncle Night comes for us all," Damian said, raising the weapon. "But not for me tonight."

Tade looked down and his eyes widened. One of the Wraiths had time to utter a curse. Then Damian squeezed the trigger. The flint struck the steel, sending sparks to light the powder in the pan, and fire erupted from the barrel. The gun kicked in his hands. Tade's coat and chest shred, and his corpse pitched backward onto the street. Cries of pain and surprise came from the fog.

Damian spared a moment to consider Tade's mangled corpse. Only by a blessing of the gods had Tade let him loose enough to bring the scatergun to bear. As the echo from the shot faded, Damian pushed himself into action. Slinging the scattergun over his shoulder, Damian drew both of his two-shot pistols. What he wouldn't give for someone to make a two-shot scattergun.

A Wraith rushed at him from the fog. Damian fired, catching him in the face. Blood, teeth, and bone sprayed a second Wraith who followed. That one stopped to wipe the gore out of his eyes. Damian stepped forward and kicked the man between the legs. As the Wraith doubled over, Damian slammed the butt of his pistol on the back of his head.

No one else appeared out of the fog. Damian strained his ears past the echoing gunshots and heard boots tromping on the cobblestone streets, retreating into the night.

Holstering the pistol, Damian ran away from the nearby bridge. They would likely expect him to flee toward the bridge to freedom. There was another bridge less than ten blocks away, but that one led to Central Isle where the Governor's Palace rested in the highest levels of the city. It was a dangerous path because ground level of that island held the barracks for the White and Red Draqons. Damian planned to skirt the edge of Central Isle, eventually making it to another bridge and getting to High Market from there, or maybe to O'lean Town where he could get smuggled out of the city.

The noise from his guns would attract more attention than he ever wanted. The Kingdom offered large rewards to anyone who aided in the capture of individuals possessing firearms. While those fortune seekers were not at the top of the list of Damian's worries, they would make it more difficult to evade the true threat. The White Draqons would also come. Even though the fog was thick, it wasn't enough to wash away the scent of his passing. They would be able to follow the scent of fired gunpowder that now clung to him. He needed to get out of the city and get out *now*.

FOUR

One of the Whites walked over to Xander and snarled. The White towered a head and a half taller than Xander. Its hair was a mass of braids spilling over its shoulders.

"You don't belong here," the White said.

"Not now," Xander's escort said. "Black Claw wants to see him."

"I am Barrier," the challenger said. "Remember my name, Hatchling. You will see me again. Then we will see what the Reds taught you."

"I will be honored to be defeated by a warrior with so many braids," Xander replied.

Barrier leaned forward, got a hand's span away from Xander's face, and sniffed. "I smell fear on you."

"Yes," Xander replied. "It is a human weakness. I hope you will teach me to overcome it."

Barrier snorted a blast of hot air into Xander's face. As Xander struggled to keep from coughing at the hot and dank air he'd just breathed, Barrier turned away from him, completely showing his back. The other Whites followed suit, turning their backs as well.

"Come, Hatchling." Xander's guide headed for a door into the stronghold proper.

Xander sighed and followed. Barrier's breath still burned his nostrils. Xander had known he wasn't going to be received with open arms, but he'd never imagined being scorned like this. He'd hoped his time with the Reds would have earned him some small bit of respect. He should have known better; they were, after all, only Reds.

Within the fortress, the compact passageways only allowed two people, or Draqons, to walk side by side, giving only room enough for one soldier to swing a sword at a time. A single individual with enough skill and endurance could defend a corridor against many foes. It would cost rivers of blood for any invaders to make it to the inner sanctuary where the Adepts would go if the city were attacked. Ensuring every corner of the fortress was cleared of Draqons might take weeks.

Walking through the winding corridors, Xander felt the eyes of every White he passed burning contempt into him. Several went out of their way to walk into him, knocking him aside. Since the Whites kept the peace within any city where the High Blood lived, they were also the Draqons who most often met with assassins wielding firearms, the surest way for a common man to put himself on equal footing with a miracle speaking Adept. Xander's name and past had surely circulated through the fortress.

Xander's guide brought him to a spiral staircase.

While ascending, they passed a young woman wearing the uniform of a White Dragon. She was tall, nearly six feet, close to Xander's height. Her flaming red hair and bright green eyes that sparkled like emeralds marked her as a member of House Aernacht. She looked close to Xander's age of twenty-five. As Xander came close to her, she leaned against the staircase wall and smiled. Her hand rested on a sword the same style as the Whites' curved two-handed blade, but forged for her size. As Xander passed her, she looked him over. Her mouth curved into a sly smirk.

His escort growled, deep in the back of its throat. The girl's smile vanished. She drew her sword a few inches out of its scabbard, bared her teeth, and hissed. The White snorted and started up the stairs. Xander followed but glanced back over his shoulder. The girl glared at the White, eyes squinting, and the smirk had returned. She caught Xander looking at her and looked him over again, slow and appraising. With a wink, she turned and walked away.

Once the girl was out of sight, Xander hurried to catch up with his escort. He pushed the girl and her inviting smirk out of his thoughts. He could not afford any distractions. Soon, his escort came to the top of the stairs and opened a door.

"Enter," the White said. "Black Claw waits."

Xander stepped across the threshold.

FIVE

Within the span of ten minutes, Damian cut through several alleys and side streets. He crossed his path three times and backtracked twice. He hoped that would confuse the Whites long enough to give him time to escape. Lungs burning, he made it to the second bridge. There, he scampered down to the water's edge and washed his hands in the filthy muck. It might take several scalding baths to remove that stench, but it would go a long way to mask the gunpowder. He took off the sailor's coat, wiped down the guns that he'd fired, and tossed the coat into the water. He took the makeshift pack from his back and put his boots and coat back on. His feet were freezing at this point, toes aching. The only thing that kept him moving was fear of capture, and now speed was more important than stealth. All of this likely wouldn't mask his scent completely, but it might give him a few extra minutes to make it to freedom.

Damian forced himself to stroll across the long bridge to Central Isle. Even in the darkness and fog, he could make out the silhouette of the Red Draqon barracks. The White barracks were further in, directly beneath the Governor's Palace. He started to question the wisdom of coming here, but then again, who in their right mind would head toward the people looking to kill him?

Once on Central Isle proper, Damian came to one of the huge stone pillars that supported the upper levels. Each of these giant structures housed several spiral staircases leading upward. At different points along the several-hundred-foot-high towers, levels spanned the whole island, completely enclosed except for high, slender windows that let in light during the day. Each of these levels housed complete neighborhoods, most of them residences of the families that served the Governor's Palace and the Komati Noble estates on the uppermost levels of Central Island.

When he reached about halfway between levels, Damian stopped and listened. There were no sounds of pursuit. Heaving a sigh of relief, he sat down and reloaded his guns. Normally, he would have done so on the run, but with the cold night air numbing his fingers, Damian worried about dropping something and marking his path. After finishing, he continued up the stairs.

Damian went up two more levels before leaving the stairway. In these middle levels, there wasn't much in the way of open air between buildings. It was more like a series of hallways connecting shops and residences. Each intersection had a compass worked into the cobblestones to keep people from getting lost in the maze.

He started north, toward O'lean town. As he ran away from the level's outer edge, the fog started to thin, but it was still thick enough to obscure details, especially in the darkness. At each intersection of corridors, lamps illuminated the crossroads well enough, but did little to light the corridor between then. When he came to an open-air courtyard, Damian stopped to rest a moment and decide on the best direction to take him to another stairwell down.

He heard footsteps approaching. Before he could run, two large forms came toward him.

SIX

"Why are you here, Xander Rosha?" a deep voice asked.

The room was sparse, furnished with only a large desk, a chair, a cot, and a chest resting at the foot of the cot. A figure stood in the shadows behind the desk, tall even for a White. Xander thought it might be over eight feet tall, easily the tallest White he'd ever seen.

"Stop gawking and answer me!"

"To prove the loyalty of my family," Xander answered quickly.

The White stepped out of the shadows, standing almost two heads taller than Xander. Its eyes had a sharp slant, and its ears came to fine points. Its lips were pulled back, revealing twin rows of sharp teeth. Its skin was whiter and the scales finer than most Draqons of its breed. The braids on its head were so fine that it looked like normal hair at first glance. The White snorted, and its neck muscles twitched, pointed ears flicking backward. Its eyes slanted even further.

"That answer may serve for your Red Draqon commanders and the High Blood. Not for me. Why are you here?"

Xander thought for a moment. What answer could the commander be looking for? What else could it want? In the end, Xander chose honesty.

"To prove the worth and strength of my name, so I can make my family great once again."

The White growled. Its whole body tensed, and then it moved. Xander tried to dodge, but the White moved with dizzying speed.

In the span of a heartbeat, the White was over the desk and had Xander pinned to the wall with one clawed hand. Xander dangled against the stone wall several feet above the floor. His breath came in short gasps as the talons dug into his throat, and he felt droplets of blood running down his neck.

The White pressed its lips right against Xander's ear and whispered, "If you lie to me again, I will spill your guts and make you use them to clean the great hall."

Xander felt himself heaved through the air. He landed in a heap in the corner of the room.

"Only once that task is done will I allow you to die," the White said in a normal tone. It might have been asking after Xander's mother. "Is that understood?"

"Perfectly," Xander said, as he rose and stood at attention.

"Good. I am Black Claw. In the morning you may see to your lodgings. As for now, get down to the dungeons, they need cleaning. Every Draqon in the fortress has been ordered to direct you there."

"Yes, Commander," Xander said.

"In the future, don't waste your breath responding to my orders. I do not require the subservience that seems necessary to human nobles or some Red commanders. I speak. You obey. Learn that, and you may earn your way out of the dungeons."

When Xander crossed the room and opened the door, Black Claw said, "Stop."

Xander turned to face his new commander.

"Sir?"

"Take out your braids."

"Sir?" Xander said. "I earned these in battle."

"You earned those braids as a Red. You have yet to prove yourself as a White. Until you do, your hair will remain unbraided. Take them out or I'll remove them, along with your head."

Xander reached up to one of the fine leather strands that kept his braids in place. He pulled the strap and untied the braid. Then he moved on to the next one and his fingers started trembling. Xander hadn't realized how much those braids had meant to him. He'd fought hard alongside the Reds in those battles. Those battles had been fought to prove himself a loyal Kingdom man, and the braids were a symbol of that. When he got to the fifth braid, Xander choked back his tears.

"Are you so sad to lose those?" Black Claw asked, a hint of mockery in its voice.

"No," Xander said. "I'm angry. My braids are important to me."

Black Claw snorted. "They were from a different life. If you are loyal, the High Blood will honor you."

"How will I earn braids down in the dungeons?" Xander asked.

"Better earn your way out of the dungeons first."

When Xander unwove the ninth and final braid out of his hair, he turned on his heel and left the room.

As he walked down the stairs, Xander said, not for the first time, and likely not anywhere near the last, "Damn you, Damian."

SEVEN

Damian fired twice, dropping both figures before they became completely visible. They were tall, almost seven feet, more than a head taller than the average Komati. Their skin was grayish-white, and they wore silk under slashed leather doublet and trousers, both leather and silk as pure white as the Draqon's eyes. Their half capes were adorned with the golden sun symbol of the Kingdom.

The strength went out of his limbs. Anyone lucky enough to kill one White rarely lived long enough to celebrate such a feat, and he had just killed two.

More Whites came out of the fog. Damian counted five, but there had to be more. White Draqons were grouped in squads of eleven. All had their long, curved-bladed swords drawn.

"I am Prince Damian Adryck of House Eras," Damian cried as he dropped his weapons.

His only hope was to let them capture him so the Kingdom could try him and sentence him to a public and bloody execution, while he planned some escape.

One of the Whites stepped right in front of Damian. Its curved, two-handed sword flicked Damian's cheek, drawing a bit of blood. The creature used the blade one-handed, though Damian would have wielded the sword with both hands. Muscles bulged under its leather armor. It parted its lips in a half grin, half scowl, and Damian couldn't help but stare at its two rows of pointed teeth. This White had a full mane of braids.

"You are fortunate my commander wishes to question you about the firearms," the White growled. Its voice came out like glass scratching against rough iron, "and that the High Blood wish to make an example of you. I would like nothing more than to hear you beg me to kill you all through the night."

There was no way to fight against this; only a miracle could save him. Damian would do anything, pay any price, to survive this.

Any price? A voice asked in the back of his mind.

Yes, Damian thought to himself. *Any price.*

Done. The other voice said, and Damian realized it wasn't his own.

At first Damian thought it was his imagination, but then other words followed, though they were in another language. Without waiting for comprehension, he cried them out.

"*Galad'thanya kuiva aen eva ruth!*" As Damian spoke, words in a spidery script appeared in the air before his mouth, as if he wrote those words by speaking them.

All the Whites froze.

Now, the voice in his mind said, *clap your hands together.*

Without question, Damian brought his hands together around the White's blade. The words exploded outwards with a thunderous *boom*. A wave of force cleared the fog in all directions. The White's arm was gone, now transformed into a bloody stump just above where its elbow had been. It stumbled back, snarling and wailing in pain as blood sprayed from the stump.

For a moment, Damian stared in disbelief, his hands holding the ruined hunk of smoking metal that had been a sword. Damian cast it away and stared as the White fell twitching and bleeding out over the cobblestones.

Eight more White Draqons lay sprawled on the street. Unfortunately, they had only been stunned and now began to recover. As they rose, a flock of crows descended from one of the windows, landing around Damian. For a moment he thought the Whites were going to rush him, but the birds started *cawing*. The racket seemed to form a barrier between Damian and the Whites.

After a few moments of this odd cacophony, the Draqons backed away into the fog.

What did this mean? Where had this power come from? He recognized two of the words he'd spoken: *Galad* meant shadow, and *kuiva* was rage or anger. The others were a mystery, but he wrapped them into his memory. He knew a place where he could find out, once he reached the Lands of Endless Summer, but that was for another time. First he had to get out of this damned city.

Damian took a step, intending to sprint away, but the crows closed in around him, blocking his attempts to escape.

More wings flapped above him and Damian looked up. A crow the size of an eagle descended out of the sky. The bird circled three times above Damian's head, then flew to perch on a window ledge across the street. At that distance, the fog should have concealed the crow, but its flight seemed to displace the fog and kept the space clear.

Then Damian heard a single set of footsteps. The gait was swift and coming closer.

The large crow squawked. All the smaller crows around Damian twitched and contorted. A few moments later, a crowd of several dozen children, all dressed in black and gray rags, stood where the crows had been. They scurried around, collecting his guns and the bodies of the slain Draqons. Within moments, the street around him was clear.

"I'm going mad," Damian said.

Moments after the crow-children had departed, a woman walked out of the fog. She wore the gray and black Adept's mantle of House Kaesiak, one of the four Great Houses of the Kingdom. She also wore the traditional silk mask of the Kaesiak High Blood. All nobles of House Kaesiak wore a mask of some kind; hers was only a few token lines of fabric

Despite her being a High Blood and an Adept, Damian could not ignore her beauty, or the air of charisma that surrounded her. She was young for an Adept, perhaps in her mid-twenties, not much older than Damian. Her long, dark hair was pulled into tight, twin braids starting at her temples and falling behind her back, as was the fashion for unmarried women of her House. Damian's gaze wandered from her high cheekbones, to her full lips, past her neckline, and imagined what hid underneath her Adept's mantle, until she cleared her throat, bringing his eyes to meet hers.

"What have we here?" the Adept asked.

Damian looked into her dark eyes, and while they were beautiful, he could not help but compare them to another pair of eyes he'd seen recently. A pair of steel-gray eyes came unbidden into Damian's mind. Faelin's words echoed up from the back of Damian's memory, *That woman is more trouble than all your father's guns combined.*

"Boy!" the Adept spoke with such command that Damian blinked back into the world. "Do you know who I am?"

Damian looked from the Adept, to the giant crow behind her, to a pool of blood where one of the Whites he'd shot had fallen. He grinned. Kahddria must have heard his prayer.

71

"I apologize," Damian found his voice at last, "I do not believe we've met, or if we have, I surely do not recall the introduction." A heartbeat later, Damian bowed and added, "my lady Adept."

The Adept opened her mouth. Her jaw worked back and forth for a few heartbeats before she closed it again. She repeated this process twice more, until she finally asked, "Do you care nothing for yourself to show me the respect I am due?"

Damian shrugged. "With all the times Old Uncle Night has breathed on the back of my neck tonight, I've lost my fear of him."

The Adept laughed. "I have no desire to kill you, boy. My reason for being here is curiosity. I felt the miracle of my god coming from this area, and I came to investigate." Her eyes pierced deep into Damian, searching. "Can you tell me what happened?"

The large crow dove, landing between Damian and the Adept. It screeched defiantly and spread its wings, creating a wall between the Adept and Damian.

"What do you want with this one?" she asked.

The huge bird squawked. "*Hano yn'tarkae.*" Its feathers ruffled, and it looked as if it were going to attack the Adept.

Damian knew part of that. *Hano* was he, and *yn* was is. He is…what? Damian struggled for the last word, but didn't know it.

"Are you sure?" the Adept asked

The crow nodded, and squawked, "*Ji.*" *Yes.*

The crow continued, faster now. Damian tried to follow the words, but he could only make out two, *vara* and *kaer*.

Well, Damian certainly knew those words. The Kaer was the training grounds and barracks of the Vara, the constabulary force of any large Komati community.

"Fine," said the Adept. Then she turned to Damian and held out her hand. "Well, boy, I suppose we should move along. It isn't a long walk to the Kaer, but long enough considering the time of night."

The crow gathered its wings and took to the air.

"I have a feeling we'll be seeing a lot of each other in the future," the Adept said. "I am Adept Czenzi."

"Call me Zephyr." If he gave her his name, she would surely recognize it. Possession of firearms was a rare crime, and those who escaped justice for it, even more so.

Czenzi pursed her lips and raised an eyebrow. She likely understood he was being evasive. *Good, let her.*

Instead of letting her corner him about it, Damian asked, "Why am I going to the Kaer?"

"Because that bird is a Stormcrow elder, a messenger from Grandfather Shadow. He commanded me to take you to the Kaer and enlist you in the Vara."

"Why?"

"I was not told why," Czenzi said, "Only that you must go. It seems you have attracted the attention of Grandfather Shadow."

As he followed Czenzi, Damian considered the night's events. He had spoken a miracle, plain and simple. Only, miracles required the use of special foci to draw power from the celestial realms and they taxed both mind and body. Even Adepts who had been speaking the power of their gods for decades would grow weary and exhausted after a time. Damian had never done anything like that in his life. He should be near to collapsing, but he felt fine. Then he stewed on Czenzi's words, *It seems you have attracted the attention of Grandfather Shadow.*

Why would Grandfather Shadow be interested in me? Damian thought. *Could Father have been right?*

EIGHT

Xander did his best to work the mop with one hand while he held his nose closed with the other. It wasn't working well, but he didn't expect any of the people coming into the dungeons to care about the quality of his work. The only Draqons he'd seen were the two deformed Greens that served as jailers. Any humans brought down here would soon have much heavier matters weighing on their minds than the stench.

Xander understood that Black Claw had assigned this detail in an attempt to break him. When a human joined the Reds, they signed a contract for a specific period of time. The only other way out of the term of service was to no longer be fit for combat. With the White Draqons it was different. Any human serving in their ranks could depart at any time they wished, because only the truly strong survived being White. Xander was now imprisoned within the ranks of the Whites, serving until the Sun Throne recognized his loyalty or he was killed. Death was just as likely to come from the Whites as it was from the enemies of the Kingdom. Whites were brutal with each other, often coming to blows over the most trivial matters. These scuffles were rarely fatal to Draqons, but could easily maim or kill a human.

Slopping the mop back and forth across the refuse-infested floor, Xander offered a prayer to Sister Wind for any kind of relief from the stench. A few moments later the door to the dungeon opened, letting in a breath of cleaner air from outside. Two Whites stood in the doorway.

Xander tensed. His gear, including his sword, was on the other side of the room. The only real weapon he had at hand was his dagger, but there was no way he could choose not to fight back. At best, his name would be ridiculed for the rest of this post. At worst…Xander wanted to think it would be his death, but death would be a blessing compared to remaining down here for the rest of his life to suffer in this filth and stench for the price of his half-brother's crimes.

"Brother Stone," Xander prayed, tightening his grip on the mop, "give me strength."

"Hatchling," one of the Whites said. "Come with us. Black Claw wants you."

Xander barked a relieved laugh. The Whites looked at each other, and then at Xander.

"You are amused by this?" the White on the right asked.

Xander couldn't help but break into a full half-crazed laugh.

"What is funny?" the other White asked in a growl, hand on its sword.

"I thought you came to test my strength," Xander replied. "I was trying to decide which end of my mop to fight you with."

The two Whites laughed. Draqon laughter made Xander's teeth clench together. It sounded like they were growling and chewing bones at the same time.

"I am Plague," the taller of the two Whites said. "This is my nestmate, Fury. You are not what we expected."

"Why are you laughing?" Xander asked.

"Because you are an idiot," Plague replied. "Proud and defiant, but an idiot."

They laughed louder as they walked away, leaving Xander to catch up. Tossing the mop aside, he snatched up his gear. "Thank you, Sister Wind, for answering my prayer."

Once out of the dungeons, he took a breath. This deep in the stronghold, the air was musty and stale, but smelled fresh as spring compared to the dungeon.

Following Plague and Fury, Xander heard them muttering together. Occasionally, they glanced back at him and laughed, then continued conspiring. Whatever name they created, Xander would be branded with it for the rest of his time with the White Draqons, unless something else he did was brave or stupid enough to overshadow this.

"Have you decided my name?" Xander asked.

The Draqons looked back at him over their shoulders.

"Yes," they said together.

"And?" he asked.

"Later," Plague said. "Black Claw must approve first."

As the two Whites laughed and led Xander from the dungeons, a whistle from down a side hall caught Xander's attention. He looked and saw the human girl once again. Before he got too distracted, Xander looked away. He had his duty to do; a pretty face would only distract him, and in this place a distraction could get him killed.

"You, Flirt, get back to your post," Fury ordered.

"Flirt?" Xander asked.

"That's her name. Black Claw gave it to her."

Xander decided he was going to stay away from anyone Black Claw named Flirt.

Leaving the girl named Flirt behind, Plague and Fury escorted Xander through the fortress and ushered him into a room.

Black Claw stood at the head of a large table. A full squad of Whites surrounded the table. The squad's leader stood at the foot, facing Black Claw. Behind Black Claw, eight Whites stood with swords at their feet, eyes cast down. For any Draqon, having its sword at its feet was the worst shame imaginable. It meant that Draqon had done something to prove it was unworthy to wield the blade.

"Come here, Hatchling," Black Claw said. "We have a situation that you have some experience with."

Xander stepped up to the table. A large map of Koma City was spread across it. The map had several markers. One marker had a gun and was placed in the warehouse district, with another similar one on Central Isle. Three markers with the White Draqon crest were spread through the Warrens and Warf District, all in very poor neighborhoods.

"Tonight we had an encounter with two Komati trying to sell firearms to the Wraiths, a gang controlled by certain High Blood of House Swaenmarch. One of the criminals is in our custody. The second escaped, but not before killing three White Draqons and depositing their bodies across the City." Black Claw indicated the three White Draqon markers.

"These cowards allowed the second criminal to escape, saying that he had the power of an Adept," Black Claw said. "This fugitive is Damian Adryck."

Xander thanked all the lesser gods at once. Surely, they were the ones that had brought Damian within Xander's grasp. How better for Xander to prove his loyalty than to hunt down the person who brought it into question?

"What assistance can I give?" Xander asked, trying to keep the eagerness out of his voice.

"Has your brother ever exhibited a talent for speaking miracles before?" Black Claw asked.

"He is Komati," Xander replied. "I thought only the High Blood could be chosen and blessed by the Greater Gods to speak miracles."

"You see," Black Claw said, turning to the eight Whites standing over their swords. "People do not spontaneously become Adepts, especially not

Komati. We all know that the Greater Gods abandoned the Komati once the Kingdom conquered them."

"Then how do you account for the death of our squad leader?" one of the standing Draqons asked.

Black Claw got up from the table and went over to the one that had spoken. They stood there, staring at each other.

Black Claw smiled, and then buried its claws deep in the other White's abdomen. With a quick jerk, the Draqon leader removed a chunk of flesh. The injured White didn't fall. It barely even winced.

"The Komati have been developing new technology in secret for some time. As much as we have tried to stamp it out, they have always retained gunpowder and firearms. I expect that they are increasing their power." Black Claw turned to Xander. "Accompany this squad and find your nest-mate. Capture him so we can learn more about this technology."

Rather than say anything, Xander nodded.

"Hatchling," Black Claw said. Xander looked up, and his commander continued. "I know you want to kill your brother. I can see it in your eyes and smell it in your blood. The Kingdom needs him alive."

"Yes, sir," Xander said.

Black Claw merely nodded. "Now where is that bloody Adept?"

A slight cough came from the back corner of the room. All heads turned to see a figure step out of the shadows. Every Draqon in the room tensed. Only the black and gray mantle and mask proclaiming him as an Adept of House Kaesiak saved the man's life.

"That *bloody* Adept has been here for some time, Commander Black Claw," the Adept said. "Now, I suggest that we stop jumping to conclusions about what Damian Adryck did or did not do, or how he did it. Divine blessing is not the only way to gain unexplainable abilities. There are many dark beings in the world willing to give power quickly and easily for one who knows how to ask."

"You think he made a pact with a Daemyn or Daevyl?" Black Claw asked.

"I'm not willing to say one way or the other," the Adept answered. "You may indeed be correct about some new technology. However, we won't know until we question him, and we won't be able to do that standing here."

Without another word, the Draqons saluted and formed together.

"Stand with me, Xander Rosha," the Adept said. "We will speak about your brother while we pursue him."

"Of course, Adept," Xander replied. "I am yours to command."

Black Claw might not desire acknowledgement from his underlings, but Xander knew better about the Adept. Every creature with power Xander had ever met, human and Draqon alike, demanded respect from those below him.

As the Squad of Draqons started out of the room, Xander dropped his gear and collected his sword. Then he fell into step just behind the Adept. Xander also knew better than to assume too great a position by actually walking next to the Adept. Except in the case of the Royal Family, Adepts always went first.

Outside the stronghold, the night was colder than when Xander had entered. He inhaled deeply through his nose. The cold stung his nostrils, but it helped drive away the lingering stench of the dungeons. He also focused his resolve. Tonight would finally see Damian's capture. It would break Mother's heart, but it was the best thing for the greater family.

"Is something bothering you, Prince Rosha?" the Adept asked.

The use of his title took Xander aback. It had been several years since anyone had referred to him as Prince.

"Nothing, Adept," Xander replied. "I'm merely enjoying the fresh air."

"Ah," the Adept said, as if that explained everything. "Mucking out the dungeons?"

"How did you know?"

"I am Tamaz, Adept of House Kaesiak. It is my duty to watch over the White Draqons of Koma City and keep them from causing too much trouble."

"Yes, Adept."

"And that's what Black Claw gives as everyone's first assignment, whether they are human or Draqon," Tamaz said. "But enough of that, tell me about your brother."

"I'm not sure what I remember that would be of use, High Blood," Xander said. "I haven't seen him in over two years. Surely he's changed much since then."

"Perhaps a bit. However, the core of a man would remain. What do you remember?"

"He is fearless, and refuses to recognize limitations. Where most people might bend underneath adversity, Damian always found a way to persevere. I think that's why he was able to escape when the Whites came for him. They weren't prepared for a single Komati to give them much trouble. Which is another thing, Damian refuses to let himself be intimidated by others."

"Intriguing," Tamaz said. "Do you know which god he holds as his patron?"

"It was Sister Wind, and I doubt he would have changed that. He was always praying to her to give him luck. The fact that he survived childhood may be an indication that she was listening."

Tamaz turned and looked Xander eye to eye. "Do you truly mean this?"

Xander thought for a moment. "At first I said it half-joking, Adept, but thinking upon it, I realize that it might be true. Only by luck did he escape many potentially lethal situations unscathed."

"This is all good to know," Tamaz said. "Is there anything else?"

Without hesitation, Xander replied, "Don't let Damian get a sword."

"Why?" Tamaz asked

"I've never seen anyone who was Damian's equal," Xander replied. "He is the youngest ever to receive the title of Maestro in Komati history. He spent three years traveling to study with the Maestros of D'fence schools all across the Kingdom and found few of them able to teach him anything he felt worthwhile. He learned from the whirling duel masters of the Lands of Endless Summer and the strange warriors across the Eastern Sea."

"We have some of the greatest Whites in the entire Kingdom of the Sun," Tamaz said. "Surely he could not best them."

"Damian faced Whites when they came for him after my stepfather's crimes were discovered," Xander said. "But I do know that Damian is more than a swordsman, he is an artist."

"Interesting."

As they walked through the fog, one of the Whites came up to Tamaz and saluted.

"Adept," it said, "we have picked up the trail. The criminal is not far."

"Lead on," Tamaz ordered. "I am most eager to meet Damian Adryck."

Xander wanted to run ahead with the Draqons, but contained himself. The Adept hadn't given him permission to go.

Thoughts of Damian made Xander smile. He remembered a time when he had taken Damian hunting. At the first sounds in the underbrush, Damian slid off his horse and began loosing arrows blindly into the brush. Moments later, a massive boar charged them, none too pleased about being shot. The creature chased them up a tree and ran off their horses. Once the boar left them, the rest of the day was spent trying to gather the horses and avoid the boar.

Xander longed for such simpler times as those, but they were gone forever. Damian and Vincent had killed any hope of them ever returning. Xander's stepfather was gone, and soon Xander would finally catch up to his wayward half-brother. Once they caught Damian, Xander would hand the traitor over to Black Claw. Once the Kingdom of the Sun finished with Damian, Xander would at last be able to put the family shame to an end.

NINE

Damian pulled his coat close around his neck. Now that his frantic escape had ended, the night chilled him to the bone.

As they walked, Damian caught the Adept examining him with a curious eye, but she asked no questions. Had her god given her the answers already?

Damian shook the thought aside. If Adept Czenzi had received information, she would be taking him to the White Draqon fortress rather than the Vara.

"Step lively, boy. I do not want to be out any later than I must."

"I understand, Adept," Damian replied. "If you wish to retire, I can present myself to the Vara alone. I know the way."

Czenzi chuckled. "You are a crafty one, and either brave or crazy to speak so impetuously to an Adept. However, I must see you there personally. It is not every day one is given a command by a Stormcrow elder."

"What's the difference between a Stormcrow and a Stormcrow elder?"

"Are you always so inquisitive, boy?"

"Nearly, Adept; sometimes more so. Why do you ask?"

"Because most Komati are not. They tend to keep to themselves and stay out of trouble."

Damian adopted his best innocent expression. "I assure you, my lady, I do my best to stay out of trouble. It attracts the attention of important people I would rather avoid."

Czenzi stopped and looked at Damian. He took a step back as her eyes bore into his. They stood for a moment, until Czenzi nodded and started walking again.

"Dear boy," Czenzi said, as Damian fell into step just behind her. "If you are trying to avoid the notice of important people, I'd say that you have failed. You are, after all, being escorted by an Adept to the Kaer to enlist with the Vara."

"I cannot speak to joining the Vara, High Blood," Damian said. "But as for meeting an Adept, I'd say the gods have favored me."

Damian had never met a woman that didn't like flattery. However, Czenzi was an Adept, and thus Damian would have to speak compliments carefully. Czenzi chuckled. Like everything about her, the laugh was pleasant. It would have been more pleasant if he were in on the jest.

"Adept," Damian said, "permit me to ask a question."

"Of course," Czenzi said.

"Why are you laughing?"

"Does it bother you?"

"It makes me a little nervous, Adept," Damian replied. "But mostly I am curious to know what you find amusing."

"More inquisitiveness," Czenzi said. "I'm laughing at you and your naïveté."

Damian opened his mouth to ask more, but thought better of it. He'd learned to speak as little about himself as possible over the last two years. Instead, he muttered Father's favorite curse, "*Kraestu kraenka yn'goska,*" and as soon as he spoke, Damian's heart sank to the bottom of his stomach. The fatigue and cold must have made him slip.

Czenzi stopped and faced Damian. "What did you say?"

Father used the expression in bad situations or to describe stupid people when nothing else fit. Damian used it sparingly, but sometimes it just slipped out.

"I said, I don't want to be a soldier." Damian hoped against hope that she believed him

"You lie!" Czenzi said. "That was *Galad'laman*. Where did you learn it? Speak the truth, or I'll flay it from your mind."

Well, if he had to tell the truth, Damian would give it to her a small spoonful at a time. "My father used it when I was a child."

"What was your father's name?"

"Vincent."

She stared at Damian, taking in his face, eyes flicking back and forth over him, calculating.

"You are Damian Adryck?" Adept Czenzi said at last.

Since she walked out of the fog, Damian knew he was living on borrowed time.

He cringed, waiting for her to speak some miracle and blast him into nothingness. After a few moments, he opened his eyes. Czenzi stood with her arms crossed, regarding him with a new light in her eyes. It was part humor, part amazement, and perhaps a little fear.

"We've been looking for you a long time," Czenzi said. "But not for the reasons you think."

"Ummm...why?" Damian asked.

"Now is not the time," Czenzi said, glancing around. "The night has too many eyes and ears. I shouldn't have even said your name. Let's get you to the Kaer. Then I must confer with my master."

Without waiting for a response, Czenzi turned on her heel and doubled her speed.

Damian looked after her for a moment, stunned. If Czenzi knew his name and crime, why was she still taking him to the Vara instead of dispensing Kingdom justice?

Damian sensed he had fallen into some strange game, only he didn't know his role. Was he a pawn, centerpiece, player, or the prize? Since he didn't know the game, the other pieces, or the players, he must be a pawn. However, in the game of Houses, a pawn had two strengths. It was the only piece that could move anywhere on the board, and it could be changed into a stronger piece if a person played well enough. In the game of Houses, a player could change their pawns into other pieces by capturing an opponent's piece and replacing it with one of their pawns, by sacrificing another pawn, or returning one of the opponent's captured pieces. The Kingdom claimed this taught young High Blood the value of holding pawns and prisoners in reserve, because in politics, one never knew when either might be useful. Damian believed it meant anyone, with proper planning, could, if the circumstances were right, raise his status above being a pawn.

Damian had no pawns but himself, so he had nothing to sacrifice. However, that didn't mean that he couldn't raise himself to a better position. It didn't matter that he didn't know the rules of this game. He didn't care. He'd play his own game. He'd force his opponents, whoever they were, to come play on his board by his rules.

Ahead of him, Czenzi stopped and looked back.

"Well," Czenzi said. "Shall we go, Your Highness?"

Damian smiled. She had stopped calling him *boy*.

"Your will is my command, Adept Czenzi," Damian said with a bow and hurried to catch up with her.

The first rule of Damian's games: Damian always won, even if he had to make up new rules.

TEN

One of the Whites jogged up to Tamaz and Xander. It paused long enough to salute before reporting. "Adept Tamaz, we will be upon the traitor in moments."

"Excellent," Tamaz said. "Let us end two years of foolishness."

Tamaz Aegotha, High Blood of House Kaesiak and Adept of Old Uncle Night, found his breath quickening to match his heartbeat. Soon Tamaz would have Damian Adryck, the most elusive traitor to the Kingdom of the Sun, firmly in his grasp. Adryck's death would not only serve to further the Brotherhood's plans and their push for Zenith, but it would also put an end to the schemes and machinations of the traitors within House Kaesiak itself. Even though Tamaz served Old Uncle Night, something he wasn't proud of all the time, at least he still served a greater god. His stomach churned at the thought of those fools who wished to raise a lesser god to be the patron of their House. Well, Adryck's death would put an end to that heresy.

Stealing a glance at Xander, Tamaz wondered what the First Adept of Old Uncle Night saw in this Komati prince. If it were up to Tamaz, both brothers would die, but orders were orders. Some Night Adepts turned a deaf ear to the voices of their superiors when those orders were inconvenient or might hamper their ambitions; Tamaz was not one of them. He understood the Brotherhood remained weak for precisely this reason. The First Adept of Old Uncle Night was a visionary, and it was not Tamaz's place to question the First Adept.

There was the matter of Xander's account of his younger brother. Could Adryck truly be that good with a blade? Doubtful, but Tamaz didn't want to risk it. Sword or no sword, he would order the whole squad to take Adryck's head.

ELEVEN

Damian stopped just short of bumping into Czenzi. To get to the Kaer, she'd brought him back down to ground level. The fog had thickened again, to the point where they couldn't see the silhouettes of the fortresses on the ground level of Central Isle. Only the closest street lanterns provided direction for them. Every neighborhood in the city had them, but only the wealthier islands kept them lit throughout the night.

The Adept had just stopped in the middle of the street, head cocked to one side as if she were listening. Damian strained his ears. He couldn't believe she'd heard something when he hadn't.

"What is it?" Damian asked.

Czenzi hissed him to silence. Damian took a breath and listened harder. Then, in the distance, he heard something. It was the faint sound of heavy footfalls. As the sound grew louder, he could tell it was a small group all marching in step.

He drew the only weapon he had on hand, his fighting knife, a wicked four-sided blade, ten inches long. Damian flipped the knife in his hand so that the blade rested against his forearm. Most people used the stiletto style blade as a thrusting weapon. Damian had sharpened all four edges to surprise people when he used it for slashing rather than stabbing. That was usually enough time for him to get in at least one good hit. If it was the right hit, one was all he needed.

"What do we do?" Damian asked.

"We wait and see who they are," Czenzi answered.

"At this time of night? They could be anyone."

Only a squad of Whites or Reds would be marching in cadence on Central Isle at this hour, but Damian had to convince Czenzi that it might be someone dangerous to both of them, rather than just to him.

"So? I'm an Adept."

"Being an Adept might hold weight in some places," Damian said, "but down in the fog, you're just another potential victim."

"I have the blessing of Grandfather Shadow," Czenzi said. "I am not a victim."

"As it pleases you," Damian said. "It was nice knowing an Adept and not dying."

With that, he bowed and turned to run.

"*Galad pita han viela*, Damian Adryck," Czenzi said.

The shadows around Damian writhed and caught his legs, became solid, trapping him. Struggling only made the clinging shadows climb higher on his body. Damian stopped before they reached his arms. His knife wasn't a sword, but he refused to go down without a struggle. A group would definitely get him, but he would kill the first person to come within reach.

TWELVE

Czenzi drew a deep breath through her nose and let it out through her clenched teeth. This was more to calm her frustration at Damian Adryck than to recover from speaking such a simple miracle. How was she going to save Damian's life with him intent on putting himself in even greater danger? Didn't he realize that staying by her side was the safest place for him? Of course he wouldn't. Not after being hunted by the Kingdom for two years.

The footsteps came closer, and a moment later a squad of White Dragons came out of the fog, curved swords drawn. When the Whites saw Czenzi, they pointed the tips of their swords toward the street and bowed their heads. This did complicate things, but Czenzi had learned well from her master so manipulating these Whites should prove little difficulty. She and Damian should be on their way after a few moments.

"Be silent and let me handle this," Czenzi muttered to Damian under her breath.

Damian rolled his eyes and then looked away. But at least he kept his mouth closed.

Czenzi turned to the first White. "What is the meaning of this?"

"Your pardon, Adept," the Dragon said. "But we are hunting that one." It indicated Damian with a wave of its sword.

"This one is in my charge," Czenzi said. "Return to your fortress and tell Black Claw that you no longer have claim to him."

Then two humans came up behind the Dragons. One wore the uniform of a Red Dragon; the other was dressed in the black and gray mantle of a Kaesiak Adept. When the Adept came closer, Czenzi recognized Tamaz, one of the Adepts who helped guide the White Dragons of Koma City.

"Unfortunately, it's not that easy, Czenzi," Tamaz said.

It never is, Czenzi thought.

At least Tamaz was from her own House. She would have to take him into her confidence. It might cause some problems with her master; however, it was the most expedient way to relieve the situation.

Tamaz continued. "He is Damian Adryck."

"Do you have proof?" Czenzi asked.

"I am Xander Rosha," the other human said. "And that is my half-brother."

Now that Xander Rosha had named himself, Czenzi could see the resemblance between them. Both had slight, upturned noses, and their chins seemed to be cut from the same mold, though Xander's chin was more slender and pointed than Damian's. Both brothers carried themselves with a natural confidence that many High Blood practiced for decades to achieve.

"Hello, Xander." Damian's tone was easy, as if Xander had come calling for afternoon tea. "What brings you out on a night like this?"

"You do." Xander's entire face tightened, and his words came through clenched teeth. "And finally bringing you to justice and clearing the Rosha name."

"How's that going by the way?" Damian asked. "Pretty well, I'd imagine, considering you're with a squad of Whites in Koma rather than on a battlefield in Heidenmarch. Did the Reds finally realize that you were too good for them so they sent you off to be with people who *might* be able to compare with your greatness?"

Czenzi clenched her fists together inside her robes. Why wouldn't Damian keep quiet? Was he trying to goad his brother into attacking him, and if so, why?

"Do not mock me, little brother," Xander said.

"Hatchling," the squad leader said. "Do not let this filth goad you."

"Yes, sir," Xander said.

Czenzi sent a silent prayer to Grandfather Shadow that Xander Rosha seemed to have more discipline than Damian. Glancing at Damian, Czenzi saw his lower lip jutting out and his eyes squint. Was he actually disappointed that Xander hadn't attacked him? She brushed those thoughts aside. She had to regain command of the situation before it got any worse.

"Tamaz, send the Draqons back to their fortress," Czenzi said. "This one is more important than you think. Hear me out and you'll agree."

"Tell me in *Galad'laman*," Tamaz said.

"*Sehan na aen Tsumari'osa*," Czenzi said.

"Really?" Tamaz said with wonder in his eyes. Then he added, glancing at Xander. "That must mean…"

"Exactly," Czenzi said. "Now send your pet Draqons away so we can talk. First Adept Kraetor has plans for these two."

Tamaz nodded, turned to the Draqons, and said, "Return to Black Claw. Tell him the situation has changed, but I am in complete control. I will deal with it. Prince Rosha, you will remain so that Adept Czenzi and myself are still protected."

"Adept Tamaz, I must protest…" the squad leader started.

"It is not your place to protest," Tamaz snapped. "It is your place to obey. Now do so before I relieve you of your command."

The Draqons saluted both Adepts and hurried away.

THIRTEEN

As the White Draqons left, Damian caught Xander's eye. For a brief moment, the seething hatred had given way to confusion and curiosity. Xander had always been a poor liar and kept his emotions easily readable on his face. It gave Damian a small bit of comfort to know that Xander was just as lost as he was.

When Tamaz turned back to Czenzi, Damian saw the cold look in the second Kaesiak Adept's eyes. Tamaz's eyes shifted too much between Czenzi, Xander, and Damian. It was the predatory look Damian saw daily down by the docks. Tamaz had lulled Czenzi into trusting him, providing the perfect moment to strike.

Tamaz spoke, "*Tzizma...*"

Damian was not about to allow an Adept of Grandfather Shadow to finish any sentence that began with Old Uncle Night's ancient name. Damian's hand flashed out, and the stiletto flew through the air. The Adept's second word transformed into a cry of pain. Damian had aimed for Tamaz's neck, but Xander had pulled the Adept aside at the last moment, so Damian only managed to hit Tamaz's shoulder.

"What are you doing?" Czenzi asked.

"He wants to kill us," Damian said.

"Liar," Xander snarled, stepped toward Damian, and drew his sword.

"I've had enough people try to kill me." Damian wished for another knife he could reach, but Czenzi's shadows covered his three other blades. "I know the signs."

Damian pointed at Tamaz, trying to get Czenzi and Xander to focus on the true threat.

"*Tzizma nu nichta,*" Tamaz cried.

The world went black. Damian squinted, straining to pierce through the darkness, but there wasn't even the faintest glimmer of light. Sometimes he hated being right.

"See," Damian yelled. "You idiots should have believed me."

"*Karkota aen pimies,*" Czenzi yelled.

Vision returned, and Damian saw Tamaz about to thrust the stiletto into Czenzi's back. Without another Adept to counter Tamaz's miracles, Damian and Xander had no hope. Damian could only think of one way to save them. The words he'd spoken earlier flashed into his mind with perfect clarity. If Grandfather Shadow had truly granted his attention and blessing upon Damian Adryck, the miracle would work again

"*Galad'thanya kuiva aen eva ruth!*" Again, the words formed in the air as he yelled them.

Without wasting a moment, Damian brought his hands together on the last syllable. The thunderclap was deafening.

FOURTEEN

Xander had danced in Old Uncle Night's shadow in dozens of skirmishes and battles during his time with the Red Draqons. The worst of them was when his unit was ordered to charge a line of over a hundred Heidenmarch soldiers armed with long-guns. Only a small handful of the unit survived and Xander still bore the scars, but the Heidens died to the last man. In that battle, as with every time the order to charge came, Xander fought without hesitation. He knew that some of the Kingdom's enemies had learned to falsely harness the power of miracles, and Xander had even fought a battle where fire and lighting had streaked across the sky and roasted humans and Draqons alive as they fought.

However, seeing the words appear in the air as Damian spoke them gave Xander pause. He'd never even heard of such a thing. Was Tamaz correct? Had Damian given himself over to the service of some dark power?

Damian finished speaking that strange language and clapped his hands together. A thunderclap boomed.

Some force lifted Xander into the air. His arms and legs flailed as he flew backward and slammed against a wall.

As Xander crumpled to the cobblestones, he struggled to remain conscious. As a White, Xander's duty was to protect all Adepts and High Blood from enemies of the Kingdom. As his mind descended into blackness, Xander prayed to all the lesser gods that some other Whites were close enough to hear what Damian had done.

FIFTEEN

Tamaz drew on the Dominions of Lies and Corruption the moment he heard Damian Adryck speaking *Galad'laman*. When the words appeared in front of Adryck's face, Tamaz broke the seal on one of the bone vials hidden inside his sleeve. The life essence of three young boys poured out of the vial and into the foci hidden under his mantle. The boys had been young street urchins, half-starved, but still full of life. He took their youth and used it to fuel his counter miracle.

"*Tuznak maaish prutos nal*" Tamaz spoke the words just as Adryck's hands came together.

The miracle of Shadow's Thunder struck Tamaz like a hand swatting a fly. He would have been flattened if not for his extra power. Even still, Adryck's miracle slammed Tamaz to the cobbles.

Unmoving, Tamaz prayed, *Old Uncle Night, please let them believe this lie.* He needed a moment to plan his next move.

SIXTEEN

As the words poured from Damian's lips, Czenzi's mask tingled with the power of Grandfather Shadow's seven Dominions. It wasn't one of the paltry imitations Adepts had spoken in the thousand years since the Greater Gods had been imprisoned, but a true miracle.

Her shock lasted until she comprehended which miracle he spoke.

Flinging herself to the ground, Czenzi prayed Tamaz didn't recognize Damian's words. As an Adept of Old Uncle Night, Tamaz deserved to be caught by Shadow's Thunder.

The thunderclap boomed, and a shockwave rolled Czenzi across the cobblestones. She'd be battered and bruised for the next few days, if not a week, but it was better than the alternative. In all the stories, being caught by the Shadow's Thunder was never good.

SEVENTEEN

Damian fought the wave of exhaustion that crashed down on him. He could wait until later to figure out why doing that hadn't taxed him the first time. Right now, he had more pressing matters to deal with, like killing Adept Tamaz. Both Adepts were down, as was Xander. If Damian was going to escape, this was the moment.

He tried to move toward Tamaz, but the shadows still clung to Damian's legs. He tried to reach one of the knives tucked into his belt, thinking that he might be able to cut his way out of the shadows. When his fingers came close to the shadows covering his knife, they moved upward, as if eager to trap him even further. Damian pulled his hand away. He refused to lose control of his arms as well as his legs.

A groan drew Damian's attention. Czenzi was stirring. Tamaz lay sprawled on his back in the middle of the street. Xander lay still against a wall, arms and legs twisted at strange angles. Damian hoped he hadn't accidentally killed his brother.

Damian's gaze shifted back and forth between Xander and Tamaz. Compared to Xander, Tamaz looked almost comfortable. Down by the Docks and in the Barrens, some thieves would appear to be unconscious from too much drink. They lay waiting for someone to come close, either to rob them or to help them. Those who did found themselves at the wrong end of a sharp knife. Tamaz looked like someone trying to use that ploy, although he did it very poorly.

"Damn it, Czenzi," Damian cried. "Let me go. Tamaz isn't hurt."

Both the Adepts looked up, and their eyes met. Czenzi's eyes widened, and she sucked in a deep breath of air. A feral grin stretched across Tamaz's face.

The gods hate me, Damian thought as both Adepts started speaking.

EIGHTEEN

Czenzi drew on Secrets, Knowledge, and Illusions and spoke them into a miracle masking her from Tamaz's perceptions. She couldn't afford to put enough power into the miracle to make it last very long. She had to keep something in reserve to fight Tamaz and defend Damian.

A miracle slid past her, but Czenzi remained focused, drawing on Storms and a small bit of Illusions. She wrapped Tamaz in a gale force wind, hoping to keep him off-balance and make it hard for him to form words aloud. She used the Illusions to make him unable to hear the sound of his voice over the wind. Speaking miracle into the world required exact pronunciation. Any faltering in the speaking of them made them fizzle.

As the wind howled around Tamaz, whipping his Adept's mantle around him, Czenzi felt someone drawing on the Dominions of Balance, Shadows, and Vengeance. Dark bolts of energy flew past Czenzi. If any one of them had struck, it would have ended the fight, if not her life. The only way he could have spoken that miracle was if she hadn't trapped him. Tamaz must have hidden using the Dominions of Old Uncle Night.

Czenzi thanked Grandfather Shadow that she had decided to mask herself before attacking. She skirted to the side, to better hide herself while she tried to think of a way to defeat Tamaz. He had almost twice as many Dominions to draw on as she did, and he would know whenever she spoke a miracle and what Dominions she drew on.

NINETEEN

Tamaz glanced back and forth, searching for any sign of Czenzi's true location. She hadn't fled. The second miracle Tamaz had spoken would tell him if anyone came or left within thirty paces.

Grinding his teeth in frustration, Tamaz realized that he should have killed Czenzi right away, even before he had sent the squad of Whites away. He had underestimated her, but he should have remembered that she was First Adept Kraetor's right hand. Now that Tamaz had given her time to prepare, he might not be able to defeat her, but he had to try. She knew he served Old Uncle Night. If allowed to live, Czenzi would reveal him to the House Floraen Inquisitors.

Creeping around the square, Tamaz worked his way against the clock. He split his attention between finding Czenzi and being prepared to defend himself against any surprises. Tamaz trod carefully as he went, for even though Adryck still screamed at Czenzi to free him, a misplaced step might reveal his position.

Even with his care, he still bumped into someone. Both Czenzi's and his miracles dissipated as they made contact with each other. They stood for half a moment, eyes locked in mutual hatred before they both spoke.

"*Mina kehia turvata!*" they each yelled as they drew on the Dominion of Storms.

Tamaz watched Czenzi get carried off her feet and away from him, as a gale force wind pulled Tamaz into the air. He should have known better and been better prepared. They had both reached for one of the earliest defensive miracles taught to new Adepts of Grandfather Shadow.

Trying to twist in the air to soften the blow, Tamaz only managed to cause his already injured shoulder to take the brunt of the impact when he collided with the wall.

Choking back a cry of pain, Tamaz pulled himself to his feet just in time to feel Czenzi drawing on Shadows, Vengeance, and Balance. He didn't need to hear her cry "*Tuska!*" to know what miracle she spoke. Ducking under the dark bolt, Tamaz felt rubble pelt him from above.

Now that he and Czenzi were face to face, the fight could truly begin. It came down to imagination and skill. But Tamaz had one thing Czenzi didn't have – the power of Daemynic Alchemy. He just had to wait for the right time to use it.

TWENTY

Damian watched divine energy fly back and forth between the two Adepts. At this point their fight had become like a knife fight rather than a duel with swords. It didn't matter which one was stronger, or which one knew more. It only mattered who was fastest.

A stream of incomprehensible words came from each Adept. Shadows and darkness ebbed and flowed throughout the street. Wind howled, clearing the fog. Lighting crackled but was short-lived, and several times both Czenzi and Tamaz blinked out of sight and appeared in another place, only to reappear in their original position.

As this strange combat continued, Czenzi's eyes looked haggard, and her breath came in shorter and shorter gasps. Damian willed her to be stronger. If she won, he had a chance to escape. If Tamaz won, he was dead.

"Excuse me," said a voice at Damian's side. "I think you lost this earlier."

Damian glanced down and saw a child, a girl of no more than ten winters dressed in black and gray rags, looking up at him with dark eyes peering from underneath darker hair. She held one of Damian's two-shot pistols. Damian snatched the weapon.

Damian smiled. "I did. Thank you."

He checked to see if the gun was loaded. It wasn't. His smile changed into a frustrated snarl. Why were they going to take his weapons only to give them back later, without any ammunition?

"Did you lose these too?" the girl asked, holding up Damian's ammunition pouch and powder horn.

Damian's smile returned. Now he had the means to enter this fight as an equal. And, he had one shot for each Adept – if the gods were kind.

TWENTY-ONE

Tamaz hunched his shoulders and kept his eyes wide to appear panicked as Czenzi struggled to speak her miracles properly. He couldn't afford to celebrate his victory too soon; she also might not be as tired as she looked. It wouldn't be the first time an Adept had feigned exhaustion to gain the upper hand. Instead, Tamaz tested her weariness.

Drawing on Storms, Tamaz spoke, "*Sata aen reakuro pala* Czenzi."

As he completed the miracle, hailstones the size of green apples rained down on Czenzi. She countered easily, sending a wind upward from her, blowing the hail away. Her quick reaction showed she wasn't as haggard as she would have Tamaz believe.

The hailstones only provided a moment's distraction, but it was long enough for Tamaz to spread a powder of ground up Daemyn bones. Daemyns were immune to the power of miracles spoken by Adepts, and parts of their bodies maintained that quality once severed from the host. Night Adepts used this trait to protect themselves from the miracles spoken by the Adepts of other gods.

Czenzi would have to exert herself more if she wanted her miracles to affect him. Tamaz would be unable to affect her as well; the protection went both ways. However, while Czenzi taxed her strength in attacking Tamaz, he would conserve himself, waiting for the proper moment to strike.

TWENTY-TWO

Damian pulled two waxed paper wrappings of ball and powder out of his ammunition pouch. He pushed one down each barrel and pulled out the ramrod.

Hold on a little longer, Damian thought as he thrust the ramrod down on the first ball. He struck once, twice, and a third time, just to make sure the ball was packed in well enough.

One barrel done. The next barrel would be loaded in a matter of heartbeats. Then Adept Tamaz would learn that Miracles weren't the only path to greater power. But that's only if Czenzi kept Tamaz occupied until the gun was loaded.

TWENTY-THREE

Czenzi's body ached from channeling so much divine energy. Her mask felt so hot she feared it might burn the skin from her face. Only the concentration instilled in her countless hours of training allowed her to form each syllable properly to continue speaking her miracles.

Like all Adepts outside the House Floraen Inquisitors, she knew next to nothing about fighting a Night Adept. Somehow Tamaz had blocked himself from all her miracles. The only good thing was that he wasn't speaking any miracles at her, but that only meant he was able to recover some of his strength while she grew more and more tired. Czenzi couldn't afford to take the time to rest. That would also put her in the position of waiting for Tamaz to attack again, putting her immediately on the defensive. She had only managed to survive thus far by lashing out with quick, vicious attacks, keeping Tamaz too busy countering her to mount any serious offense.

Drawing on Shadows, Illusions, and Vengeance, Czenzi tried taking control of Tamaz's shadow. The first word of her miracle caught in her dry throat. She tried again but only managed a hoarse croak. She locked eyes with Tamaz, and the Adept of Old Uncle Night smiled.

TWENTY-FOUR

The moment Czenzi became unable to speak her miracle, Tamaz drew on Old Uncle Night's Dominions of Corruption and Sickness. He wanted to kill Czenzi outright, but feared expending that much power would leave him without the means to deal with Adryck.

Kicking at the dust that formed the barrier between them, Tamaz spoke, "*Zumak nitch crusag nu tzomadir.*" The miracle filled Czenzi with a disease created during the First War of the Gods. She would be dead within an hour, but even better, she would be unable to stop Tamaz from killing Damian.

Just as Tamaz had hoped, the miracle met no resistance. Czenzi's skin became yellow and cracked as parchment. She dropped to her knees. Her lips moved, but she couldn't form any words. She only managed an anguished cry as she dropped on the cobblestones.

TWENTY-FIVE

Czenzi's scream drew Damian's attention as he finished loading the first barrel. He looked up from his gun to see Tamaz turning toward him. Damian slung the powder horn over his shoulder, slid the ramrod between his teeth, and took aim. Tamaz started chanting, his eyes intent on Damian.

Damian pulled the trigger. Flint scraped against metal. A shower of sparks erupted in the pan, but there was no shot, only a puff of smoke.

Juggling the pistol, powder horn, and ramrod, Damian hurried to load the second barrel.

TWENTY-SIX

Tamaz saw the flash come from the gun and ducked out of pure instinct. He had been shot once before and had no desire to repeat the experience. Even if the shot did not kill him, another injury would prove the end of him.

When he did not hear the gun's report, Tamaz realized the weapon had misfired. He turned his dive into a roll and came up on his feet. Drawing heavily on the Dominion of Death, he turned his eyes on Adryck's torso. With one miracle, Tamaz would kill all of Adryck's internal organs.

Tamaz opened his mouth to end this foolishness, when a little girl dressed all in rags ran toward him out of the shadows. She had a knife. Backing away, Tamaz loosened his draw on the Dominion of Death and turned the attention of his miracle on the girl. It took less power to kill children than it did adults.

He spoke the words, but nothing happened.

The girl dashed forward and sank her knife into his thigh.

Tamaz cried in pain. He turned back to Adryck only to peer down two dark cylinders.

TWENTY-SEVEN

Damian pulled the second hammer back, took a deep breath as the little girl fled from Tamaz, then squeezed the trigger. The gun spat flame and smoke. A large chunk of flesh vanished from Tamaz's neck, and blood fountained from the wound. Tamaz dropped to his knees. His hands pressed at his throat, as if he could somehow keep the blood inside. Tamaz glared hatred at Damian. Damian shrugged. What use was a miracle, if your enemy's finger was faster?

Then reality came back. Even if the Whites hadn't heard the thunderclap and gunshot, somebody else would have. Somehow Damian imagined that talking his way out of this situation would prove difficult. He had to get out of there, but as far as he could tell, there was no way out of the shadow bonds.

The girl returned to his side.

"Can you get me out of these things?" Damian asked.

"No," the girl said. "But you can."

"How?"

"Have faith in *Galad'Ysoysa*," she answered.

"Grandfather Shadow?"

The girl nodded.

Damian's father had worshipped Grandfather Shadow in secret. Damian wanted to worship the Greater Gods, but he was only a Komati. All his life he'd been told that worshipping above your station would lead to ruin. While this was all dogma spat out by the Adepts of the Kingdom, worshipping too high had ruined his father. Then again, this very night an Adept had told Damian that he'd attracted the attention of Grandfather Shadow.

"I have faith," Damian said. "Teach me the words."

"Speak, *Galad an karkota'vastinus*," the girl said.

Damian nodded. He drew in a breath and spoke the words. Nothing happened.

"What went wrong?" Damian asked.

She looked at him gravely. "You do not believe."

"If it will get me out of this mess, I'll believe anything you want me to."

"That is not *faith*, Damian Adryck," she said. "That is desperation. Yes, *Galad'Ysoysa* has chosen you. But you must also choose Him. Release your fear."

Damian took a deep breath. The miracle hadn't worked because he didn't believe strongly enough. Well, he had something at hand that he did believe in. Bending over slowly, so the shadow binding him to the waist didn't creep any higher, Damian picked up the powder horn. He cleaned his handgun quickly, and then loaded it. Just as he finished with the second barrel, he heard footsteps coming closer at a run, lots of them.

"Wonderful." Damian tucked the gun inside his shirt.

For the third time that night, a squad of White Draqons came out of the fog. An Adept wearing the black and gray of House Kaesiak walked in their midst. However, unlike Czenzi, this Adept wore a mask that covered most of his face. His only visible features were a bemused smile, dark, piercing eyes, and short black hair with just a touch of gray at the sides. Where Czenzi's presence was mostly due to her beauty, something about the way this man examined the scene without blinking an eye radiated *power*. He looked around with no more expression than a man examining a stable for the best horse.

93

Finally, the Adept's gaze fell on Damian. A weight fell on Damian's shoulders, like the Adept could pry out Damian's darkest secrets with his eyes.

"What is your name?"

The Adept's voice was so calm and reasonable, that for a brief moment, Damian wanted to give this man all his secrets. Damian just wanted to have this ordeal over with so he could get out of the cold and have a hot meal. They wouldn't quietly cut him down in the middle of the night. The Kingdom would want to make a spectacle of his trial and execution to prove that no one, not even the prince of a Great House, was above Kingdom Law.

The girl poked Damian in the side. He glanced down at her and she shook her head. He looked back at the Adept and shrugged.

"You are playing a dangerous game," the Adept said.

Damian craned his neck, making it obvious that he was examining the Whites, then looked back at the Adept. "Depends on your perspective."

"I will ask one more time," the Adept said. "What is your name?"

Damian remembered a term being used in reference to him. He thought back and pulled the words to the front of his mind. *Sehan na aen Tsumari'osa.* But that didn't sound quite right. One of the words was wrong if Damian were going to say it. Which one was it? In a flash, one of the few lessons his father had given him came back.

"*Mina na aen Tsumari'osa,*" Damian said.

"Truly?" Amusement filled the Adept's voice. "Who told you this?"

Damian saw no reason to lie. "A really big talking bird told her," Damian waved at Czenzi, "that I was."

"Do you know what this means?"

"No," Damian replied, then added, "but she said that I'm blessed by *Galad'Ysoysa.*"

"Then it is my pleasure to make your acquaintance, Prince Damian Adryck. I am Kraetor Ilsaen, First Adept of Grandfather Shadow."

What was the First Adept of any god doing in Koma, away from the capital? The First Adepts were the Sun Throne's voice to the gods. How could the king maintain his rule of the Kingdom if he didn't have access to the gods' wisdom?

"Forgive me for not bowing, High Blood," Damian said. "But I am lacking that ability right now."

"I see." Kraetor walked over to Damian, looked at the shadow bonds, and nodded. "*Galad aen carcota'vastinus.*"

The shadows trapping Damian's legs faded back into the fog. He dropped into a deep bow. "Thank you for my freedom, First Adept. Now if you'll excuse me, I'll take my leave and trouble you no more."

"Contain your haste, Prince Adryck," Kraetor said. "If you are the *Tsumari'osa,* you are too important to run about unguided. Stand by while I rouse my assistant."

Damian hadn't expected Kraetor to let him go so easily. He took two steps back, making sure the bulge from his two-shot faced away from Kraetor and the Whites.

Kraetor knelt beside Czenzi and whispered into her ear. She sat up, blinked a few times, and then looked at Damian.

"Is your brother okay?" she asked.

Damian glanced at Xander. "He doesn't look comfortable, but he's breathing."

"Good," Czenzi said, as Kraetor helped her to stand.

"What happened?" Kraetor asked.

"Damian spoke Shadow's Thunder," Czenzi replied.

"Intriguing." Kraetor turned back to Damian. "Yet, not completely surprising or unexpected. How do you feel, my boy?"

"Tired," Damian replied, "like I've been up all night. Wait, I have been up all night. Why do you care?"

"I have an insatiable curiosity about everything." Kraetor's flat tone gave the impression that he was done answering questions.

Damian decided to hold his tongue. Time would give him the answers, time that he might not have if he tried Kraetor's patience.

"What happened to Tamaz?" Kraetor asked.

"I don't know," Czenzi answered, glaring at Damian. "He attacked me with miracles spoken in a tongue I didn't understand. I tired before he did, and then one of my miracles failed. The next thing I knew, you were standing over me."

"Truly?" Kraetor went and examined the body. Shaking his head, Kraetor looked up at Damian. "Do you still have the firearm?"

Grinding his teeth, Damian reached under his coat and pulled out the two-shot. As soon as the firearm was visible, the Whites drew their swords and rushed forward. Damian backpedaled, wishing he'd had time to reload. As it was, he veered toward Xander. If he could reach his brother's sword, Damian might survive a few moments while Kraetor and Czenzi called the creatures off.

"*Galad pita an Draqonti viela,*" Kraetor said.

Every shadow in the area surged and enveloped the Draqons. The Whites fought against the shadow bonds, but the more they fought, the tighter the shadows became. A small part of Damian's sympathy went out to them, but not much. He'd spent the last two years running from the Whites.

"*Galad tuceduta hene,*" Kraetor said.

The shadows holding the Draqons rippled. The Draqons struggled, hard at first, but after a few moments, the struggling became weaker, and finally they stopped twitching altogether.

"Now that they're dealt with, we need to decide what to do with you and your brother." Kraetor turned to Czenzi. "Where were you going with this one?"

"A Stormcrow elder told me to take Damian to the Vara," Czenzi answered.

"Curious," Kraetor said. "Why?"

"I don't know, but I wasn't going to argue."

Kraetor nodded. "Yes, yes. Neither would I. The Stormcrows have a much closer tie to *Galad'Ysoysa* than the rest of us. Well then, if that is the task that you have been set upon, by all means, set back upon it." Kraetor stepped up to Damian. "Don't do anything foolish to get yourself killed. Think of some other name to call yourself by the time you get to the Kaer. Your name carries a certain amount of notoriety."

"I am called Zephyr, First Adept." As Kraetor turned away, Damian cleared his throat. "Might I be permitted a question, Adept?"

Kraetor turned back to Damian, his expression spoke that he would suffer little foolishness.

Damian took a deep breath. "Why are Xander and I so important that my crimes are being forgotten?"

"You are the *Tsumari'osa*. Your brother is *Galad Setseman'Vuori aen Keisari*."

Damian opened his mouth, but Kraetor raised his hand.

"Now is not the time for questions. I know this shall be a challenge for you, but now is the time to do as you are told. Please don't protest. Just this once, Prince Adryck, please accept that someone from the Kingdom is acting in your best interests. If you have any doubt of that, consider that you are still alive while they are not." Kraetor gestured at the squad of Whites. "Go with Adept Czenzi. You and I will speak again, when we have more time."

In the distance, Damian heard more footsteps. Czenzi grabbed his arm.

"We need to go," Czenzi said. "Now."

Damian let her pull him into the fog and away from Xander. He watched Kraetor walk over to his brother and kneel down, and then the fog obscured them from Damian's sight.

Following Czenzi, Damian considered Kraetor's words. Yes, the First Adept was correct: Damian was still alive. However, he didn't think this had anything to do with the purity of Kraetor's heart, or Czenzi's either. Those two planned to use both Damian and Xander to further their own ends. Well, as much as they thought he had fallen into their web, he was trapping them as well. Damian doubted it would go over well at court if two high ranking Adepts of House Kaesiak were discovered giving aid and succor to a traitor prince.

TWENTY-EIGHT

Xander woke, feeling the same as he had his first morning after joining his first unit of Red Draqons. Two squads had taken turns beating him through most of the night. Their only order had been to make sure that Xander was fit for duty the next morning. After that beating, Xander couldn't find any part of his body free from ugly, purple and blue bruising. Sitting up, Xander's head felt like it had been used to ring all the bells of the Sun Palace.

He sat against a wall in a short alley. Looking about, he saw it was still night and the fog hadn't lifted. Close by, light shone from the streets in both directions. Taking a quick inventory, Xander made sure he was still armed.

Xander's last clear memory was of Damian chanting like an Adept. Then the deafening boom came, and everything went black.

Xander stood, and the throbbing in his head lessened and his senses returned to normal. As the ringing in his ears subsided, he heard a muffled moan down the alley. Then he heard the sound of skin slapping skin, followed by a gasp of pain.

"Shut up old man," said a gruff voice, and then came another slap.

"That's it," said a second man. "Keep him from speaking while I get this gag on him."

Xander drew his rapier and crept forward.

From the sounds of the struggling, some street toughs had managed to waylay an Adept. The Adept wasn't truly in danger. If the men had wanted the Adept dead, they wouldn't be bothering with a gag. Most often, anyone who attempted to kidnap and ransom an Adept received death as their reward. However, every so often the culprits escaped with their lives and a ransom. Those few successes encouraged others to try.

In the silhouette of the lights, Xander saw four men. Two held a struggling man wearing the mantle of an Adept of House Kaesiak while the fourth tried to secure a gag around the prisoner.

Lunging, Xander impaled the man holding the Adept's right arm. The force of the thrust sent the blade through the man's chest and into the wall beyond. Xander backhanded the man with the gag across the jaw. Releasing his sword, Xander followed the backhand with a solid punch to the throat. Cartilage folded underneath his fist, and the man went down, clawing at his crushed throat.

Drawing his dagger, Xander turned to the last man just in time to see him flee out of the alley. Flipping the blade and catching it between his thumb and first two fingers, Xander took careful aim. He cocked his arm back and, flicking his wrist, sent the blade end over end through the air. The blade caught the escaping traitor just behind the ear, and he stumbled to his knees before flopping face-first to the cobblestones.

Xander went to retrieve his dagger. The man was still alive, though blood flowed from the wound in a dark river. He weighed the chance of getting anything useful out of this man against the effort of saving his life. He had assaulted an Adept and would be executed for that. Xander decided that he just wasn't worth the effort. Xander tilted the man's head back and thrust the knife up under his chin.

When he pulled the knife free, Xander cleaned it on the dead man's coat and then turned back to the Adept.

Now that the excitement had died down, Xander saw the Adept had drawn his own knife and busied himself with cutting up the man Xander had pinned to the wall. And from what Xander could see, the Adept had no intention of giving this other traitor a quick death.

"Adept," Xander said. "Are you hurt?"

The Adept turned, revealing that he wore the ornate mask and black i-ron chain of office of the First Adept of Grandfather Shadow.

"First Adept Kraetor?" Xander said.

"Good morning, Xander my lad," Kraetor said in his always cheerful tone. "It seems that I am twice in debt to you for saving my life."

"There is no debt, my lord," Xander said. "It is my duty."

"Ahhh," Kraetor said. "*Velka*."

"Excuse me, First Adept?" Xander asked.

"*Velka* is a sense of duty and loyalty so strong that you have no choice but to follow it," Kraetor explained. "Grandfather Shadow gave his faithful this word because, while many know their duty deep in the shadows of their heart, young Xander, very few of them possess the courage to fulfill their duty. I tell you this, because I see so few people, even amongst the High Blood of my own House, who have displayed *velka* as you do. I commend you."

"Thank you, Adept Kraetor," Xander said. "But I am unworthy to learn this word."

"Nonsense," Kraetor chuckled. "I am the First Adept of Grandfather Shadow. I will determine what words you are to learn, especially if I am going to petition the First Seat of House Kaesiak to name you High Blood once the Sun King is convinced of your loyalty."

Xander blinked several times, unable to speak.

"Don't look so surprised," Kraetor said. "You and your mother would both make fine additions to House Kaesiak."

Xander dropped to one knee. "This is too high an honor for me."

Kraetor pulled Xander back to his feet. "Of course it is. At least, it is while you wear a Draqon uniform. However, once you have proven your worth, you will be worthy of this honor and many others. But let us not speak of this any further. Instead, tell me about your time with the Whites."

"But what about these men?" Xander asked.

"Oh, they won't survive but a few more moments. I'll send some Greens to attend to their corpses. Retrieve your blade, and you can tell me about your adventures thus far as we return you to the White Draqon stronghold."

"Yes, First Adept."

Xander pulled his blade free, and they left the alley. As they walked, Xander told Kraetor about all that had happened that night, including seeing Damian's apparent casting of a miracle. Xander couldn't quite believe his story, even though he had seen it all.

"Interesting," Kraetor replied. "I feel the gods are at work here. To what end, I do not know. I will confer with Grandfather Shadow. Until then, keep your brother and his miracle to yourself. I will speak of it to those who need to hear this news."

"As you command, Adept Kraetor."

"Even to Black Claw. I may be forced to use some subterfuge when we come face to face with Black Claw. I will need you to corroborate anything I say. Is that understood?"

"Yes, First Adept," Xander replied. "But—"

"Now is the time for silence," Kraetor snapped. "I must think."

As they walked through the fog, Xander couldn't help but wonder what reasons Kraetor might have for hiding Damian's miracle. Well, it wasn't Xander's place to question the motives of his betters. As long as he wore the uniform of a Draqon, his duty was to follow orders.

DANCE AMONG
THE LIGHTNING BOLTS

"Fanatics are the easiest people to convince to kill and die for the smallest and greatest reasons. My whole life is an example of this truth." – Vincenzo Salvatore

Stories and legends speak of individuals who catch a god's attention, a god who claims those mortals as their agents in the physical realm. In the stories, these mortals either embrace this or fight against the god's will, which almost always ends in tragedy for the mortal. However, there are a few stories where the mortals prove themselves more cunning than the gods and escape their ire.

There are those who are chosen by a god that neither reject nor embrace that god's attention. They dance on a fine edge between the god's pleasure and ire, doing just enough to stay the god's vengeful hand. There are few stories of this kind because few people are brave enough or foolish enough to toy with the gods in such a way.

That changed when the King of Order imprisoned the Greater Gods. The mortals who knew this had happened eventually lost their fear of the gods' wrath. For those who knew the truth, the gods became tools of mortals. Once the Greater Gods became free from their prison, they played their same old game of choosing mortal agents and expecting blind obedience.

An excerpt of *Chosen by the Gods*
by Julian Adryck
and Cathan Rosha

ONE

Faelin sat in the corner of the common room tuning his harp. Every other evening since they'd come to Bastian's inn, Faelin would have already been entertaining, but tonight there was no custom other than the Morigahnti. Prince Sandré had used his title and his coin to have Bastian clear the inn of all other guests. While that conversation had happened behind a closed door, Bastian's muffled shouts told the story of how he felt about the arrangement. But in the end, he was only a common innkeeper and Sandré was a prince and First Seat of his House.

A crash and laughter took Faelin's attention away from his instruments. Nathan sprawled on the floor next to an overturned bench. Thyr, perched on a chandelier made from an old wagon wheel was in his Stormcrow form and squawked down at Nathan. Wynd, who had been creeping up behind Thyr, hopped onto the table and leapt for the chandelier. Thyr flew away just as Wynd's fingers closed around the spokes. Shadows danced around the room as Wynd swung from the chandelier. While she wasn't a heavy woman, the pulley supporting the light groaned under her added weight. She dropped to the table with a heavy *thunk*.

Faelin shook his head. He knew far more about this game than he wished to. Whichever of them, Nathan or Wynd, caught Thyr would be able to command the other for the rest of the night. Faelin also knew more about the nature of these commands by overhearing Nathan bragging to Korrin and Wynd tormenting Aurell the morning after. The best nights for everyone, well everyone besides Nathan and Wynd, were when neither managed to catch Thyr.

During this chaotic game, Alerick came down the stairs leading up to the rooms. He took in the sight of Nathan and Wynd stalking the crow and sighed. Alerick's stature was almost the mirror image of his father, tall and broad shouldered, but his face did not have the sharp ruggedness of Allifar. Alerick's face was softer around the nose, cheeks, and chin, and his hair was the color of sanded pine wood.

As Alerick descended the stairs, his gaze settled on Faelin. The young Morigahnti walked straight to Faelin.

"How did my father die?" Alerick asked.

The young count may not have his father's features, but he had definitely inherited his father's bluntness.

"You should probably speak with your uncle about this," Faelin replied.

"If I wanted my Uncle's council on this matter," Alerick said, "I'd be asking him. I am asking you."

Alerick's tone suggested that he had received another trait from his father. For as long as Faelin could remember, count Allifar Thaedus possessed a spirit of command that few men could deny. Faelin saw that quality in Alerick now.

"Why me?" Faelin asked

"Because you are not Morigahnti." Alerick's face was stone.

"I don't understand," Faelin said.

"You've been gone a long time, Faelin vara'Traejyn. The Morigahnti are even more fractured than when you left. A Morigahnti, perhaps even one from my father's own Fist," Alerick glanced over at Nathan and Wynd, "might tell me what they thought I might want to hear if they imagined it could bring my favor."

"And you think I will be different?"

Alerick nodded. "I do. I heard what the Lord Morigahn said about Grandfather Shadow sending you to protect her. I believe that Grandfather Shadow knows the worth of all those who follow him. As a true Morigahnti, I will trust my god's judgment."

Faelin took a long look at Alerick Thaedus. If he was going to be so straightforward, Faelin would pay him the same respect.

"Your father and many of his people died so the Lord Morigahn could escape Shadybrook and not fall prisoner or worse to the Brotherhood of the Night," Faelin said.

"Then Grandfather Shadow truly blessed my father," Alerick said with a wistful smile. "He always hoped to serve another Lord Morigahn worth dying for."

"Another?" Faelin asked.

"My father always said that Maxian Taraen was the last Lord Morigahn truly worthy of the scar."

"The Lord Morigahn is even—" Faelin started, but Parsh burst through the doors.

"Brotherhood," Parsh gasped. "Coming with at least a squad of Reds and more Nightbrothers."

Faelin stood. He ignored his harp when it fell from his lap and clattered to the floor. The discordant *sprong* still rang from the impact as he stepped over it and dashed toward the stairs.

TWO

Julianna sat reading from the Tome of Shadows. From what she read, it seemed every Lord Morigahn had been in an almost constant spiritual dialogue with Grandfather Shadow. Yet the God of Storms and Vengeance had marked her with his own hand. Why wouldn't he speak to her?

She rubbed her eyes with her left hand and reached for the teapot with her right. It was empty. How long ago had she had her last cup? Shortly after

Sandré departed, Julianna recalled. She'd wanted to go to bed, but she suspected Smoke had yet to return. She glanced at the door, wondering if anyone might be in the kitchens so she could get more tea. Faint light shone through the crack under it. After a moment, the light grew brighter.

Julianna straightened and grabbed her rapier which lay on the table.

Faelin entered, carrying a lamp. Korrin came in behind him, *Galad'fana* wrapped around his face.

"The Brotherhood attacked Parsh," Faelin said. "He reports reinforced numbers of Reds and Nightbrothers from what we defeated at Shadybrook."

"Do the others know?" Julianna asked.

"Word is spreading," Faelin replied

"We are prepared to fight or flee, Lord Morigahn," Korrin said, "on your order."

"We cannot fight in the town," Julianna said. "Too many innocents could be harmed. We flee, and rob them of the chance to kill us. Korrin, inform the Morigahnti of my plan. Getting the horses from the stables is the priority. We don't want to get trapped in there."

"Yes, Lord Morigahn," Korrin saluted and hurried from the room. "I'll make sure Vendyr is saddled first."

Julianna hurried to pack the *Galad'parma* into its satchel.

"You know Sandré is going to use this to discredit your choice to stay," Faelin said.

"Had I chosen to leave," Julianna said, "we would still be waiting for Parsh."

She slung the satchel over her shoulder, belted on her rapier, and wrapped her *Galad'fana* around her head. This was the wrapping that had been Khellan's, not the one Smoke had given her. That *Galad'fana* lay hidden at the very bottom of her satchel. She feared it might be too tempting a prize for an ambitious man such as Prince Sandré Collaen. When Nathan and Wynd had arrived at Bastian's Inn, Nathan had brought her Khellan's *Galad'fana*. Thyr had retrieved it and Allifar's *Galad'fana* from their fallen bodies on the battfield of Shadybrook. The Stormcrows often did this after battles so that *Galad'fana* could not be used against the Morigahnti.

"I'm ready," Julianna said.

"Your clothes?" Faelin asked.

"Bah. They are replaceable. My life is not. Let us go."

They crossed the room, and as Faelin reached for the handle, the door opened. The hallway beyond was crowded with men. It took Julianna only a moment to take in the off-white leather helms of the Brotherhood of the Night. Carmine D'Mario stood at their head wearing his black Adept's mantle. His gaze met hers. Julianna felt herself smiling in mirror to him, a grim smirk of hunger and satisfaction.

Carmine opened his mouth, but before the Adept of Old Uncle Night could speak, Faelin smashed the lamp into Carmine's face. The glass shattered, and oil sprayed. An instant later, the flame from the wick caught the spilt oil. Carmine screamed. Faelin kicked the door shut and then barred it.

"The window," Faelin said.

Something thudded against the door.

Together they hurried across the room. They were not so high up that they couldn't jump safely.

Faelin flung the double windows open. A bolt flew past him, barely missing his face. Julianna chanced a quick glance outside. Five men and two Red Draqons waited below, trapping them. They were armed with crossbows and carried torches.

"What now?" Faelin asked.

"I don't know," Julianna said.

Three torches flew through the window. Two landed on the floor. The third hit the bed. As they landed, they splattered flaming bits of tar and pitch. Flames licked at the floor, but the bedding flared quickly ablaze.

Julianna forced her breathing to remain steady, counter to her pounding heart.

"There's no option but to fight," Julianna said, "and attempt to contain this as quickly as possible."

"We don't know how many Morigahnti are dead," Faelin said. "Korrin is almost assuredly gone. We have to assume that we can only count on each other."

"You're right," Julianna said, drawing on Grandfather Shadow's Dominions swirling in the *Galad'fana* around her head. "It's time to see how much I've learned."

She knelt in the corner furthest from the burning bed. The flames had already spread to the walls. Julianna opened herself to the flood of Grandfather Shadow's language. In the jumble of words, phrases, and miracles of *Galad'laman* in her head, there had to be some way to get them out of this room safely. Heat rose steadily in the room until one sentence became clear. She focused on the blessings placed upon the *Galad'fana*, pulled upon the Dominions of Shadows, Balance, and Illusion. She willed Grandfather Shadow's divinity to descend from his celestial realm through the holy relic, into her mind, and spoke the words into a miracle.

"*Galad aen Faelin anta na vartalo.*"

Faelin gasped as the miracle transformed him into a murky image of himself. He looked down at himself, and back at her. His mouth moved, but she only heard hisses and whispers.

"*Galad aen mina anta na vartalo,*" Julianna said.

All the air rushed out of her lungs, and Julianna felt as if she floated in a pool of cool water.

"Julianna?" Faelin asked. Now that she was in the same form, she understood his whispers. "What?"

"I transformed us into shadows." Her voice was a faint whispered echo of her normal tone. "Now we can pass by our enemies unhindered."

She moved to the window. The five men and two Reds were still there. One of them saw her and fired his crossbow. The bolt passed through her body and lodged in the ceiling. She turned back to Faelin.

"You see," Julianna said.

By then, the blaze had spread across a good third of the room. As Faelin came toward her, one of the bedposts exploded. A shard of flaming wood caught Faelin on his shoulder. Instead of passing through him, smoke smoldered from the wound. Julianna saw charred flesh instead of shadow.

Faelin howled in pain and pitched forward toward a clump of burning embers. Julianna reached out, grabbed Faelin's arm, and pulled with all her might. Faelin was nearly weightless, and the force of her effort sent them out the window.

Several more bolts passed through her as she floated to the ground. She wondered *were any of these men at Kaeldyr's Rest the night Khellan was murdered?*

When she reached the ground, she weaved back and forth, screaming at the Nightbrothers. She could only imagine the hissing bouncing off the walls and echoing in the inn yard. The final two Nightbrothers loosed their weapons. With all the crossbows empty, Julianna smiled.

"*Galad ulos mina vastan na vartalo*," Julianna spoke.

Her body became physical again, and a wave of fatigue crashed against her. She gasped for breath and blinked away the brightness in her eyes. Even though it was night, the light seemed blinding after seeing through the eyes of a shadow. The two Reds rushed for her, swords drawn.

Julianna slapped her hands together. "*Galad'thanya kuiva aen eva ruth!*"

The blast was deafening, and a shockwave knocked the Reds and the Nightbrothers off their feet. Julianna dropped to one knee. Every muscle in her body cried in protest. She felt like she'd been beaten with a bag full of bricks. In her last battle against the Floraen Inquisitor, she's been using the great *Galad'fana* and had become accustomed to drawing on that level of power. She couldn't afford the time to draw it from the bottom of her satchel.

With a few moments to spare, she glanced around. Faelin lay writhing a few paces away. One of the torches had been blown backward and had hit him full in the chest. Even though the torch had dropped to the ground, the wounded part of his chest had become solid again. Julianna crawled over to him, preparing to cast one last miracle.

Just before Julianna reached Faelin, another form stepped out of the night.

It was a woman wearing the black mantle of a Night Adept and carrying a short sword. The woman was slight of build and her dark hair and eyes made her appear almost Komati.

"Good evening, Lord Morigahn," she said. "You look tired. Speak too many miracles?"

Julianna opened her mouth, but her voice was too raw.

"A pity you haven't built your strength against the rigors of channeling divine energy." The Adept raised the tip of her sword level with Julianna's eye.

Julianna sent a silent prayer to Grandfather Shadow. *I cannot be meant to die this way.*

"Now, you pathetic little Komati," the Adept said, "it is time for you to dance with Old Uncle Night."

Julianna heard someone whistle from the far side of the inn yard.

The Adept looked that way. The hilt of a knife sprouted in her throat. A second later, another blade impaled her eye. The Night Adept crumpled to the street.

A moment later, a pair of hands grabbed Julianna from behind. She was turned around to see Tar, the innkeeper's daughter, looking down on her.

"I saw you change out of a shadow," Tar said. "And I saw you knock those men back. You have to save my father's inn."

Julianna looked past Tar. The fire from her room had spread to the rest of the inn. She swallowed the last saliva in her mouth, hoping to wet her throat a little. The one miracle that she thought might do some good would likely drain her completely.

"I will try, if you promise to protect me afterward," Julianna said.

"By killing an Adept, I have already thrown my lot in with you," Tar said.

Julianna nodded. She drew on Storms, raised her voice to the sky, and cried, *"Galad'Ysoysa, leheta aen myrscri na sinun suinasi!"*

The moment she spoke the miracle, her throat burned as if she'd just swallowed burning lamp oil.

A flash of lighting turned the night as bright as noon. Just behind the lightning came the first rumble of thunder. A moment later, rain poured from the sky. She felt a small bit of Grandfather Shadow in every drop. Craning her neck, Julianna looked to the sky and opened her mouth. Some of the rain fell inside her mouth, and took the edge off the rawness of her throat. Within moments, the rain soaked her hair and clothes, but it also moistened her throat enough to speak.

Unconsciousness threatened her, but Julianna forced her eyes to remain open. Though she had just witnessed the deadly accuracy of Tar's daggers, Julianna did not completely trust them against the Brotherhood. She crawled to Faelin. The rain had put out the torch, though his wound still smoldered.

Julianna drew on Shadows, and spoke, "*Galad ulos Faelin vastan na vartalo*."

Faelin solidified as Julianna descended into darkness.

THREE

Morigahnti from all three Fists fought in scattered groups throughout the burning inn. Wynd was with the largest group and couldn't imagine ever fighting in a worse situation. Flames licked at them from the walls, smoke choked them and threatened to blind them, and they were in a cramped hallway fighting in pairs. It seemed that neither Grandfather Shadow nor Old Uncle Night looked on their followers with favor this night.

Her rapier slipped out of her blood-soaked hand, but thankfully it was not her blood. The Nightbrother who had disarmed her cackled with feral glee as he took a step toward her.

A hand pressed on her shoulder and pushed her down. She did not resist, allowing the hand to guide her toward the floor. A gunshot rang out above her. The Nightbrother fell back, blood spraying from a hole in his skull-faced helmet.

She snatched up her sword again while pointing a finger at the Nightbrother who fought her husband. She drew a trickle of power from Shadows and Vengeance, and cried, "*Tuska!*"

The dark energy struck the Brother's sword hand. It exploded like an overripe tomato dropped to the street. Nathan skewered his now unarmed opponent.

The hand pulled Wynd off the front line, and two more Nightbrothers stepped forward to engage the Morigahnti. This technique of fight-and-switch was a common Morigahnti tactic. Even though they possessed more skill than their enemy, their opponents had the advantage of numbers. Every time a Morigahnti killed one, a fresh Brother took his place. If the Morigahnti did not rotate their front line, fatigue would eventually cause them to make a fatal mistake.

A bestial roar chilled Wynd's blood, and six Reds burst through the door behind the Nightbrothers.

Wynd heard Charise Garieth call, "Prince Sandré, we can't fight these odds!"

"I know," the aging prince yelled back. "Detryck, Maesyn, Tyral, Nathan! Hold this line."

"No!" Wynd cried.

"Do not question orders," Parsh snapped. "Aurell, take her. Nathan, hold with the others."

A pair of arms wrapped around Wynd's shoulders. She struggled to stay with her husband, but couldn't match her friend's strength.

"A Morigahnti does not let a brother face danger alone!" she screamed, but the Fist captains seemed uninterested in obeying that particular law tonight.

Aurell pulled Wynd through a door, and someone slammed it shut as Nathan and three other Morigahnti engaged with the six Reds.

FOUR

While the building proper of Bastian's Inn burned, Yrgaeshkil and her companion slipped into the stables. The flames had not reached here yet, giving her time to put her plan into motion. Wrapping herself and Alyxandros Vivaen in a Lie that covered all the senses, Yrgaeshkil carried her sole-surviving Saent in her left arm and a sword of Faerii steel in her right. The blade was just as thin, though only half as long as *Thanya'taen*, and while it might not be as deadly to any celestial or infernal being, it would allow her some modicum of defense if something happened to perceive past her Lie. Yrgaeshkil decided carrying such a weapon was prudent after witnessing Grandfather Shadow kill Saent Raena the Sacrificial.

Yrgaeshkil took Saent Muriel the Destroyer to the stall furthest from the door. It was empty. She made a little nest out of straw and placed the Destroyer. Muriel fussed a bit, but made no other sounds. As a Saent, the infant had no need of nourishment.

"And you're just going to leave her there?" Alyxandros asked.

"That is my intent," Yrgaeshkil replied.

"Is that wise?"

Yrgaeshkil fixed Alyxandros with her most disapproving stare. The mortal didn't even have the decency to look away. She sighed. So much would change once she grew fully into her power as a Greater Eldar.

The stable door opened.

"Perhaps," Yrgaeshkil replied. "Perhaps not. However, if you plan to be my first high priest, you should probably learn to trust that I have a reason for everything I do, considering how long I spent planning and implementing Grandfather Shadow's release."

I did not mean to speak out of turn," Alyxandros said with a bow. "I only wish to aid you, and I can better do that if I know your plans and intentions. My question was poorly worded. Forgive me, goddess."

"This once," Yrgaeshkil replied. She arranged the straw to look less like someone had made a bed for the child. "But I will answer, because your reason for asking shows merit.

"If the Morigahnti want to escape the Brotherhood of the Night and their Draqons, they will need horses. When they come for the horses, they will find this darling child. At their core, the Morigahnti are not nearly as harsh as my husband's followers. At least one of them should have compassion enough to care for the baby. That will be their undoing."

"I still fail to see how this little one is going to serve to undo them," Alyxandros said.

"She will live up to her name," Yrgaeshkil replied. "There are so many ways to destroy. Who knows what one small thing will cause the Morigahnti to fall to bickering and infighting."

She scooped up a handful of straw and scattered it across Muriel. Then Yrgaeshkil paused. Alyxandros had not retorted or replied. The Goddess of Corruption and Lies spun.

A figure wearing a Dosahan shaman's mask stood behind Alyxandros, who was coughing up blood and had a blade sticking out of his chest.

"I name you—" Yrgaeshkil started, but the shaman said, "Now," in an all-too-familiar voice.

Before Yrgaeshkil could complete naming Alyxandros Vivaen as her high priest, and thus raising him to Saenthood upon his death, the air around her head whipped away in a rush of wind. She felt herself lifted off her feet and flung toward the other end of the stable. As she spun end over end through the air, the Faerii steel blade slipped from her fingers. Never being one to remain and fight when her enemies clearly had the upper hand, Yrgaeshkil shifted from the physical realm to her throne room.

Her momentum did not slow, and she crashed to the floor in an undignified heap.

The entire Realm of the Godless Dead shook with her outraged scream.

Moments later, her son Nae'Toran flew into the throne room.

"Mother?" he asked, "is all—"

She flew to meet him, grabbed him by the throat, and slammed him into a wall. The only thing that saved him was that he was her favored child, and that only because he'd managed to orchestrate Grandfather Shadow's freedom, which in turn, had allowed her to become a Greater Eldar.

"Go," she snarled. "Go deep into whatever hole you have Kaeldyr tucked away in. I have greater need for him than your amusement."

"Yes, Mother," Nae'Toran managed to croak out.

Yrgaeshkil flung her child away and put him out of her mind.

In one well orchestrated ambush, Kahddria and Maxian had robbed her of not only the man she'd intended for her high priest, but also her Saent, for they would surely kill Muriel. The Mother of Daemyns flew to her husband's throne, a throne that would soon be hers, and settled in to think.

She'd already had thoughts on how to replace one of those pieces of her game, but how to replace the other? Oh, and she could always go and kill

111

another baby, but she'd been caught doing that and couldn't do it again so soon. She would have to watch events unfold and be ready to move if an opportunity presented itself. She needed to tread more cautiously than she ever had before, as it was only a matter of time before Kahddria informed Grandfather Shadow that he hadn't managed to kill the Goddess of Lies.

FIVE

The moment he saw Bastian's Inn burning, Kaenyth rushed forward. He made it two quick steps before a hand landed on his shoulder and held him back.

"Remember what I told you, boy," Uncle Staephyn whispered in his ear. "The girl is in the gods' hands, as are we. Keep your head down and perhaps they will ignore us."

A gunshot sounded from somewhere ahead of them. Kaenyth's feet refused to move. He'd seen a man get shot once in a tavern, and the weapon took half the victim's face off. Kaenyth had barely been a young man, but he remembered it with stunning clarity.

Kaenyth heard the Inquisitor mutter, "All Father, why must you test me so consistently."

He was certain that Inquisitor Luciano hadn't intended for any of the Vara to hear those words. If he hadn't rushed forward in his concern for Tarshiva, Kaenyth wouldn't have heard it at all. He stepped back. Kaenyth suspected he should do his best to hide witnessing the Inquisitor openly questioning his god.

Uncle Staephyn pushed past Kaenyth and stepped up next to Inquisitor Luciano.

"Begging your pardon, Inquisitor," Staephyn said, "but my boys aren't ready to walk into that."

Inquisitor Luciano turned to face the Vara. He did not look like a man afraid, or who had just a moment ago doubted his faith. To the contrary, the Inquisitor stood straight, head high, hand on the hilt of his rapier.

"The enemies of the Kingdom battle each other in and around that blaze," Luciano said. "We will allow them to do so. All Father Sun will guide me safely to the one I seek. Once we have her, we may depart, and the Crown and the Holy Order of the Dawn will not forget your loyal service. The Kingdom of the Sun treats its heroes well, and heroes you will be if you aid me in bringing the leader of all fanatical traitors to justice. However, if you men do not believe yourself equal to the task, the Crown will not fault you for that. This is an extraordinary stretch of your duties. Return to your dice or your beds as you prefer, should you feel the need. Those who would share in the glories that the Kingdom of the Sun has to offer, well then, those men follow me into All Father Sun's glory!"

With that, the Inquisitor turned and started off for the burning inn.

"Well then," Rayce said, "I'm for dicing and drinking again. Anyone else?"

Uncle Staephyn slapped the back of Rayce's head.

"You damned fool. We cannot leave, no more than we could refuse to help back in the Crows' Court. He'll remember your faces and find your names. You may not be carried away, but for the rest of your lives you'll be branded suspicious, and the Kingdom of the Sun will watch you, all of you, until the day you die. We have to follow. And it might not be so bad. If you do really well, the Inquisitor might take word to the Sun King and he will actually reward you. Now hop to it. After him, quickly."

As the squad of Vara hurried to catch up with the Inquisitor, Kaenyth held back and walked next to his uncle.

"There won't be a reward, will there?" Kaenyth asked in a whisper.

"Doubtful," Staephyn replied. "Possible, but doubtful."

"Then why tell the lads there would be?"

Uncle Staephyn stopped and grabbed hold of Kaenyth's shoulders. "Because they need the hope to believe that there's something waiting for them past dawn so they won't be so scared they give up already."

"And why be honest with me?" Kaenyth asked.

"Because you're smart enough to keep your head down without a bloody Faerii story." With that, Uncle Staephyn pushed Kaenyth after the others. "Keep an eye out for your cousin. He's not nearly as clever as you."

SIX

Kahddria solidified and scooped up the Faerii steel sword Yrgaeshkil had dropped. It would be just like the Daemyn Goddess to reappear and ambush them at an inopportune moment. She stepped up behind Maxian as he leaned over his brother-in-law, who lay in a pool of his own blood. Maxian's shaman's mask hung from his neck so that Alyxandros could see his face, and he had taken Alyxandros's firearm, sword, and *Galad'fana* and tossed them aside. Alyxandros glanced from Maxian to Kahddria. His expression held the tiniest glimmer of hope as he reached out.

"Sorry," Kahddria said. "I like Maxian much more than you."

"I'd ask why," Maxian said, "but you decided to serve the Mother of Lies, and that makes any explanation you give suspect. I trusted you. Julianna trusted you."

"Please," Alyxandros said, coughing up blood. "I..." but he couldn't finish.

"*Kostota*," Maxian said. "I may have walked away from the gods, but some truths transcend the gods."

With that, Maxian thrust his knife into Alyxandros's eye. Alyxandros shuddered, twitched, and lay still.

"Satisfied?" Kahddria asked.

"Not even remotely," Maxian replied, "but it's a start. I still owe Yrgaeshkil for setting all this in motion. I'll call her to a reckoning, starting with that abomination of a Saent. May I borrow that Faerii blade for a moment?"

Kahddria tried to keep her face still, but she felt herself tighten around her eye and mouth. Kavala's attack was still too fresh for her to be completely trusting.

"Fine," Maxian said. "You do it."

Kahddria nodded and went over to where the infant Saent lay in the straw. The child looked so pure and innocent, staring up at Kahddria with large brown eyes, face gaunt from hunger.

"Don't see a child," Maxian said. "It is a creature that should not exist. Yrgaeshkil is toying with celestial precedence."

"Right," Kahddria said.

She shifted her grip on the Faerii steel weapon, raised it above her head, and gritting her teeth, brought it down with all the strength she could summon.

The blade shattered a few inches above the child. Shards of the reddish metal flew in all directions, some impaling her.

She cried in pain as small pieces of her vanished as the metal cut her.

"Bloody damn!" Maxian cried.

A sliver of the sword as long as his forearm pierced his thigh; another smaller piece stuck out from his left shoulder.

"What was that?" Maxian asked, limping closer to the child.

"I don't know," Kahddria said. "I've never seen anything like that happen before."

"I've never heard of anything like that happening before." Maxian gritted his teeth and grunted as he gripped the shard in his shoulder with two fingers and worked it free. "I think we'd better find out more about this little creature." He gingerly touched the piece sticking out from both the front and back of his leg and sucked in a quick breath through his teeth. "Damn." He pulled on the metal just the smallest bit. His entire body tensed, and he couldn't quiet suppress a pained grunt. "Partially in the bone. Have to leave it for now."

Maxian drew in a deep breath through his nose and let it out though pursed lips. He shook his hands and flicked his fingers at his sides.

"Alright then," Maxian said, his face its normal stoic mask. "Let's see what this thing is about." He drew another breath, and spoke, "*Aeteowian ic seo wat sodlis ikona.*"

While she had never heard Maxian speak the *fyrmest spaeg geode*, his knowing it didn't surprise Kahddria in the least.

A multitude of Yrgaeshkil's symbols, with their sharp points and angles, floated in the air throughout the stables, coming from the door, presumably where Yrgaeshkil had entered. Kahddria hadn't seen the Daemyn Goddess, but her Dominion of Lies couldn't hide her from Maxian. Kahddria's symbol, a spiral ever twisting in on itself, flowed all around the place where she'd blasted Yrgaeshkil and kept her from naming Alyxandros her high priest.

"Lords and Princes," Maxian swore.

Kahddria floated over next to Maxian. She expected to see a variation of one of Yrgaeshkil's Dominions surrounding the infant Saent. Instead, she saw words in a script she'd never seen before. It resembled Old Uncle Night's divine language, but the letters were not quite the same, and the structure, as she could tell, was different as well.

"That's not good," Kahddria said.

"No," Maxian said. "With only one Saent now, it's drawing an immense power from Yrgaeshkil. Thankfully this creature is trapped in an infant's form. It likely has as much celestial power as many lesser Eldar."

"Celestial power?" Kahddria asked. "Don't you mean infernal?"

"For being so long-lived and supposedly wise, you gods and goddesses aren't very quick. Yrgaeshkil is a Greater Eldar. She's no longer an infernal being. You can thank the Ykthae Accord for that."

Kahddria sighed. "Fine. How did she break the sword?"

"I don't know," Maxian said. "Probably has something to do with that," he waved his hand at the writing swirling above the Saent. "But I don't read Yrgaeshkil's divine language, do you?"

"Does anyone?" Kahddria asked.

"Yrgaeshkil likely does," Maxian replied. "And this changes everything."

Maxian picked up the Saent and cradled it in his arms.

"Are you sure that's a good idea?" Kahddria asked.

Maxian fixed her with a withering stare.

"Right," she responded.

"I think I know a place to take this thing," Maxian said. "I'll return here after I deliver it and ensure that Yrgaeshkil keeps herself out of this conflict."

"I'll make sure the other Eldar are leaving the brothers alone," Kahddria said.

"Good thought. This conflict is going to draw enough attention as it is without the Eldar sticking their noses in."

Maxian nodded at her. She smiled at him. He continued to look at her. The goddess of wind shook her head and vanished, heading for Koma City.

SEVEN

The old man and the dog that looked much like a wolf watched in silence as Yrgaeshkil placed the baby in the stable, just as they stood witness to the fighting and Alyxandros's death and did nothing when Maxian took the child. The dog sniffed at the air.

"The child is a Saent," the dog said.

"Yes," the old man agreed.

"What will you do about it?" the dog asked.

"Nothing for now," the old man replied. "I am surprised to see Yrgaeshkil still living, but now she has piqued my curiosity. She and I are the only two Greater Eldar free with Saents active in the world. There is a certain semblance of balance to that. Besides, this provides another opportunity for Julianna to justify my faith in her. Speaking of Julianna, will you excuse me?"

"Of course," the dog said. "You do not require my leave."

"I know. I have decided to experiment with mortal courtesy. It intrigues me."

"By all means, then," the dog said, "don't let me keep you."

"Thank you," the old man said. *"Kun vaen ovat kuten makaesti."*

"Medan kerta voida tas johta," the wolf replied.

The God of Shadows stood tall, taller than the old man could have been on the best day of his life, had he been mortal, and stepped to the side and vanished.

EIGHT

Pain burned in Faelin's chest and shoulder, but not nearly as much as when he was a shadow. His first few breaths came in heavy gasps, as if he'd been holding his breath for a long time. He gained control of his breathing, rolled to his feet, and drew his rapier.

Tar backed away a few steps and looked ready to throw the knife in her hand.

"This isn't for you," Faelin said. "Now, run and fetch our horses."

"But..."

"If you want to live, do as I say. If you want to die, argue with me long enough for them to wake." Faelin swept his sword in the direction of the Reds. Without further argument, Tar ran back toward the stable.

As Faelin struggled to get Julianna's deadweight over his shoulder, two forms stepped out of the shadows near the inn. He nearly dropped Julianna in order to fight them, then he saw they were Morigahnti. He couldn't see their faces — each wore a *Galad'fana* — but both were tall. The men lowered their veils, revealing the faces of Korrin and Alerick.

"Let me help you with the Lord Morigahn," Alerick said.

After a moment's consideration, Faelin nodded.

Alerick said, "Kill them," to Korrin as he moved toward Faelin.

"Wait," Faelin said. He looked at Korrin. "The Brotherhood attacked our room moments after you left? How…what?"

Korrin grinned his I-know-more-than-you grin. "I heard someone scream after I went down the stairs. I came back up to see the Brotherhood filling the hallway. I killed one from behind and did my best to pull some away from you. Two of them chased me to the common room, where Alerick and I fought and killed them. When we felt the miracle of Shadow's Thunder down here, we didn't bother going back upstairs."

Korrin sheathed his sword. As Alerick came over and took Julianna's burden from Faelin, Korrin drew a square bladed assassin's dagger from his boot. He went to the nearest Red and stabbed the blade into its eye, then thrust the blade into the Red's throat.

"Where are the others?" Faelin asked.

"Some are dead," Alerick said with no more emotion that if he had said, *it's raining*. "I don't know what happened to the other Fists, but we're trying for the stables. There are Nightbrothers and Reds all over the inn. We have to find a place to hide and call the others to regroup. "

"How will we get them the word?" Faelin asked

"The Stormcrows," Korrin said.

"I have a place," Faelin said.

"Where?" Alerick asked.

"The abandoned theater behind the inn," Faelin replied.

"I should have thought of that," Korrin said.

"Why there?" Alerick asked at the same time Faelin said, "You knew about that?"

Korrin nodded. "Thyr and Raze have been keeping an eye on you while you wandered around the town."

He thrust his knife into the last Nightbrother's throat.

"I should have suspected." Faelin couldn't help smiling a bit. "The townsfolk believe it's haunted by the ghost of an actor that died during a performance. Since coming to town, I have encouraged this by letting passersby hear odd noises and see flashes of light at night."

"Why would you do that?" Alerick asked.

"Because that's where I've been storing all our travel supplies so as not to draw too much attention to ourselves."

"Didn't your buying it all raise any suspicions?"

"Who said I bought it all?" Faelin gave a grim smile. "I'll meet you after I retrieve the horses."

"Well enough," Alerick said. "We will meet you there. However, if Lord Morigahn wakes and gives us a course before you arrive, we will assume you are dead."

"Well enough," Faelin said.

He drew his sword and hurried toward the stables.

NINE

Inquisitor Luciano Salvatore, Inquisitor of House Floraen, led the squad of Vara toward the burning inn. He glanced down at the Detector. The hands on the enchanted pocket watch spun between the Symbols of Old Uncle Night, Aunt Moon, and Grandfather Shadow, mostly Grandfather Shadow. The second largest of these hands pointed almost directly forward, toward where he'd heard that thunderclap and seen the lightning descend from the sky. The Lord Morigahn would likely be there. He'd learned from questioning a few of the survivors of Shadybrook that the Lord Morigahn had survived their battle.

"We are here only to take one woman," Luciano said, glancing back at the Vara. "Once we have her, we will depart and let the Morigahnti and the Brotherhood of the Night destroy each other. We will avoid them as best we can."

The Vara glanced up at the flames and back at him.

"Do not fear the flames," Luciano said. He drew on All Father Sun's Dominions of Light and Justice and spoke them into miracle. *"Mishark Amhyr'Shoul protus nodris ip flagrio."*

Including the Vara in the miracle rather than just himself taxed Luciano more than he'd wanted, but they wouldn't help defend him or provide distractions if the fire burned them alive while hunting for the Lord Morigahn.

"I have protected you from the flames," Luciano said. "As I will attempt to protect you from other threats as well."

Luciano returned his Detector back to his coat pocket and tightened his grip on his sword cane. He hadn't wanted to bring the weapon into this fight, but he'd seen too many Daemyn hounds running about lately and didn't want to chance encountering one without it to defend himself.

He hurried to a door at the back of the inn, glancing over his shoulder once to ensure the Vara followed him. They did, though that Sergeant Staephyn Rool looked about constantly in all directions. He was a crafty one, smarter than any commoner had a right to be. Smart men like him could be dangerous if pressed. Luciano would have preferred to have found another squad of Vara, one with a more docile sergeant, but sometimes the other gods thwarted All Father Sun's grand design. And with the fighting breaking out, he had no time to locate another. It would be what it would be. Luciano had grown used to making light with whichever wick he'd been given.

Luciano arrived at a side door to the inn and opened it. Two women wearing Morigahnti veils stood not three paces on the other side. One was tall and slender, the other shorter and stocky.

Instinctively, Luciano drew on Light and Duty and spoke, "*Mishark Amhyr'Shoul clapious pyr lusias!*"

Both Morigahnti's eyes grew wide at the sight of light and flames gathering over Luciano's head.

As he reached for the Dominions again, the taller of the two women raised her arm. For the first time in his career, Inquisitor Luciano Salvatore stared down the twin dark barrels of a Komati firearm. His breath caught in his throat at the sight. He swallowed and drew in a breath to speak a miracle, but the woman pulled the trigger first.

Fire spouted from the barrel.

But I'm protected from fire, Luciano thought as some force slammed into his chest.

TEN

Wynd's breath caught in her throat as the Floraen Adept collapsed at her feet. She panicked for the space of a single heartbeat and then acted. The Inquisitor hadn't been alone. She sneered at the *Vara'Morigahnti* who stood looking dumbfounded at the Inquisitor's body. Them with their hoods of gray wool, pretending at being protectors of the Komati people

All the pain and rage of the loss of leaving her husband behind reared up at seeing these, her countrymen, standing with a House Floraen Inquisitor, one of those who actively hunted Komati who *worshipped above their station.*

Wynd drew on Shadows and Vengeance through her *Galad'fana,* and spoke, "*Tuska!*"

A shadow bolt caught the oldest of the Vara, likely the Sergeant since they tended to base rank on time spent in service, in the abdomen. Intestines and other organs spilled to the ground at the Vara's feet.

Wynd stepped through the door, choked down bile that rose from the noxious stench of freshly spilled organs, and lifted her arms to the sky as she reached through her *Galad'fana* and pulled from the Dominion of Storms.

She screamed, "*Fulgur aeculis!*"

A thunderclap boomed as a flash of shining ribbons descended out of the night sky among the Vara. Three of them screamed. Two of the others could not, as they fell next to the sergeant, bodies smoking.

Someone grabbed Wynd from behind. She spun, drawing her fighting knife from her sleeve. It was Aurell.

"Calm down," Aurell snapped. "You will be bring more Adepts or the Brotherhood here with such a display of power."

"The Lord Morigahn herself used the Miracle of Shadow's Thunder," Wynd said. "She shows us the way, giving us the edge we need to take our country back. If Sandré had let us truly be Morigahnti, my husband would still be alive."

"You don't know he's dead," Aurell said.

It was a false hope, and Wynd knew it – a ploy to help calm her. She wanted to scream miracles, to draw enough celestial power from Grandfather Shadow to lay this neighborhood to rubble, but she bottled the rage inside her. There would be time for her *kostota* later.

"I will watch," Aurell said, as she reloaded the spent barrel of her two-shot pistol. "You search the Inquisitor."

Wynd picked up the Inquisitor's cane. It felt heavier than it should have. She grasped the top with one hand and halfway down the cane with the other, twisted and pulled. She gasped when she saw the blade's redish color flickering in the firelight.

"What is it?" Aurell asked.

"Faerii steel."

Wynd had only seen one other blade like this in her life. That was when the last great Lord Morigahn, Maxian Taraen, came to visit Count Allifar and had shown the whole household his ancient weapon from the War of the Gods.

She returned the sword blade back into the cane, slid it into her belt, and continued to search him.

She found his purse easily enough and slung that over her shoulder; there would be time to go through it later. Then she found a pocket hidden in his Adept's mantle. A pocket watch lay inside the pocket. Wynd didn't bother to examine it, though she suspected it was more than it seemed. Kingdom High Blood leaned away from using any technology that might remind their conquered people that the world held other paths to power than the Adepts. She couldn't find anything else.

"Done," Wynd said, standing. "Let's go."

As she stood, a crow descended out of the rain and darkness. A few feet from the ground, the crow shifted into human form. Raze looked at Wynd.

"The Morigahnti are gathering in the abandoned theater. Faelin is headed toward the stables, and a group of Nightbrothers is right behind him."

"The Lord Morigahn?" Wynd asked.

"In Parsh's care," Raze replied.

"We should aid Faelin," Aurell said.

"But Parsh will want us to gather with the Morigahnti," Wynd replied.

"You didn't see the Lord Morigahn's reaction when the Brotherhood took Faelin in Shadybrook," Aurell replied. "Parsh would only want us to gather because it's what Sandré wants. Allifar would want us to do what the Lord Morigahn would want."

Wynd nodded. "The stables then."

If nothing else, it gave her a chance to kill more Nightbrothers.

ELEVEN

I hate fighting in the rain, Gianni D'Mario thought as he ducked and weaved between the Nightbrothers.

He couldn't dare to stop and fight just one, so he danced and ducked and rolled amongst them, slashing at legs and arms with his short sword and spinning his cudgel on its leather thong to block and parry his enemies' attacks. He couldn't stop long enough to speak a miracle to heal either of the two acolytes: Kahtleen or Shaemys.

Moments before, while heading toward the glow of the burning building and following the trail of the celestial energy of Old Uncle Night, Gianni and the other Aernacht Adepts had stumbled into a squad of Nightbrothers. The squad numbered perhaps ten to a dozen – combat had erupted before he could get an exact count of his enemy.

Now Gianni fought alone, his fellow Life Adepts cut down.

Run you idiot, Gianni told himself, as he parried a slash at his neck and brought his cudgel down on the attacker's elbow.

But he couldn't run. His cousin Carmine might be in this neighborhood somewhere, and it was the duty of all Adepts to protect their fellow man from the corrupted worship of the Brotherhood of the Night.

In that moment of concern for his cousin, Gianni hesitated a heartbeat too long. A sword bit into his thigh. Gianni stumbled. A pair of arms, thick around as oak saplings, wrapped around him from behind, pinning his sword arm to his chest. Two Nightbrothers rushed forward and plunged their blades into his stomach.

His blood pounded in his ears as it always did when the battle rage of his Aernacht ancestors overtook him. The cut in his arm received early in the fighting, the wound in his leg, and the two swords in his stomach felt like nothing more than pinpricks and scratches.

Gianni swung his free hand up from his elbow and slammed his cudgel into the face of the man holding him. It tore the wounds in his stomach even more. Something gave way with an audible *crunch* followed by a satisfying grunt of pain. However, the grip on him did not loosen.

The Nightbrothers in front of him withdrew their blades. Gianni hated when his enemies pulled their weapons free. It always seemed to hurt more pulling them out than when they pushed them in. Blood flowed down his stomach into his breeches. He hated fighting in clothes that stuck to him even more than in the rain, especially if the clothes stuck because of his own blood. Thankfully, and Gianni never thought he'd think this, at least it was raining.

He went limp and more blood flowed from his wounds, soaking further into his *laenya*, releasing the enchantment woven into its threads. Had this fight taken place six months or so from now, Kahtleen and Shaemys would have had similarly enchanted garments, but Mother Earth had not blessed them with the quick wit and intellect that she had given Gianni.

The Dominion of Life washed over Gianni, and his skin began knitting back together. As he healed, he relaxed his body more and more – until he finally felt the grip holding him loosen. Gianni lifted his leg and drove the heel of his boot onto the toes of the man holding him in a great bear hug. Mother Earth smiled on Gianni, for that enemy had soft boots – better for sneaking about in, Gianni supposed, but bad for a battlefield. Many men could train themselves or be trained to remain unflinching against a multitude of injuries suffered at the hands of other men, but a few well-placed blows could break even the toughest warrior. Toes were one of those places.

While the man holding him didn't release Gianni completely, Gianni was able to twist enough to get in a good, solid strike with his elbow. House Aernacht and House Swaenmarch were the only Houses who still believed brawling to be worthy of study.

Twisting his body three times in rapid succession, Gianni pummeled the Nightbrother with his elbow. Thank all the gods and goddesses that the Brotherhood of the Night still had their minions wearing those near-useless leather helmets. On the last strike, Gianni landed a very well-placed blow and felt something give way under the helmet. The man released him.

By this time, the two Brothers who had stabbed Gianni realized that he was not out of the fight. They moved toward him, circling to flank him. Gianni attempted to fling himself to the side to avoid getting trapped between them. He slipped on cobblestones slick with rain and blood.

Even before landing, Gianni was set to scramble away, to put enough distance between himself and the Nightbrothers so that he could defend himself with miracles. He hit the cobbles at an awkward angle. Something inside his right forearm snapped. He howled in pain and frustration. The enchantments in his *laenya* would not heal broken bones; it only healed wounds that pierced or sliced his skin and muscle. Healing broken bones and blunt trauma was another sort of enchantment altogether.

As it was, slipping had likely saved Gianni's life. The two Nightbrothers completed their attack. Their blades passed through the space where Gianni had been a moment ago, and they wound up skewering a third Nightbrother, who had been sneaking up behind Gianni, through the neck.

That third Brother dropped next to Gianni, coughing and clawing at his throat.

A Red Draqon pushed its way between the two Nightbrothers who came toward Gianni. It looked down at Gianni and drew its sword. Even with the blade free of its scabbard, the Red stared down a few moments longer.

"What are you waiting for?" Gianni asked. "Attack!"

"You heard the Adept," said the Brother on the left. "Attack."

Gianni became suddenly very, very cold, and it had nothing to do with the wind or the rain. He tried to scramble away, but the Red shifted its grip on the sword and plunged the blade through Gianni's chest. Gianni coughed blood and sent a silent prayer of thanks to Mother Earth that the blade hadn't pierced his heart.

TWELVE

Carmine stumbled up the stairs to the porch of the house across the street from Bastian's Inn. Everything about this attack had gone wrong. How could the Morigahnti have countered the Brotherhood's every move with such near-perfect precision? Half the Brothers were dead or too injured to fight, they'd lost Draqons, and Rosella lay dead in the inn's courtyard while the inn burned around her. Even with the downpour, the inferno created more than enough light for Carmine to see his ruined face reflected as he passed a window. The burning and scars had mostly remained on the right side of his face. He'd turned just as Faelin struck, and luckily had gotten a hand over his eyes before his face caught fire. He could still see out of both eyes, but that was the only blessing. His face still burned in his mind as if it were still on fire, and there was no way to reach an Adept of House Aernacht in time to heal his face. True, Gianni was somewhere in the city, but Carmine would have to explain how he'd come by the injuries and he didn't think he could come up with a reasonable lie that would also keep Gianni and any other Adepts with him from investigating. Carmine resigned himself to the knowledge that he'd bear these scars for the rest of his life.

Carmine turned away from his reflection, stared past the blazing inn, and vowed to send Faelin's soul to the God of Death.

A noise from the front door caught his attention. He spun to find Sylvie watching him from the doorway.

"Leave me alone." Carmine turned and faced the street so that he would not have to see her, or his reflection.

Sylvie's soft footsteps crossed the porch.

"I will not leave you alone, Carmine D'Mario," Sylvie said, putting her hand on his shoulder. "I love you."

"Liar." He jerked away from her touch. "You gave yourself to me in order to save yourself. Self-preservation and ambition were your only motives. Well, you succeeded in both, more than I could ever give you. Now, just go."

She grabbed him by the arm and spun him around. Her blue eyes looked right into his, and Carmine saw no shock or pity looking back at him.

"I won't deny that's why I offered myself to you on that first night, and why I seduced you later. But that's not why I kept coming to your bed. I *do* love you, Carmine D'Mario. I love you for your ambition. I love you for your cunning. And I love you for the way you make me feel. Listening to you speak of the Brotherhood, I understand why you chose that path. I want to walk that path with you. When we are both fully High Blood and Adepts of Old Uncle Night at the right hand of the Night King, who will stand in the way of our desires?"

Sylvie reached her hands behind Carmine's head and pulled him into a kiss. At first it was tender, almost timid, as if they were childhood sweethearts kissing for the first time. Then, as the fire spread from his lips down to his groin, he wrapped his arms around her and crushed their bodies together. The kiss became strong, full of need and desire.

Breaking the kiss, Carmine looked into Sylvie's eyes. She didn't love him. She might believe she loved him, or she might not. There was strong lust between them. She did love power. Whatever her motives, he didn't care. He did care that she was young, beautiful, and had enough ambition to see past his now-hideous face. Even if she weren't a countess, being able to look past his deformity was enough, and at sixteen, she was still young enough to be trained. His earlier panic and flight had been foolish, bordering on stupid.

"Excuse me, Adept Carmine," Jorgen said, coming out of the rain. Water dripped from his armor. The Skull mask hid his face, but Carmine recognized his voice easily, and the bow Jorgen gave when Carmine looked toward him. Of all the Nightbrothers, Jorgen gave him the most respect. "Please forgive my interruption, but Adept Hardin is coming and wishes to speak with you."

"Thank you, Jorgen," Carmine said. "Would you do me the kindness of watching over Sylvie?"

"My honor on it, Adept," Jorgen said. "And take care. Adept Hardin is in one of his moods."

"He always is." Carmine clapped Jorgen on the shoulder as the Nightbrother passed.

As Jorgen escorted Sylvie back into the house, Hardin stepped onto the porch out of the rain. His robes were soaked, giving him the appearance of a drowned dog rather than a ranking Adept. Graegyr followed. The Kaesiak's eyes held a faraway look. As much as Carmine had lost, Graegyr had lost more.

Carmine gazed past Hardin into the night. Looking at the decrepit Adept reawakened the desire to put a dagger in his eye.

"What do you have to say for your failure?" Hardin demanded.

"*My* failure?" Carmine's breath quickened. His hand tightened on the hilt of his short sword.

"Yes." Hardin jabbed his finger into Carmine's chest. "Explain how you let them slip past you."

"I hardly think—" Graegyr started when another voice interrupted.

"What about your explanation, Adept Hardin?" The voice came from out of the night beyond the other end of the awning.

Carmine, Graegyr, and Hardin turned to see a man step into view. He was dry and impeccably dressed in yellow and orange silk and leather, declaring his allegiance to House Floraen. The twisting and spiraling pattern of the hilt indicated his weapon had been crafted by a master artisan. Despite the rapier's obvious worth, the man twirled an assassin's dagger with a solid black blade between his fingers.

Hardin paled. "Please, Roma. There is no failure," his voice cracking on the last word. "I can bring a victory out of this."

Roma. Every Adept of Old Uncle Night knew that name. Roma was the right hand of the First Adept. Rumor had it no miracle could affect him. Not from Old Uncle Night or any other god.

"No, Hardin," Roma said. "And for that matter, my master doesn't want *you* to."

One moment Roma stood at the awning's edge, the next he was face to face with Hardin. He thrust the dagger into Hardin's chest. Hardin's body twitched and began to shrivel. Heartbeats later, it crumbled to dust and his Adept's robe drifted to the porch.

Roma faced Carmine and Graegyr. "The First Adept does not fault you for this. In his youth, he also had the tendency for impetuousness. He will give you one chance to make this right in his eyes."

"I live to serve the First Adept and Old Uncle Night," Carmine said.

"The First Adept's will is my single command," Graegyr said.

"Excellent. Fix this mess. Do not call any further attention to the Brotherhood. Do not allow the Lord Morigahn to leave this city. Are you two capable of this?"

"It shall be done," Carmine and Graegyr said together.

"Good." Roma stepped back into the darkness and vanished.

Carmine and Graegyr looked at each other, and though the mask hid Graegyr's face, Carmine saw the Kaesiak's eyes squint as he looked into the night, thinking.

"What is the easiest way to make sure they won't attempt a fighting escape?" Graegyr asked.

"Put them on equal footing with us," Carmine replied as he regarded the burning inn. The fire hadn't reached the stables yet. "Their horses."

"Yes," Graegyr said.

Carmine nodded and called to the Reds standing guard at the foot of the porch. "You!" He pointed to the one in the middle. "Go to the stable. Kill anything or anyone you find there."

The Red saluted and headed into the rain. Why must they always be fighting Morigahnti in the rain? Such concerns would soon be over. He had a thought that would ensure the Morigahnti lost this battle.

"You six," Carmine called to the squad of Nightbrothers they'd held in reserve.

The squad came forward and saluted.

"Gather anyone you find in the field. I don't care if they are Morigahnti, Brothers, or just some poor sod who chose to stay in that inn on the most unlucky night of his life. Nor do I care if they are dead, wounded, or just have some strange predilection for walking in the rain. Just bring them."

"Yes, Adept Carmine." They saluted again and went off on their task.

"What is that about?" Graegyr asked.

"We're going to give the Morigahnti something they are completely unprepared for." Carmine couldn't suppress his smile as he anticipated undertaking his favorite part of being an Adept of Old Uncle Night.

"Hardin has, *had*, a complete set of Daemyn summoning tools. He never used it to its fullest potential, because he was a coward. I won't let fear hold me back. We won't waste our time with Daemyn hounds."

THIRTEEN

Sylvie stood in one of the upstairs bedrooms looking out of the window at the street and the burning inn, watching as the Nightbrothers moved through the darkness collecting bodies. She had no idea what Carmine might want with those bodies, but then, she was such a novice in the ways of the Brotherhood of the Night. Even the thought of being associated with the Brotherhood of the Night in any form made her shake her head in wonder. With the amount of time she had to herself, Sylvie understood that she'd had no choice. From the moment the Brotherhood attacked Julianna's birthday celebration and took Sylvie captive, she stood at the head of two diverging paths, one that led to mothering a Daemyn-born, the other to becoming Carmine's woman in the hope that the Zenith shifted during her lifetime and the Kingdom of the Sun became the Kingdom of the Night. She would do whatever she needed, anything she needed, to ensure being named High Blood.

"Why do you let him direct you as his puppet?" Colette asked behind Sylvie.

Sylvie spun, ready to lash out at the servant girl. Only Colette hadn't been the one who had spoken. It had been Colette's voice and Colette was the only person present in the room, however Colette would never dare look directly at Sylvie with that self-satisfied smirk. An ashen hue had washed over Colette's face, and her eyes held the same strange glow a cat's did when reflecting lantern light.

"Back, my lady," Jorgen said as he stepped between them.

Colette who-was-not-Colette laughed. "Oh, now that is sweet." She looked at Jorgen as if he were a morsel at a ball she'd never seen before and was considering if it were worth tasting.

"Stay calm, Jorgen," Sylvie asked. "Who are you? A Daemyn?"

"Simple Daemyns and Aengyls cannot come to the physical realm unless bidden."

"Then who?"

"A Daemyn." The thing in Colette's body smiled even more. "After a fashion."

Sylvie stifled an irritated sigh. Since she'd seen Adept Hardin deal with a Daemyn to create a pack of Daemyn Hounds outside of Shadybrook, she knew better than to raise the ire of these otherworldly creatures, and also knew their fondness for feeding on human flesh and bone.

"You'll have to be a better liar than that to survive amongst the Brotherhood of the Night."

"A better liar?" Sylvie asked. "But I didn't say anything."

Colette laughed. "What a wonderfully sheltered and naïve little thing you are."

She walked across the room. Jorgen tensed with his hand on his sword as whatever the thing in Colette was passed between him and Sylvie. At which Colette laughed again and flung herself on the bed, stretched out for a moment before sitting, and then patted a spot beside her. Sylvie folded her arms and cocked her head. Again, Colette patted the spot next to her on the bed.

"I've learned enough to know not to give something for nothing with your kind," Sylvie said. "What will I get if I sit next to you?"

"At least you aren't a complete idiot," Colette said. "I will answer one question honestly."

"Alright." Sylvie crossed the room and sat down. She looked at her possessed servant girl and asked, "Who are you?"

Colette leaned in just next to Sylvie's ear, and said slowly, "Yrgaeshkil."

Sylvie stiffened. The room was quiet for some time, the only sound being the rain pattering on the roof above them.

Finally, with a swallow, Sylvie looked at Jorgen, and said, "Get out."

"But, my lady," Jorgen started.

Sylvie pointed to the door.

Jorgen bowed and left. Sylvie followed him to the door and closed it behind him.

With some semblance of privacy, Sylvie dared to look at Cole—at Yrgaeshkil, the Daemyn Goddess, wife of Old Uncle Night and Mother of Lies.

"Why are you here?" Sylvie managed to ask without her voice cracking too much.

"Aren't you the forward and demanding little thing?" Yrgaeshkil said. "Not at all the meek thing so many of your countrymen have become." The goddess stood, walked over to Sylvie, and took her hands. The godess's touch was cool, her skin feeling more like clay than skin. "I've been watching events and people surrounding this new Lord Morigahn and have taken notice of you."

"Why me?"

Yrgaeshkil smiled at Sylvie as if they were old and dear friends. "Because I have need of someone like you. Have you not yet wondered why all this is happening in Koma? Why is it happening now?"

"Why what is happening?" Sylvie asked.

"The gods are walking among you," Yrgaeshkil replied.

"Aren't you always walking among us, pushing and pulling on all aspects of our lives?" Sylvie asked.

Yrgaeshkil rolled her eyes. "I'd forgotten how insanely short mortal memory is. Quick history and theology lesson in one: All that the Kingdom has told you about the gods and goddesses, especially the Greater Gods, has been lies. The Komati are Grandfather Shadow's favored children, and until the night of Julianna's twenty-first birthday celebration, he, like all the Greater Eldar – those are the Greater Gods – was imprisoned. Now he walks the earth, seeking to make his precious Komati great again."

Sylvie nodded, trying not to think about that too much, even though much of it made a certain amount of sense. It made the Morigahnti's covert war against the Kingdom Adepts much more understandable.

"How did Grandfather Shadow escape this prison?" Sylvie asked.

"Well, there are many layers to that question," Yrgaeshkil said, "but the simplest answer is, I arranged it. I didn't do the deed. But I did set events in motion that would lead to his freedom."

"Why would you do that? I mean, if the Greater Gods were all trapped, doesn't that mean the lesser gods could rule in their place? Why would you want to become subservient again?"

Yrgaeshkil stood and turned on Sylvie.

"I am subservient to no one, and I mean to keep it that way. With Grandfather Shadow free, I have become Greater Eldar. I have begun to worm my way into ruling the hearts and minds of the followers of the other gods and goddesses, but I would have followers who are not polluted by those other religions. I would have a strong people, people yearning to be free, to follow me. In you, I see a reflection of my own ambition and thirst for power. Follow me, and I will ensure that you sit next to a husband on the Daemyn Throne."

"What of the Night Throne? Won't your husband be upset with you u-surping his place if he ever becomes free like Grandfather Shadow?"

"Should that actually come to pass, *Ahk Tzizma'Uthra* won't have the power necessary to oppose me. So many of his followers already favor my influence rather than his."

"Why tell me any of this?" Sylvie asked.

"I've watched people and events surrounding Julianna Taraen," Yrgae-shkil said. "Follow me, bring more people into the fold, and I will give you the power to do what even the Kingdom has not been able to do, no matter which House sits at the Zenith."

"What is that?" Sylvie asked.

"Conquer an entire continent and have every man, woman, and child on that continent blessing you and praising you."

Sylvie licked her lips. "What must I do?"

"First, learn to lie," Yrgaeshkil said. "Learn to lie with your entire body to the point that your mind both believes the lie and holds the truth in its darkest corners. That, and begin to bring Komati to follow you."

Sylvie knelt. "Yes, my goddess. I am your loyal servant."

"And before I leave you, I'll give you the first true gift of being my foll-ower. I will teach you to protect yourself against the miracles of other gods and goddesses." Yrgaeshkil placed a chain around Sylvie's neck. It had an amulet with a strange symbol on it that made Sylvie's head ache as she tried to follow the weaving lines in the metal. "Now, repeat after me."

A short time later, Sylvie opened the door. Jorgen still stood at his post. In the room behind her, Colette lay in the bed, asleep from the strain of playing host to a goddess in her body.

"Are you well, Your Excellency?" Jorgen asked.

"I am," Sylvie said, and for the first time in a long time, she meant it. "Let us go find Adept Carmine. I have news for him."

FOURTEEN

Faelin heard voices inside the stable. He strained his ears to understand the words in spite of the cacophony of raindrops that echoed on the street and the stable's roof.

"We need to flee, Father," Tarshiva said. "They brought this upon us. The inn is gone. The rain came too late. That woman ruined us."

"No," Bastian snapped. "The Brotherhood of the Night ruined us. We cannot fault the lady for that."

"I fault her," Tar said. "Her and all of those that came after her, lording around the inn, scaring away our custom. I tried to be patient for you, Father, but this is too much. We must flee."

Faelin couldn't let them leave yet. He'd need them to help with the horses. Once he got at least enough horses for Julianna and those Morigahnti he was fairly certain were loyal to Julianna and not to Sandré, he didn't give a damn what the Bastians did.

He burst through the door. Bastian jumped and raised his cudgel. Tar held a knife between two fingers. They stood in the center of the stable, halfway to the other pair of doors. Faelin hated the stables in Komati and Heidenmarch inns with their wide, double doors at opposite ends. Granted, they weren't intended to be tactically sound for fighting, but he'd found himself fighting his way out of them more times than any man would expect.

"Please," Faelin said. "I need your help. My lady needs your help. She tried to keep your inn from burning the best way she knew how."

"We've helped you already," Tar snapped. "We helped you for a week, and this is how you and the gods repay us?' She gestured with her neck toward the inn proper. "We don't owe you anything."

"If you help," Faelin heard his voice rising in pitch, "my lady will see you repaid for the damage. She is that kind of woman, but that's only if we can all escape." It might not be the truth, but in all likelihood Julianna would repay them for their loss, and then some, as soon as she was able. She seemed to be taking to *kostata* more seriously than any Morigahnti Faelin had met.

Before either of the Bastians could respond, the double doors at the far end of the stables flew open. Three Red Draqons rushed into the stables, blades drawn and braided hair flowing behind them. The Red in the middle went right for the Bastians, while the two on the flanks veered to the side to go after the horses.

Tar's arm became a blur, two knives appeared in the center Red's chest, and a third in the side of its neck. Blood spurted. The Red faltered for a moment, then recovered and rushed forward with no noticeable lack of speed.

Horses screamed from either side of the stable.

Tar threw another knife, hitting the Red in the shoulder and the upper jaw. The Red didn't slow. Tar dove to the side as the Red reached them. Master Bastian was not so fortunate.

The Red's sword flashed in the lantern light. Donal Bastian's gasp turned to a cough, and then a pained whimper. His intestines and other organs spilled onto the stable floor. He dropped to his knees and tried to scoop his innards back inside his stomach.

Tarshiva's screams echoed along with those of the horses the other two Draqons were maiming as they moved down the stalls.

The Red that killed Bastian turned to Tarshiva.

Faelin broke into a sprint. He lunged at the Red, knowing full well that his rapier wouldn't do much against the creature. The blade slid deep into the Draqon's back.

The Red snarled. Spinning, it backhanded Faelin, striking with such force that black spots danced in his vision.

Faelin stumbled back, head spinning, a detached part of his mind a-mazed that the Red hadn't shattered his jaw. He blinked rapidly, attempting to clear his vision, praying he wasn't moving back toward one of the other Reds.

A gunshot roared. Faelin dropped. Guns meant some of the Morigahnti had arrived. He couldn't know which, Julianna's or Sandré's, and Faelin did-n't want to run the chance of getting *accidentally* caught in the crossfire.

After a few heartbeats, Faelin looked around.

The Red that he and Tar had skewered lay on the ground, a pool of blood spreading out beneath it.

Faelin glanced around. Two figures stood in the doorway where the Reds had come from. Both wore a *Galad'fana*. One was thin and taller than the other, though definitely female. The other could only be Aurell, broad in the shoulder, and stocky, but unable to hide her bosom.

Aurell reloaded a two-shot pistol, while the other Morigahnti pointed at one of the Reds rushing toward them.

"*Tuska!*" she cried. Faelin clearly recognized Wynd's voice even over the screaming horses.

A bolt of dark energy crackled through the air and caught the Red full in the chest, lifting it off its feet even as scales and flesh shred off its bones.

Aurell finished loading when the final Red was only five paces away from Wynd. She took aim and fired. At that close range, half of the Red's face evaporated an instant after the gunshot.

Wynd and Aurell came forward, cautiously looking for any other possible threats.

Faelin scrambled to his feet. He wobbled a little, still unsteady from the Red's blow, but he would live and felt he could move well enough. Nothing felt broken.

"We have to go," Aurell said, as she and Wynd came up to Faelin. "The Brotherhood is regrouping."

Tarshiva sat in a pool of blood and gore, cradling her father's head.

"Tar," Faelin said.

Tarshiva looked up, tears streaking her face.

"Damn you," the innkeeper's daughter snarled. "Damn you all to the godless dead."

She leaned over, kissed her father's forehead, and fled.

"Tarshiva!" Faelin yelled. "Come back!"

"Let her go," Aurell said. "She's angry and bitter and will be no help to us now. We need to see if we can save any of the horses."

Faelin quickly glanced about. Each and every horse in the stable was screaming, all rolling in their stalls. The Reds had severed the tendons on all their rear legs. He also noticed that many of the stalls that should have had horses in them were empty.

"Convenient that it seems Sandré's Fist managed to get their horses out," Faelin said.

"And Parsh's," Wynd said. "Maybe we can steal others."

"Maybe," Faelin said. "For now, we need to get out of here." He retrieved his rapier then turned to Aurell. "Give me the gun for a moment."

He'd expected an argument, but Aurell handed over the two-shot pistol. Faelin walked to Vendyr's stall. The magnificent animal struggled to get to his feet, despite his injuries. His eyes rolled into the back of his head as he thrashed about.

It had been years since Faelin had last fired a gun, but his muscles held the memory well. He took aim and fired a shot into Vendyr's head, easing the animal's suffering.

"Would that we could do that for them all," Wynd said, as Faelin returned the gun to Aurell.

"If only," Aurell said, "but we don't have the time, nor the ammunition."

"Where now?" Wynd asked.

"Follow me," Faelin said.

He ran for the doors, praying that he'd not made a mistake putting Julianna in Alerick and Korrin's care, because now that he thought of it, that was actually putting her in Prince Sandré Collaen's care.

FIFTEEN

Pain was nothing new to Gianni D'Mario, Adept of Mother Earth. Still, he bit his tongue hard enough to nearly split it in two, filling his mouth with the iron taste of his blood. A pair of Nightbrothers carried him, one holding his legs, the other his arms. Every step sent shocks of pain up his injured arm. If he cried out with anything more than a whimper or a groan, the Nightbrothers might decide to check and see if he was actually as injured as he seemed. Then they would discover most of his wounds had healed completely and take it upon themselves to ensure he wouldn't recover from a sudden case of death. The enchantments on his *laenya* could heal a lot, but they would not cure death.

"Put him by the other one," someone said.

The two Nightbrothers carrying Gianni swung him twice, and he felt the lurch of being flung through the air. Gianni loosened the grip his teeth had on his tongue and bit the inside of his cheeks instead. He landed on his broken arm. It felt as if the pain stabbed from his forearm directly into his brain. Even with his eyes closed, white light flared in his vision and he tore a chunk out of his right cheek. He settled as the pain faded from a stabbing agony back to a throbbing ache.

Footsteps receded, and Gianni pushed his senses out just a bit. He lay in the center of a crowd of dead and dying people. His skin prickled and stomach churned at the sensation of life trickling away from those around him. Gianni pulled his awareness back into himself. He hadn't felt a completely healthy individual within ten paces. He was sure at least one guard would be standing close by, but not close enough to interrupt the speaking of one miracle, two miracles if Mother Earth smiled on him tonight.

Gianni opened his eyes enough to take a quick glance around. He almost burst out laughing when he saw the sun symbol of a House Floraen Inquisitor fill his vision. The Inquisitor was still alive, but barely. A small, round hole in the middle of the Inquisitor's breastplate looked back at Gianni like the eye of some dark creature, hungry for the life of others.

With a steadying breath, Gianni reached out with his good arm and touched the Inquisitor's hand. He estimated enough left in him for one last miracle, and figured he had a better chance of escape with an Inquisitor and a broken arm rather than with two healthy arms.

"*Gyth'Imyrthae*, hear my prayer," Gianni spoke, drawing on the Dominions of Life and Strength. "*Spreacah agys saol seo ar aes chuig curah fyr caele ionas gyr faedyr leis cavro laom ghiolla chun laemh yn naeme rus baethoa.*"

Exhaustion crashed down on Gianni.

The Inquisitor sat up, wide-eyed and gasping.

"Night below," someone cursed behind Gianni.

Forcing himself to move despite his pain and exhaustion, Gianni rolled to his knees. His left hand scrambled for anything it could find. His fingers closed around something solid. Without waiting to see what he'd grabbed, Gianni flung it in the direction of the voice he'd heard.

It was one of the leather skull-faced helmets of the Brotherhood of the Night, and Gianni had thrown with surprisingly good aim. Not close enough to actually hit the Nightbrother standing watch, but close enough to make his instincts take control of his body. He ducked.

This gave the Inquisitor time to get to his feet and cover the distance between them. The Nightbrother recovered quickly. He slashed at the Inquisitor, who twisted so that the sword clanged off his breast plate. Before the Nightbrother could bring the blade around for a second attack, the Inquisitor wrapped his arms around him, lifted him off the ground, and slammed him to the cobbles. The Nightbrother's head whipped down a second after his body, hitting with a nerve-grating *thud*.

This didn't seem to satisfy the Inquisitor. He stood, arched back, and dropped his full weight, crushing the Nightbrother's head under his breastplate.

Gianni took in his surroundings as he stood. He and the Inquisitor were between two buildings, houses Gianni thought, though they could be shops of some kind. Here, the wind and rain weren't quite so prevalent. The inn still burned across the street, and Gianni could see that he and the Inquisitor had been tossed into a pile of bodies.

"Damn," the Inquisitor said, his hands searching his clothes as he returned to Gianni.

"Time for regrets later," Gianni said. "We should flee to my mistress while we can. We can arm ourselves, rest, and return."

"But the Morigahnti—"

Shouts came at them from out of the darkness.

"Almost killed you," Gianni said, "if that hole came from a gunshot. The Brotherhood will be more than pleased to finish the task for them."

As if summoned by his words, four Nightbrothers and two Reds came around the corner of the building. They broke into two groups, one headed for the Inquisitor, one for Gianni.

The Inquisitor looked around frantically, his eyes settling on the burning inn.

"*Mishark Amhyr'Shoul clapious pyr lusias!*" the Inquisitor spoke.

Light, fire, and heat all leapt from the burning inn and flew into a ball swirling and twisting above the Inquisitor's head. The Nightbrothers slid to a stop on the rain-slickened cobbles and began scrambling to retreat. The Reds continued forward at a run. Gianni wondered if he would ever get used to seeing Draqons attacking a High Blood.

The Inquisitor didn't hesitate. He thrust his hands forward, and spoke, "*Lusias bruiarce al aedifecta!*"

The ball of light, flames, and heat blew outward, enveloping the two Reds and four Nightbrothers.

The Inquisitor dropped to one knee as the victims of his miracle writhed and screamed as they burned. Steam rose from the ground and off the walls where the flame blast had dried and even, in the case of the walls, charred the surfaces it had passed. Raindrops popped and hissed as they landed between the buildings.

Gianni swallowed, mostly to keep from retching at the scent of burnt flesh, as he moved over to the Inquisitor.

"As I was saying," Gianni said, helping the Inquisitor to his feet with his good hand, "bless and thank your god and my goddess that we were placed together and the Brotherhood had some desire for us outside of our corpses. We can hunt Brotherhood of the Night and Morigahnti later."

Shouts came from out of the distance. The Inquisitor nodded, and they fled together.

"I'd offer my hand," Gianni said through gritted teeth as they ran, "but it's seems to be broken. Don Gianni D'Mario yp Caenacht."

"Don Luciano Salvatore," the Inquisitor said. "Where do we go?"

"My mistress, Sabina Maedoc, is not far," Gianni said. "With her, perhaps we can entreat the Kingdom Representative in the City to call up her household Reds to aid us."

"We will find no aid or succor from Rosella Andres," Luciano said. "I went to her manor upon entering the city. Her abode reeks of the Dominions of Old Uncle Night, but perhaps we can enlist her Reds against her and these Nightbrothers."

"Oh," Gianni said. "I think those might have been some of her Reds that attacked us."

"Draqons fighting for the Brotherhood?" Luciano asked. When Gianni nodded, the Inquisitor said, "We are truly alone here."

"Excellent," Gianni said. "I love an adventure."

"Are you mad?"

Gianni nodded. "More than just a little."

SIXTEEN

Kaenyth waited in the shadows as the men in black armor and the bone-colored skull helms carried his uncle and cousin along with all the other bodies toward the house opposite Bastian's Inn. Some of the bodies wore the strange black leather armor of the Brotherhood of the Night, some looked like commoners, some wore the livery of that noble who had ridden in toward the end of the day, and finally, Master Donal Bastian, his guts trailing a bit behind.

Seeing Master Bastian there felt like dropping his heart into ice. Where was Tar?

Two figures ran past his hiding place. One was that damned Inquisitor who had brought Kaenyth, his cousin, and their uncle into this mess. Kaenyth's grip tightened on his cudgel. What god would allow all his family to die yet spare this man who had brought them into the middle of a fight they hadn't needed to be involved in in the first place? Kaenyth wanted to scream, to rush in and fight all the Nightbrothers at once, then find the Morigahnti and fight them.

He took a breath to steady himself. What would Uncle Staephyn do? Kaenyth controlled his breathing as he considered that. Uncle Staephyn would thank luck or chance or whatever strange thing he'd gotten into his head was greater than the gods at that moment. Then, he would mourn the loss of his family, get on with his life, and stay bloody well out of it. That's why Staephyn had been there as Rayce and Kaenyth had grown and why their fathers had not. Their fathers had decided to get involved.

Moments passed, and the way remained clear. It seemed the Brotherhood had collected all the bodies they needed or could find. He glanced about, doing his best to see well into the dark shadows in the awnings of buildings, to ensure that he was actually alone. He saw nothing, heard nothing.

He tensed, ready to take his first step when he heard sounds. He stilled himself, even holding his breath.

A pair of Nightbrothers came into view, leading Tarshiva between them. She walked under her own power and seemed unharmed, but that did nothing to hold back Kaenyth's gasp of surprise. He hadn't meant to, but sometimes the body reacts faster than it's possible to control. He stilled his breath again. Tar had glanced over to where he hid, but the two Nightbrothers hadn't seemed to hear him.

This changed everything. Uncle Staephyn was dead. Rayce might be. He hadn't been moving at all when Kaenyth had seen the Nightbrothers carry him away. Tar was a different matter. She was healthy, fully under her own power, and Kaenyth had heard whispers of what the Brotherhood did to women they captured. Kaenyth couldn't leave Tar to that fate.

Kaenyth drew in a deep breath, readying himself to charge the two Nightbrothers. Something touched his shoulder, and Kaenyth saw the blade of a sword stretching out past his neck.

"I thought I heard someone shuffling around out here," a voice whispered behind him. "Don't make me kill you, boy."

Kaenyth weighed his chances as the two Nightbrothers led Tarshiva into the house. The man behind him pressed the sword's blade into Kaenyth's neck. Kaenyth dropped his cudgel.

"Smart lad," the man said. "Now, after your sweetheart."

"She's not—"

"I've been watching you," the man said, pushing Kaenyth forward. "You've been pining for that one, standing where you think she can't see you. That's why we brought her last."

The man led Kaenyth into the front room of the house.

The Brotherhood of the Night had heaped a pile of corpses in the far corner, well away from the hearth where a modest fire burned. Uncle Staephyn was one of them. Tar knelt by the pile, weeping and cradling her father's head. Rayce huddled near the hearth with three other men and one old woman, trying to warm themselves. Rayce barely acknowledged Kaenyth. A Red Draqon watched over the prisoners, sword drawn,

"Over there," the man leading Kaenyth said.

As Kaenyth joined the group near the fire, a young woman descended the stares. She was a slip of a girl and couldn't possibly be over the Komati age of adulthood. She had the dark hair of a Komati but piercing blue eyes. A man wearing the black armor and skull helm of the Brotherhood of the Night followed her.

"Is this everyone you could find?" She did not speak with the accent of a Kingdomer, yet these Nightbrothers seemed to show her deference.

"Yes, Excellency," the man said. He gave Kaenyth a nudge toward the hearth.

Excellency? Kaenyth sifted through his meager knowledge of nobility and the honorifics that went with each specific title? Was she a duchess or a countess? Was *Excellency* a greater title than *Grace?*

"Well done, Brynn," the young woman said. "I believe these will do nicely."

She turned to address Kaenyth and the other prisoners. "I am Countess Sylvie Raelle. Welcome to the Brotherhood of the Night."

"I'm not joining you," one of the men said.

Kaenyth inched away from the man. This could not end well. It had been the kind of night that such predictions came easily.

The countess looked at each of the prisoners, her gaze settling on Tarshiva last of all.

"I understand your shock," the countess said, as she walked over to Tar, "and even your reluctance."

In a very unnoble-like gesture the Countess placed her hands on Tarshiva's shoulders. Tar looked up at the touch. Tears streaked her face, and her eyes seemed sunken and more tired than Kaenyth had ever seen. Tar's shoulders pressed back against the countess's touch.

"He was important to you?" the countess asked.

"M...m...my father," Tar said, and then added a belated, "Your Excellency."

"Sylvie," the countess corrected. She turned to the rest of the prisoners. "Please call me Sylvie. Until any of us are blessed enough to be raised to the High Blood, we are all equal in the eyes of death." She turned her attention back to Tar. "I recently lost my sister. The Brotherhood of the Night trampled her to death when they were attacking the Morigahnti."

Tar blinked in surprise. Kaenyth glanced at Rayce. Rayce shrugged.

Sylvie laughed, drawing everyone's attention to her. "I can see you all wondering. *Why?* Why would I join with those who have wronged me? I began my time with the Brotherhood of the Night as a prisoner, like you, but my heart is full of ambition. I listened. I learned. Death is not the end. It is only one step on the continuous journey of the cycle of Life, Death, and Rebirth." She took Tar's shoulders, turned the innkeeper's daughter away from her father, and pulled her into an embrace. "Mourning is not a sign of weakness. It is a celebration of the life that has moved on. By releasing the pain, we honor those who will soon be born again."

Tarshiva sobbed into Sylvie's shoulder. The countess who wished to be counted an equal among them – which Kaenyth didn't completely believe for a moment, but she offered more comfort than any other noble might have done – stroked Tar's hair and whispered softly as Tar's shoulders heaved as she wept.

"You have all likely lost people dear to you tonight," Sylvie said. "You might blame the Brotherhood, the Morigahnti, and perhaps even just blind chance. These are all lies. You lost them to Old Uncle Night. He alone chooses the hour when each mortal will pass through the cycle of Life, Death, and Rebirth."

The room was quiet save for the soft sounds of Tarshiva's grief.

After a few moments, Sylvie regarded the man who protested. "Do you see now? All men and women serve Death. I am offering you an opportunity to serve knowingly and to reap the benefit of the Uncle's blessing before you pass to your next life."

"Whatever sugarcoating you place on it," the man who protested said, "it's still blasphemy, and the Kingdom will sentence us to the Rite of Undoing."

"Not if we ensure the Brotherhood rises to the Zenith, and show them that we Komati can embrace the truth of Life, Death, and Rebirth."

"You are mad! You've spent too much time with them!"

Sylvie smiled patiently at him. "Only long enough to see the truth of things as they are. Join me and you will become enlightened as well."

The man spat toward her. "That is the only service you will ever gain from me."

Sylvie sighed. She leaned her head close to Tar's ear, and though her tone was soft, Sylvie spoke loud enough for everyone in the room to hear, "I'm sorry dear, but you must let go for a moment."

Tar pulled her arms from Sylvie. When free of Tar's embrace, Sylvie stood and faced the man. The care and concern washed away from her face and the noble lady returned. Her bright blue eyes glared at the man who defied her. Once, shortly after Kaenyth had joined the Vara, he'd helped to settle a tavern brawl near the dock. After all was said and done, one of the men had tried to break from the Vara and murder another. Kaenyth had managed to stop him because he'd seen the cold, calculating look in the man's eyes. Countess – for she'd become a noble once again – Sylvie Raelle glared at this man before her with such a cold calculating stare that he stepped away from her and his hands came up as if to shield himself from her ire.

The Countess cleared her throat and waved her hand absently at the man. In one swift motion, the Red Draqon stepped forward, its sword swept up, then down, and then it stepped back to where it had been a moment before. The protestor's head hit the floor. His neck sprayed blood as it toppled forward.

"Well, there goes one perfectly usable corpse," the Countess sighed. "Please don't damage any others beyond what Adepts Carmine and Graegyr can use."

The Red nodded.

"The Adepts can make use of the head as a sentry, your Excellency," Jorgen said.

"Well then," the Countess said, "you can serve Old Uncle Night in life or in death. The choice is yours. Which do you prefer?"

Before anyone could answer, a man in a black mantle wearing the mask of a House Kaesiak High Blood stormed into the room.

"What are you doing?" Graegyr demanded.

"I am converting these worthy people to the Brotherhood of the Night," the Countess replied.

"You overstep yourself, thin-blooded whore," the masked Adept turned to one of the Nightbrothers who had come with him. "Kill them all."

"No," Sylvie said. "As they are commoners, I claim them as my vassals under Kingdom Law. If you harm my people, we will see this to an Imperial court."

The room became very quiet as the nobles stared each other down. Kaenyth and Rayce looked at each other.

"We survive," Kaenyth mouthed to his cousin.

Rayce nodded. Unfortunately, that meant backing this crazed countess.

SEVENTEEN

Carmine D'Mario smiled as his vision returned to his own eyes. Through his Nightbat, he knew the Morigahnti numbers and their locations. They gathered at an abandoned theater where they waited for Julianna to recover. Faelin made his way there with the last of the surviving Morigahnti who hadn't gone there already. They were unlikely to move until Julianna regained consciousness. Pockets of Nightbrothers stalked the streets discouraging the Vara and any others from getting involved.

Carmine looked down at Hardin's ashes. He went to kick Hardin's remains to the wind, but stopped short.

"What are you doing?" he heard Graegyr demand from inside.

Sylvie said something, but soft enough so that Carmine couldn't make it out.

"You overstep yourself, thin-blooded whore," Graegyr said.

Then Carmine heard flesh striking flesh, and Sylvie cried out in pain.

Carmine rushed into the front room.

Sylvie was backing away from Graegyr, rubbing her cheek.

Already people were moving to one side of the conflict or the other. Four Nightbrothers flanked Graegyr. Carmine didn't recognize the way they moved, so they must be from the ones that followed Rosella. Jorgen and Brynn, the last surviving Nightbrothers who had followed Carmine and Hardin in the attack on the Morigahnti at Julianna's birthday celebration, stepped next to Sylvie, their short swords out and threatening. As intriguing as that was, it wasn't nearly as intriguing as the two prisoners wearing Vara hoods moving as if they were going to join the fight. The taller of them shuffled slightly toward a chair. The other one, who crouched by the hearth, leaned toward the logs and grabbed one.

The Reds were staying out of it. At least for now.

"I agree," Carmine said. "What are you doing? We have enemies enough without turning on ourselves. And you better have one damn good reason for striking Sylvie."

"This one," Graegyr said, pointing at Sylvie, "is overstepping her station to the point of blasphemy. She dares to preach the word of the Uncle and recruit these thin-blooded folk into our Brotherhood."

"Carmine," Sylvie said. "These thin-blooded creatures are countrymen to half your blood. They are strong enough to survive amidst warring Nightbrothers and Morigahnti. Just as the Morigahnti continue to survive waves of Nightbrothers. The First Adept of Night must see something in the Komati, why else would this be the place he comes to solidify his power to take the Zenith. He must see that in you, as you, with half your blood being from Koma, are his chosen apprentice."

"You cannot seriously be listening to this heretical woman," Graegyr snapped. "She dares to pollute our faith with her blasphemy!"

"It is not blasphemy," Sylvie said.

"It is!" Graegyr retorted.

"Truly?" Carmine bellowed. "You sound like a schoolyard bully, Graegyr. Can you not defend your position with more eloquence than that? Both of you, quiet. This is not helping us at all."

Graegyr drew in a deep breath. "This is not over."

Sylvie pursed her lips in that way she did when calculating some scheme, weighing her options. She reached into her shift and drew out a pendant Carmine hadn't ever seen before.

"I've been visited by Yrgaeshkil," Sylvie said. "She spoke to me of her plans for the Kingdom and our place in them. We must have enough of the Komati loyal to her husband to undermine the Morigahnti."

"Lies!" Graegyr said.

"If so, Syr Adept Graegyr," Sylvie said. "Speak a miracle from any god you choose and see what good it will avail you."

"Attack," Graegyr said.

The four Nightbrothers around him moved forward: two at Sylvie, two at Carmine.

Carmine leapt back. Jorgen placed himself between Carmine and the attackers.

"*Tuska*," Graegyr cried, pointing a finger at Carmine.

Even before Graegyr completed the miracle, Sylvie screamed, "*Erzni zazrak!*"

Carmine's mantle tingled with the power of Lies and Corruption.

A dark bolt of energy flew at Carmine. Jorgen flung himself at Carmine, knocking him away from the bolt. If only divine power obeyed the laws of the physical world like man-made weapons. The miraculous attack veered in the air. Carmine lifted his arms in a futile attempt to shield his head. Just before the bolt hit Carmine, it blasted back toward Graegyr, as if repulsed by some shield.

The bolt caught Graegyr's arm at the elbow. The limb exploded, showering the wall with blood, flesh, and bone. He dropped to the floor, bleeding and moaning in pain.

Nobody moved.

The Nightbrothers, both Carmine's and Graegyr's, stood looking between Graegyr and Sylvie. The Komati all looked as if they were trying to shrink in on themselves, anything to avoid notice. Carmine's breath came in shallow gasps. He'd never been so close to meeting the Uncle, and Sylvie alone had postponed that introduction.

"You," Carmine pointed to one of the Reds, "remove his tongue and staunch that bloody stump." He waved at Graegyr. "I don't want him speaking miracles or dying...at least not yet."

Carmine turned to Sylvie. "How?"

"I am an Adept of Yrgaeshkil, Mother of Daemyns," Sylvie replied.

Carmine opened his mouth. He looked at Sylvie, truly looked at her for the first time. She stood taller, straighter. She met his gaze, and while she had never flinched away from him looking at her, she had always held the slightest bit of defiance that she could never truly banish. Her defiance was gone.

"Jorgen," Carmine said. "Is this true?"

"I know not, Adept Carmine," Jorgen said, "but something did possess the servant girl. It said it was a Daemyn of sorts, but not a regular sort of Daemyn as they can't come into the world without being summoned. Sylvie sent me out of the room before I could learn who it was."

Carmine took this in and decided that he was going to have to tread very carefully around Countess Sylvie Raelle from now on. Luckily he had planned on summoning a Daemyn anyway.

"Well then," Carmine said. "Come, my love. Let me show you the path to the greatest power you will ever know."

If she could stomach what he was about to do, she might be the woman for him.

Looking about, everything seemed well in order. The Red Draqons stood against the wall, watching everything. The Nightbrothers had not come to blows, which pleased Carmine. The two Vara were back by the hearth, and they had the innkeeper's daughter with them. However, the old woman lay near the hearth, not moving, eyes staring at nothing.

"What happened to her?" Carmine asked.

One of the Vara, the taller of the two, stepped forward a little. "It looked as if her heart gave out in fear during the fight."

"Well enough," Carmine said. "Do you wish to serve the Brotherhood of the Night as Adept Sylvie suggests?"

"I speak for all of us when I say we wish to live," the Vara said.

"As most men do," Carmine said. "What is your name?"

"Kaenyth, Adept."

"Well, Kaenyth," Carmine waved to the pile of bodies, "put the old woman there." He turned to the four Nightbrothers who had stood by Graegyr. "You, Reds. Kill them."

The Nightbrothers didn't have a prayer. Carmine wished it could have been different, but he couldn't trust them. It seems that he was having trouble trusting anyone from the Kingdom with the exception of Brynn and Jorgen, and perhaps the First Adept of Night.

"Brynn, bring Graegyr. Jorgen, go get the servant girl." He gave Kaenyth a last look. "Are you still willing to serve?"

"I'm sure we all prefer it to the alternative," Kaenyth replied. He gestured to the growing pile of corpses where the Reds tossed the four fresh Nightbrothers' bodies. "You seem to have more than enough there, and they don't seem to be begging for company."

"Excellent. Welcome to the Brotherhood." Carmine offered his arm to Sylvie. "Let me show you something spectacular."

EIGHTEEN

Faelin stormed into the abandoned theater.

Morigahnti jumped, and several of Sandré's Fist aimed firearms at him. Faelin wondered if Aurell and Wynd hadn't been with him, would those Morigahnti have fired, and if so, what excuse would they give Julianna – a sad story about a horrible accident brought on by fatigue and a night of fighting?

He saw a group of Morigahnti near the stage, Parsh and Korrin standing taller than the other three.

Faelin headed toward that group, walking down the wide isle between the rows of chairs facing the stage. Morigahnti sat in small groups, two near the door to Faelin's right, three closer to the stage, also on the right, with the final group clustered on the stage. He couldn't count them, but it seemed there was at least a Fist there. Faelin craned his neck, trying to look around the Morigahnti on the stage and between their legs. Thankfully, the supplies he'd gathered seemed dry. Only one stream of water fell onto the stage, and that was toward the back corner.

The group of Morigahnti faced Faelin as he came up to them. More accurately, Korrin, Parsh, Charise, and one of Sandré's Fist faced Faelin. Prince Sandré Collaen made a point of turning completely away from Faelin vara'Traejyn.

The Morigahnti Faelin did not know stepped forward and met Faelin well before he reached the group. The man was shorter than Faelin by a half a head and had a deep, rusty beard, neatly trimmed. While shorter than Faelin, the man carried himself with the same tense stance of being ready to move that most Morigahnti developed.

"The prince is not giving audiences at this time," the Morigahnti said.

"What's your name?" Faelin asked.

"I am Lord Karstyn Agostan'Kolmonen," the man replied.

"Lord Karstyn," Faelin said. "Get out of my way, or you and I will have a disagreement and I will seek satisfaction."

"I hardly think that you will find anyone to stand as your second," Lord Karstyn said with a sneer.

"I will," Wynd, Korrin, and Aurell said without hesitation.

Karstyn glanced back and forth between the Morigahnti of Parsh's Fist.

Sandré turned. "You would put Morigahnti against Morigahnti when we have enemies hounding us, preparing to strike at any moment."

"When some of those Morigahnti are favoring themselves over the rest by ignoring the third law, I will do so without hesitation. Besides, as someone likes to remind people, I am not Morigahnti."

"I will not be baited into risking my man in your childish need to prove yourself," Sandré said. "What do you want?"

"Where is the Lord Morigahn?" Faelin asked.

"She is in one of the dressing rooms backstage," Sandré replied. "Count Alerick is guarding her. He insisted on taking up that honor in your absence."

Well that was something. Alerick seemed to be cast from the same mold as his father. Even still, Faelin couldn't be sure, considering Alerick's time as Sandré's ward.

"Thank you, Your Highness," Faelin said.

With that, Faelin gave a deep and formal bow, turned on the ball of his foot, and headed toward the ramp leading onto the stage.

"Is that all?" Sandré asked.

Faelin turned back. "Yes, Your Highness. I have feared for the Lord Morigahn's safety since we parted."

He'd considered lashing out at Prince Sandré, but no good would come of it. If Parsh and Charise, the other Fist captains, were not going to address the issue of Sandré's favoritism, any arguments Faelin made would only come across with the appearance of him being a petulant child attempting to overstep his place in the order of precedence. The best outcome from calling Sandré to task that Faelin could likely hope for would be to get cast out. More likely, Sandré would kill him, damn the consequences with the Lord Morigahn.

"She will never be in danger when Morigahnti are near her," Sandré said.

"Of course, Your Highness." Faelin decided not to point out any of the times Morigahnti had turned on each other. He bowed again and headed toward the backstage area.

When Faelin reached halfway across the stage, several boards dropped from above.

The Morigahnti on the stage began tromping around, sending vibrations through the stage and the noise of their pounding echoed through the theater.

Faelin drew his sword and readied himself.

Something blurred through the air from above, screaming feral fury, landing among the rubble of the boards that had fallen moments before.

Men shrieked and cried out at the Red Draqon now snarling in their midst.

The Red launched itself at a Morigahnti and slid its curved sword all the way down the man's side, taking off his arm and slashing open his hip. Blood sprayed, and any training he had received vanished; when faced with the sudden pain and the snarling Red Draqon, the man screamed and bolted. As if sharing a herd mentality, the other men on the stage followed, heading for the only place that offered safety from the predator among them. As the Morighanti fled, the Red chased them, slashing and cutting at them from behind. Several fell before the rest reached the edge of the stage and leapt, clearing Sandré, Parsh, and the others. The Morigahnti ducked and huddled beneath the lip of the stage.

One Morigahnti landed amongst the first two rows of seats. His legs got tangled up and snapped.

Without thinking, Faelin rushed the Draqon.

As if sensing the oncoming attack, the Red turned to face him, but a moment too late. Faelin drove his rapier into the Red's torso almost up to the hilt. The wound wouldn't kill the thing immediately but would at least slow it down some.

Snarling, the Red twisted, pulling the hilt out of Faelin's grip. It counterattacked. Its sword came down. Faelin ducked inside the Red's guard. He collided with the Red, driving his shoulder into its abdomen. He felt more than saw the thing shift its grip on its sword. Before it could strike, he stood up, lifting the Draqon off its feet. The Red struggled in his grip, legs kicking and arms flailing. Faelin arched his back and then slammed the Red into the stage floor. The Red dropped its sword on impact. Faelin kicked the weapon across the room. The Draqon leapt up, slashed at Faelin with its claws, and tore a chunk of flesh from his left shoulder.

"Faelin!" Parsh yelled from the edge of the stage. "Move!"

Faelin dropped.

"*Tuska!*" four voices cried.

Parsh, Korrin, Charise, and Karstyn all had their *Galad'fanati* wrapped around their heads and were pointing at the Draqon. Four black bolts flew from their fingers. Two hit the Draqon's hands, exploding in a shower of blood, bone, and claws. One hit it squarely in the chest; its ribs ripped open, spilling gore onto the floor. The last hit it in the head. The Draqon's face melted, and the back of its skull blasted outward.

The theater was a chaotic mess. Morigahnti moved about, seeking other foes who might have rushed in during the confusion. Horses screamed.

Faelin rushed toward the backstage area. Alerick stood in front of a closed door, a two-shot pistol in his hand.

"Is she?" Faelin asked.

"Well," Alerick replied. "There are no other ways in or out of that room."

Faelin looked in on Julianna anyway. She lay on a couch, still unconscious, but otherwise unharmed. He shut the door.

Galad'Ysoysa, let her wake soon, Faelin prayed to himself.

"What happened out there?" Alerick asked.

"A Red Draqon attacked," Faelin replied. "It seems the Fist captains did not feel it necessary to set a guard or sentry patrol."

"And they always seem to be one step ahead of us," Alerick said. "They have Adepts, Nightbrothers, and Red Draqons. How can we win this fight?"

"We cannot just give up," Faelin said.

"No, we cannot," Alerick said. "Moriganti do not flee from battle."

Faelin nodded and clapped Alerick on the shoulder. He was Allifar Thaedus's son. Would that all Morigahnti were like him, Koma might never have fallen to the Kingdom. But the world never coincided with wishes and dreams.

Faelin went to a corner to think.

They might not all be able to escape, but a small group might be able to slip by the Brotherhood of the Night. Might. The trouble was, he would need help from some of the other Morigahnti. Some of them served Julianna faithfully, but Faelin's plan would require a betrayal, if only a betrayal by omission. Could he trust any of the Morigahnti with that?

NINETEEN

Carmine had just placed the final skull onto the top of his, formerly Hardin's, altar to Old Uncle Night when the Red brought the sixth and final body into the room. He placed it against the wall with the others, as Carmine had ordered when he'd begun erecting the altar.

"Lay the bodies with their heads facing the altar," Carmine said, as he went to the black lacquered boxes and carefully lifted the draperies cured from human skin, one for each of the six ages of man. "Three on each side of the brazier."

Each corpse had suffered a relatively clean death, making hiding the death wounds fairly easy. The sixth body, and the one that held the greatest interest for Carmine, was one of the Morigahnti they'd killed. Thankfully, the four Morigahnti corpses the Nightbrothers had found died fighting so the other Morigahnti could escape, and none of their fellows had seen them fall. The Morigahnti fought as Morigahnti do, making victory on the skirmish as costly as possible. The other three wouldn't serve for Carmine's plans, but this one had fallen to one of Graegyr's plague miracles, and so his body was clean of any injuries. Perfect for Carmine's needs.

As the Red placed the bodies, Brynn brought Graegyr into the room. The Kaesiak Adept was so close to death that his pathetic struggles seemed more like an epileptic fit than any actual attempt to escape. Jorgen followed shortly after, leading the servant girl by the arm. Colette took one look at the altar of Old Uncle Night, screamed, and began to struggle against Jorgen.

"Brynn, help hold her," Carmine said.

Brynn dropped Graegyr in an unceremonious heap and ran across the room to take hold of Colette's other arm. Still she fought.

Carmine drew on the Dominions of Lies and Corruption, and spoke, "*Zpanek zhu nahs.*"

Colette went limp, a deadweight in Jorgen and Brynn's arms.

"What did you do to her?" Sylvie asked from the corner where she'd been watching Carmine construct the altar.

"I convinced her that being awake is a lie," Carmine replied. "Now put the girl on the cot."

Once the Draqon laid the corpses out on the floor and Colette slept on the cot in the far corner, Carmine said, "Now."

"What are you going to do?" Sylvie asked.

"Summon a Daemyn and bargain for power," he replied.

"I saw Hardin do that at Shadybrook," Sylvie said.

"Not like this," Carmine said. "Summoning Daemyns to come to the world as Daemyn hounds is the first task any new Night Adept learns. This will be so much more. Now, you have to be quiet now, no matter what. Any interruptions could be disastrous, making death seem like a blessing."

Sylvie nodded, and by the fear he saw in her unblinking eyes, he knew she would sit in her chair and do nothing.

Carmine would have preferred to have more time to perform a summoning, but he did not have the luxury to wait. Just before preparing, he'd learned from his Nightbat that Gianni and the Inquisitor had made it to the inn where Gianni's mistress was staying. If they joined this fray before Carmine had proper reinforcements, all would be lost.

Going to his baggage, he brought out the tools needed for the summoning. He placed the two iron squares laced with silver on the floor, one crosswise on top of the other so that the corners of each formed small triangles. Next, he placed the gold circle on top so it touched each corner of both squares. These items would bind the Daemyn in place during the negotiation. Next, he placed the summoning brazier into the center of the circle, and filled it with coals and incense. Taking a candle from the table next to his cot, Carmine lit the coals. The scent of smoke and herbs filled the tent.

"Brynn and Jorgen," Carmine said. "Ensure that I'm not disturbed."

Alone except for Sylvie and his victims, he set about the actual summoning.

He went to Graegyr.

"I'm sorry," Carmine said. "But some things are greater than any one man, greater than the Brotherhood of the Night. Some things are about family, true family."

He took his ceremonial dagger out of his belt and cut off a portion of Graegyr's scalp. When he tossed it onto the brazier, Carmine wondered if his Komati blood caused him to put all things aside to get revenge on Julianna for killing Nicco. Was such a thing as *kostota* burned into the soul of everyone born of this nation?

The stench of burning flesh and hair mingling with the scent of smoke and herbs brought Carmine from thoughts of revenge to focus on the task before him.

Carmine once sickened at this smell, but now he reveled in its heady rush. Most Night Adepts felt that speaking miracles was the pinnacle of their power. Not Carmine. Summoning and bargaining with Daemyns was. Miracles were always certain once you knew the proper words. Dealing with Daemyns was always a challenge, even when you knew which one you were summoning. Each word in the negotiations had to be selected with the utmost care. One misspoken word could easily cost his soul.

As the scalp smoldered, the smoke coalesced above the brazier but did not billow out into the rest of the room. It remained within the confines of the gold circle. Small tendrils of smoke snaked out, as if testing the barrier, but none could pierce through the summoning circle. A pair of luminous green eyes formed in the smoke.

"Who do you seek?" a voice rasped.

"I would prefer to deal with," Carmine stopped a moment to make perfectly sure of his pronunciation, "Nae'Toran'borlahisth. But I will conduct business with any who possesses the same power as he and who will give me their full name."

There was a chuckle. "I have the power, but I will not give a pathetic creature such as you my name. What will you give me to fetch Nae'Toran for you?"

"I have a fresh body here," Carmine gestured to Graegyr. "A still living Adept of House Kaesiak, knowledgeable in the ways of Grandfather Shadow and Old Uncle Night. You may have any one part of him you wish."

"Intriguing that you bargain with a fellow Night Adept," the Daemyn said. "And even with such a prize, to be your messenger I want two parts."

"Which two?"

"His eyes and his ears."

"That's actually four parts," Carmine said. "Two of each one."

"You are a sharp one," the Daemyn said. "You've either dealt with us before, or have been well trained."

"Both," Carmine said. "But we're getting off the subject. If I give you the requested pieces off of this man, will you bring Nae'Toran'borlahisth to this negotiation."

"For this price, I will tell him you wish to speak with him. Are we a-greed?"

"No. For the named price, I demand you deliver Nae'Toran'borlahisth to this negotiation."

"Fine," the Daemyn said. "Who shall I tell him is calling?"

"Never mind. Just bring him."

"Payment first."

"State the nature of our bargain first."

"Very well," the Daemyn said with an exasperated sigh. "I will bring Nae'Toran'borlahisth to you for negotiation in exchange for two human eyes and two human ears of a Kaesiak Adept."

"I'm afraid that won't be good enough," Carmine replied. "Agree by your name to bind our bargain."

"Then you will need to give me your name as well."

"No," Carmine said. "You are not enhancing me or granting me any personal power. You don't need my name to complete our bargain."

"You *are* good, mortal," the Daemyn said. "The best negotiator I've dealt with in a long time, and entertaining as well. I will bind myself to this bargain by name in hopes that you will someday want to deal with me again. In exchange for two human ears and two human eyes from a Kaesiak Adept, I, Taelan'sha'Naeporishn shall bring Nae'Toran'borlahisth to this negotiation."

"Agreed."

He went to Graegyr with his knife and removed his eyes and ears. Ignoring Graegyr's moans of pain and the blood that poured over his hands, Carmine tossed the eyes and ears onto the brazier. The Daemyn, Taelan'sha, made a gurgling sound, full of contentment, and its eyes closed to mere slits. When Graegyr's ears and eyes burned away, Taelan'sha focused on Carmine again.

"I will return with Nae'Toran." The Daemyn's eyes disappeared.

Carmine sat back in his chair and waited.

He looked over at Sylvie and smiled. She opened her mouth, but before she could speak he held his fingers to his lips. She remained silent.

So far, this had gone well. He hadn't expected to learn another Daemyn's name. That made four that he could call on for favors and power. Let the other Adepts command men and Draqons, he would command Daemyns, a power that neither men nor Draqon could match.

Thinking of building a power base among the Daemyns, Carmine went over to Graegyr's body. Taking the knife, he cut off Graegyr's nose. Apparently, Taelan'sha had a fondness for facial features. When he returned, Carmine would give him a gift. Like men, Daemyns were also susceptible to bribery and flattery.

A few minutes later, much sooner than Carmine expected, a presence returned to the summoning circle. Taelan'sha's eyes looked at him from within the smoke.

"I've brought the one you seek," the Taelan'sha said. "You bargain well, mortal. It is a rare pleasure to have a bit of a challenge. I hope one day to bargain again."

"Perhaps," Carmine replied. "In hopes for the mutual benefit of our future dealings, I have a gift."

He tossed Graegyr's nose onto the brazier. Again, there came the sound of contented gurgling. When the nose burned away, the eyes looked back at Carmine.

"Thank you for the morsel. You have more manners than most of your kind. I think you will go far."

With no further words, Taelan'sha's presence left. Six heartbeats later, another pair of eyes, these glowing a sickly yellow green, appeared in the smoke. Carmine bowed.

"I know you," the Daemyn said. "Hardin Thorinson is your master. Where is he?"

Carmine knew the deep, rumbling voice of Nae'Toran'borlahisth. He'd learned the name by watching Hardin summon and bargain with the Daemyn.

"Hardin offended the First Adept of *Ahk Tzizma'Uthra*," Carmine said, using the ancient name of Old Uncle Night. Daemyns sometimes became offended when one used their god's modern name. "You will no longer have the pleasure of dealing with him."

"Pity," Nae'Toran said. "He was a crafty one. Why should I deal with you?"

Carmine took a deep breath. This was going to be the most detailed negotiation he had attempted. The gifts he wanted from the Daemyn would cost him, most likely cost him in ways he would not fathom until long after the bargain had been struck. Carmine understood that. Power didn't come to those who refused to take risks.

"Because I have most of a fresh body for your pallet, a woman for you to bed, and a request that will give you some continued influence over the mortal realm."

"Not even Hardin would offer me a woman," Nae'Toran said. You are brave, desperate, or foolish. Most likely the latter two."

"I am the former two," Carmine said. "I am also ambitious. I have a thirst for revenge that I cannot quench on my own. Will you aid me?"

"Taelan'sha told me that you were well prepared. Name your terms."

Carmine took a moment to collect his thoughts. In his time as apprentice, he had watched three other would-be Adepts perish from poor dealings with Daemyns. Carmine decided to always proceed with patience when bargaining with Daemyn.

"I wish for six minor Daemyns to inhabit these corpses I have provided, for as long as the bodies remain functional," Carmine said. "They will obey both the letter and spirit of my commands, not seek to harm me in any way, and return to your realm upon my death."

"And in return?"

"As I said, I have a nearly unspoiled, living body, and a fertile human woman."

"Insufficient," the Daemyn growled. "You have shown foresight, so I will give you my terms for sending four of my underlings into your service indefinitely. These are final and not open to negotiation. First, I will lie with this human girl. Second, you will provide me with a fresh human girl on the anniversary of this pact for the next six years. Third, you will provide me with an interesting soul within one month of our agreement, and that sad excuse for an Adept does not qualify as interesting. As far as the Daemyns I send into your service, they will obey the letter of your commands at all times and the spirit only if they feel inclined. If any of these terms are not met, then your soul is mine."

Weighing those conditions, Carmine calculated the potential difficulties of each and saw most easily met. While the obedience of the Daemyns to only the letter of his commands would be tricky, he always chose his words carefully. Only one term of the agreement gave him pause.

"Would you define an interesting soul?"

"That is something you'll have to discover," Nae'Toran said.

"What if that soul was trained as a Taekuri?" Carmine saw his revenge growing even sweeter.

Nae'Toran's eyes flashed. "Now that *would* be interesting."

"Then I will agree to all your terms," Carmine said. "However, there is only one part of the bargain missing, what if your end of the bargain is not met?"

"I will not fail in my part."

Carmine expected that reaction. Powerful Daemyns were not accustomed to mortals questioning them. However Carmine saw an opening for even greater power out of this bargaining, one that the Daemyn, in its pride and arrogance, probably did not see.

"But, just for the sake of argument," Carmine said. "There is a condition in the agreement if I fail. It is only prudent for me to request the same of you, however unlikely that might be."

"True, true," Nae'Toran said. "Just to amuse you, if any part our agreement is broken by myself, I will personally serve you for one month's time."

"A year."

"*What?*"

The growling deepened to the point where Carmine thought the Daemyn might try to escape from the summoning circle.

"If I fail in my part, you get my soul for eternity. I think a year is an equal trade, and you must serve the spirit of my commands, as well as the letter."

The growling persisted for a moment longer. The slitted eyes glanced over at the girl, and the growling changed in tone. It sounded less angry and more predatory, with an underlying hunger.

"Agreed, but I want the bargain signed in blood."

With that, Carmine knew that Nae'Toran did not see his mistake.

Carmine went over to the altar and took the ceremonial quill and page of skin. He winced but gave no other reaction. He let his blood flow, covering the tip of the quill thoroughly. He had to do this three times in the course of writing.

> *This agreement stands binding between Nae'Toran'borlahisth and Carmine D'Mario of House Floraen. Nae'Toran'borlahisth will provide four Daemyns to inhabit four human corpses. These Daemyns will obey Carmine D'Mario's commands to the letter, and they shall not harm Carmine D'Mario in any way. These four Daemyns will remain in service so long as the shells they inhabit are functional. In exchange for these granted boons, Carmine D'Mario will provide a fertile human woman for Nae'Toran'borlahisth's pleasure upon the signing of this agreement and on its anniversary for the next six years. Carmine D'Mario will produce one human soul for Nae'Toran 'borlahisth within on month's time; the only requirement for this soul is that it is interesting. Carmine D'Mario will also provide the four Daemyns in his service one day and night to slake their lusts and pleasures. Should Carmine D'Mario violate any of these agreements, he will forfeit his soul to Nae'Toran'borlahisth. Should Nae'Toran 'borlahisth violate any of these agreements, he will serve the letter and spirit of Carmine D'Mario's commands for a term of one year.*

Completing the document, Carmine took the page over to the summoning circle and held it before Nae'Toran's eyes.

"I accept your wording of this agreement," Nae'Toran said. "Now, sign in your blood."

Carmine stabbed himself again and signed his name.

"Now you." Carmine passed the parchment and quill into the summoning circle.

Some of the smoke gathered around the quill, and a moment later, Nae'Toran's full signature appeared just below Carmine's. The parchment shimmered, then became two.

Four of the six bodies spasmed and sat up.

"You four, know your duty to this human," Nae'Toran said.

"Yes, Master," they all said as one.

"Now," Nae'Toran said, as the smoke in the summoning circle gathered together and took on a humanoid shape, "I will thank you all to leave me to my pleasure."

The four Daemyns bowed. Carmine took the sheet of leather, folded it carefully, and put it in a small pouch on his belt containing the other two agreements he'd made with other Daemyns. He then reached out with his foot and nudged the circle apart slightly so that Nae'Toran could escape it, but did not disturb the brazier that created the gateway between the physical realm and the Realm of the Godless Dead.

Once outside, the four Daemyns blinked and stretched. Carmine stepped up to them "My Nightbat will lead you to a house. I want you to bring me the one called Faelin vara'Traejyn." He pointed to the one inhabiting the Morigahnti corpse, "Infiltrate them and learn all you can about them. Fight only to defend yourselves. Brynn, gather more Nightbrothers, and you three go with them to round out the escort to six Nightbrothers. Five would arouse suspicion, especially if they discover that three are Daemyns."

"Yes, Master," they said. Brynn looked nervous, but Carmine didn't care. Soon, very soon, he would have Faelin, and then after that, Julianna when she came to rescue him.

As the Daemyns followed Carmine's Nightbat, the cries of a woman in ecstasy came from inside the house.

"You're letting the Daemyn rape her?" Sylvie asked.

Carmine chuckled. "Does it sound like she's being raped?"

"No. It sounds like she's enjoying it, and that confuses me. Why is it so important for it to lie with her?"

"There is some ancient treaty among the celestials that says that Daemyns cannot affect the physical realm unless a human asks them to. We must be very careful what words we use in asking, because Daemyns are cunning and seek to use our words against us. They also never do anything without some sort of payment, and every Daemyn has different *tastes* in how they like to be paid. However, they all seek out any chance to impregnate a human girl. If a Daemyn sires a child, that gives them a permanent link to the physical world. They still can't affect the physical world unless their child asks, but they can speak to the child and usually do so from a very young age."

"But why does it sound like she's enjoying it so much?"

"Because Daemyns have the power to seduce the human soul. This will be one of the greatest moments of the girl's life. She will never know greater joy and will believe she's with a normal man. If I guess right, she probably thinks it's me."

"You wouldn't ever use me in a bargain, would you?"

"Of course not," Carmine lied. He had no plans to ever offer Sylvie, but would if the price was right. "I love you."

She pulled him into a deep kiss. The mixture of her lips on his and the sounds of ecstasy coming from inside the house made his blood boil. He pulled from the kiss and swatted Sylvie's bottom. There would be time for that later. Right now he needed to remove all distractions. The Daemyns might bring the Morigahnti on their heels, and he needed to be prepared to deal with that.

In the meantime, Carmine hoped that Nae'Toran was enjoying himself. At some point the Daemyn would also be his to command. Carmine had carefully worded the advantage into the agreement he'd drawn up, and he meant to use it.

TWENTY

Julianna found herself in a large hall with a long row of stone columns lining each side. Everything was in shades of gray, and the light coming through the high windows near the ceiling was the half-light of twilight or perhaps dawn. At the far end of the room, she saw a huge throne, also carved from gray stone. A cloaked figure sat on the throne.

"I am dreaming," Julianna said.

"What makes you think so?" a voice boomed throughout the room, sending vibrations through the floor.

"I was fighting a moment ago," Julianna said. "No, I had just turned Faelin back to flesh. The effort was too much for me."

"Again, what makes you think this is a dream?" This time the voice was even louder.

"What do you mean? What else could be happening?"

"You might be dead."

"No," Julianna said. "I would know it if I were dead."

"How? Have you ever been dead before?"

Julianna had no answer to that. She looked up at the cloaked figure, and whispered, "Please let me be alive." When the figure gave no answer, Julianna asked. "Grandfather Shadow?"

"Not I," the voice softened to a normal tone, not the booming sound that filled the hall. Now Julianna could tell the speaker was a female.

"You're the one who has been in my dreams," Julianna said.

The cloaked figure stood and walked toward Julianna. As the figure approached, it seemed to grow smaller, more frail.

"Yes, dear," the woman said. "I am."

"What should I call you?" Julianna asked.

"Well, since I've been in your dreams for so long, why don't you just call me Dream, or perhaps Grandmother? I've been both before and find a familiar comfort with each."

"Grandmother, then," Julianna said. "Something I've never known, but always wanted. Perhaps you'll be sweet against Grandfather Shadow's sour."

"That's very sweet," Grandmother said. "And while your dig at Grandfather Shadow amuses me, you might want to watch how you describe him."

Julianna shrugged. "Are you a goddess?"

"I am."

"Of what?"

"Of a great many things," Grandmother answered. "But I'd prefer not to name them. Such naming by my kind resonates throughout the realms and calls the attention of beings I'd rather avoid the notice of."

"You speak in riddles," Julianna said. "Is that some requirement for being a god?"

Grandmother laughed.

Lightning flashed outside, and thunder rolled behind it. A biting wind swept through the chamber.

A fluttering sounded in the hall, and a massive crow appeared from the shadows near the ceiling. The crow dove toward Julianna. She instinctively ducked, but the bird veered just before reaching her. It landed, turning into a gentle old man. When she looked at him, she saw deep power in his steel-gray eyes.

"*Galad'Ysoysa*," Julianna gasped, dropping to her knees and looking to the floor.

"Oh, get up," Grandfather Shadow's voice reflected none of the power she saw welling behind his gaze. "Several of my siblings require such humility from every single follower they attract, and I suppose I might from my lesser followers, but you are the Lord Morigahn. Our relationship is different than that."

Julianna stood. She noticed that Grandmother wasn't there any longer.

"I'm not dead, am I? Or are you here to name me a Saent?"

"No, but you came near enough, and had you killed yourself tonight, I would not name you a Saent. You came close to channeling enough of my divinity in such a short time to burn your soul away. Take care, Julianna, you must build up your resilience to the rigors of speaking miracles before exerting so much power."

"But if I hadn't, I might have died."

"By doing so, you almost did," Grandfather Shadow said. "What is my Second Law?"

"A sharp sword is nothing without a sharp eye," Julianna replied. "Miracles are nothing unless tempered by faith. True power is found in the heart and mind."

"You should do well to not only know my laws, but also ponder them," Grandfather Shadow said. "They seem straightforward at first, but each one has layers of meaning. My laws can help guide you through every situation if you keep your heart and mind open to the hidden wisdom they carry."

"I'm sorry I failed you."

"You have not, as of yet, failed me. If you had at any point, we would be having a much different conversation."

Julianna looked at her god. She chewed her lower lip and regarded him. "But you have sent the pain of my marking to me again and again. Why would you do that if I hadn't failed you?"

"That is a holdover from the Ykthae Accord," Grandfather Shadow said. "It is not completely my doing. The nature of that particular effect of being the Lord Morigahn is something I don't fully comprehend. While I do not suffer idiots in my service, and you are an intelligent young lady, Julianna, that doesn't mean you are flawless. Mistakes happen, and for you, mistakes can be deadly. You are not only a young Morigahnti, you are also a young woman. I understand that you are going to have the impulses of youth, but you must fight those urges. Never forget that your mind is your most powerful weapon. It will stand by you when all others fail you."

"All others?" Julianna asked. "Can't I work miracles as long as I possess a *Galad'fana?*"

Grandfather Shadow chuckled. "Too often the servants of the gods rely on the power of miracle. The divine powers granted by the gods are not the only path to power. The Ykthae Accord also dictates restrictions on the workings of miracles. Look within the *Galad'parma*. Read the writings of Saent Julian and those who bore the title after him. If I tell you everything, you would come to rely on me too much."

Grandfather Shadow led Julianna between the pillars. Once past them, Julianna saw a row of doors along the wall, stretching away in each direction. Grandfather Shadow walked up to one and opened it. Julianna saw only swirling gray mist on the other side.

"Now," Grandfather Shadow said, "I'm sending you back to lead my children. Watching over you this last night has convinced me that I chose you well. Go and lead the Morigahnti to greatness, for in you, their time has come again."

"*Ji Galad'Ysoysa*," Julianna said. "Is there anything else I should know?"

"Avoid casting a miracle for the next few days at the very least," Grandfather Shadow replied. "A week would be even better. Even with the first *Galad'fana*, your soul may not be able to handle the strain."

Julianna took a deep breath and steeled herself to that. She'd managed to not speak miracles during their time at Bastian's Inn, but she'd also not been fighting for her life. When the Brotherhood had attacked, her first instinct had been to reach for Grandfather Shadow's Dominions. She hadn't even thought to use her mother's gift of jaunting back and forth in time and space. Not that it would have worked, but at one point not long ago, that had been her instinct. How quickly she had changed.

"Remember my laws," Grandfather Shadow said, as if he sensed her thoughts. "Miracles are not the first, last, and only weapon of the Morigahnti."

Julianna nodded. She crossed the door's threshold and found herself floating in shadow. She looked back to Grandfather Shadow to see the door close behind her.

PRIDE AND FOLLY

"Sometimes, when two people share the same sin, they will share the same punishments until they both repent." – Saent Julian the Courageous

The stench of pride
hangs on your words
as strong as any onion or garlic.
Gods and wise men smell keenly
the words of the clever man,
no matter how sweet he thinks them,
when corrupted by pride.
But if a man's meaning is pure,
and his words spoken from his spirit,
the gods and great men
will hear past clumsy and tripping speech
to know the truth of his conviction.

- Talmoinan the White

ONE

As the sun's first light rose in the east and pierced through the fog, Damian studied the Vara fortress. It was more like a group of warehouses haphazardly connected by a series of hastily constructed wooden walls. A dozen towers rose from inside the compound, some attached to the walls, others attached to the buildings. Here and there, men carrying spears and crossbows walked the walls, though not enough to make any kind of real defense if an enemy actually attacked the compound.

This sad place housed Koma's pathetic excuse for a constabulary, but that's how the Kingdom wanted it. The Kingdom title for the soldiers here and other pitiful units in other Komati cities was "the Vara." And while most of the Komati accepted that as the official name, Damian knew enough to know the Kingdom was mocking them all, shortening the name from *The Vara'Morigahnti*, or false Morigahnti.

Czenzi pounded on the gate. A few moments later, it slid open a bit and Damian couldn't help rolling his eyes. The gate should have opened outward. While sliding open wasn't as bad as opening inward, it was still ridiculous, bordering on idiotic.

The young man, younger even than Damian, put his head out through the small opening. He took in Czenzi's mask and mantle, and his eyes went wide. Something about him seemed familiar.

"Good morning, Adept," the youth stammered. From the way that his voice cracked, Damian suspected this Vara hadn't yet reached the Komati age of maturity. Times must be desperate for the Vara if they were willing to accept applications under the age of maturity. It wasn't illegal, and hadn't been for some time. However, the practice was frowned upon, especially by the nobility. This could be especially dangerous for the Vara, who relied heavily on donations from Komati nobles to function even at their meager standards.

"I wish to speak to General Dyrk," Czenzi said. Her tone indicated she expected to be obeyed without delay.

The young Vara swallowed. "The general is not in, my lady Adept. However, I can show you to a sitting room and provide refreshments until he returns."

As the boy spoke, Damian examined his black and gray leather armor. Some pieces were hard leather, while others soft. Damian doubted that armor would provide much protection against any but the most inept attack against him. But just as the Kingdom didn't want the fortress to be fuctional, it also didn't want the Vara getting delusions of adequacy as a military force.

"I suppose that will have to do," Czenzi said. "However, if the general is not informed of my presence upon his immediate return, I will be most displeased with those responsible for delaying the message."

"There will be no delay," the Vara said, his voice cracking again.

He slid the gate open wider so that Czenzi and Damian could pass. There were no other Vara anywhere near the gates as he and Czenzi entered. Normally this would have disgusted Damian, however, this morning it proved to be a blessing. As Damian entered the Vara compound, the youth looked him over and his eyes grew even wider than with Czenzi.

"Prince Damian?"

His voice sounded as if he were addressing a god.

Then Damian remembered how he knew this boy. He was a minor lord, a baron if Damian remembered properly, and his name was Gabryl Raesu. The Raesu were another family from Damian's House of Eras. Gabryl's parents had sworn themselves to Xander's father, and Gabryl had grown up worshiping Xander, and to a lesser extent Damian. In truth, both Damian and Xander had treated Gabryl poorly, but the boy cried out for it. He had so little in the way of social graces, and even less in the way of self-confidence, yet he always managed to attach himself to the two brothers at balls, picnics, and banquets. His weasel-like features, oozing pimples, and nasally laugh had chased off more young ladies than Damian would care to count.

"No," Damian said. "I'm Zephyr. If I'm a prince of anything, it's nothing more than a gutter in the commons."

"Don't lie, Your Highness," Gabryl whispered. "Don't worry. I won't tell anyone."

Damian looked at Czenzi and shrugged. What passed for her High Blood Mask did little to hide her frustration. She placed her hand upon his forehead.

"Give us a moment," Czenzi said.

Gabryl bowed and stepped away.

"Kneel before me," Czenzi said.

"I hardly think…" Damian started, before he caught hold of himself. Better to get it over with and be out of this woman's hands so he could come up with a plan to get out of this city and to another continent.

Damian knelt. Czenzi placed her hands on his forehead.

"*Kaeki jotka tavahta Damian Adryck lulevat vaensa varasa,*" Czenzi said. "*Sinun vaen ajatela se on ikava, eta ne naetavat samalta.*"

When she finished speaking, Damian's skin tingled.

"What did you do?" Damian asked as he stood.

"Placed a miracle on you so that nobody will recognize you," Czenzi answered. Then she turned to Gabryl. "The man is not Damian Adryck. Prince Adryck is a traitor to the Sun King and is marked for death. I would hardly keep company with such an individual."

"Ye… ye… yes, my lady Adept," Gabryl said, bobbing his head with each word.

"Now, show us to this sitting room."

"Right this way," Gabryl replied, leaving his post and the gate opened.

Czenzi started after Gabryl, but her leg buckled with her first step. Damian caught her before she stumbled to her knees. She grabbed his shoulder for support. They stood for a moment, and Damian heard Czenzi's breath come in ragged gasps. Their faces were close together, and this close, he saw the dark circles under her eyes.

If there was ever going to be a perfect moment for Damian to escape, this was it. He could throw Czenzi to the ground, dash out the gate, and disappear into the Warrens. As if sensing his thoughts, Czenzi gripped Damian's shoulder and looked into his eyes.

"Don't," she said, her voice almost pleading. "We need you to do this."

"We?" Damian asked.

"Fine," Czenzi replied, some of the steel returning to her voice. "*I* need you to do this."

That wasn't the confession Damian had wanted. He'd hope to get her to reveal who else was in on this little plot revolving around him. However, her eyes held his, and his stomach twisted.

"Alright," Damian said, barely above a whisper. "But only for you. And you owe me one straight answer."

"It's yours," Czenzi replied. "Though not now. Another time, and I'll answer one question honestly."

Damian helped Czenzi to her feet. Gabryl stood about ten paces away, having traveled that far before noticing that they hadn't followed yet. Before they started off, Damian slid the gate closed. Gabryl shuffled his feet and stared at the ground. Something told Damian that it wasn't the first time Gabryl had left the gate open.

"Well," Damian said. "Shall we see what sort of refreshments come with Vara hospitality?"

TWO

Xander and Kraetor walked in silence until they came to the White Dragon stronghold. The guards at the gate did not question Kraetor's presence, but they did give Xander curious looks.

Soon they stood in Black Claw's planning room. Black Claw entered shortly after them and saluted Kraetor. Kraetor nodded. Black Claw ignored Xander's presence.

"I am Kraetor, High Blood of House Kaesiak and First Adept to *Galad'Ysoysa*. Where is the Adept assigned to this stronghold?"

"Tamaz is dead," Black Claw said. "We found him surrounded by a squad of Whites, also dead, though none of them from my stronghold. The Whites had been strangled and Tamaz shot in the head by a firearm. This was found around his neck."

Black Claw held out a medallion. Kraetor took it and gave it a close examination.

"This is the Symbol of Old Uncle Night," Kraetor said. "Either Tamaz served Uncle Night, or someone wishes us to believe this. Let no one into his quarters. I will send my assistant to examine them."

"Yes, First Adept," Black Claw said, and then turned to Xander. "What of this one? How did you come upon him?"

"I particularly enjoy walking at night, when the world is quiet," Kraetor said. "Unfortunately, I am unfamiliar with your city, and so I wandered out of the reputable areas of town. Three ruffians managed to waylay me. This young man came to my defense for the second time in as many months. This is a sign from Grandfather Shadow that we are bound together by fate. As long as I am within Koma, this man will be a member of my honor guard."

"As you command, First Adept Kraetor." Black Claw gave Xander a hard glare. "I will set him to that duty."

Several of the other Whites growled deep in the backs of their throats. Being named to an Adept's personal guard was a rare honor, usually hard won by great deeds bordering on suicide. Xander imagined the resentment these Whites held at seeing him accepted above them all. He would definitely have to turn around corners carefully from now on.

"Settle down, before I settle you down," Black Claw ordered, though never taking his eyes off Xander. "What of Damian Adryck? The squad that went with Tamaz reported that you found him in the company of another Kaesiak Adept."

Xander was at a loss for what to say. He'd been so distracted by the thought of being named High Blood that he had not thought up a story to cover his meeting Damian. For a moment, Xander wished he had Damian's talent for creating complex and believable lies without any forethought.

"There is nobody in this City who could have seen Damian Adryck for at least the last fortnight," Kraetor said. "Kaesiak agents have placed him in Heidenmarch, smuggling firearms and teaching the rebels how to use them."

Black Claw seemed to accept Kraetor's explanation, not that the White would have challenged the story. Draqons did not question High Blood, much less an Adept. Hopefully, that also meant that Black Claw wouldn't question Kraetor's word once the First Adept was no longer present. Xander would lie for his patron, but Black Claw was a Draqon and would likely smell Xander's lying.

"Congratulations on your new post, Hatchling," Black Claw said, though there was no sincerity in its voice. "Retire to your quarters. It looks like you're going to be very busy for the next few weeks."

"Why?" Xander asked.

"Why else would I be here instead of at the Sun Palace?" Kraetor said. "The Sun King is coming to Koma."

THREE

Damian paced back and forth across the sitting room. He and Czenzi had been ushered into the small room where they'd been waiting at least an hour, and the energy that came from the night's excitement had worn off. He was hungry; the refreshment Gabryl provided had been nothing more than a pot of tea, tea biscuits, and a small helping of cheese. Damian had offered all the food to Czenzi. She looked like she needed it more than he did. Damian was beginning to regret that decision, just like he was also questioning his sanity for not running when he had the chance.

Now he was trapped in this small room, waiting for only the gods knew how long, when all he wanted was a meal and a bed.

"Would you sit down?" Czenzi tone made it clear that it wasn't a request.

Stopping in midstride, Damian took a deep breath. He put his foot down, turned to face Czenzi, and somehow managed to contain the half dozen retorts that sprang to mind. Her dark eyes bore into his. The minor token of a mask did nothing to hide the dark circles underneath her eyes. Still, she made it clear that she expected to be obeyed. When he didn't move, her lips tightened, and she gestured toward the chair next to hers with a flick of her hand, palm toward the ceiling.

Damian gave her a deep bow and returned to his trek back and forth across the stone floor. Moving was the only thing keeping him awake.

"Very well," Czenzi said. "Work yourself into a panic. You have nothing to worry about. I will speak, and they will listen. I am an Adept."

Again, Damian stopped and looked at Czenzi. She appeared to actually believe that her mantle would get her anything she wanted in Koma. In reality, people would be far more likely to give a lone Adept the sharp end of a blade rather than help her.

"Don't be too confident in that mask or that mantle," Damian said. "There are places where they won't help you as much as you think."

"The power of Grandfather Shadow will protect in such places."

"My lady," Damian said, "I fear that one day you may learn that all the power granted from any god won't do much against an angry rebel with a gun."

As he spoke each of those words, Damian's voice sounded odd to his own ears, like someone else was saying them along with him.

Czenzi sniffed.

He bowed again, and said, "Forgive me, High Blood. The late hour has robbed my tongue of any censure."

She glared at him. Not a bit of the tenderness she'd shown in the courtyard remained, but Damian was too tired to care. Shaking his head, mostly to clear his mind of how odd his voice sounded, he went back to pacing. His exhaustion was to blame. He had to keep moving.

Only his quick wits and the gods' blessing had allowed him to survive the night, and if he wanted to survive further, he needed to keep his wits ready. The gods would not bless him forever, but he could rely on his wits if they remained sharp. To keep his mind focused, Damian kept shifting his gaze to different parts of the room, trying to notice minute details of the stone walls, the weaves on the tapestries, and gilding on chairs and table.

The door opened. Gabryl entered.

"General Dyrk has returned," Gabryl said. "Please follow me."

"Thank you." Czenzi stood and glanced at Damian. "You see. They weren't going to leave us here all day."

"I have the feeling this isn't going to get any better," Damian muttered underneath his breath. Again his voice sounded odd, as if coming from far away and too close all at the same time.

Damian and Czenzi followed the Vara down a hallway and through a set of double doors. Each door was almost twice as high as Damian was tall. Their guide opened the doors and ushered them through.

The room he entered was a large chamber. Dozens of Vara, all dressed and armed the same as their escort, milled around three large tables covered in food. Damian's mouth watered as the smell of fresh bacon and sausage enticed his stomach. Vara poured themselves steaming mugs of geleva. Damian couldn't remember the last time he'd had a decent cup. Geleva was either exceptional or terrible. From the smell, this was the former.

As Damian plotted to get a mug of caffé and a heaping plate of food, the crowd parted. In the center of the room stood a man in a much finer outfit than the other Vara. His outfit was all silver and blue, made out of silk and velvet. The only similarity between that man and the others was that he wore the suede hood of a Vara. His rapier had a swept hilt of gold and jewels on the scabbard. The man's black eyes studied Damian and Czenzi with a predatory gaze.

"I am Dyrk," the man said. "General and High Commander of the Vara. To what do I owe the pleasure of a visit from an Adept of House Kaesiak?"

"I have brought you a new recruit," Czenzi said.

"And why should I take such a sad sight as this into the Vara?" Dyrk asked.

"Because I am asking you to," Czenzi replied.

Damian rolled his eyes. Czenzi was destroying any chance for Damian to gain any kind of rapport with these men. He had to do something to save himself.

"If you'll permit me, Adept," Damian said, "I think I can give some reasons why the Vara might accept me."

Dyrk shifted his view from Czenzi to Damian. "Do tell."

"Part of the Vara's duty in Koma is to help the White Draqons ferret out rebels and criminals," Damian said. "However, the Whites have a terrible time infiltrating the underside of the City. You help them as best you can, but even that is minimal."

"Really?" Dyrk asked. "And how do you know this?"

"Because until recently, I lived in the underside of the city," Damian said. "Even though my appearance makes me seem a poor asset, my former life makes me a storehouse of information and contacts."

"And how does this help me?" Dyrk asked.

"I know how to listen and remember most of what I hear," Damian said. "Accept me and I can give you something the Whites could never get."

"And that is?"

"I can lead you to several groups of rebels, General Dyrk."

Dyrk leaned back and squinted at Damian, as if appraising some item he meant to purchase on a whim. "I won't accept a turn cloak into our ranks."

"I am no turncoat," Damian said. "I am a business man, and Adept Czenzi has convinced me that a military career is the true calling of my life."

"Perhaps I will consider it."

"What is there to consider? You need me." Damian's voice changed. It echoed like it had when he'd spoken to Czenzi. This time his words sounded like they carried physical weight. "If you accept me, I can bring you glory undreamed of by the White Draqons. Turn me away and you will fall into ruin."

Dyrk studied Damian. The Vara leader locked eyes with him, seeming to search for something. Damian held that gaze. He needed to be accepted. There was no telling what Czenzi would do to him if Dyrk rejected this petition, and he would more likely be able to escape the Vara and get out of the City than he would from under Czenzi's nose.

At last, Dyrk nodded.

"It is rare to hear a man speak with the guile of Sister Wind, the smoothness of Sister Wave, the weight of Brother Stone, and the passion of Brother Flame all at the same time. However, I'm not sure if we could find a place for you."

"Excuse me," Czenzi said, stepping between Dyrk and Damian. "From what I've heard, the Vara aren't terribly picky about who they accept."

Why was she helping again? Damian had everything under control. Was she trying to get him tossed out on his backside?

"We *are* very picky, my lady," Dyrk said, smiling. "But if you like, I will take this young man into my care, as a personal favor to you."

Dyrk's smile sent an icy chill through Damian's chest. He didn't know what game the Vara leader was playing, but it couldn't be good.

Damian felt the coin of fate being tossed again. Where would it land this time?

"As a favor then," Czenzi said, accepting Dyrk's offer. The coin flipped, but was it for good or for ill? "I will look in on him now and then."

"I would speak with you a moment alone before you depart," Dyrk said to Czenzi. Then he turned and whispered something to one of the Vara near him. That man was close to forty, and was missing the ring and pinky fingers on his left hand. The thumb and other two fingers were missing on the other. He nodded.

"Of course," Czenzi said, and followed Dyrk out of the meal hall.

Damian watched them leave with a sinking heart. When the double doors closed behind them, the Vara with a mangled hand stepped into Damian's view. "I am Paedrik Sardon, General Dyrk's second in command. The General thinks you need to be taught that your wagging tongue may have served you well living with the dregs of the city, but here it will only get you into trouble."

"I don't suppose you'd only let me off with a warning?" Damian asked

"You won't receive a warning from the scum on the street and in the canals," Mangled-hand said. "Just thank the gods the punishments here aren't fatal."

You'd be amazed at what you can live through, Damian thought, and for a moment he considered speaking the thought aloud but held his tongue. The last thing he needed to do was invite more of the wrong type of attention. Besides, whatever punishment they found for him couldn't be any worse than what he'd already been through tonight. As soon as Damian thought that, he regretted it. His entire life seemed to prove that no matter how grim things became for him, they could always get worse.

FOUR

Czenzi followed Dyrk to a room. Two chairs and a table sat in the middle of it. Off to one side was another table with quills and ink, along with a few bottles, presumably holding some sort of spirits. Czenzi had heard of the rooms like these where the Vara'Morigahnti bargained with the Komati nobility over detailed contracts. The Draqon breeds were far more efficient.

"What do you want, Dyrk?" Czenzi asked.

Dyrk flopped into the chair facing the door. "I want to know the real reason you want me to take in this insolent son of a dock-side whore."

Czenzi took a deep breath. How dare this man question her like this? She dug her fingernails into her palms to focus her anger rather than lash out. She wanted to wipe the insolence from him, but there were other considerations besides her pride. Kraetor had a plan for Damian Adryck and Xander Rosha, and Czenzi couldn't let Dyrk goad her into acting rashly.

"Because I said to. I am not in the habit of explaining myself."

She had little patience to politic with this self-styled Lord Morigahn. Though the general didn't claim the title outright, he carried himself as though he was one of the heroes of old. However, with an heir to the Komati Throne and a younger sibling to make the pronouncement, the true Lord Morigahn could come forward and bring the true Morigahnti to serve them. When the true Morigahnti emerged, they would obliterate this pathetic affront to their name. She longed to see the shell of a man Dyrk would become on that day.

"If you want me to keep him in our ranks, you answer every question I ask," Dyrk said.

"We have already reached an agreement," Czenzi said. "You said you would sponsor him as a favor. If you cast him out of your ranks, then you will no longer have my favor. Which would you rather have, my favor or my ire?"

"Your favor, of course, my lady," Dyrk said. "You don't mind if we draw this up as an official contract, do you?"

It was rare for those not of Kingdom noble blood to ask that a favor be drawn up as an official contract, but it was not unheard of. The practice had originated with the High Blood of different Houses to keep each other honest when trading favors. The trading of favors was the true currency of the High Blood, Low Blood, and Adepts.

"Of course not," Czenzi replied. "Allow me."

She went to the table and took paper, quill, and ink. She spread two sheets of paper next to each other, with a little space in between. She placed the ink and quill in that space. She wrote two contracts, one in *Galad'laman*, and one in the Kingdom's common tongue.

Dyrk's copy read:

> *I, Czenzi Vaesna, High Blood and Adept of House Kaesiak, owe General Dyrk of the Vara'Morigahnti one favor, so long as it does not break any vows of loyalty I have made to Grandfather Shadow, the Kingdom of the Sun, or House Kaesiak.*

She signed it, held one hand over each of the documents, and focused her faith through her mask. When she knew for certain that she acted in the name of Grandfather Shadow, Czenzi spoke, "*Hano ken latia hano nimeta on kostota var mina.*"

Czenzi's legs trembled. She gripped the edge of the writing table in order to remain standing. Though the words were simple, the miracle's effect was far reaching.

"What did you do?" Dyrk asked.

"Cast a miracle to ensure this contract is beyond tampering," Czenzi replied. "It is a common practice among Kaesiak Adepts and High Blood."

That was true enough. The High Blood of all the Great Houses had ways of ensuring that agreements were beyond tampering, but none so efficient as House Kaesiak. Members of the House of Shadow were the least trusted in the kingdom. The High Blood of the other Houses used that distrust to gain a political edge every chance they got. Czenzi had learned very quickly to protect herself in all her dealings.

"How do you expect me to read this second paper?" Dyrk asked.

"I don't," Czenzi answered. "That is my copy. I prefer to read in *Galad'laman*. Now, if you would kindly sign, I've had a very long night and very much look forward to retiring."

"Of course, High Blood," Dyrk said through gritted teeth, and signed.

"Thank you for a smooth business transaction," Czenzi snatched the copy written in *Galad'laman*. "Don't bother showing me out; I remember the way, and I know that you are a very busy man."

"Yes, High Blood," Dyrk said.

As she left the *Kaer*, Czenzi considered what she'd witnessed in the dining hall. Damian had begun to exhibit his abilities of the *Tsumari'osa*. She'd heard the change in Damian's voice when he'd spoken a fate, but had he realized it? Doubtful, unless he'd witnessed a Speaking before, which was unlikely. Fate-Speaking was a rare gift.

In less than one full day, Damian had spoken the miracle of Shadow's Thunder without the use of a divine focus and he had proclaimed a fate. Such close timing between those events made Czenzi wondered how closely Grandfather Shadow watched them.

With things moving more quickly, they also needed to find the true Lord Morigahn. He was the only one who could bring the Morigahnti to fight for Xander and Damian. However, before that, Kraetor and Czenzi needed to find a way for the two brothers to settle their difference.

FIVE

Something warm and soft brushed against Xander's cheek. Dreams of chasing Damian through the foggy streets of Koma's underworld faded as Xander woke. Whatever was on his face moved to his ear, and Xander thought he heard breath there. Blinking the sleep from his eyes, Xander turned his head and looked up. In the soft glow of candlelight, he saw Flirt's face right next to his, her full lips smirking at some private jest.

For a moment, Xander let his gaze linger over her face. Her green eyes seemed to invite him to dive in. He longed to feel her full lips against his. It had been so long since he'd known the touch of a woman that Flirt's closeness tempted Xander to let go of his duty.

No matter how he might be tempted, Xander forced himself to remain strong. He pushed her off of his bed. Once he restored honor to his family, Xander would have many beautiful women yearning to tempt him.

"What do you want?" Xander demanded.

Flirt looked back at him with a smirk. Her eyes matched the smile, like she knew exactly what Xander was feeling.

"You were out late last night. I came to make sure that you didn't over-sleep your first day on First Adept Kraetor's honor guard."

Xander snapped awake like Flirt's father had caught them together.

"What hour is it?"

"Early enough for you to wash and get something to eat if you hurry," she answered. "If you choose not to eat, you might not have to run up the stairway to the palace."

Xander couldn't think of eating. His stomach was a churning mass of excitement and nervousness. He'd been assigned to the personal guard of one of the most powerful men in the Kingdom of the Sun. Kraetor had only three equals, the First Adepts of the other Greater Gods, and two superiors, the Sun King himself, and the Speaker for the Sun. Xander was the first person not of the four Great Houses to be granted such a post.

Jumping out of bed, Xander went to the washbasin and the pitcher of water he'd gotten just before retiring the previous night. He poured a third of it into the basin and wet a cloth. Before pulling at the strings of his night-shirt, Xander turned to Flirt. Her smirk had changed to a soft smile of amusement.

"Shall I help you with your toilet, Prince Rosha?" Flirt asked. "We wouldn't want to look bad on our first day."

"I haven't had a servant in two years," Xander said. "And I don't need one now. Besides, I hardly think humility is one of your virtues."

"You are correct." Her grin widened, lighting up her face. "Perhaps his lordship could punish me if I displeased him."

Xander picked up the pitcher. With one hand, he held it threateningly. With the other, he pointed to the door.

"Out," he said, "but leave the candle."

She gave a mocking bow and left his chamber. Now free from distraction, Xander soaped himself up and rinsed off. Once he was clean, he donned his White Dragon uniform. It had been left in his room while he had been out hunting Damian the night before. While there was no mirror to ad-mire himself, Xander imagined he cut a dashing figure. He would have to wait and see what the reactions were from the servant girls in the Governor's Palace.

Leaving his room, it didn't take long for Xander to find the stairway leading up to the palace. The Whites gave him sidelong glances as he walked by. A few snarled at his passing. Even though he'd earned a position of dis-tinction, the rest still held him in the contemptuous role of a traitor to the Kingdom.

Xander made his way up the long spiraling staircase to the Palace of Ko-ma. Draqons were not allowed to use the balloon lifts that connected the various levels of the city. Only nobility and merchants with special permits were given access to the lifts.

Stopping at one of the arrow slits, Xander looked out over Koma City.

The early morning sun had burned away the upper levels of fog, giving a view of the great towers and platforms of the greatest city in all the known lands.

This momentary rest gave Xander a moment out of time when all the world's problems faded beside the marvel of Koma. The lands of the Ko-mati had been settled in a valley surrounded by two great mountain ranges. The seven highest peaks in those ranges became the ancestral homes of each of Koma's great noble Houses. In the early times of the Komati, all the leaders of the Great Houses met at the lowest point in the land, where the land met the sea at the mouth of a great river delta. As time went on, they decided that they should meet at one of the mountains, but none could decide which House should be the first host. After much debate, the Houses decided that Koma City should be transformed into a mountain of buildings, becoming the eighth mountain, belonging to no House and to all Houses at the same time.

Koma City was a marvel unparalleled in any known land. Even though the technology that created Koma had long since been forgotten, the city still remained as a monument to Komati drive and ingenuity. Perhaps when he returned to noble life, Xander would seek to uncover some of the forgotten technology. Of course he would work within the constraints of Kingdom Law. The last thing he wanted was to follow Damian down the road of be--trayal.

Taking a deep breath of crisp morning air, Xander resumed his journey up the staircase.

Reaching the top of the stairwell, Xander stepped into the courtyard of the Governor's Palace of Koma. A pair of Draqons guarded the outside doorway of the stairwell that led down to the White Draqon fortress. They nodded to Xander, each of them wearing a strange expression he'd never seen on any breed of Draqon.

"What is it?" Xander asked.

"We feel the same threat that you do," one of them said.

"What do you mean?"

"The other Whites envy our position," the other said, "and so they plot for ways to kill us."

"We are the oldest besides our commander," said the first Draqon. "They think we will be easy to kill. They are wrong."

"I am Hatchling," Xander said.

"I am Hex," said the first White. "This is Heart."

"Hex?" Xander asked.

"Yes," Hex replied. "I am Hex-Upon-the-Life-of-My-Enemies."

"And I am Heart-that-Refuses-to-Stop-Beating."

"I am honored to know your full names," Xander said.

If a Draqon of any breed gave you its full name, it meant that it wished no hostility. Xander took great comfort in having these Whites give him their full names. He had enough problems watching himself in the fortress below. He didn't need to be watching his back while protecting Lord Kraetor.

"I am merely, Hatchling," after a pause, he added, "for now, only for now."

Both Whites nodded.

"You're not exactly what I expected," Xander said.

"You thought us to scorn you like those below?" Hex asked.

Xander nodded.

We cannot afford to squabble like those who remain below," Heart replied. "We must save our fury for those who would harm the High Blood."

"And besides," Hex added. "If you are not worthy to serve with us, you will be dead soon enough."

"I understand," Xander said.

"No," Hex said, "but you will, sooner than you'd like."

"Then you'd best be on your way," Heart said. "You don't want to keep Smiles waiting."

"Smiles?" Xander asked.

"Yes. Smiles is the captain of the palace guard."

"Thank you," Xander said, and hurried to the nearest door to the palace.

Xander marveled at the beauty of the palace. He'd been here several times before when he was much younger, but that was before Octavio Salvatore had become the Governor of Koma. Before, the palace was sparsely furnished. Now, Xander barely recognized the place. Paintings, statues, and tapestries depicting the glories of the gods adorned every free space. The most prevalent were idols and images of All Father Sun. Not surprising, as Governor Octavio Salvatore was a High Blood of House Floraen, therefore he would be preparing for the Sun King's arrival.

As Xander wandered the halls, he realized he had no idea of where to report. The Palace was huge, taking up space both vertically and horizontally. At this time of the morning, people in the halls were scarce, which was good. Anyone he came across was likely to be a servant and would be easier to get directions from without offending them. Kingdom nobility could be very touchy about protocol, and Draqons did not speak to their betters unless spoken to, or in case of a current threat.

Stopping at place where four hallways stretched out and staircases went both up and down, Xander waited for someone to come by. After a moment, a young woman in House Floraen livery came down one of the hallways carrying a tray of food. Xander straightened his back and put his hand on the hilt of his rapier. She had golden blond hair pulled back into a braid and deep blue eyes that threatened to suck him in as easily as Flirt's. Thankfully as a servant, this girl wouldn't be in as much a position to tempt him as Flirt was.

"Excuse me, miss," Xander said. "I'm somewhat lost."

She looked him up and down. Her expression didn't contain the admiration that he'd hoped it would.

"Somewhat lost?" she asked. "You better get out of that uniform before Smiles beats you out of it."

"I need to find Smiles. He's my new commanding officer. And if he beats me, it will be because I'm late, not because of my uniform."

"Oh, you're the new one." Her expression changed. It might have been amusement, but Xander couldn't tell for sure. Like most women, you didn't know what was going on until it was too late. "Was your brother really a traitor?"

"*Half*-brother. And yes, he's a traitor."

Though, somehow, last night had placed a seed of doubt in Xander's mind. The girl Adept seemed to think Damian was worth protecting from a squad of Draqons. Why?

"It's very noble for you to try and save your family honor. If you go up those stairs two flights," she said, pointing with her chin, "High Adept Kraetor's suite is to the right of the landing."

"Thank you," Xander said. "What's your name?"

"Larayne. What's yours?"

For a moment, Xander struggled with which name to give her. With a deep breath, he answered, "Hatchling."

She gave him a strange look, then smiled.

"I am please to meet you, Hatchling. I'm sure I'll be seeing a lot of you around the palace."

She walked past him and Xander bowed. He watched her go and thought he saw a little exaggeration in the sway of her hips.

Following Larayne's directions, Xander soon arrived at the landing of Kraetor's wing. A White Draqon stood at the double doors leading into the First Adept's suite. It was nearly as tall as Black Claw, but not as big in the shoulders. As Xander got closer, he noticed the Draqon's face was a criss-cross of wrinkles and scars. One of the Draqon's ears had been cut off, so instead of a sharp point, it was a mangled scab. The other ear had a slight droop to it, reminding Xander of a faithful dog instead of a soldier bred for killing.

"You are Hatchling?" the White asked. Its voice was coarse, likely from more scars underneath the metal gorge protecting its neck.

"Yes," Xander answered.

"I am Smiles-While-He-Rips-Your-Throat-Out. Smiles. I am not so strict as Black Claw, unless you give me reason to doubt your loyalty to the Kingdom of the Sun. I know only one punishment for that."

"I understand," Xander said. "I will do my best to make you and the First Adept proud."

"I have no pride," Smiles said. "I only have duty to House Kaesiak. Worry about making Adept Kraetor proud. Worry about making me believe that you are as loyal as First Adept Kraetor thinks you are."

"I will," Xander nearly added, *do my best*, but reconsidered. Whites did not care about trying, even if it was trying your best. Whites cared about success and failure, so Xander added, "I will."

"Good." Smiles gave a brisk nod. "Your first duty is to stand at this door and allow entrance only to those people who wear the Kaesiak livery, a High Blood of Kaesiak, or an Adept of any House."

"Yes, sir," Xander said, and took a position in front of the twin doors.

Without another word, Smiles walked away.

Xander stood and looked down each direction of the hallway. The day had just begun, so there was little sign of anyone moving around besides servants. Even if the hallway got busier, would he actually do anything besides stand at this door? How would he prove his loyalty standing in front of a door for days at a time?

SIX

The acrid vapors of soap mixed with stale urine and excrement burned Damian's eyes and nose as he scrubbed out the priv. He'd lost track of how long he'd spent at the revolting task. His knees hurt from constantly kneeling on the stone floor, and his back ached from being hunched over for so long. His only consolation was the row of small windows at the top of two walls that allowed a small bit of fresh air to waft into the room.

Damian brought his hand up to rub the tears from his eyes, but then he remembered what his hands had just been touching. He stopped his hand before it touched his face. He didn't care that he'd been up to his forearms in soapy water; he wasn't going to touch his face with his hands for at least a fortnight. Instead, Damian used his shoulder and upper arm to wipe his face. That might be the one part of his upper body that hadn't been contaminated yet.

Yawning, Damian examined his work. Seven of the ten privs were clean – or at least as clean as any mortal might get them using only water and soap.

Damian stood and stretched. His muscles seemed to groan in protest.

I am a Prince of House Eras, Damian thought to himself. *How did I come to this?*

It wasn't the first time he'd asked himself that question. He wondered if Xander ever asked himself the same question. Possibly, but Xander likely blamed Damian – or more to the point, Damian's father – for giving him the guns in the first place. However, blaming Vincent Adryck was too easy. Those guns had been Adryck family heirlooms since before the Kingdom conquered Koma. What right did the Kingdom have to deny them to Damian?

Had anything good ever come out of the Kingdom of the Sun?

In answer to his question, Czenzi's face appeared unbidden to his mind's eye. Damian knew nothing would ever come of his fantasy, but he allowed himself the dream that he might one day see Adept Czenzi of House Kaesiak without her…mask on. That might almost make this work worthwhile. Almost. On the other side of the coin, he didn't plan on remaining here long enough to ever see Adept Czenzi again.

Shaking his head, Damian pushed the bucket with his foot to the next priv.

Another face came to his mind, pushing Czenzi away. This face had striking steel-gray eyes and a scar down one side of her face. Ever since Damian fled Shadybrook, Faelin's friend, the one he said Damian wanted no part of – as if that warning would actually dissuade Damian at all – kept creeping into his mind.

"Gods and goddesses be damned," Damian said. "You're all a cruel lot."

"Be careful with what you say about whom," a woman said behind him.

Damian spun around.

A woman wearing an Adept's mantle stood in the center of the room. Damian instinctively dropped into a bow before he realized that no Adepts wore robes of deep purple with strange symbols of gold woven throughout, nor did Adepts wear two-shot pistols hanging from their belts. He straightened, and looking past the mantle, saw a lady with shocking white hair staring at him over triangular spectacles. She was the lady who had given him the gun outside of Shadybrook, the gun he'd used against the Daemyn

Hound. And if he wasn't mistaken, the gun on her hip looked like the very same gun she'd given him that night, the one the little crow-girl had taken.

"My lady," Damian bowed, honestly this time, not the impulsive response so many Kingdom subjects learned when faced with an Adept's mantle. "I would like to say it's a pleasure to see you again; however, I was told it's impolite to lie to a lady."

"I've watched you for some time, Zephyr," the lady said. "I've never known you to hold back a lie for the excuse of being a gentleman. I seem to recall you lying to Kahddria on occasion."

Damian barked a laugh. He hadn't even tried to suppress it.

"Kahddria might be a goddess," Damian said, "but I hardly think she qualifies as a lady."

"While I can't disagree with you, I wouldn't say that where Kahddria can hear you."

"So, what? Never speak my thoughts anywhere that might be touched by the wind?" Damian asked. "Kahddria knows my opinion of her."

The lady chuckled. "I'd forgotten that honesty is a weapon you tend to use as deftly as any sword."

"Truly?" Damian asked. "I thought gods and goddesses knew everything."

"Ah, the naïveté of mortality," the lady said. "How wonderfully refreshing."

Damian waited a moment for her to elaborate. She said nothing. Instead, she wandered around the priv, looking into corners, sniffing, and wrinkling her nose.

"Interesting," she said. "Even without my guidance, you all come up with such wonderful inventions, yet you can't come up with a better way to clean up after yourselves."

Rather than be drawn into that discussion, Damian asked, "What do you want?"

"Always to the point," the lady said. "I'm here to try and convince you to remain in Koma City."

Damian blinked. "Why would I do a damnable bloody stupid thing like that?"

"I could go on about how your brother is going to need you," the lady said, "but that wouldn't do any good. I doubt you'd do it for your mother, either. You've not cared enough for them these last few years to turn yourself over to Kingdom Justice."

"I love my mother," Damian said. "And even if he's an insufferable boor, I love Xander, too. I also love breathing. I think it's possibly the thing I love most in this world. I've had a lot of practice over my whole life to become very good at it. If I turn myself over to Kingdom Justice, the Inquisitors will probably want me to stop breathing, and I'd hate to see my life's work go to waste on their account."

The lady laughed, still not looking at him. "Oh, you are going to drive all the worlds mad once you come into your own. I think you may become the most feared *Tsumari'osa* in the history of Koma."

"What is a *Tsumari'osa*?" Damian asked.

"That is something for you to discover later. Someone might not be pleased with me if I spoiled that surprise for you." The lady turned to face Damian, and her tone became low and serious. "Who, besides Kaeldyr the Gray, would you say is the most influential man or woman in all of Koma's history?"

Damian considered this, and replied, "Julian the Courageous, or the man who we came to call Kavala."

"Interesting? Why would you name Kavala?"

"Two reasons," Damian replied. "One, if Kavala hadn't abandoned his responsibilities, Saent Julian would have never risen to become Lord Morigahn at the end of the Second War of the Gods. Two, he orchestrated Koma's fall to the Kingdom. You didn't ask who influenced us for the positive."

"You're correct," the lady said, "I did not. And why Julian?"

"He gave us gunpowder and firearms," Damian said. "And by *us*, I mean mortals."

"Both fine answers." The lady smiled. Damian didn't like that smile. He'd been in enough rigged gambling games to know that smile. "If you stay, you could become more influential than Saent Julian the Courageous and Kavala, not just to Koma, but to the entire world."

"How?" Damian hated her for piquing his curiosity.

"I have no idea," the lady said. "We gods and goddesses do not know everything. However, some of us are very good at predicting things. If you stay, I predict great things for you. If you flee, I predict a life of running. Running from the Kingdom and running from your conscience." She took his face in her hands. "I won't lie and tell you that staying will be safe. People will try and take away your favorite pastime, but no man ever became great without some risk. Some people are still trying to make Kavala stop breathing, and it's been a long, long time since he achieved his greatness."

She let him go and walked to the door.

"Consider it," she said, and left.

"Damn, and bloody damn," Damian said.

He held his mop firmly and beat his head against the handle. Seven times he struck his forehead to the wood. It actually made him feel a little better. Then he remembered a question he'd wanted to ask her: *Why had the firearm been able to hurt the Daemyn hound back in Shadybrook?* Beating his head against the mop handle again, Damian suspected he'd see that goddess again.

Just as he finished abusing his forehead and was about to attack the next priv, Damian heard the door open behind him.

He turned to make some quip at the goddess. Instead, he found three Vara looking at him.

They were all bigger than he was, and all three carried wooden practice swords. The largest stood in the middle, and his left eye twitched a little and his mouth drooped a little on that side. The one on the right had dark, coarse hair that sprouted from his head at awkward angles, like weeds from an otherwise finely trimmed garden. The smallest of the three stood on the left, and he walked with a slight limp.

The two on the sides moved away from Droop Mouth, no doubt circling so they could trap Damian between them.

"So it's to be like this?" Damian asked.

"Like what?" the short one asked.

"Three against one unarmed man. Well," Damian let his mouth curve into his most feral grin, "at least seemingly unarmed."

The two flanking him paused at that. They should be worried. Damian had faced worse odds than these within the last fortnight, and he suspected these Vara would provide less challenge than the Nightbrothers outside of Shadybrook.

"We're here to welcome you," the one in the middle said. His tone told Damian all he needed to know about what kind of welcome these three wanted to give him.

"I'm afraid you won't be able to beat me right now," Damian said. "General Dyrk ordered me to clean the privs. Come back when I'm finished. Perhaps you can catch me before he orders me to some other menial task."

"Can't do that," Droop Mouth said, glancing at his leader. "It's a tradition. Right?"

These three had the look of those who frequently came to make new recruits feel welcome among the Vara. The three leered at him with all the anticipation of men about to engage in a favored pastime, and with none of the hesitation of men unused to bullying or of those acting with new companions.

Taking a deep breath, Damian centered himself. He would only have one chance to escape from this unscathed, but even that was risky. He didn't want to call any undue attention to himself. Hopefully nobody knew these three men had come after him. If he beat them soundly enough, they wouldn't tell anyone about the incident for fear of losing face in front of the other Vara.

"You hear me, boy?" Droop Mouth screamed.

Damian's foot hadn't moved from where he'd been pushing the bucket of water to the next priv. He kicked it at Droop Mouth. Droop Mouth ducked. Most people would assume an attack was aimed for chest or head.

Damian aimed for the hand holding the practice sword. The bucket struck true. Droop Mouth cried in pain, water, soap, brush, and practice sword scattered across the floor.

Even before the sword touched the ground, Damian was moving. He slid to a stop where the sword had landed. As Damian snatched the weapon up, Droop Mouth kicked at him. Like most large men, Droop Mouth moved slower than he should have, likely believing the myth that his strength didn't require him to focus on quickness. Damian easily avoided the blow.

Dropping into a ready stance and testing the practice sword's balance, Damian smiled. The weapon was modeled after a hand-and-a-half broad-sword rather than the more popular rapier. It was designed for combat on the battlefield for the purpose of bashing through armor, a weapon that re-lied mostly on strength and was perfect for beating an unsuspecting soul helpless. Well, that was the case with a real version of the weapon. The prac-tice sword was considerably lighter than a real weapon of the same make. Hunger, thirst, and exhaustion lost their hold on Damian as the sword forms from half a dozen different schools flowed through his mind.

Damian moved. He reveled in being able to unleash his full talent on these poor fools who happened to choose the worst possible day to attack Damian Adryck and allow him to get his hands on anything close to resem-bling a sword.

After a few moments, the three Vara lay on the floor, groaning in a state of semiconsciousness. Damian looked them over with disappointment. They hadn't been any challenge at all. Even the two men with swords hadn't been able to mount any reasonable defense. If all the Vara were this incompetent, he was going to have to work harder than he first thought masking his skill from these people. On the other side of the coin, it had been amusing to watch them trip all over each other as they realized how outmatched they were. Damian hadn't spared them a single joint. Their headaches might fade by sunset, but all three would suffer aches and pains for the next few days.

He rapped each of them on the head once more for good measure and then slid the practice swords out a window. Then he grabbed the mop and slapped them with soapy water. Considering some of the Vara he'd seen, Damian could probably convince most of them he'd beaten them with the mop.

He went back to cleaning. A few minutes later, the door opened again. This time, Paedrik Sardon entered the priv.

"Gods be damned," Damian swore. "What now?"

Paedrik ignored him. Instead, he looked over the three bodies writhing on the floor. He snorted with displeasure.

"What happened to them?"

"Them?" Damian replied as if having three bodies sprawled on the floor he was trying to clean was the most natural thing in the world. "I think they slipped."

"Slipped?" Doubt dripped from Paedrik's tone.

Damian didn't care. "Yes. They came to welcome me to the Vara, I spilled the bucket, and they slipped."

"Really? Did they also hit the bucket several times on the way down?"

The bucket lay almost in the center of the three men.

"Well, they might have. They might have slipped a couple more times trying to get up. The water is very soapy, and that makes the floor very slick."

"Well, I'll ask them about it once they wake up," Paedrik said. "As for you, General Dyrk wants you to get out to the practice yard."

"Practice yard?" Damian asked.

"Yes. He wants to see what kind of a swordsman you are."

If there was any way for someone in this ragtag group of misfit mercenaries to figure out who Damian really was, despite Czenzi's miracle, it was by seeing him use a sword.

"But the priv isn't clean yet," Damian said. "I'll be out just as soon as I've tidied it."

"Don't bother with it," Paedrik said. "I'll have this lot do it when they wake up, to punish them for being so careless with a bucket. You get out to the yard. That's an order."

"Well, orders are orders," Damian said, offering Paedrik a crisp salute. "Can't keep General Dyrk waiting."

SEVEN

Bordering on the verge of exhaustion, Czenzi made her way through the Governor's Palace toward Kraetor's suite. It was moments like this when Czenzi missed her simple life as a printer's apprentice. All she wanted right now was a warm cup of spiced tea and her bed, but duty took precedence. Kraetor would want his report about Damian Adryck getting into the Vara, and Kraetor's wishes always came before Czenzi's comfort.

Upon thinking of her report, Damian's face came unbidden into her mind. Though his clothes were not much better than a beggar's and he had smelled of cheap wine, Damian Adryck carried himself with more noble bearing than most High Blood in the Kingdom could dream of. Throughout everything that had happened since she'd encountered him, Adryck never seemed to doubt himself or believe that anything was going to go wrong for him.

Shaking her head, Czenzi forced her mind to other things.

Turning around the final corner leading to Kraetor's suite, Czenzi saw Xander Rosha standing guard just outside the doors. Grandfather Shadow's blessing must have still been with her, for Xander was looking the other way, giving her time to leap back out of his view. Kractor had gone to extreme lengths to keep the two of them apart. Czenzi didn't know why, but it didn't matter. While she held Kraetor's confidence, the First Adept did not give her the minutia of every plan and scheme that he was involved in. It wasn't her place to know everything, only her place to obey the man who had brought her to a higher station in life than she ever could have dreamed of.

All that was beside the point. Right now Czenzi had to figure out a way to get around Xander Rosha. Had it been earlier in the night, she would have drawn on the Dominions of Secrets and Illusions and spoken a miracle to sneak past him. However, after the night she had had, Czenzi didn't possess the endurance to speak even the smallest miracle.

Czenzi hit herself on the forehead. What was she thinking? Her first inclination was to use a miracle, and that went against Grandfather Shadow's teachings. The second law warned against overindulgence or reliance on either brute force or divine power. Ever since entering Kraetor's service, the First Adept had taught Czenzi that her mind was her foremost weapon. As soon as Czenzi turned away from the thought of using a miracle to bypass Xander, a solution presented itself.

Czenzi made her way to the servants' quarters. She ignored the bows and curtsies she received from servants and the few Low Blood she encountered. Czenzi came across a pair of High Blood, one of House Swaenmarch and the other of House Floraen. She knew neither of them. Normally, this would have raised some suspicion in her mind. House Swaenmarch and House Floraen usually found themselves at odds, especially lately with Kraetor publicly being such close friends with Mateo Andres, Speaker of the Sun. However, these two High Blood were engaged in a heated debate about the strengths of their Houses' respective patron deities. The High Blood nodded at her passing, and she returned the gesture.

When Czenzi finally reached the servants' level, she headed to the wing that housed those who served the uppermost levels of the Governor's Palace.

"Leave," Czenzi ordered, as she entered her destination.

Servants either scurried out of the hallway or into their rooms. They all kept their eyes downcast and did their best not to trip over each other in their haste to obey Czenzi. With the servants gone, Czenzi entered one of the sleeping chambers. As she opened the door, the single occupant bolted upright, a dagger in her hand.

"Calm down, Layla," Czenzi said. "I need your help."

"My apologies, Adept Czenzi." The edge in Layla's green eyes softened, and she lowered the knife. "You startled me."

Layla slid out of her bed, smoothed out her night dress, and pulled her brown hair into a bun. Her grooming completed, she dropped into a respectable curtsy. It pleased Czenzi that Layla kept up the appearances of her role even when they were alone together. It made it much less likely that she would make a mistake when they were in public.

"It's quite alright," Czenzi replied. "However, you are supposed to be playing the part of the civil servant girl. Won't the other servants start to wonder if you keep drawing a knife at the first sign of trouble?"

"Oh, that's nothing to worry about," Layla explained. "I have the others thinking that I was raped at my last post. I actually overplay being skittish, and every time I get startled, or at least I let them think I get startled, my hand strays to my knife. It's even become somewhat of a cruel game for them."

"Well, just see that you don't draw too much attention to yourself," Czenzi said. "Now help me get out of my clothes and into your livery."

"Why?" Layla asked.

Czenzi almost snapped as though Layla were actually a servant, or perhaps even a Low Blood. That wouldn't have done at all. Doing so might have cost Kraetor this girl's father, and House Kaesiak required the loyalty and assistance of certain Komati families.

"There is some place I need to get inside the palace, and it's easier as a servant than as an Adept."

Layla nodded, and they both began to remove the various layers of Czenzi's clothing. Though Czenzi liked the way she looked and felt while wearing her proper Adept's attire, she despised getting into and out of it.

After a few minutes, Czenzi had completely shed her Adept's mantle and donned one of Layla's servant's outfits. The only thing that remained was for Czenzi to remove her mask.

"You must turn away," Czenzi said.

"Are you suddenly modest?" Layla asked.

Czenzi knew that wasn't the question that Layla really wanted answered. Kaesiak Adepts also used misleading or misdirecting questions to gain information that the person being questioned didn't necessarily want to reveal. Perhaps somewhere deep in the past, Grandfather Shadow had taught all his previous worshipers the same lessons.

"You know very well I have no modesty of the flesh," Czenzi said.

"You're actually going to remove your mask?"

Most Kaesiak Adepts reviled the thought of removing their mask. It was their connection to Grandfather Shadow, and most felt weakened too much by its absence. In her service to First Adept Kraetor, Czenzi frequently removed her mask so that she could go places and observe events that would have been difficult for an Adept of House Kaesiak. She was no stranger to playing the part of a servant.

"Yes," Czenzi replied. "And I would prefer that you didn't see me with it off."

"But your mask barely covers your face at all," Layla said. "Anyone who takes a good look at you will know you as Adept Czenzi of House Kaesiak."

Czenzi gave Layla a faint smile. "If that is how you see things, then you have not learned *Galad'Ysoysa*'s lessons very well. Those who see me wearing my mask see an Adept of House Kaesiak, not the girl underneath. When they look at me in this," Czenzi gestured to the servant's livery she wore, "they will only see a servant girl. It is the same reason you have been undetected in the palace so far, even though you number some acquaintances among the Komati nobles residing there. They do not see you because they do not want to see you in this role.

"It is much the same with your *Galad'fana*. When you wear it, the cloth does not hide your identity. There are many other features you possess that a keen-eyed or cunning observer could use to ascertain who you are beneath that gray cloth. However, this symbol of the *Galad'fana* creates a disguise that is nearly impenetrable, even by followers of Grandfather Shadow."

Layla pursed her lips and blinked rapidly, as if mentally digesting Czenzi's words. After a moment, Layla nodded and turned her back to Czenzi.

Adept Czenzi of House Kaesiak removed her mask and vanished. In her place stood Czenzi, apprentice printer and loyal servant of anyone of higher standing. Her shoulders slumped forward, and her gaze lowered to the floor. Falling back into her old life, as easy as donning the Kaesiak livery, Czenzi curtsied to Layla, who was in truth Countess Yllaylaena Vitonen'Thaems, and left.

Czenzi's return journey to Kraetor's suite took at least twice as long as to the servants' quarters. Adept Czenzi walked with confidence and pride, standing aside for almost no one; she was the right hand of Kraetor Ilsaen, First Adept of Grandfather Shadow. However, Czenzi the printer's apprentice was a timid creature who curtsied for almost everyone, including the other servants who looked as though they were more important or had higher rank than a printer's apprentice.

Finally, Czenzi turned around the corner that led to Kraetor's suite. This time, Xander Rosha stood looking right at her. The printer's apprentice inside Czezni saw the lost heir to the Komati Throne dressed in a White Dragon uniform, and the timidity of her former life seized control of her body. She could not move.

Xander cocked his head to the side and gave her a puzzled look.

The Adept within Czenzi came forward just enough to give the printer's apprentice orders. *Curtsy, you fool.*

Czenzi heeded the command.

"Oh, stop that," Xander's voice called from the other end of the hall. "I'm just a guard."

Czenzi gave three brisk nods, rose, and started down the hall toward the doors behind Xander. She kept her eyes downcast for the entire journey, and it felt like a journey, for no matter what she had said to Layla, deep down Czenzi feared that Xander would recognize her despite having only seen her in the dark of night and wearing her Adept's mantle and mask. By the time she reached a few paces of the doors, her nerves had overcome her to the point where she could barely keep moving. Somehow, her foot caught on the edge of her skirt, and she stumbled forward. Her hands came up to brace for the impact, but she never struck the floor. Xander had rushed forward and caught her.

As he helped Czenzi to her feet, she looked into his eyes. *Oh shades,* Czenzi thought. *I'm caught.*

The next moment, Czenzi found herself drowning in Xander's eyes. His eyes were such a pale shade of blue that they looked almost steel-gray.

"Are you well?" Xander's voice was firm but patient, and it took Czenzi a moment to realize it was the second time he had asked the question.

Czenzi's lips moved, but she couldn't manage to speak. *Answer him, girl,* the Adept ordered from the back of her mind.

"Yes," Czenzi said weakly. "Thank you."

"You should be on your way before anybody comes along," Xander said with a sly smile. "We'd likely become the next entertaining scoundrel scandal amongst the Komati families and High Blood alike. And the last thing I need is to be in the center of yet another scandal."

Czenzi managed to get herself back to her own two feet, curtsied again, and hurried into Kraetor's suite.

Her master was sitting at his breakfast. Even at this early hour, Kraetor had on his mask. Kraetor looked up when she entered, took in her outfit, and grinned.

"It appears as though you've had an eventful evening," he said.

Czenzi's stomach yearned to devour the pastries and bacon piled on the table where Kraetor sat. He loved Floraen pastries and had been taking adventage of Governor Salvatore's cooks since arriving in Koma City. However, Czenzi resisted, and bringing her own mask out from the folds in her skirt, she returned it to her face. Now that the mask had returned to its rightful place, the Adept returned fully to her mind.

"It had its entertaining moments," Czenzi replied.

"Did Rosha recognize you?" A touch of concern entered Kraetor's voice. He rarely spoke with anything less than the utmost confidence. Czenzi had studied her master's voice so much in their years together that she could read his moods by the inflections of his words. She could almost always guess his moods. For some reason, the subject of Xander and Czenzi's meeting filled him with great concern, almost dread. Why was that?

"Not in the least."

"Excellent." Kraetor clapped his hands together. "Go and dress properly, join me for breakfast, and tell me of your adventures."

Sleep would have to wait.

EIGHT

Damian stepped into the Vara practice yard. Closing his eyes, he took in a deep breath and let his mind float on the sound of wood cracking on wood and steel ringing on steel. Any sort of swordplay had a rhythm. Early in his travels to learn the sword styles of various lands, Damian had learned to tell the worth of a school by the rhythms of its practice yard. In a good school, the wooden rhythm would ebb and flow slowly as the younger students went through their exercises, while the steel rhythm would punctuate its presence now and then as the more advanced students tested each other under the careful supervision of the school's Maestros. In the very best schools, the weapons became instruments in an orchestra, and the Maestros were not instructors, rather they were conductors who created great music while their students learned the art of swordsmanship.

The Vara sounded like a crowd of street urchins who had been given sticks and crates and pots and pans and were told to play a symphony.

On his way from the privs, Damian had decided that it would be best to play at being in the lower end of the skill level of those present. Now that he'd heard the Vara at practice, Damian doubted his training would let him do that. There were certain things his body would just *do* when put into a situation where he had a sword in his hand. Sometimes he could overcome those reflexes by concentrating on limiting his performance. However, as tired as he was, Damian didn't trust his concentration to overcome his training for any length of time.

"There you are," a voice called out above the cacophony. Damian easily recognized Dyrk's deep voice over the chaos of practicing Vara.

Opening his eyes, Damian saw Dyrk striding toward him with a practice sword in hand.

"What were you doing?' Dyrk asked.

"Praying that this was just a bad dream," Damian replied.

"I promise you that you are very much awake," Dyrk said. "Take this sword and join that line."

Dyrk gestured with the practice sword toward a clump of Vara. It was the least line-like formation that Damian had ever seen.

Taking a quick head count, he saw perhaps ten to a dozen Vara. The three largest stood in the center. Two held the others at bay with wide slashes which, wielded by their powerful arms, might crack bones if any of them had skill enough to connect. The third man, larger than the others, stood beating someone who lay curled at his feet. With his size, he could have been the twin of the ringleader of the bullies who had just attacked Damian in the priv – unfortunately his poor victim didn't have the skill or the confidence to fight back.

Damian sighed. What was it about these packs of bullies in the Vara that made them travel in threes? And was their Maestro so incompetent that he couldn't teach the small, less powerful men here to dart past the bullies' wide, clumsy strikes. Watching this horrific display made Damian want to challenge the current Maestro for his position, but he could not. He could only stand by while this travesty took place.

"Well," Dyrk said, handing Damian the practice sword. "Get in there."

"Yes, General," Damian said through clenched teeth.

As he approached the sad excuse for a training session, Damian realized that Gabryl was on the receiving end of this beating.

Logic and reason fled Damian's mind. He shifted his grip on his practice sword and rushed into the melee.

In three steps, Damian came within striking distance of the maniacs swinging like children at a House Floraen name day party. He went between them, and when they each swung, Damian dove forward into a roll. Two loud cracks and two cries of pain told him that his ploy had worked.

Rolling to his feet, Damian found himself facing the third. If this brute was brother to the ringleader earlier, he was certainly the uglier of the two. His uneven hair clung to his head in oily lumps. His eyes were sunken into his head further than anyone Damian had ever seen, and when he sneered, he showed two rows of crooked, decaying teeth with several gaps on both the top and bottom.

Gap Tooth swung at Damian, his arms pulled over his head to strike with what most people would think was an obvious, overhanded blow. However, Damian noticed Gap Tooth had his forward foot pointed slightly to his own right and his left shoulder pulled back ever so slightly. It was a common technique that most who trained with broadswords learned early on, especially if they ever thought they would be facing opponents using rapiers or other lighter blades.

It didn't fool Damian for a moment.

Damian lunged forward, and Gap Tooth's attack transitioned from an overhead attack to a slash at the abdomen that was intended to slice through the victim's sword and disembowel him. Parrying the blow with ease, Damian countered first by slapping his blade down on Gap Tooth's wrists – the blow caused Gap Tooth to cry in pain and surprise and to drop his own sword – then by slashing upward along the arms with a vicious cut to the neck.

Gap Tooth dropped to his knees, gasping and clutching at his throat. He was lucky that Damian had come at him out of a roll. If it had been a full charge, the blow would have crushed Gap Tooth's throat, likely killing him.

Spinning, Damian prepared to face the follow-up attacks from Gap-tooth's friends. Those attacks never came. Everyone in the practice yard stood staring at Damian and Gap Tooth.

Ignoring them, Damian knelt down next to Gabryl.

"Are you alright?" Damian asked, putting his hand on Gabryl's shoulder.

Gabryl looked up. A dark purple bruise swelled on his forehead, and a steady stream of blood flowed from his nose. He groaned as he pulled himself into a sitting position.

"It's not the worst beating I've taken in this yard," Gabryl said. "My thanks."

Damian nodded and helped Gabryl to his feet.

"That was impressive," Dyrk said. "I can't wait to see what else you know."

The Vara leader had come over to them. Damian's heart sank. He was going to have to work hard and talk fast to overcome this display of swordsmanship. The temptation to resume Gabryl's beating came upon Damian, but he resisted. He should have maintained a closer reign on his emotions.

"You won't see much more of that from me, General," Damian said. "Give me a knife to fight with, and I'll carve up any man who will try to take my purse. When it comes to swords, I know a few tricks, but mostly my swordsmanship consists of knowing which end to hold. And even my tricks are unreliable at best." Damian opened his eyes a little wider and deepened his voice. As he spoke his next words, he lifted his face to a little toward the sky. "Sister Wind must have guided my hand and my blade to help teach everyone here some humility. We mortals never know when another might come along who is an agent of the gods to teach us a well-deserved lesson."

Damian blinked several times and twitched a little. He looked at Dyrk as if he was surprised to see the Vara leader.

Dyrk fixed Damian with an unbelieving stare. "We'll see about that. Everyone, on the line. Now!"

As the Vara scurried to obey the order, Dyrk pushed Damian into a place in one of the lines. With a sigh, Damian looked up and down the line of Vara standing against his line. All of his potential opponents were looking at him, some with eagerness and some with nervousness and fear, but one thing was true for each and every one: Damian had gained their attention.

"*Kraestu kraenka yn'goska,*" Damian muttered under his breath.

And he thought cleaning privs was going to be a long day.

NINE

Being assigned to the Governor's Palace was not the glamorous adventure Xander expected. He'd been standing his post several hours, and now his legs grew weary and his mind wandered, flitting from one thought to another with no direct correlation between. Many people walked by his post, most of them giving Xander a confused or wide-eyed look before hurrying on to whatever task they were about. Only two people went through First Adept Kraetor's door that morning. The first was a servant wearing Kaesiak livery, carrying Kraetor's breakfast. The second was Kraetor himself. After breakfast he left the suite to worship at the temple of Shadow and returned within the hour.

At least Xander was free from the White Dragon fortress below the palace. Who knew what sort of torments he'd be suffering were he still stationed there? As Xander's thoughts created endless scenes of what the Whites might do, part of his mind remained aware of his surroundings. He snapped to attention even before he was consciously aware of three people walking directly up to Kraetor's door. One of them was Smiles, which was why he didn't immediately challenge them.

When they stopped several paces away, Xander took a moment to look over the other two. They were humans, a man and a woman, wearing the red and gold of House Floraen. Xander forced his gaze to stay on the man, but he didn't really notice what the man looked like as he couldn't keep from glancing at the woman. She had the same dark hair and dark eyes that dominated the High Blood of House Floraen. Her lips curled into a half-smile that seemed to say she was keeping the world's most important secret to herself.

"Hatchling," Smiles said, "This is Portia Salvatore, High Blood of House Floraen, wife to Governor Octavio, and this is Dante Salvatore, High Blood of House Floraen. They heard about your rescue of First Adept Kraetor and wished to see you."

"I am honored, High Blood," Xander said, and gave a formal court bow.

As he was introduced to the governor's brother, Xander took a better look at the man. Dante Salvatore appeared close to his thirtieth winter, clothes perfectly tailored with enough lace and trim to befit the second most powerful man in Koma, yet not enough to make him seem flamboyant. The jewels and gold wiring on his rapier disguised a decent weapon, not a great one, but one capable of actually holding up in a fight, unlike the court swords many High Blood wore, especially those of House Floraen.

Both the High Blood nodded at his courtesy.

"You are Prince Xander Rosha of House Eras," Dante said. Xander had been inspected enough times in the Reds to recognize Dante's appraisal of him.

"Yes, High Blood," Xander replied.

"Why did he call you, Hatchling?" Dante asked.

"That is my Draqon name, High Blood."

"Why Hatchling?" Portia asked.

"I have not earned a greater name yet," Xander replied.

"From what I hear of your career in the Reds," Dante said, "you will soon earn a name with the Whites. It has been a pleasure to meet you."

"The honor is mine, High Blood."

Portia stepped to the side, making as though she might head for the door to Kraetor's suite. Xander recalled Smile's order from earlier: *Allow entrance only to those people who wear the Kaesiak livery, a High Blood of Kaesiak, or an Adept of any House.*

Xander shifted himself as to block the door, and said, "Your pardon, High Blood, but I am commanded to keep out anyone who is not Kaesiak."

Portia looked at him as though amused, as if she were sharing her own private jest about the situation. He didn't know what she might find humorous about this, but he didn't really care. Orders were orders, and Xander would follow them so long as they did not lead to his own treason.

"I wasn't trying to go through the door," Portia said. "I just wanted a better look at your hair. Why don't you have it braided yet?"

"High Blood?" Xander asked, confused and a little hurt. He still felt the pain from when Black Claw forced him to remove the braids he'd earned while serving with the Reds.

"You saved a High Blood last night. That should earn you the right to wear one braid."

She was right. In the rush of emotions from seeing Damian and then rescuing Kraetor, Xander hadn't thought of a new braid.

"I may not decide to braid my hair, myself," Xander said. "I must be given permission by my commander, or a High Blood."

"I give my consent for you to wear one braid, Hatchling," Smiles said. "Now turn."

Xander pounded his fists together over his heart, saluting Smiles. This would give the Whites something to talk about once Xander returned to the fortress.

When he turned his back to Smiles, Xander saw a lone noble walking toward them from the far end of the hallway. He was too far away for Xander to make out his features, but he wore the red and gold of House Floraen. A rapier hung on the man's hip, but even at this distance, Xander could tell it was only a ceremonial court sword, not truly fit for real fighting and only good as a last hope weapon.

As the noble walked toward them, he looked intently at Xander. Seeing a White getting braided was a rare thing, and seeing a human wearing a White uniform receiving that honor was even more so. The noble watched Xander so intently that he didn't seem to notice the two servants appearing from side hallways and heading right toward him. Both servants were men and were carrying bundles of laundry.

"That's odd," Xander said, wincing a little as Smiles pulled his hair back.

"What's odd?" Smiles asked.

"I thought the women servants usually did the laundry."

"They do," Dante answered. "But it's not uncommon for the men to help, especially when one has a fancy for one of the lady servants. It's actually quite amusing to watch their romances."

Xander heard Portia say something, but he ignored her. He hadn't taken his eyes off the two servant men. Something was not right about them. One shifted his burden, and Xander saw something underneath the bundle glint in the sun coming in the wide windows. Xander cocked his head and leaned a little to his left to get a better look at whatever it was. The glimmer faded, and Xander thought he saw something thin and metal in the bundle, a long dirk or even a short sword, but that didn't matter.

Without hesitating any longer, Xander reached back and grabbed Smiles's sword. Normally the White would have stopped Xander from touching the hilt, much less drawing it. However, Smiles was busy braiding Xander's hair and so the sword came free of its sheath. Rushing forward, Xander stifled a cry as he pulled away from Smiles's grasp. He was sure the White's strong fingers pulled out several clumps of hair. Ignoring the pain, Xander heaved the large sword at the servant with the blade.

Smiles, Dante, and Portia cried out as the sword spun end over end through the air. Xander didn't stop to see if it would hit the servant, he drew his own sword and dagger and ran down the hall. He had to protect the High Blood from these assassins.

The sword struck hilt first, knocking the assassin to the floor. His laundry flew into the air and scattered all over the hallway. Not seeing the blade in the assassin's hand, Xander assumed it was buried under the pile of clothes and blankets. The servant didn't bother to look for his own blade, but grabbed Smiles's sword instead. The second servant glanced over his shoulder. His eyes widened at seeing Xander racing toward him, blades drawn. He dropped his laundry and ran at the High Blood with a wicked looking curved-bladed dirk.

Xander flipped his own thin dirk, catching it by the blade without missing a stride. He flicked his wrist and the dirk flew spinning end over end. It made a better throwing weapon than a sword, and the blade plunged into the second servant's back. A patch of dark red blossomed around the hilt. The servant stumbled to his knees.

The first servant faced Xander, now holding Smiles's sword. It was obvious from his stance that he wasn't accustomed to such a large blade. The tip was too low, barely above the knees, and his arms trembled with the effort of keeping it that high.

"Surrender," Xander said, skidding to a stop just outside of the assassin's reach. "You can't hope to win."

"You're right," the assassin said, and slowly turned the sword around, offering the hilt to Xander.

Xander reached out for it, taking care to be ready in case this was a ruse. As soon as his left hand closed around the hilt, the assassin tried to push the pommel into Xander's stomach. Xander reacted by tightening his grip and resisting, pushing the sword away from himself. As soon as he did, the assassin dove forward, impaling himself all the way up to the hilt. Now his face was only a few inches away from Xander.

"*Aen Keisari*," the assassin said, coughing blood, "you betray us all by wearing that uniform." He took a last rasping breath and slumped on the end of the sword.

Xander put his foot squarely on the assassin's chest and pushed the corpse off Smiles's sword.

"What is the meaning of this?" cried the Floraen High Blood.

Xander held the bloody sword out to his commander. After Smiles took it, Xander turned and saluted the High Blood with his sword pointed to the floor and his neck bared.

The High Blood walked right up to Xander. The Floraen looked to be in his early forties, but only barely. His beard and moustache were trimmed neatly around his lips and chin, leaving his cheeks bare. Many Floraen nobles wore their beards in this fashion. Xander had heard it was how the Sun King cut his, and of course the nobles of his own House absolutely *had* to imitate him. The High Blood's dark brown eyes fixed on Xander.

"I know who you are," the noble said. "Why are you killing my servants?"

"Calm down, husband," Portia said, coming around to Xander's right side. "They both had swords."

"Husband?" Xander asked. His breath came out in a whisper. If this man was Portia's husband, that made him...

"Governor Salvatore," Smiles said, drawing the High Blood's attention. The White knelt down and pulled aside some of the spilt laundry, revealing the assassin's blade. "These men were assassins."

Duke Octavio Salvatore, Kingdom Governor of Koma, looked at the two men and their weapons. He stroked his beard. His eyes darted to Xander and back to the would-be killers.

"Well, young man," the governor said, "it seems that you need to take that braid out."

"What? Why?" Xander couldn't believe what he'd heard. He knew he should stay silent, but couldn't keep his indignation bottled up. "I earned the right to wear this braid by saving First Adept Kraetor last night. Like any other White, I'll remove it with my death."

"Stand down, Hatchling," Smiles growled. "You will *not* speak that way to a High Blood."

"It's alright," Governor Salvatore said. "He misunderstands me. You need to take the braid out so you can wear two. It seems that like First Adept Kraetor, I am also in your debt. Thank you for your keen eye." Octavio Salvatore gave Xander a slight bow then offered an arm to his wife. "Shall we to dine my dear?"

"Of course," Portia said, lacing her arm through her husband's. "But shouldn't we deal with these assassins."

"I have every confidence that the Whites will handle it, my dear," the governor said. "But only after putting that other braid in that young man's hair."

Smiles nodded as Governor Salvatore led his wife away. Then the White commander turned to Xander.

"Put the sword away," Smiles said. "Then turn around."

Xander slid his rapier back into its sheath and turned his back to Smiles. This was the second braid he'd earned in two days. At this rate, he'd have more braids than any White in the whole Kingdom in less than a year.

TEN

Damian didn't ever remember hurting this bad. Even breathing was painful, so he was careful to take shallow breaths, going so far as to hold his breath for ten heartbeats after every fifteenth breath. That continued ritual allowed him to focus his mind away from the pain.

Through all the years he'd studied swordplay, Damian couldn't remember receiving a beating like the one he'd suffered today. Even the time he and Xander fought half a dozen boys from House Collaen hadn't resulted in pain like this. Also, both Xander and Damian had given just as good as they had received; only numbers had helped the Collaens that day.

"That was quite the dramatic presentation," a gruff voice said above Damian.

Damian opened his eyes. General Dyrk stood above him.

"What do you mean?" Damian asked through clenched teeth.

Dyrk sat down on Damian's cot, hard, jostling the whole bed. Damian sucked in a pained breath.

"Well, you have almost everyone believing that you don't know how to use a sword. That bit about Sister Wind guiding your hand to teach Boris a bit of humility was actually a touch of genius. However, I recognized the maneuver you used. It wasn't a lucky strike. It was a maneuver from the Jinarii School from the Taitsu Empire. I've known three men who could perform that maneuver. Each was a master of at least two different schools of swordplay. I heard one of those men even taught it to his grandson, though I can't verify the validity of that rumor."

Damian's mind raced. He should have realized that even among this group somebody was going to recognize that maneuver. But that didn't mean he was discovered.

"Of course it was a real maneuver," Damian said. "I told you that I know a few tricks and that's all, I've paid a pretty penny to learn them all. Most real swordsmen decide they want nothing to do with me after they see me use that on someone, which is good, because you've seen how bad I am with a blade."

"Well," Dyrk said. "That would explain it, but this isn't why I came to talk to you. Get up and walk with me."

"Why?" Damian asked.

"Because I told you to," Dyrk replied. "I want to show you something."

Damian forced himself up from the cot. His muscles protested. He almost succeeded in holding in a groan, though letting the groan out might have been the better choice. By trying to hold it in, the sound came out as a tired whimper.

Dyrk watched this with a bemused smile.

"What?" Damian asked.

"I was just thinking that the best way to keep most people from thinking you are really an expert swordsman would be to let yourself get beaten as badly as you did today."

"If I was, why would I want to hide it?" Damian snapped, perhaps a little more forcefully than he meant to.

"Why indeed?" Dyrk shook his head. "But you say that you are not, and because we are all brothers within the Vara, I will take your word on the matter."

Damian peered into Dyrk's eyes, but try as he might he could not sense any deception. However, this did not remove Damian's suspicions that Dyrk was hiding something. In his travels, Damian had learned that powerful people, just like those who lived in the underside of society, not only lied with ease to others, they could even convince themselves the falsehoods they spoke were true. Exceptions existed, rare exceptions – like Xander, as an example.

Thinking of his brother's straightforward, sometimes brutally honest approach to dealing with people made Damian stifle a laugh.

"Something amuses you, Zephyr?" Dyrk asked, his dark eyes probing Damian.

"No, sir," Damian replied. "Just grunting from the pain of getting up."

"We'll have to arrange for you to have practice time every day until you are better able to defend yourself."

"I can't wait," Damian muttered, and followed Dyrk out of the barracks.

Each step was a chorus of all his aching joints and muscles. By the time Damian reached the door, he wanted to lie down again.

Dyrk led Damian across the Vara compound. It was late afternoon now. Being on the ground level of Central Island, shadows were already growing so long and dark that lanterns and gas lamps alike assisted in lighting the Vara fortress.

They took a path that wove between several of the buildings until Dyrk brought them to a point where they could see a small area secluded from the rest of the compound. In that alcove, Damian watched about a dozen young men facing off with practice swords in two rows. He recognized some of them from the practice session earlier that morning, including Gabryl.

"What are we doing here?" Damian asked in a low voice.

He kept his voice down because Dyrk kept them both out of sight as much as possible. Not that it mattered. The group was so fixated on their practicing that Damian and Dyrk could have likely walked into their midst before being detected.

"I wanted you to see what you have started," Dyrk replied. "The new recruits have sword practice three days out of every week. Afterward, they are given the rest of that day to recuperate, so long as they do not leave the compound. This is the first time any of them, much less a group of them, have continued practicing after being dismissed from the official session."

"So?"

Dyrk glared at Damian. "So, this is the highest morale has been for any batch of new recruits in recent memory. Look at their faces."

Damian looked. Each of the Vara was covered in bruises and cuts, but their eyes shone with excitement. Damian recognized that look. He'd seen it in dozens of academies in over a dozen different lands.

"I see," Damian replied. "What do you want from me?"

"I want you to teach them." Dyrk held up his hand, cutting off Damian's retort. "I know. I know. You don't really know how to use a sword. You only know a few tricks to keep from getting in a real fight. That's fine by me. The Vara aren't supposed to be a military force. We're meant to keep the peace. Your philosophy of swordplay is actually perfect for what the High Blood expect us to do. I want those lads, and any that come after them, to be able to put a criminal down, quickly and decisively, *before* the situation gets out of hand. More to the point, I also want to reinfuse some semblance of pride within the Vara. Are you my man?"

"Perhaps," Damian said. "What do I get out of it?"

"For starters, I'll make sure you don't have to clean any more privs. And I'll consider making you a sergeant."

"No thank you, General. The last thing I want is any accolades or quick rewards. I'll do it because I think that life here will be much harder for me should I refuse, and because I'd hate to see any of them killed when I could have shown them something that might have saved their lives."

Stepping back, Damian saluted. Then, without waiting for Dyrk to return the salute, Damian marched around the corner of the building. All of the pain from his earlier beatings faded a bit at the thought of molding these potential swordmasters. The only question now was how to teach them to actually be dangerous without ever giving away his identity or true skill.

As he got closer to them, their practice slowly came to a stop. Damian stopped about ten paces from them and gave his best smile.

"Take a rest lads," one of them said to the others. "I'll see what he wants."

When the speaker separated himself from the rest of the group, Damian recognized him. Like Gabryl, Baronet Coltaenan Tuada was the youngest son of a family from House Kaeski. Most people who knew Coltaenan even remotely well called him Colt. Colt's father was a viscount who had served Damian's father. The last Damian had heard, Colt's father had died and Colt's older brother had squandered away the family's meager inheritance on risky business ventures and even riskier greyhound coursing wagers.

Though Gabryl and Colt were the only ones in the group that Damian recognized by name, he did see some other familiar faces from when he had been at court. It seemed that the Vara was becoming the place for the younger sons of less-than-well-to-do noble families. Hopefully Czenzi's miracle would hold strong against all these people who might otherwise recognize him as Prince Damian Adryck.

"Hello," Damian said.

"Greetings," Colt replied. "That was—"

"Believe me," Damian said, "I wasn't trying to impress anyone."

"Oh, I do believe you," Colt said with a sly smile. Then he added with a whisper, "Your Highness."

A spear of solid ice pierced Damian's heart. He quickly scanned the compound for a way to escape, but the only two ways out of this alcove were through the new recruits or back through Dyrk. Damian doubted he would have much luck in either direction without killing someone.

"Relax," Colt whispered. "Only Gabryl and I know, and neither one of us will betray you."

"Well," Damian said, regaining his composure, "that's a comfort. Call me Zephyr."

Colt nodded. "What do you wish of us?"

"Dyrk has given me the task of teaching you the tricks that I know," Damian replied. "Though I wish I could teach them all to be at least competent with a sword."

"We could do it together."

Damian eyed Colt. "How do you mean?"

Colt smiled. "You teach them the tricks, then I explain the basic principles behind why the tricks are so effective. I have the most experience with a sword, so they'll believe me. I'll put on a show of being confused about it every once in a while."

"Sometimes it might not be an act, and those moments might come more often than you expect. Some of my tricks are fairly complex."

"Well then, we should get started." Colt's smile never faded.

Damian decided right then that he liked Colt. The baronet's mind worked in a similar fashion to his own.

"I suppose we should," Damian said.

Colt turned back to the group. "Lads, this is Zephyr. He's agreed to show us a few things that he knows."

Damian glanced over his shoulder. Dyrk still stood there, watching him, only now Paedrik Sardon stood next to the general. Sardon whispered something in Dyrk's ear. Dyrk nodded. He smiled at Damian and gave a half-wave.

What was that about?

So many people were scheming and plotting with Damian feeling himself at the center of those webs. Czenzi and Kraetor, Dyrk and Sardon, that goddess with the spectacles, and if Damian allowed himself the idiocy of believing Czenzi, even Grandfather Shadow had plans for Damian. Ever since the Kingdom Inquisitors discovered his father's firearms, they'd had plans for Damian Adryck, and those plans hadn't come to fruition after years of hunting him, mostly because those plans didn't coincide with Damian's plans for himself. Let those others plot and scheme around him, even the gods; Damian Adryck danced his own dance regardless of the tune being played, everyone else be damned.

ECHOES OF THUNDER

A storm is coming...
It is always coming, just on the horizon.

Bring the pure wine,
We'll raise our glasses to the storm,
that terrible brother that comes.

Bring the wine, pure and strong,
like the storm
full of terror and joy.

Like lightning, your lives will be quick and bright.
Like thunder, I last beyond your brief time.
Like lightning, your beauty fades before it can truly be seen.
Like thunder, I linger. My voice is heard across the heavens.

It matters not to me
whether the storm rages or not
for the storm cannot touch me.

You, however, you, my brothers and sisters,
will sit in a congregation of the dead,
where one handful of dirt says,
I was once a head of hair.

To this I say,
More wine!
Bring more wine, strong like the tempest,
and I'll teach the lighting
to fear the echo of my passing.

- Kavala

ONE

Faelin stood in a circle with six others: Parsh, Korrin, Wynd, Alerick, Aurell, and Charise. Wynd's wedding ring, the only thing they had that had any attachment to Nathan.

"Nathan was the better at everything," Korrin said, "even if he was unwilling to acknowledge that I was older." Korrin's tone and Aurell's, Wynd's, and even Parsh's soft laughter gave the feeling that this was an old joke between the brothers.

Faelin took a breath. Wynd and Korrin had asked him to stand in the ceremony, and with this being the fourth time around the circle of seven, Faelin was struggling to come up with things to say of Korrin, though he didn't have nearly the trouble Charise did.

"Nathan accepted me for myself," Faelin said, "and he made poor wagers on knife throwing."

"Nathan helped me refine my sword technique," Alerick said, "and he made poor wagers on almost everything."

This brought more laughter from members and servants of House Thaedus.

Before Parsh could speak again, one of Sandré's Morigahnti on watch called from the theater's door, "Seven men approach. Looks like six Nightbrothers and a Morigahnti."

"I'm to the Lord Morigahn," Aurell said, and dashed toward the back of the theater.

Everyone else rushed to the front of the theater. Faelin looked out of one of the windows. In the light of predawn, he saw seven people coming toward the house. Six of them wore the hardened leather armor of the Brotherhood of the Night without the skull helmets. The fourth man was bound between the others. His hands were tied behind his back and the three Nightbrothers held ropes tied around his neck.

"Nathan!" Wynd cried.

As Wynd cried the name, Faelin recognized Nathan. His face was muddy, and likely bruised underneath the mud, but it was Nathan. Wynd pushed through the Morigahnti crowded at the door. Korrin and Alerick grabbed hold of her.

"Wynd!" Parsh bellowed. "Stand down!"

She struggled against Korrin and Alerick for a few heartbeats and then relaxed.

The Nightbrothers made no attempt to come any closer. They just stood in the middle of the street, waiting.

"What do you make of this?" Charise asked.

"It may be a ruse to lull us," Parsh said.

"Perhaps," Sandré said. "This might be a distraction. Morigahnti, prepare for others. Get the Stormcrows in the air to see if we're being flanked."

Raze and Thyr flapped their wings and took to the sky. Two others from Charise's Fist flew, one out of a window, one out of a hole in the roof.

"What now, Your Highness?" Parsh asked.

Sandré glanced at the Morigahnti in the theater and scratched at the few hairs remaining on his head. Faelin recognized that look. He'd seen it years before when Sandré had driven a wedge between Faelin and the rest of the Traejyn family. That was the last time Faelin had seen his family. Sandré's gaze locked on Faelin, then glanced to Nathan and settled on Faelin once again.

"I will speak with them," Sandré replied, "and discover their purpose."

"I don't think that's a good idea, Your Highness," Parsh said.

"Your concern is noted, baron," Sandré said. Faelin swallowed at Sandré's slight smile, a smile he'd also seen before. "But they have one of my Morigahnti, and I mean to see him freed."

"Yes, Your Highness."

Faelin didn't bother to say anything. Sandré was in complete control until Julianna woke – if she woke.

Sandré walked into the street, and his Fist fell into ranks behind him. Several produced pistols and moved to flanking positions.

Sandré stopped about thirty feet from the Brothers. "What do you want?"

"An exchange," one of them said. "We will trade this prisoner for the minstrel, Faelin. He has offended our master."

Faelin didn't even bother to suppress a chuckle. Carmine D'Mario must be seething about his face. That took the sting off whatever Sandré had schemed up.

"Give us the Morigahnti," Sandré said, "and I will let you leave with your lives."

Faelin blinked and shut his mouth.

"We cannot accept those terms," the spokesman said.

"Lord Agostan." Sandré pointed to one of the Nightbrothers. "Kill him. Make it bloody."

Karstyn stepped forward, arms outstretched, and spoke *"Galadti'mina hoita hanen pansa."*

Though faint in the early morning light, Karstyn's shadow surged forward and wrapped around the Nightbrother's neck, closing and tightening. A few heartbeats later, the Nightbrother let out a deep, hearty laugh. Karstyn's shadow released the Nightbrother and slithered back to its master. Few things could resist the power of miracle. Fewer still would associate with the Brotherhood of the Night.

"Daemyn," Faelin whispered.

Were all six of the Nightbrothers Daemyns, or just that one?

"We were ordered not to fight the Morigahnti," the spokesman said. "But I was also ordered to bring the minstrel back to my master. I am able to defend myself against any who attack me, which my colleagues and I are hoping you'll do. It's been a long time since we've tasted human blood."

If it came to a fight, these Daemyns would slaughter the Morigahnti. They wouldn't care how much punishment the Morigahnti dealt upon their physical shells. Once the Daemyns finished with the Morigahnti, they could walk into the theater and take Julianna.

Faelin stepped between the Morigahnti and the Daemyn. "Take me and free your prisoner. I will go to Carmine."

"Faelin, no," Korrin said.

Faelin turned around. All the Morigahnti looked at him. All of them, even Sandré Collaen had paled.

"It is the only way. You cannot win a battle with these creatures."

"I'm glad at least one mortal has some sense," the spokesman said.

Faelin went to Nathan and removed the ropes from the Morigahnti's neck. Nathan's eyes pleaded an apology to Faelin. Gripping Nathan's shoulder, Faelin said nothing. He put the ropes around his own neck.

Without looking back, Faelin let the Daemyns lead him away.

TWO

Julianna's eyes snapped open. She was wet and shivering. A steady stream of what sounded like raindrops drummed on something above her. Beneath her, she felt a lumpy mattress. Every muscle in her body felt battered. She wanted to fall into the sleep of oblivion but forced herself to stay awake.

Sitting up, she found herself in a room that looked as if it had been deserted for years. Aurell stood by the door with a two-shot pistol raised and ready.

"What's going on?" Julianna croaked, her voice scratched as she spoke.

Without turning from the door, Aurell said, "We are in an abandoned theater Faelin used to store provisions he's been gathering for the last week. Our horses are dead. We were waiting for you to wake before we attempted to escape Johki. Now there is a squad of Nightbrothers outside."

Julianna pulled herself to her feet. Her body screamed in protest. Julianna stumbled on her first step, caught herself on the wall, took a breath, and steadied herself. Then her heart nearly leapt into her throat.

"My pack." Julianna wasn't sure if it was a statement or a question.

Aurell pointed with her free hand toward the corner, and Julianna saw her pack. She rushed over as quickly as she dared on her still unsteady legs. The *Galad'parma* was still safely inside. Julianna heaved a sigh of relief.

"Now," Julianna hoisted the pack onto her shoulders, "let's go and see about these Nightbrothers."

"Lord Morigahn," Aurell spoke with the same tone a parent used when trying to be patient with a child.

"Now," Julianna said.

Aurell nodded and headed out into the theater proper. Julianna followed close behind.

Bodies lay in a row down one side of the stage.

"Where are the horses?" Julianna asked.

"Only Sandré's Fist's horses made it out of Bastian's Inn," Aurell said. "The Reds attacked the rest, crippling all the horses that remained behind."

"Vendyr?" Julianna asked.

"Faelin put Vendyr down so the animal wouldn't suffer."

Julianna took several slow breaths. She only felt a small stab of sorrow in her breast. Mourning required energy, of which she had little, and she must expend that little on other matters. If they lost the horses, then they must have lost some of the Morigahnti in the fighting

"How many Morigahnti are gone?" Julianna asked.

"Nathan that you know," Aurell said. "Two of Viscountess Charise's Fist." She gestured to the bodies. "And those men who came from Sandré's riverboat."

"I'm sorry," Julianna said.

Aurell shrugged. "We are Morigahnti. Few of us die of old age."

That much, Julianna knew from reading the old stories, and the not so old. From the Tome of Shadows she'd read how the Morigahnti had continued to fight against the Kingdom. The battles were small and covert, but they happened all the same.

"Where are the Nightbrothers?" Julianna asked.

"Just outside the front," Aurell said.

Julianna didn't hear any fighting. She didn't know whether to consider that a good or a bad sign. A few of the Morigahnti she recognized from Charise's Fist came in.

"What's going on?" Julianna asked.

Charise came back into the theater a moment later and came up to Julianna.

"We had to let them take him," Charise said. "Please believe me. We couldn't do anything."

"Let them take who?" Julianna asked.

Charise opened her mouth, but instead of speaking, she closed her mouth and looked away.

Julianna understood immediately. "Faelin."

She rushed for the door.

"Stop her," Aurell said.

Charise jumped in Julianna's way. Julianna spun around her, though this slowed her just enough for Aurell to catch up. Aurell grabbed one arm, Charise the other. They nearly pushed Julianna to the floor to keep her from rushing outside.

"You don't understand," Charise said. "The Brotherhood sent a squad of Daemyn-possessed Nightbrothers. They had Nathan prisoner. We exchanged Faelin for Nathan. If we didn't, they could have destroyed us. Six, Julianna. Six Daemyn-possessed Nightbrothers."

Julianna relaxed a bit. Charise and Aurell loosened their hold on her. The moment they did, she forced her way past them and made it to the door before stopping.

Wynd held Nathan tight, weeping as she cradled him.

The Squad of Nightbrothers led Faelin away down the street. Tears welled and threatened to spill down Julianna's face. She bit her cheek to staunch her emotion. It seemed Faelin had been right, that some would seek to use Faelin as a weapon against her.

As soon as the Nightbrothers led him out of sight, Julianna pulled her *Galad'fana* around her face, using the motion to dry her eyes. She stepped out into the street.

Parsh was the first to notice her.

"Lord Morigahn." The Morigahnti snapped to attention when Parsh spoke her name, with the exception of Wynd, Nathan, and Sandré. "Faelin gave himself willingly to keep the Daemyns from slaughtering us."

"Do you see that sacrifice done to protect me?" Julianna asked. She faced Sandré Collaen. "You shall not dare to shame yourselves to speak against Faelin's loyalty again. How many of you would do the same for me or your fellow Morigahnti." She paused, looked at Sandré, Parsh, and Charise in turn. "I charge you with creating a strategy for rescuing Faelin."

"But the Daemyns and Draqons," Parsh protested.

"Allifar would have already had his Fist moving at my command," Julianna snapped. Parsh reddened and opened his mouth, but Julianna raised a hand, cutting him off. She lowered her *Galad'fana*, stepped up to Parsh, and put a hand on his shoulder. "I understand you have a huge weight on your shoulders. Try to live up to the strength of your sword, Baron Thaedus, as I know you can." She stepped back and addressed all three captains again. "I want it done. I don't care how. Do it."

She stepped away, leaving them to determine their strategy, not actually expecting them to come up with something, especially with Parsh busy trying to curry favor with Sandré and Charise too terrified to stand up to the Prince. In truth, setting the captains to this task was a ruse so that Julianna had time to search the *Galad'parma* for something she'd remembered reading about the battle of Ykthae Wood. She remained outside, where the light was better.

After a few minutes of flipping through the pages, Julianna found what she was looking for and it would do nicely. It would serve her in battle, as well as serve to solidify her claim on being the Lord Morigahn. She considered several courses of action, weighed them, chose, and acted.

Ready, Julianna slapped the *Galad'parma* closed. The sudden movement made Aurell start.

"Lord Morigahn?" Aurell asked. "Is all well?"

"Nothing is well," Julianna replied, as she walked into the street a bit. She took a deep breath and yelled. "Captain Parshyval! Summon your Fist to me!"

Moments later, she heard footsteps on the cobbles behind her. She saw people looking out of windows up and down the street. Hopefully, she would live and not regret this ploy. Julianna turned. Parsh, Aurell, and Korrin stood with her. Raze perched on Korrin's shoulder. Wynd helped Nathan from where they'd sat against the theater wall and moved to join them. Thyr perched on a windowsill near them, head cocked at an angle as he watched Nathan. Julianna held up her hand.

"Go back and rest," Julianna said. "You can give the Brotherhood *kosto-ta* another time."

Nathan saluted and went back to his resting place.

Sandré and Charise also came to stand with Parsh and his Fist.

"What are you doing?" Sandré demanded.

"I need to know, right now, if you are with me," Julianna said to those gathered around her. She looked each in the eye, seeking any hesitation.

"We should do this inside," Sandré said. "Inside, away from prying eyes and waggling tongues."

"No. We do this here and now." She faced Parsh. "Yours is the first Fist to fight for me and beside me, the first to lose friends and family in defending me. Where do you stand?"

"We have all sworn to you, Lord Morigahn," Parsh said, though she noticed he paused and glanced over her shoulder before he added, "we are yours to command."

"Good," Julianna said. "We're going to rescue Faelin."

Parsh sucked in a deep breath, and let it out. "Yes, Lord Morigahn."

Sandré Collaen pushed his way between Korrin and Wynd. "No. You cannot do this. We cannot risk true Morigahnti for one bastard who refuses to join the true followers of Grandfather Shadow."

Julianna wrapped her *Galad'fana* around her head, covering her face, and turned to Sandré. "Hold your tongue. It is not your place to order me. I am the Lord Morigahn." Julianna spread her gaze to encompass all the Morigahnti. "I know some of you question my claim. The time for questions and split loyalties is over. Those of you who are true-blooded Komati and children of Grandfather Shadow, follow me. Those who wish to hide yourselves, depart, but leave your *Galad'fana*. You do not deserve the honor of wearing them."

Aurell, Wynd, and Korrin saluted. A moment later, Parsh straightened and saluted. Over by the theater, Nathan stood and saluted. Charise stepped forward, her Fist behind her, and they saluted. Prince Sandré Collaen lifted his *Galad'fana*, covering his face, stepped in line with the other captains, and saluted. His Fist followed his example. Julianna held his gaze for just a moment. His eyes never turned from her, nor did he blink. Covering his face so she could not read his intentions was a masterful ploy. Most would see that as a greater sign of his support, approaching her as a Morigahnti, but Julianna understood Sandré far more than she believed he would credit her. At least publicly he had given his support to her, and she would spend that coin for as much as it would buy her.

Julianna glanced over her shoulder.

"Korrin."

"Lord Morigahn?" Korrin stepped forward.

"Send your Stormcrow into the air. I want an accurate assessment of the Brotherhood: their numbers, location, and deployment."

Korrin saluted. He turned his head and whispered something to Raze who was sitting on his shoulder. The Stormcrow took flight.

"I am the Lord Morigahn!" she yelled. Her growing rage smothered any care she still had for stealth or subtlety. She refused to run and hide any longer. Grandfather Shadow wanted her to free Koma and unite his people. She couldn't do that with the Morigahnti alone. "We are Grandfather Shadow's first and most favored children. Not the Morigahnti. Not the nobility. All of the Komati. I have come to free you from the lies the Kingdom of the Sun has used to rule you. I am going to end the Brotherhood of the Night who attacked your town and murdered your friends and family as they did mine." She turned to Korrin. "Lead me to Faelin."

Korrin saluted and headed toward Bastian's Inn. Without looking to see who joined her, Julianna followed toward Carmine and Faelin. She prayed that Carmine took a long while in deciding what to do with Faelin.

THREE

Carmine waited on the porch. Sylvie stood next to him. They held hands, and he smiled despite the pain in his scarred cheeks. Finally, he was beginning to see the truth behind the First Adept's words. To struggle in life was the truest way to honor Old Uncle Night. The greater the struggles a man survived, the more times a man could ignore the Uncle tapping on his shoulder, the greater he was rewarded. Carmine D'Mario must truly be one of Old Uncle Night's favored children, for his wife, Yrgaeshkil, the Daemyn Mother, had come and taken Sylvie as her first known Adept. Together Carmine and Sylvie would stand at the forefront of a Kingdom of the Night unlike the world had ever known.

When he saw the three Daemyns hauling Faelin vara'Traejyn through the street, Carmine's mouth split into a wide grin. Pain flared as if the oil spilled across his face again. He reveled in the pain knowing that Faelin was going to know so much more agony.

"Well done," Carmine said. "Was the fourth able to infiltrate the Morigahnti?"

"Yes, Adept Carmine" Brynn said. "They never questioned the exchange."

Faelin's head snapped up. "The captured Morigahnti was a Daemyn?"

"That's right, boyo," one of the Daemyns said. It grabbed a fistful of his hair and gave his head a violent shake. "And you traded yourself for him."

"Enough," Carmine said. "Bring him inside."

Nae'Toran sat in a chair sipping a glass of blood. Jorgen leaned against the far wall bandaging his hand.

Carmine raised his finger.

"Calm yourself, Adept Carmine D'Mario," Nae'Toran said. "Your man gave me his blood in exchange for a portion of my name. Bargained almost as well as you did. You might consider him as an apprentice." The Daemyn raised his glass to Jorgen, then drained it in one large swallow. "You have brought me this Taekuri?"

"I have," Carmine answered, then he called back out the door. "Bring him."

The three Daemyn brought Faelin into the room. They threw him down at Nae'Toran's feet. Faelin sprawled on the floor. Nae'Toran reached out one taloned hand and lifted Faelin's chin. Faelin locked eyes with the Daemyn. Carmine saw no fear in his former friend. Most people would be wetting themselves by now.

Faelin snapped the ropes that bound him – the ropes split as easily as if they were nothing more than yarn – and grabbed Nae'Toran's wrist. The Daemyn gasped, and slashed its claws across the minstrel's throat, splashing blood across the room. Faelin let go, hands coming to his throat, trying to staunch the blood spilling down his chest. Nae'Toran backhanded Faelin on the side of the head, sending him flying through the door.

"You mortal idiot," Nae'Toran growled. "That is no Taekuri. His soul belongs to another, and because you brought me that *thing*, there are only two souls I will find interesting enough to settle your account. The heir to the Komati throne serves as a White Draqon. The one who can name him serves as a Vara. Find both in Koma City. Bring them to me or your soul is mine."

Carmine's throat became very dry, and he had trouble breathing. Still, he managed to croak out. "Will you give me the names?"

"No. I have given you more than I should have. You have one month."

Upon that, Nae'Toran vanished, leaving only smoke in his place.

Carmine turned his attention to Faelin. "What is he?"

From the echoes in the smoke, Nae'Toran's voice came as a whisper, "Something that was once human. You are lucky it is new to its power, or you would be dead."

Faelin lay on the porch, gasping for breath. His hands pressed against his neck trying to stanch the flowing blood. Carmine watched as the bastard bled to death.

Suddenly, Carmine's vision blurred. He was looking out through his Nightbat's eyes. Julianna was coming. A crowd of Morigahnti followed her.

"Night feast upon her soul," Carmine snarled.

Once again Julianna had robbed Carmine. Now he could not enjoy Faelin's lingering death.

"Brynn," Carmine said. "Give me your sword."

Brynn handed the weapon over. Carmine grasped the sword in both hands, blade pointed down. He stabbed through Faelin's chest, pinning him to the porch. After one violent shudder, Faelin was still, his eyes staring vacantly into the overcast sky. Carmine spat on the bastard, inflicting one final revenge.

"The Morigahnti are coming," Carmine called out. "We should depart. Brynn, get Jorgen and gather up the items holy to Old Uncle Night. Reds, get our new *recruits* and make sure they don't cause any problems. Daemyns, cover our escape. Only engage the enemy as they approach, and only long enough to ensure the rest of us can escape. I mean to be in Koma City within the week."

He had one month. It was a week to Koma City under favorable conditions. He could shave off a few days if he didn't worry about killing the horses. Once in the city, the search would be difficult. If anyone else from the Kingdom learned of a Komati heir and a younger sibling, both would be quietly assassinated. While that wouldn't make the task Nae'Toran set him impossible, Carmine would have to discover who was next in the Komati order of precedence, which would be very difficult in less than a month.

"What of Colette?" Sylvie asked.

"Leave her," Carmine said. "She's served her purpose."

They went to the back door through the kitchen. A fire still burned in the hearth, left there at Carmine's orders. A dozen torches were propped up next to it.

"Take those torches," he said to the Daemyns. "Set fire to the building as soon as you see the Morigahnti, and every building we pass until they are spent."

Julianna and her Morigahnti would have a difficult time tracking him through a burning town. It would be too much to hope that the fires would blaze out of control and take them also. There had been too much rain the night before.

Sylvie laced her arm in his, stood on her tiptoes, and kissed his cheek.

"What?" Carmine asked.

"I feel more alive and in control of my life than ever before," Sylvie said. "If not for you, I would only be dreaming of marrying as best I could and providing my fat, sweaty husband with sons. Now we are preparing to rule an empire."

"If I can find the Komati heirs," Carmine said.

"We'll find them," Sylvie said. "They will die, and we will gain the favor of the First Adept of Night."

Carmine nodded. As they hurried to where they had hidden the horses, she laid her head on his shoulder. Having danced back to solid footing, Carmine smiled, reminding himself again that the Uncle favored him enough to keep testing him. He recalled one little piece of his bargain with Nae'Toran. If he couldn't manage to find the heirs, Carmine might have to exploit the weakness in the Daemyn's bargaining sooner than he'd planned.

FOUR

Faelin floated in a sea of warm darkness. He'd never been so at peace, until sounds of fear and panic pierced his peace. He tried to shut them out, fought to ignore them. He wanted to stay here, free from all the pain and suffering he'd ever known.

"You are needed, Faelin vara'Traejyn," a voice rumbled throughout the void.

Faelin's eyes snapped open, and daylight momentarily blinded him. He lay on a hard surface. The crisp air had that right after the rain smell. He tried to breathe but only managed a bloody wheeze. A dull ache throbbed in his chest. He tried to roll over, but the ache turned into a searing pain, cutting against his ribs. Instead of screaming, blood erupted from his mouth.

Slowly, his sight returned. Lifting his head made him want to vomit, but he managed to control the urge and looked down. A sword protruded from his chest. His head dropped back to the hard floor beneath. He grunted, and pinpoints of light flashed before his eyes.

Gritting his teeth, Faelin reached up and grasped the sword. He couldn't reach the hilt, so he wrapped his hands around blade. His palm sliced open as he tightened his grip and pulled. The blade grated on two of his ribs and the pain flared beyond anything he could imagine. He nearly passed out again with the first tug. His grip slackened, and every part of him slumped to the floor.

He settled back to let the darkness overcome him. Sometimes you had to give up.

Before sweet oblivion washed over him, the voice spoke again. "Will you abandon Julianna to those who betrayed your family?"

"Never!" Faelin spoke in a strong, clear voice.

Faelin grabbed the sword again. Blocking the pain, he pulled the blade free.

FIVE

Julianna stood in the smoking ruins of Bastian's Inn. The last remnants of the rain she'd summoned the night before hissed and popped as drops of water fell out of the sky. Parsh stood to Julianna's right, with Aurell, Charise, and Sandré right behind her.

She looked at the house where the Brotherhood had been hiding and watching her for at least a few days. More smoke rose from behind the house, and Julianna believed she saw the occasional flame flicking up. It was as if the inn had only been a prophecy of the fate waiting to befall Johki City, or at least this part of it. People crowded the streets, some panicking and some setting up water brigades. The crowd that had followed her had dispersed to help contain the flames. Stormcrows circled above, flying through the smoke. Those that had come with Charise's Morigahnti had joined Raze in scouting the Nightbrothers' positions.

"Why?" Julianna asked.

Alerick jogged up to her and saluted. The young man looked so much like his father, tall with a proud bearing.

"My Stormcrow reports that a few Nightbrothers remain in that house," Alerick said. "They're at the upper windows armed with crossbows trained on the street below. A man with a burned face wearing House Floraen colors is several blocks away, leading a band of five Red Draqons, two Nightbrothers, two Vara, and the innkeeper's daughter."

"Tarshiva?" Julianna asked. "What is she doing with Nightbrothers?"

"I cannot say, Lord Morigahn," Alerick replied. "The flames are worse than they look from here. The Nightbrothers are setting fire to every building they pass. Citizens are fighting the flames on every side, and to the west a group of Aernacht Adepts and one Inquisitor are helping to quench the fires."

"The Brotherhood means to keep us from following," Sandré said.

Julianna wanted to blame herself for the destruction and the innkeeper's death, but she could not completely bring herself to accept responsibility for the Brotherhood of the Night. As with so many centuries upon centuries before, when Kaeldyr the Gray went in search of aid against an outside threat, followers of All Father Sun and Old Uncle Night brought chaos and strife to Koma.

"It will gain Carmine D'Mario only a temporary reprieve from my vengeance," Julianna said. "Where is Faelin?"

"We must leave now." Sandré confronted Julianna directly. "You've caused enough damage with your little temper tantrum and public confession. Now you've given the Kingdom cause to hunt us in earnest instead of focusing on its other conquered territories."

"Let the Kingdom come for me with their Inquisitors and Draqons," Julianna snapped. "My god is free, while their gods wallow in the King of Order's prison." Sandré blinked in confusion, and before he could press the matter, Julianna turned to Korrin. "Where is Faelin?"

"Faelin is on the front porch," Alerick pointed to the Nightbrothers' house. "He's covered in blood, but moving."

"We need to move now," Julianna said. "If he's still alive, we can save him."

"Lord Morigahn!" Sandré stepped in front of her. The left side of his face twitched. "You cannot risk Morigahnti lives to rescue that *bastard*." He said the word as a curse.

Julianna sucked in a deep breath. Her jaw clenched so tight her teeth hurt. When she spoke her teeth did not separate. "You will move out of my way, *Prince*." She used the same infliction for his title that he had used for Faelin. When it looked like Sandré wasn't going to step aside, she added, "Or I will move you."

Sandré placed his hand on the hilt of his rapier. "You caught me by surprise once. It will not hap…"

Julianna cut Sandré off by hitting him with the *Galad'parma* square on the side of the head. The blow sent him sprawling. She took two steps and put her foot down on his throat. Sandré's Fist stepped forward, hands on their weapons.

"Morigahnti, stand down!" Julianna's voice sounded strange to her own ears.

The Morigahnti glanced at each other as if looking for someone to tell them who to side with.

Julianna looked down at Sandré. His eyes bulged wide, seeming ready to pop from their sockets. He gasped for what little breath Julianna allowed him. She fought the urge to crush his throat under her heel. Smoke's words came back to her, "Murder is only an easy way to exchange one problem for another." How many more problems would she bring upon herself if she killed – no, not killed, this would be murder – murdered a prince of House Aesin? She took a deep breath to steady herself and her anger.

"I am going to rescue my friend," Julianna said. "And I'm going to kill anyone who gets in my way." She put more of her weight down. "Do you understand me, Prince Sandré Collaen of House Aesin?"

Sandré nodded as best he could. Julianna removed her foot from his throat. He started to rise, but she pushed him back down again with her foot on his shoulder.

"Stay. Right. There. If you can manage that, I won't strip you of your *Galad'fana*. If you can't... Lord Agostan."

"Lord Morigahn," Karstyn said.

"Give me your gun." Julianna held out her hand and glanced to the two-shot pistol he had shoved into his sword belt. Karstyn opened his mouth, and for a moment, it looked as if he was going to resist her. Julianna slowly shook her head from side to side. "Now, Lord Agostan. We don't have time for this."

Karstyn handed the weapon over. Julianna gave it to Aurell.

"I have a firearm, Lord Morigahn," Aurell said.

"I know," Julianna said, not taking her gaze off Karstyn. "This is not about who has a weapon, this is about obeying. If his Highness cannot follow my last order," Julianna said, "as simple as it is...shoot him."

"Yes, Lord Morigahn." Aurell pointed the gun right at Sandré.

Julianna turned to face the Morigahnti. "Sandré's Fist will precede me. Charise, your Fist will move out to protect against any flanking Nightbrothers the Stormcrows might have missed because they are hidden by miracle. Parsh, you and Alerick are my guard. Korrin, return to the theater to help protect your brother and sister in case the Nightbrothers or Kingdom attacks there. Are my orders clear?"

"Yes, Lord Morigahn!" came a chorus of replies.

"Morigahnti," Julianna said, "what is the sixth law?"

"Cowards take prisoners," the Morigahnti recited. "Morigahnti do not. Morigahnti are born to fight and conquer. Killing is not too good for your enemies."

"I expect nothing less today. Let's make this swift and clean."

The Morigahnti snapped to attention and saluted. Sandré's Fist moved through the wreckage of Bastian's Inn. Charise's Fist moved to the flanks. The Morigahnti moved with precision, alternating fluidly between moving and covering each other.

These were the true chosen of Grandfather Shadow. How she was ever going to fall into step with them she did not know. Would it ever feel natural for her?

You were born into it, Grandfather Shadow's voice whispered in her mind. *Do you think I would raise just anyone to be my Lord Morigahn? You are more suited to bear the mark than anyone alive.*

"Lord Morigahn?" Parsh asked.

"I'm ready."

She opened the Tome of Shadows and followed her Morigahnti into battle. Carrying the book cradled with one arm out in front of her was awkward, but necessary. She had to have it open to the proper page if she was going to make any difference. Though she couldn't cast miracles through herself using the *Galad'fana*, the Lord Morigahn possessed certain abilities granted by Grandfather Shadow. It was time to start using them.

When she was most of the way through Bastian's Inn, Julianna stopped. Sandré's Fist was trading crossbow and pistol fire with the Nightbrothers across the street. Two of her Morigahnti had received minor wounds.

Looking across the street, Julianna saw Faelin on the porch struggling to get to his feet. Even from that distance, she saw him soaked with blood.

The Morigahnti weren't gaining ground fast enough. She had to inspire their courage.

"Alerick, give me your hand," Julianna said.

Alerick offered his left hand. She took his hand in hers. Alerick had strong hands, with the calluses and blisters of someone used to swordplay and hours upon horseback. She placed both their hands upon the *Galad'parma* and kept her hand on top of his.

"Morigahnti, down!" Julianna called.

When all the Morigahnti dropped to the ground, she placed her hand on the open page and called forth Grandfather Shadow's divine power, only she didn't pull it through her own body but focused it through the *Galad'parma*.

Heedless of the weaponry flying back and forth across the street, Julianna started toward Faelin at a steady pace, and spoke. "*Thanya'haeth suojata aen Morigahnti!*" Alerick echoed her words.

She waited for the exhaustion of speaking the miracle to crash down upon her, perhaps even sending her back into unconsciousness. Instead, next to her, Alerick gasped and stumbled a bit, but Julianna kept his hand firmly pressed to the book she carried. If his hand slid away, the miracle would fail.

A moment later, a wind swirled in front of her. It didn't feel very strong, but she put herself in Grandfather Shadow's hands.

She stepped into the street, and a rain of bolts flew at her. Julianna flinched, but the bolts scattered off course, blown harmlessly away. After taking a few more steps, another hail of bolts flew at her. The winds buffeted them aside as well.

As she continued forward, the Morigahnti fell in behind her. Even with the wind protecting her, she couldn't rush to Faelin. If she moved too quickly, the winds would dissipate. There was a limit to how much change even wind could endure before blowing itself to stillness.

Across the street, Faelin made it to his feet. He looked tired, as if he'd been beaten or tortured for hours. Still, he looked grateful as he stumbled into the street. When he was halfway to her, Faelin looked up, seemingly into the sky and glanced from side to side.

"No!" Faelin yelled.

Pain speared through Julianna's left shoulder as something hit her, knocking her to her knees. A warm fountain poured from her shoulder, soaking the back of her dress. The Tome of Shadows fell from her hands, and the shield of wind blew itself out.

Someone crashed into her, forcing her down. As she fell, her palms tore as they scraped across the cobblestones, but the *Galad'parma* saved her face and chest. Whoever knocked her down stayed on top of her. It was a man. She knew because she felt a man's muscular chest instead of breasts. Several impacts hit his body and then he went limp.

Voices around her screamed in *Galad'laman*, but the words jumbled together. Her *Galad'fana* hummed as divine power surged all around her. Three miracles spoken so close Julianna could almost taste their Dominions flowed past her.

Time lost meaning.

SIX

Nathan sat back against the wall. The Daemyn had another name, the one he used while in the Realm of the Godless Dead, but he rather liked using Nathan's name just as much as he liked using the Morigahnti's body.

Carmine had given Nathan pure freedom. His orders were quite specific. "Infiltrate them and learn all you can about them. Then return." The Adept gave no time frame for Nathan to return with any of the gathered intelligence, nor did the Adept indicate how Nathan was to gather this intelligence. He would torture information out of these pathetic excuses for Morigahnti, well, the male ones anyway; the females would give Nathan everything he wanted to know while begging him to love them. It had been such a long, long time since Nathan had been free to walk the world, and he'd never been able to with such impunity. Night Adepts did not bargain with the same skill that they had when *Ahk Tzizma'Uthra* walked free; those were days when mortals trembled at the whispered mention of the Brotherhood of the Night.

Nathan sifted through his host's memories of all the times his wife Wynd had shared her body with him. Oh, she was a talented little thing, wild and passionate. He couldn't wait to see what happened after he trained her, imagined using Wynd to sire a gaggle of half-Daemyn children and teach them to wreak havoc on the physical realm. For that matter, Nathan didn't plan on limiting his lust and procreation to just Wynd. He would plant his seed in any woman who would lie down and spread her legs. Granted, he wasn't as well practiced in the art of seduction as his master Nae'Toran, but Nathan was a Daemyn and seducing the mortal soul was a talent they all had.

A boy of ten or eleven winters entered the room. No matter how much Wynd and Nathan had protested, the boy who was not a boy would wear nothing but the rags he had on now, and no amount of grooming could satisfy Wynd's fixation on straightening the boy's unruly mass of black hair. Nathan smiled. The boy smiled back at him. The Stormcrow had been the one part of this infiltration that made Nathan nervous, but here he was coming toward Nathan with arms open, fooled as everyone else had been. It wouldn't last. The bond between the Morigahnti and their Faerii kin companions was too strong for Nathan to fool the boy for long. The boy would have to go, and go soon. Now was a perfect time.

Kneeling down as this body had hundreds of times before when Thyr the Stormcrow had come at him, Nathan also held his arms out. Thyr ran to Nathan and launched himself into the air, slamming into Nathan's embrace. Nathan shifted at the last moment, catching Thyr's neck, rather than his torso.

As if sensing the danger, Thyr began transforming into his bird form. Nathan grinned, having anticipated this reaction. Had Thyr been a Stormseeker instead of a Stormcrow, the transformation would have been nearly instantaneous, but as it was, the change took several seconds, seconds that allowed Nathan to get one hand around Thyr's neck and the other hand around Thyr's head. The Stormcrow's neck made such a pleasant popping sound as Nathan twisted the head one way and the body the other. He was just about to twist the other way – not to ensure the Stormcrow was dead, as he went completely limp in the Daemyn's grip, but because Na-than just liked the sound of it – when he heard footsteps come into the room.

"What is going on here?"

Nathan's mortal memory recognized his wife's voice.

Perfect.

"Hello my love," Nathan said. "Won't you tell me a secret?"

SEVEN

Wynd watched, stunned as Nathan dropped Thyr's body to the floor and turned to face her.

"Damn," Wynd muttered when she saw his eyes.

Whoever or whatever it was looking at her through Nathan's eyes, it wasn't her husband. Between the two brothers, everyone always thought Nathan was harder than Korrin. People said Nathan's gaze could break steel. Wynd knew what they saw. She had seen that same look fixed on countless men, but never on her. His hardness always softened with love whenever his eyes fell on her. The eyes looking at her now held neither hardness nor tenderness. They held desire, pure and uncaring lust.

"Wynd, is everything well?" Korrin asked from just outside the theater.

"Get out of my husband's body," Wynd said.

"But Wyndolen, my love. It's me."

Damn, but she almost believed him. She wanted to believe him. In Grandfather Shadow's name, she *needed* to believe him. But she couldn't. Those eyes weren't Nathan's, and only one creature could ever make her believe otherwise, even for a moment.

Daemyn.

"No," she said. "You're not my husband."

As soon as the words left her mouth, she felt the creature's power over her fade. The haze shrouding her mind was still there, though not as strong.

"Well, I guess that puts an end to our marriage," it said. "I don't want to fight. Do yourselves a favor and just let me leave."

"No," Korrin said, as he rushed into the theater. "You will free my brother's body."

"No, Morigahnti. You will let me pass."

"A Morigahnti does not run from his battles," she said, and thought of Count Allifar.

Count Allifar had sacrificed himself because he believed Julianna was the Lord Morigahn. This Daemyn was a threat to the Lord Morigahn, and though Wynd wouldn't survive, perhaps she could weaken it so that the other Morigahnti could destroy its shell and send the damn thing back the Realm of the Godless Dead.

Korrin made a motion of drawing a blade from a sheath with both hands. Wynd tried to keep her face smooth, but felt her lips curling into a smirk as she realized what Korrin meant.

Korrin called, "If you are afraid to die, you are already dead!"

This drew the Daemyn's attention away from her.

She met her brother-in-law's eyes and smiled. As one, they pulled their *Galad'fanati* across their faces and drew their rapiers. Raze landed on Korrin's shoulder and lightning crackled around his beak.

"You can't be serious," the Daemyn said, shifting his head from side to side, trying to keep them both in view. "You have no hope of survival, much less victory."

"*Kostota*," Wynd said.

"*Kostota*," Korrin echoed, his eyes dancing with mischief.

As she lunged forward, she remembered Allifar's last words.

"The strength of my sword!" She screamed the battle cry of the family she'd served her whole life.

Korrin followed with, "Thaedus! Thaedus!"

The Daemyn first turned its attention to Wynd, just as she'd hoped. She may have lunged first, but Korrin was faster and had the longer reach. She cut her movement short. The ruse worked. Expecting to meet the resistance of her attack, the Daemyn stumbled, off-balance.

Wynd leapt away, scrambling on the stage and heading for where she'd hidden the walking stick in the baggage.

"Not so eager," the Daemyn snarled.

Wynd heard a deep thud on the stage behind her and footsteps pounding toward her. Her hand closed on the walking stick. She spun around. The Daemyn was within striking distance.

Korrin rushed up behind the Daemyn, his sword drawn.

Wynd attacked with a wide, overhanded swing, bringing the stick down toward the Daemyn's head. The thing caught the stick in its left hand.

"Clumsy," the Daemyn said. "I remember you being better."

"And if you really were Nathan," Wynd said, "you'd be smarter."

The tip of Korrin's blade slid out of the Daemyn's chest. It looked down, blinking in surprise for a moment, then it grinned.

"Truly?" the Daemyn asked.

"Truly." Wynd pulled the sword free of the cane.

The Daemyn took in the weapon in Wynd's hand and scrambled backward, colliding with Korrin, slowing his escape.

Wynd lunged, her arm fully extended. The Daemyn caught the Faerii steel weapon with the palm of its hand. It howled as the thin blade caught on the bone in its palm. Wynd had expected to slide the blade easily into her enemy, but the impact jarred the weapon from her grip and she tumbled off-balance. The Daemyn stepped forward, pulling her into his embrace with its free hand. The tip of Korrin's sword protruded only three fingers away from her face.

While trapping her in its iron grip, the Daemyn pulled the Faerii steel sword out of its hand with its mouth. She had never been squeamish, but hearing the creature's teeth grinding on the metal and the squelching *pop* as it came free of its bone sent waves of nausea rolling through her stomach.

Spitting the sword to the floor and still clutching Wynd's head, the Daemyn spun on one foot, kicking out with the other. It caught Korrin in the hip. His hip twisted with a sickening crunch while his torso did not move. Korrin grunted as he collapsed and, even as he hit the stage floor, began to claw his way away from the Daemyn.

The Daemyn steadied itself and stepped toward Korrin's head. Before it could kick again, Raze was there, flapping in its face. Lighting flashed from the Stormcrow's beak and talons, scorching the fiend's face. It tried to swat the bird away, but Raze surrounded himself with lightning. Each time the Daemyn tried to strike, its arm sizzled and burned, leaving Raze free for the moment. But the Stormcrow couldn't keep at it for long. Using that much of his energy would take its toll soon.

"Raze, move," Korrin yelled.

Heeding Korrin, Raze dropped toward the floor, shifting from his bird form to his human form. When he landed, Raze looked like a boy between eight and ten winters. He crawled to Wynd's discarded weapon and picked it up.

Wynd kicked and clawed at the Daemyn as it turned to chase Raze, and Wynd heard a squishy thud just above her right ear. The Daemyn screamed, and its grip loosened just enough for Wynd to squirm free. Scrambling away, she saw one of Korrin's throwing knives embedded in its eye.

The Daemyn pulled the blade free with one hand and reached for Wynd with the other. Raze dashed forward and thrust the Faerii steel blade through the back of the Daemyn's knee. The creature howled in pain, making Wynd's skin tingle from the eerie sound of it.

"We can't fight in here," Raze said, as he pulled the sword from the Daemyn's leg and sent the weapon sliding to Wynd. "And you need to stay out of its reach."

Raze ran to the edge of the stage and dove off it. Midway between the stage and floor, he shifted into his bird form and took to the rafters.

The Daemyn faced her as she lifted Korrin's sword in a mock salute. "Don't stay away from me, my love."

Raze was right. They needed to take the fight out of here, or the damn thing was going to pummel them into pulp one by one. She sent a silent prayer to Grandfather Shadow that there weren't any innocents in the street outside. Wynd focused her faith through her *Galad'jana*, drew on the Dominion of Storms, pushed her palms toward the theater's outer wall, and spoke, "*Kraeston kansa aen thanya'haeth!*"

It was the strongest miracle she knew and speaking it took its toll on her body, but it was a calculated necessity that worked better than she could have hoped.

The Daemyn was between her and the wall, but she never expected the miracle to affect him. She intended to blow out the wall, allowing for her and Raze to lead the fiend away from Korrin. The center of the wall blew outward, just as she'd hoped, and despite all she'd ever heard about miracles not affecting Daemyns and Aengyls, the creature wearing Nathan's skin was blown, first against the theater wall and then into the street beyond, as the wind blew the wall outward. Rubble fell upon the Daemyn, and the creature lay unmoving.

Wynd rushed toward the Daemyn, hoping that she could get to it and thrust the Faerii steel blade through its head before it recovered.

When Wynd was still ten paces from it, the Daemyn flung rubble away and stood, glaring hatred and rage at her. Wynd felt ice along her spine and in her stomach. Until now, the Daemyn seemed to treat everything, even its injuries from the Faerii steel, as though it were a damn game. But Wynd had changed the rules. She had discovered something that might let her win this fight after all. She just had to choose her miracles carefully so she didn't fall from exhaustion before the Daemyn died.

She pointed at the Daemyn's foot. Let it chase her after she removed its ability to walk.

"*Tuska!*" she cried.

Her fatigue grew as the bolt of dark energy flew from her finger, hitting the Daemyn's leg.

Nothing happened.

"Damn," she said, "and bloody damn."

She didn't have time to wonder why it didn't work. The Daemyn charged.

Raze jumped up and shifted back into his bird form. Lightning crackled all around him as he collided with the Daemyn. Most of the hair on Nathan's head burned away, and some of the flesh charred. The Daemyn grabbed Raze out of the air. Despite its smoldering hand, the fiend snapped one of Raze's wings. The Stormcrow shrieked in pain and thrust his beak into the Daemyn's hand. Giving a shriek of its own, the creature threw Raze away. He landed a few feet away from Korrin, who had stopped writhing and was now inching toward the back of the room.

"*Galad pita han viela Daemyn!*" Wynd yelled, trying for a less taxing miracle. But she grew even more tired, and her throat burned.

All the shadows in the house and those cast from other buildings in the street reached out for the Daemyn, but none of them could hold him. They all slid past him as if he were nothing more than a shadow to them. She'd just wasted even more energy on another failed miracle and didn't have the energy to speak any more.

The Daemyn surged forward faster than she imagined possible. It grabbed her sword arm and wrenched it at an angle it was never meant to turn. Wynd screamed as bones pulled free of their sockets and muscles tore. As the sword fell from her grasp, Wynd counted her blessings that it hadn't ripped her arm off completely. She held no doubt that it could have done so if that was its desire. But now she couldn't concentrate through the pain in order to speak a miracle even if she might think of one that would affect it.

"Confused, my pretty wife?" the Daemyn said as it pulled her *Galad'fana* from her head.

"You're not my husband," Wynd muttered.

Its fingers sizzled where he touched the divine object. In that moment, Wynd knew one way they might win this fight. But before she could say anything about it, the Daemyn let go of the veil and hit her in the face.

"Oh, I'm your husband," it said, hitting her again. "And we'll make many happy babies together."

"Let her go," someone said, a man's voice, from the street.

Both Wynd and the Daemyn looked to see who spoke. The Inquisitor Wynd thought she and Aurell had killed the night before stood in the street. Soot streaked his breastplate and cloak.

"Oh, this is funny," Wynd said.

The Daemyn laughed and threw Wynd aside as if it was a child discarding an unwanted toy.

EIGHT

"Lord Morigahn," someone said in Julianna's ear, "this is going to hurt."

Without any more warning than that, whatever was lodged in her shoulder was pulled out. Her mind reeled as her nerves shrieked. She cried out. Someone spoke next to her, but the words sounded far away, like an echo called from one mountain to another. "*Galad'Ysoysa tsenki kin ystae li sinan Morigahn'uljas.*"

Then the pain was gone. Blood still soaked her clothes. Julianna pushed herself to her knees. Morigahnti surrounded her. Some sat chanting in *Galad'laman*, recreating her shield of wind. Others stood facing outward, weapons drawn.

Parsh and Charise came into the circle. The two captains saluted. Julianna nodded back.

"Lord Morigahn, we must withdraw," Parsh said.

"Do we have Faelin?"

"I'm here," Faelin said. "And we have a problem, two actually, but one is more immediate."

"More than what we're facing here?" she asked.

"Nathan is dead," Faelin replied. "A Daemyn lives in his body now."

"Impossible," Aurell said. "Thyr accepted him. Nathan's Stormcrow would have sensed the Daemyn."

"Not right away," Faelin retorted. "Daemyns are the creatures of Old Uncle Night, the God of Lies. By the celestial treaty, only Aengyls and the lesser and Greater Gods can use mystical or divine means to pierce the lies spoken and illusions cast by any creature from the Realm of the Godless Dead. All others must rely on logic and knowledge to protect themselves."

"How did you learn this?" Julianna asked.

"Carmine told me. He thought I was dying," Faelin said.

Julianna's heart sank as she realized she had likely sent Korrin and Wynd to their deaths. Her throat closed, catching her breath. She blinked several times and shook her head. Her body twitched and seemed to freeze up. She would *not* be paralyzed by fear. Taking hold of herself, she scooped up the Tome of Shadows and started for the theater.

While she couldn't save them herself, she had three Fists of Morigahnti at her command. Remembering the first night the Morigahnti had fought for her, Julianna yelled Allifar's cry, "To arms, to arms! Morigahnti to arms!"

She didn't look back to see if they followed. She only clutched the *Galad'parma* close to her chest so she wouldn't lose it. Even if the Morigahnti did follow her, she might be the only one of them with the means to fight a Daemyn.

NINE

Despite his earlier injury, which seemed completely healed almost the moment he had pulled the sword out of his chest, Faelin overtook Julianna and the Morigahnti. And though he ran at his full speed, he did not tire. He felt as fresh as if each step were his first in this race to Korrin and Wynd. It was one more piece of the strange puzzle that had begun when he had first found Julianna. Grandfather Shadow had gifted him. That much was obvious. But how great was the gift? Faelin pushed these concerns away for later. Korrin and Wynd were most important right now.

Turning a corner, Faelin expected to see the abandoned theater. Instead, he looked upon the ruins of Bastian's Inn.

What was going on? He spun in circles, trying to determine where he was and what wrong turn he'd made. Crushing the urge to blindly act, Faelin sat in the street. He ignored the looks he got from the people rushing about in the aftermath of the fire and the battle with the Brotherhood. Using a technique he'd learned from the Taekuri, he imagined a fire with a low wall encircling it. The wall cast a shadow across his mind, smothering all his thoughts and feelings until his mind was still. Somewhere in that shadow was a memory that held the answer. Moment by moment, he shed the light on everything that had happened to him, starting from sitting down and working his way back.

As soon as he saw it, Faelin knew when it had happened. He had touched Nathan as he traded himself for the Daemyn. In that moment, the Daemyn had done something to Faelin. Now, his only way to help Julianna was to think through the effect.

Faelin knew that he was Julianna's only hope for surviving an encounter with the Daemyn inhabiting Nathan, but he couldn't get to her unless he could outwit the Daemyn's enchantment.

TEN

Luciano Salvatore saw his sword not even two paces behind the Daemyn, just out of reach of one of the Morigahnti women who had shot him the night before. He recognized her dark eyes and the way her hair poked out of her *Galad'fana* just above her ears. That meant his Detector might lie somewhere close by. Now, he had to get past this Daemyn, get his sword, kill the Daemyn, and then get the Morigahnti girl to give the Detector over before any other Morigahnti arrived. All Father Sun had blessed Luciano many times during his years as an Inquisitor, but he was not so proud to believe that his god favored him that much.

"I've never killed an Inquisitor," the Daemyn-possessed man said.

Luciano gripped his sun pendant tightly in his right hand to reassure himself that he acted as All Father Sun's agent against the darkness.

"And you won't today." Luciano had no illusions he would die an old man in his bed. Inquisitors rarely did, but this would not be the day he died.

In all his years as an Inquisitor, Luciano had dealt with a Daemyn possessing a human body only once. However, Luciano could live a hundred lifetimes and he would never forget that encounter.

The Daemyn leapt for him, arms outstretched. Even though he was male, and the Daemyn inhabited a male body, its touch could be just as seductive to Luciano as it would have been had either of them been female. Such was the nature of Daemyns.

Luciano spun, dodging the Daemyn's attempt to grapple him, coming to face the Daemyn as it stumbled through the space where Luciano had just been. He let his sun pendant fall from his hand, and still gripping the chain, Luciano lashed out at the Daemyn with the divine focus. Many people other than House Floraen Adepts and Inquisitors scoffed at the size of the sun pendants, calling the symbol of Floraen faith ostentatious. In truth, the sun pendants had been crafted during the Second War of the Gods to be a last-ditch weapon against otherworldly creatures who sought to sew chaos and strife in the physical world.

The flames pointing out from the sun pendant caught the Daemyn just between the shoulder blade and spine. Smoke and flame flared up from the wound.

The Daemyn howled. It kicked back at Luciano faster than he could have anticipated, striking him in the left side. The blow bent Luciano's breastplate inward and sent him sprawling in the street. Only having the chain of his sun pendant allowed Luciano to keep his hold on it. He coughed and wheezed, and pain shot through his entire left side. The creature had likely broken two or three bones.

Pushing his mind and body past the pain, Luciano rolled to the side just in time to avoid the Daemyn's pounce. He came to his knees right next to his Faerii steel blade, swinging the sun pendant in two wide arcs. The Daemyn skidded to a stop on the wet cobblestones and lurched backward. Luciano smiled and snatched up the Faerii blade in his left hand. He would have preferred to have each weapon in the opposite hand, but a man did not quibble the details when All Father Sun sent his blessing.

"You think those will help you against me?" the Daemyn asked.

"You don't seem so eager to attack," Luciano replied.

Oh, Lord of Light, he thought, *my side hurts.*

He dared not take his eyes off the Daemyn for even an instant to check the injury. Snarling, the Daemyn began circling, searching Luciano up and down, likely looking for some other weakness to exploit. Luciano kept the Faerii steel blade raised toward the Daemyn and swung his sun pendant at his side to keep it moving and ready to strike.

Movement over the Daemyn's shoulder caught his eye. A lone woman rounded the corner of the next street down. Even at this distance, Luciano could make out the woman who called herself the Lord Morigahn.

In that brief moment of distraction, the Daemyn dashed forward. It grabbed Luciano's sword arm in one hand and his breastplate in the other and lifted him off the ground. Luciano tried to attack the Daemyn with the sun pendant but didn't have the leverage to use it effectively. He managed to strike it just once before the creature slammed him against the ground.

At the same time as air burst from his lungs on the impact, Luciano felt his left forearm snap as the Daemyn wrenched it. Even his concentration wasn't enough to keep hold of the Faerii steel sword. It slipped from his numbing fingers and clattered to the cobblestones.

Luciano wanted to cry out but didn't have enough air. He just coughed again. This time he felt something wet and frothy spill over his lips. He prayed those Aernacht Adepts had gotten the fires under control and were coming to aid him.

The Daemyn dragged Luciano a few feet to where the Morigahnti girl lay. It grabbed her hair with its free hand and pulled her to her knees.

"I should take her right here in front of you, Inquisitor," the Daemyn said, "while you are helpless to stop me."

"You are doomed," the Morigahnti girl said. "She comes for you."

The Daemyn turned and let go of both its captives. Luciano managed to turn his head in time to see the Lord Morigahn throw something at the Daemyn.

ELEVEN

Julianna rounded the corner leading to the theater. Faelin was nowhere in sight. He had outdistanced her early in their flight and should have been here already.

Part of the theater's front wall was missing, debris scattered about the street.

Nathan stood in the middle of the street, holding Wynd by a fistful of hair in one hand and the House Floraen Inquisitor by the arm in the other. Injuries covered the Daemyn, but blood didn't pour from any of them as it should have, especially from its eye and throat. At the theater, Korrin braced himself against the wall, his left leg hanging limp. Raze hopped in bird form between Korrin and the Daemyn, screaming at the infernal creature. Lightning crackled around the Stormcrow's beak and talons. One of Raze's wings hung as limp and useless Korrin's leg.

Julianna glanced over her shoulder. She saw an empty street. None of the Morigahnti who had followed her were there. She didn't have time to consider this. She had a Daemyn to kill.

Julianna charged and heaved the massive book at the Daemyn.

The thing in Nathan's body spun with preternatural speed and flung Wynd and the Inquisitor away. Both collapsed as if they were sacks of grain. It grabbed the *Galad'parma* out of the air, and its hands started smoking. It flung the book away, and its pained snarl turned into an amused chuckle.

"Come to me, Lord Morigahn." The Daemyn took a step toward her, eyes full of lust and desire. "Come wrap your legs around me."

Julianna backed away and drew her mother's dagger. Nathan's mangled face tightened as he stopped short.

"I've used this to kill Daemyn hounds," Julianna said. "I'll happily add you to my tally."

"You think to best me with that tiny weapon?" the Daemyn asked, weaving back and forth.

Julianna did her best to keep the point of her dagger between her and the Daemyn.

"No," she replied. She only needed to stall a few moments longer. "I have so many more weapons than this."

"Tell me," the Daemyn said, lunging at her, testing her speed and reaction. "What other weapon do you have besides your Faerii steel blade?"

"Her Morigahnti," Wynd said.

Wynd had crept up and lifted the *Galad'parma* from where it had fallen. The Daemyn spun, but that only opened him up to Wynd's attack. The *Galad'parma* caught the creature full in the face.

The book connected with a sickening *crunch*. The Daemyn howled as its face crumpled with the impact. The cry embodied a tortured existence of burning fires and freezing winds. The sickly sweet stench of burning flesh arose, mixed with something that smelled like fermented vomit and spoiled entrails.

Julianna lunged at the Daemyn's back, but the thing moved with dizzying speed. It dove into Wynd, catching her middle with its shoulder, lifting her off her feet. The Daemyn spun, and flung her at Julianna.

Julianna tried to move, but Wynd slammed into her and they tumbled to the ground together. Both had lost their grip on their weapons in the impact. Wynd gasped for breath and had a dazed, faraway expression that looked absolutely foolish on her normally stern face. Julianna tried to squirm out from underneath her, but they were too tangled together.

The Daemyn loomed above them. The Tome of Shadows had burned away the mortal flesh and revealed the creature's true nature. Its bat-like face was the color of dirty dishwater, and a black ram's horn protruded from the side of his head where the *Galad'parma* had struck it. Its eyes glowed a mix of black and orange, as if they were two embers in a dying fire. The Daemyn's thin lips pulled back in a feral snarl.

Julianna craned her neck, looking down each street and to the mouth of each alley nearby. She sent a prayer to Grandfather Shadow to send the other Morigahnti to help her fight this foul creature.

The thing wearing Nathan's skin chuckled. "Looking for someone?" It reached for Julianna. The *Galad'parma* had also burned the humanness away from its fingers, revealing sharp talons. "The Morigahnti will not come. They are trapped in a lie and will wander the streets this entire day and will never come even close to us. I will take you and my wife away. You will both bear me a dozen children and beg to give me more."

Its smoking digits grabbed Julianna's throat. With one hand, it yanked her out from underneath Wynd and lifted her off her feet and pulled her *Galad'fana* with its free hand. Its hand sizzled at the contact, and more smoke wafted from its flesh. Then it flung the *Galad'fana* away. The Daemyn wound its fingers through her hair and pulled her to within inches of its face. Julianna had to stand on the tips of her toes. The creature's face was only a hand's span away from hers.

"You are mine," the Daemyn whispered in her ear and gently kissed her cheek. "Tell me you are mine."

When the Daemyn's lips brushed her face, a wave of pleasure surged through her body. The pain from her hair was forgotten. She only wanted its lips to touch her again. She wanted to give herself over and couldn't understand why she'd fought so hard against it.

"I am—"

Pain seared her face, white-hot and cutting, as if Grandfather Shadow was slicing the knife down her face again.

"This behavior ill suits the Lord Morigahn," Grandfather Shadow's voice whispered all throughout the street.

Julianna wailed as the agony burned away her desire to lie with this soulless creature. Only the power of her god had freed her from the Daemyn's power. As the pain faded from her face, Julianna realized that mortals could not defeat the creature on their own. So knowing that it might mean her death, ignoring that she did not possess her *Galad'fana*, she opened herself to the power and blessing of Grandfather Shadow.

"*Galad'Ysoysa tuska kin Daemyn.*" Julianna snarled the miracle past the pain and shoved her finger into her enemy's eye.

The monster winced and laughed at the same time.

"Still striving for your miracles? They will not—"

"As you ask, Julianna Taraen," Grandfather Shadow's voice whispered from everywhere and nowhere at the same time. "But do not make a habit of this."

Part of the Daemyn's face exploded, showering Julianna with gore.

For a brief moment, the creature looked at her with shock through its remaining eye. The Daemyn snarled. "You die for that!"

Something gold flashed between Julianna and the Daemyn. The Daemyn's head jerked back. A golden chain pressed into its throat, smoking and burning.

"Not while I can stop you," the Inquisitor said, almost in a growl. He pulled the chain back, yanking the Daemyn away from Julianna.

TWELVE

Faelin sat, breathing steadily, thinking of nothing, letting his mind wander. Then a pair of revelations came to him. He opened his eyes, stood up, and considered the one phrase in *fyrmest spaeg geode* he knew by heart. He rolled the words around in his mind to ensure he pronounced the words correctly and took a deep breath.

"*Aeteowian ic seo wat sodlis ikona,*" Faelin said.

Words appeared, hanging in the air around him. Multiple languages stretched around Johki's streets. Some of the lettering was small and almost inconsequential; other letters loomed as large as people. These declared the strength and source of the speaker. Faelin ignored the words – especially the word *suojelija* – of Grandfather Shadow's spider-web script, the block lettering of All Father Sun, with its sharp angles, and the dizzying and spiraling letters of Old Uncle Night. Here and there, Faelin spotted the graceful, sweeping script of Mother Earth's language near the fires glowing in the distance.

Hidden underneath all those letters, lurking near to the ground, swirling about his feet was a strange lettering that Faelin had not seen before. The lettering was reminiscent of Old Uncle Night's language, but was even more difficult to make out – mostly because the letters seemed to shift and ripple so that he couldn't focus on them for very long without his head swimming and stomach churning. He did manage to make out one word, *lezet*; or, at least, he thought that's what it was. If Faelin remembered his lessons correctly, *lezet* was the term for lie in Old Uncle Night's tongue, which was also the base of what the nomads in the Lands of Endless Summer called Yrgae-shkil, the Mother of Lies.

He took a step, making sure to watch only his feet and the words that surrounded them. Even though Faelin was certain he walked a straight path, his feet turned and twisted so that he wandered about, with no noticeable pattern to his movement.

"Bloody damn," Faelin said.

He stopped and looked at the letters again. They swirled and twisted a-way from his feet in all directions. Faelin couldn't keep his eyes on any one stream of letters to follow them for very long, but he'd wager much that there was one strand of letters and words for each of the Morigahnti who had gone with Julianna.

The implications of this discovery chilled Faelin to the very pit of his stomach. He shook his head, unwilling to follow his suspicions to the end of that thought. This was not a time to panic blindly in his fear of what might be. He couldn't do anything about that anyway, not now and likely not ever. Besides, if Grandfather Shadow was actually free, the Greater God was un-likely to take this well, if Faelin's suspicions were correct.

Rather than worry about matters that were beyond him, Faelin decided to turn his thoughts toward matters that were not beyond him. As terrifying as the prospect might be, Faelin took another deep breath, and embracing the word *suojelija*, that spun around him again and again, he reached down and took hold of the word *lezet*.

"*Galad'Ysoysa, mina sasta suoje Morigahn'uljas*," Faelin said.

He yanked on letters. The letters snapped and began unraveling all along the strands of words that wound away from Faelin into the distance.

"Well done, Faelin *aen Suojelija*," a voice whispered in the back of Faelin's mind. "Thank you for proving my confidence in you was not mis-placed."

Ignoring the voice, Faelin dashed down the street. Now, without those strange letters manipulating his steps, he maintained a sure and steady course. Almost screaming in relief, Faelin raced for the theater. Somehow, he knew that two Fists of Morigahnti were also free from whatever trap had been woven around Faelin. Would it be enough to defeat the Daemyn if he didn't arrive before them?

THIRTEEN

Luciano pulled back with all his might. The chain from his sun pendant cut even deeper into the Daemyn's neck, causing the flesh to burn and pop. Acrid smoke burned Luciano's eyes. He blinked away the tears.

As he struggled with the Daemyn, Luciano wished for two things. He wished the tears had come a few moments earlier, and he wished he had the capacity to lie to himself, even if just for a little while, but he could not. Luciano recalled the words he'd spoken over and over to Santo and other Inquisitors he'd trained, *The most important truth to know is the truth within ourselves.* He'd heard the Lord Morigahn call out to Grandfather Shadow, and the Greater God had not only answered her, he'd come to her aid, granting her a miracle without the use of a divine focus. The miracle had harmed the Daemyn. This might be the first such incident of this kind since the Battle of Ykthae Wood.

The truth Luciano knew within himself crushed him to the core.

"Firearms," the Inquisitor said, hands straining as the Daemyn struggled to free itself. "Firearms can harm it."

"What?" the Lord Morigahn.

"You're an idiot," the Daemyn snarled as it drove its claws into Luciano's thigh.

He laughed rather than cry out in pain.

"I saw it happen," Luciano said, and pulled back as hard as he could on the chain.

The Daemyn fought against him, but Luciano held on despite his weakening limbs. If he let go, the Daemyn would escape. He would not allow that to happen. The Daemyn tore a chunk of flesh out of the Inquisitor's leg. Luciano merely laughed the pain away.

"I am an Inquisitor of All Father Sun. I do not lie, and I give you this, high priest of the god of knowledge, so that you may kill this thing."

Adept Luciano Salvatore of House Floraen, and Inquisitor of All Father Sun prayed to a god he knew to be imprisoned within the mind of the Sun King to grant him the strength to hold the Daemyn long enough for the Morigahnti to kill it.

FOURTEEN

Firearms? Julianna thought as she gasped for breath. *How could he know that?*

"Korrin?" Julianna called.

"I heard," Korrin said from the theater. "On it!"

"Inquisitor," Wynd yelled. "Face the Daemyn to me."

The Daemyn twisted in the Inquisitor's grip, trying to lash out. The Inquisitor pulled the Daemyn off-balance, turning it toward Wynd, who had wrapped her *Galad'fana* around her fist. Wynd grinned and punched the Daemyn in the face. The fiend screamed as its face burned. It lashed out with its claws, grazing Wynd's face. Four thin lines of blood crossed her cheek. Wynd stumbled back to avoid another blow.

With Wynd no longer attacking, the Daemyn snapped its head back, smashing the Inquisitor's nose with its horn. Luciano's hands went slack, and the chain slid out of one of his hands and away from the Daemyn's neck. The Inquisitor blinked blankly and dropped to his knees as blood gushed from his shattered nose.

Free again, the Daemyn rushed forward, scooped Wynd off the ground and above its head. It brought her down into its rising knee. The broken rapier blade jutting out of its knee pierced her middle. Wynd coughed blood, and her arms went limp. The Daemyn flung her into the Inquisitor. They collapsed in a heap.

At last Julianna caught her breath again. All she could think of were the images of Allifar and Taebor's shadow selves blinking out as they died while fighting the Daemyn hounds in Shadybrook. Julianna would not allow her Morigahnti to die in her stead ever again. Not while she could stand and fight with them.

"Lord Morigahn," Korrin yelled from over by the theater. "Get down!"

Julianna dropped.

A gunshot roared behind her. A chuck of the Daemyn's left shoulder sprayed black ichor.

Julianna grinned wide. The Daemyn reached up with a talon and winced as it poked the wound. Its face twisted into a mask of sadness and confusion; it looked like a child who had been playing a game by the wrong rules all his life only to be beaten by someone who knew the proper rules. The Inquisitor had just made the Morigahnti the primary danger to Daemyns brought into the physical world

Julianna stood. She reveled in the smirk she felt creep across her lips. This movement pulled the Daemyn from its shock. They stood in the street, Julianna and the Daemyn, facing each other.

"I will still kill you," the Daemyn snarled, and leapt at Julianna.

The Inquisitor sprang up, swung his sun pendant in a wide, overhand arc. The chain wound around the Daemyn's injured shoulder. The black blood hissed and popped as the divine focus came into contact with the Daemyn's form. The Daemyn screamed as the Inquisitor yanked on the chain, pulling the creature off-balance. The Daemyn turned and smashed its fist into the Inquisitor's face. Teeth flew from his mouth and his jaw hung loose and limp, but he held on.

Julianna looked back to Korrin, who was busy reloading his pistol. He wouldn't be in time. Julianna scrambled to her *Galad'fana*. If she could help keep the thing trapped long enough for the Morigahnti to reach them, they had enough firearms to end this thing. They had to be almost here. Shades, they should have been here already.

She got to her *Galad'fana* when she saw Aurell, Lord Karstyn, and Prince Sandré round the corner up the street.

"Shoot it!" Julianna screamed.

All three of them looked at her as if she were mad. Standard Morigahnti practice was not to waste weaponry as expensive as firearms on Daemyns that they felt could just shrug of those injuries anyway.

"Don't argue. Don't think. Just do it!" Julianna yelled.

"Shoot, damn you!" Korrin yelled, as he pointed his firearm at the Daemyn.

The shot *boomed*. Fire erupted from the barrel. The Daemyn spun, pulling the Inquisitor off-balance.

The shot hit the Inquisitor in the lower back. Now that the Daemyn understood that firearms could hurt it, catching it off guard would be even harder now. They had to kill it before it got away and spread its seed anywhere it could, leaving Daemyn-born children in the wake of its passing.

Alerick and Parsh came around a corner from the other end of the street.

"Shoot the gods-be-damned-fucking Daemyn!" Julianna yelled.

Gunfire roared like thunder. Bullets tore through the Daemyn and the Inquisitor, spraying blood, red and black. Both spun in the middle of the street and fell to the cobbles, twitching.

Julianna rushed over and scooped up her mother's dagger. She slid to her knees next to the Daemyn, grabbed it by the horn for leverage, and stabbed it up to dagger's hilt in both eyes. It stopped twitching,

She turned to the Inquisitor. His last breath came in a ragged gasp, and his eyes lost focus. Better this for him, as she didn't want to consider what Sandré would have done to him. While the Inquisitor had been her enemy, he'd been honest about it.

"May All Father Sun have mercy on you," Julianna said, gritting her teeth, expecting pain to flare in her scar. The pain did not come. She whispered, "Interesting," as she closed the Inquisitor's eyes.

"Lord Morigahn," someone yelled. "Move away!"

Julianna glanced up and saw a group of three Adepts at the other end of the block, two men standing to either side of a woman. The Adepts' mantels were the forest green and deep brown of House Aernacht. All three held cudgels of white oak, so big that they were almost staffs. Those cudgel-staffs were only one of the holy symbols of their House's goddess, Mother Earth. The three stood, watching, doing nothing to enter the fight. No. One of the men, a young man, perhaps close to Julianna's age, seemed eager to enter the fight: he leaned forward on the balls of his feet, bouncing up and down and shaking his cudgel. The woman reached her arm out, blocking him.

The Aernacht Adepts sang together. "*Gyth'Imyrthae tine teas as o brionn!*"

Julianna didn't understand the words of Mother Earth's language, but she felt the tingling of divine power through her *Galad'fana*. The Aernacht Adepts must have been calling forth an immense amount of power from their goddess.

The earth rumbled. The cobblestones beneath the Daemyn and Inquisitor cracked open, and a pillar of fire erupted out of the earth, enveloped both corpses, and spread outward in a wall of molten, liquid heat, surrounding Julianna, Wynd, and the Aernacht Adepts. It cut off the Morigahnti who seemed too stunned by this display of power to move. A blur came from an alley, flew between the closing ends of this wall of heat, and stopped next to Julianna. It was Faelin.

"How?" Julianna asked.

"Later," Faelin replied.

"Hold fast!" the woman in the center called.

Julianna stopped and faced the Adepts walking toward her.

The woman shouted, "I command you to halt in the name of the Sun King!"

"Will this never end?" Julianna groaned.

"Not so long as you are Lord Morigahn," Faelin replied.

The Adepts came closer. The pale-skinned woman, who was only two fingers taller than Julianna but looked decades older, had deep brown eyes and long brown hair streaked with gray. She walked less than a pace before the others, but her posture and the tilt of her head told Julianna that this woman was the superior.

The first man behind her drew Julianna's attention because he was huge. Not tall, but just *big*, with wide shoulders and a walk that made him seem to fill up the street. He had a shock of reddish blond hair and beard. In addition to his Aernacht short sword and cudgel, he wore a massive, two-handed sword strapped to his back.

The other man was short and thin, and appeared younger than Julianna. With his black hair and darker skin, he looked more Floraen than Aernacht, despite his deep green eyes. Where the woman fixed her eyes only on Julianna, the young man's eyes kept shifting, trying to look everywhere at once.

Julianna bowed when the Adepts stopped a few paces away. She composed herself and drew to the front of her mind every lesson of being a proper lady her aunt had ever taught her. She was going to need all that knowledge if she was going to deal with these two.

"How may I serve the High Blood?" Julianna asked.

Faelin stepped between Julianna and the Adepts.

"I, Sabina Maedoc, by right granted me as an Adept of the Realm," the woman said, "arrest you of high treason in the name of the Sun King. Stand down and…"

Faelin burst out laughing.

"What do you find humorous?" Sabina demanded.

"Who can tell, High Blood," Julianna said, before Faelin could speak. "He is a bit daft. See to Wynd while I serve this worthy Lady."

Faelin managed to control his outburst, bowed to Julianna, and went to look after Wynd.

"Stop!" Sabina barked. "You will not take leave until I give it." Then she said to the other Adepts. "If he moves, burn him where he stands, Gianni."

The smaller man looked at her as though she were mad, drunk, or both.

"Did you not see this man move as if he were blessed by Sister Wind herself?" Gianni said. He had the appearance of House Floraen, but his accent marked him of House Aernacht. "Or perhaps the Komati Lady standing behind him who fought against that Daemyn? I'm fairly certain they don't consider us a serious threat."

When Sabina spun toward him, Julianna thought she saw the Aernacht lady's eye twitch.

"You dare defy my words, disciple?" Sabina demanded.

"Of course not, Mistress." Gianni bowed in deference, though Julianna detected a hint of sarcasm in his voice. Sabina seemed too consumed by her fury to notice that subtlety. "I am merely urging caution."

Sabina glared at Gianni. He shrugged at her in return, a look of pure innocence etched on his face. The Aernacht lady sighed and faced the large man next to Gianni. Julianna glanced at Gianni. He smiled sweetly and winked at her, gesturing with his chin toward Sabina. Or was that just some nervous twitch?

"Lancyl," Sabina said. "You burn her."

"Gladly, Mistress," Lancyl said, glaring at Julianna with just as much spite as Sabina had.

"You will not…" Sabina started.

Julianna slapped her across the face. If she wasn't going to suffer Sandré, she refused to suffer this old hag. Julianna was the Lord Morigahn, first chosen of Grandfather Shadow, and the only true High Priest in the entire world.

"I'm tired of hearing you whine, *tsyhaema*," Julianna said. "That Daemyn was summoned by Carmine D'Mario…"

"*Gyth'Imyrthae tine faen—*" Lancyl started, but Faelin rushed at him, slaming both hands into the Aernacht Adept's chest, which sent him flying into the wall of heat.

Julianna couldn't decide which was worse, the scream he wailed as he burned or the stomach-churning stench.

Sabina hissed. She raised her cudgel to Julianna.

Gianni brought his own cudgel down on his mistress's head. Sabina's eyes rolled into the back of her head and she crumpled to the cobblestones. As she dropped, so did the wall summoned by her miracle, draining away back into the crack she'd summoned it from.

"What?" Julianna stood blinking and confused, trying to determine this young Adept's motivation for betraying his mistress. "Why?" She only became aware of the Morigahnti who had rushed in as Gianni dropped his weapons a moment before Parsh half tackled him and wrenched the Adept's arms behind his back. Charise placed the tip of her rapier on Gianni's shoulder, barely a breath away from puncturing his throat. Alerick pointed a pistol against Gianni's head.

Sandré walked up, knife in hand, face tight, lips curled into a feral sneer. Behind him, members of his Fist and some of Charise's glared murder at Gianni.

"If my lady would call off her valiant warriors," Gianni spoke with such speed Julianna could barely make out the words, "I would be more than pleased to explain my motivations."

"Stop," Julianna said, holding up a hand. She understood how they might feel with all the decades of oppression the Morigahnti and Komati had suffered under the Kingdom Adepts. They yearned for the tiniest scraps of vengeance anywhere they could find them; however, Grandfather Shadow was also the god of knowledge.

Surprisingly, Sandré Collaen stilled himself. He also raised a hand, stopping the Morigahnti behind him.

Julianna looked this Adept Gianni over. He smiled at her.

"I've never had the pleasure of making the acquaintance of a Lord Morigahn before," Gianni said with a wide grin. "You'll forgive me that circumstance conspires to prevent me from observing proper formalities."

Parsh tightened his grip on Gianni's arm, and Charise prodded Gianni's neck with her rapier, not enough to draw blood but enough to cause Gianni to suck in his breath. He might have pulled his head away, but Alerick's pistol prevented that.

Julianna smiled despite herself. Hearing an Aernacht accent coming from a man whose dusky skin and dark eyes screamed the he should be in House Floraen red, gold, and orange, while at the same time he used three or five words in a situation where one or two would have been enough, warmed Julianna to this strange little man.

"Release him," Julianna said.

The Morigahnti, every one of them, looked at Julianna as if she were mad.

She rubbed her eyes and sighed. "Don't ignore him. Keep an eye on him. But we're not going to kill him – at least not yet. I'll speak with him once we tend to the wounded."

Alerick and Charise drew their weapons away from Gianni, and Parsh released him with a push.

Gianni stumbled. He straightened himself, turned to face Parsh, and gave a perfect courtly bow, offering the perfect stretch of leg for Parsh's position in the order of precedence.

"Thank you, my lord," Gianni said. "So very kind."

"Adept Gianni," Julianna said. "Don't push my benevolence too far."

Gianni squinted at her and pursed his lips as he studied her. Finally, he gave a brisk nod. "Of course, Lord Morigahn. My apologies."

"Now," Julianna said, facing the Morigahnti, "the wounded."

"Have the Morigahnti watch the Adept," Faelin said. "I'll see to the others."

"Are you going to use some Taekuri trick?" Karstyn asked.

"No," Faelin answered. "Something much more than that."

With that, Faelin went and knelt next to Wynd and opened her shirt enough to expose her left breast. Julianna stood next to Faelin, looking down. She almost protested, but she trusted him to have some good reason for this. Faelin placed his hand over Wynd's heart and closed his eyes. Next to Julianna someone began to speak. Julianna held up her hand. The individual stopped before completing the word.

Faelin took a deep breath in through his nose and let it out through his mouth, then took his hand away. A gray handprint remained on Wynd's breast where he had touched her. The gray spread, quickly covering her, turning her and her clothes the color of ash. A moment later, color returned to her, but the gray handprint remained on her chest. Her eyes opened.

"Stay there a moment," Faelin said, as he closed up her shirt. "The dizziness should pass quickly."

He went to Korrin and repeated the strange ritual. When Korrin's color returned, all his wounds were healed and he had the same handprint on his chest as well.

"Did we win?" Korrin groaned.

"Barely," Faelin answered. "You'll be fine in a few moments."

"Raze?" Korrin asked. "Where is he?"

"He's fine," Julianna said. "His wing needs mending, but he'll live."

"And Nathan?" Wynd asked, pushing herself into a sitting position. "Is the creature out of his body?"

"It is."

"Soon we will mourn," Wynd said.

"But not today," Korrin echoed.

"No," Wynd agreed. "Not today."

As the two Morigahnti got to their feet, Julianna turned to Gianni. "Explain yourself. Why have you turned against an Adept of your own House?"

"Wait," Aurell said, and wrapped her *Galad'fana* around her head. She placed her hands on either side of Gianni's face. He looked uncomfortable, but did not resist or protest. Aurell closed her eyes, and spoke, "*Galad'Ysoysa rus hano keskustelu aen totus sanati.*"

When she removed her hands, Gianni asked. "What was that?"

"A miracle to make you speak only true words."

"But what if I have sworn to the Brotherhood of the Night? Then the gift of my god will not allow you to detect any falsehood I might say."

"That's why I spoke the miracle to affect you, not me. It is affecting what you say, not what I hear."

Gianni shrugged. He didn't seem concerned in the least.

"Well," Julianna said. "Your explanation?"

"That is a simple thing. She is an idiot." Gianni pointed at Sabina. "I have every confidence that the leaders within the Blessed Church of Mother Earth will punish me for my actions, but what is one life next to that of all those Carmine D'Mario will harm with these Daemyns that he's summoned. To learn that he is an Adept of Old Uncle Night is grievous news indeed. It causes me to ask many questions of the Kingdom's dealings in Koma and why Mother Earth has placed me in your company."

"Some might say you have forsaken your vows," Wynd said.

"I crave your pardon, lady," Gianni said. His indignation caused his voice to rise slightly in pitch. "I have forsaken nothing. I swore to oppose corruption wherever and whenever I witness it. Sabina was more concerned with following the Floraen and Kaesiak agenda in her obsession with bettering her status. I, on the other side of the coin, serve Mother Earth in my every action and word. We have a common enemy. You and the Inquisitor fought together against an evil brought to our world. I am at least the equal of an Inquisitor.

"You have told me that Carmine D'Mario, my father's wife's brother's son, incidentally, is an Adept of the Night Brotherhood and has several Daemyns at his command."

"If you are a D'Mario of Floraen," Sandré asked, "why do you wear the mantle and colors of House Aernacht?"

"I am Gianni D'Mario yp Caenacht. My Father is Steaphano D'Mario and my mother is Triona Caenacht. I felt the call of my mother's goddess more strongly than that of my father's god.

"Today I witnessed the carnage of one Daemyn working alone. Also, it is known within my father's House that Carmine D'Mario and Octavio Salvatore, have a rather intimate friendship, one not usually formed between the Royal Governor of a Kingdom protectorate and a half-breed so low in the order of precedence he is blessed to be considered High Blood at all. This raises some concerns about the governor's publicly professed loyalties. I am loath to speak my suspicion more plainly than that, considering the governor's close relation to the Sun King. However, it is my duty as an Adept to help you defeat Carmine and his Daemyns and my duty as a High Blood to penetrate this plot surrounding Governor Salvatore."

"Long-winded, this one is," Korrin said.

Julianna shot the lanky Morigahnti a disapproving glance. Korrin returned Julianna's attention with that half-smile he wore that made him appear as if he knew some amusing secret.

Gianni chuckled. "I confess that I have on more than one occasion been accused of having an overzealous enjoyment of my own pontification."

"I like it," Korrin said. "I've always wanted a pet Adept. I promise to feed it. Can I keep it Lord Morigahn?"

"I'm already house-broken," Gianni said, with a lopsided grin.

Julianna shook her head and sighed. She felt she might be doing more of that in the future.

"And what of the laws against Low Blood and those of common blood worshipping too high above their station?" Julianna asked. "As I'm sure you have already noticed: we all serve Grandfather Shadow."

"What of it? Are you afraid of me turning on you once I am with others of my order or perhaps a few squads of Draqons?"

"That thought had occurred to me."

"Well then, my lady," Gianni said with a wide grin, "allow me to ease your concern. I care not at all whom you choose to worship or serve, so long as you do not actually move against the Sun King. As for those laws of worship, those are tools of the politicians. I am a man of piety and faith. If any of the gods truly do not wish you to follow them, *they* will punish you. It is not my place to pass judgment on those who break the laws of men, but it is my duty to correct those who break the laws handed down by the gods, which Carmine D'Mario has done by summoning the Daemyns."

Julianna turned to Aurell. "Well?"

"He's telling the truth as he believes it," Aurell replied.

Julianna faced the Adept. "You intrigue me, Adept Gianni of Houses Floraen and Aernacht. You will come with us."

"Is he our prisoner?" Sandré asked.

"No," Julianna replied. "We do not take prisoners. Captains, have your Fists gather their belongings. We leave in five minutes."

The captains barked the order, and even Sandré did so without protest. That surprised Julianna a bit. Perhaps she was finally winning him over, but she didn't really believe that. Now she stood with Parsh, Charise, Sandré, Faelin, and Gianni.

"If he is not our prisoner, Lord Morigahn," Charise asked. "Who is he?"

"He's my pet Adept," Korrin said.

Julianna sighed. "He is our ally and my guest."

"This man cannot come with us," Sandré said. "His presence at your trials will be unacceptable."

"We aren't going to the trials," Julianna said. "We're going after Carmine."

"No!" Sandré snapped.

"Prince Sandré," Julianna said. "What do I have to do to impress upon you that I am the Lord Morigahn, or at least worthy enough for you to give me the benefit of the doubt? I have learned obscure Morigahnti lore in only a matter of weeks. I have spoken the miracle of Shadow's Thunder. I just fought a Daemyn, which nearly cost me my life. What more do you want?"

"Proof," Sandré said. "There are too many people who wish to see the Morigahnti destroyed once and for all. Many times they have almost succeeded, and putting an imposter in the place of the Lord Morigahn has been done before."

"You will have proof once we stop Carmine D'Mario," Julianna promised. "Then I will take the trials."

"Finding him will be nearly impossible," Parsh said.

"We might not know where he is," Faelin said, "but I know where he's going. He travels to Koma City and intends to sacrifice the souls of *Galad Setseman'Vuori aen Keisari* and *aen Tsumari'osa* to a powerful Daemyn Lord."

"I don't know what that string of fancy words meant," Gianni said, "but we can't allow Carmine to sacrifice anyone's soul. That will only serve to make the Realm of the Godless Dead even stronger."

Julianna looked Sandré right in the eye. "Surely, Your Highness, you cannot argue with saving *aen Keisari* and *aen Tsumari'osa*."

"No," Sandré said, "I cannot."

"But we can only have one leader," Parsh said. "Who will it be?"

Everyone was quiet for a moment as they looked back and forth at each other.

"Not that my opinion matters for much," Gianni said, "but I will only follow the Lord Morigahn." He bowed to Julianna. She nodded at him as though he were a Morigahnti.

"Your opinion does not carry weight in this matter," Sandré said.

Gianni shrugged. "I would think, Prince Sandré, that you would welcome having a High Blood Adept to aid you in this rescue of these two obviously important personages. I could be useful in so many situations."

Sandré ignored him.

"Let the Fist captains decide," Faelin said. "Let them each speak their choice for leader."

Julianna nodded. She should have thought of that. It was one of things she had read in the *Galad'parma*. It was a tradition used when more than two Fists came together. And none of the captains were allowed to choose themselves. The worst part was that Julianna was not a captain, and so she had no vote.

"Lord Morigahn," Parsh said, without hesitation.

"Charise," Sandré said.

They all looked to Charise. If she spoke for Sandré, the vote would be considered an impasse and the Fists might separate. And where Julianna wouldn't mind being free of Sandré, his experience and his Morigahnti would be very useful in hunting Carmine and the Daemyns.

"Lord Morigahn," Charise said.

Sandré sighed, and looked defeated.

"Can you follow me, Prince Sandré?" Julianna asked. "If you cannot, please leave us. We cannot afford inner strife if we are to succeed."

"I will follow you for *aen Keisari* and *aen Tsumari'osa*."

"Fair enough," Julianna said. "And then to the trials. If I don't succeed, you can kill me yourself."

By that time, the Morigahnti had collected their belongings and had gathered outside the house. The streets were still clear of people, and the town was quiet. Who knew what stories would grow from the fighting here? Julianna did know that they had to keep ahead of most of them on the way to Koma City.

"What about her?" Parsh asked.

"Leave her," Gianni replied. "She'll wake up in a bit with no more of a headache than she gets from her morning hangovers. Besides, I never really liked the old hag anyway."

"Very well," Julianna said. "Sandré. Charise. I want each of you to set one from your Fist to act as Gianni's chaperone, to protect him from any overzealous Morigahnti and keep our deepest secrets from his eyes."

"Yes, Lord Morigahn," they said together, although Sandré seemed reluctant to do so.

When the two Morigahnti were selected and led Gianni away toward the boat, Julianna pulled Aurell aside.

"Yes, Lord Morigahn?" Aurell asked.

"Stay behind us a bit," Julianna whispered. "Once all are out of sight, kill her." Julianna indicated Sabina.

While she wanted word of the Morigahnti and the Lord Morigahn to spread through the Komati, Julianna did not want the High Blood hearing of her in any way that was anything other than a whisper upon the wind.

Aurell saluted. Julianna nodded and hurried to catch up with the others.

As Julianna passed the place where the Inquisitor's body had been burned away by the Aernacht Adepts' miracle, she pulled her *Galad'fana* across her face.

"Rest well in All Father Sun's Hall," Julianna said.

FIFTEEN

The old man in the worn cloak walked with the dog at his side. He looked up at the smoke rising from the burning and smoldering buildings, darkening the early morning sky. He sighed.

The dog looked up at him, tongue lolling out of its jaws in that awkward way that is as close to a smile as dogs can get.

"You have something to say?" the old man asked.

The dog sat on its haunches and regarded the man. It snorted.

The man looked back at the dog, which looked much more like a wolf than it had moments before. The man stood straighter and crossed his arms, no longer looking worn and frail.

"What?" the man demanded.

Light flashed around the wolf, and a small clap of thunder peeled, shattering windows and knocking a few tiles loose on roofs above them.

Razka stood in his wild leathers looking Grandfather Shadow nearly in the eye. The Stormseeker smiled.

"I've never heard you sigh before," Razka said. "It's refreshing to see you perform such a simple, human action."

Grandfather Shadow pointed at Razka in that way he did when about to admonish one of his followers. He opened his mouth, then closed it at the same time he closed his hand into a fist. He rubbed his fingers against his palm, and then rubbed his chin.

"I think you're right," Grandfather Shadow replied. "Intriguing."

"Refreshing," Razka said. "It seems the Lord Morigahn is coming into her own."

The Stormseeker didn't even bother to hide his smile, the proud grandfather. Seeing that smile pleased Grandfather Shadow. He felt the Stormseekers needed something to take pride in, this particular Stormseeker most of all.

Grandfather Shadow returned the smile. "So it does. I knew that I had chosen well."

"Very well," Razka said.

"Are you still angry with me?"

The Stormseeker eyed the god. "Does it actually matter?"

"No," Grandfather Shadow replied. "It does not. A sigh does not mean that I have changed that much."

"Perhaps," Razka said. "What will you do now? Even with her growing power and confidence, Julianna still has dissention within the Morigahnti and many threats from without."

"In that, she is no different from any other Lord Morigahn," Grandfather Shadow said. "Well, perhaps she has to worry a bit more than most have about traitors and dissention within the ranks. However, these are difficulties she must deal with on her own. The King of Order is no doubt still watching me very closly, waiting for the opportunity to call the Lords of Judgment down on me again. From this point on, I will only intercede on Julianna's behalf if other Eldar come into play that Saent Faelin cannot deal with."

"He knows," Razka said.

"He does," Grandfather Shadow replied. "I'm actually a little surprised it took him this long to put it all together. As it is, I will retreat to my realm and observe events as they unfold from the Well of Knowledge."

"So then," Razka said, "we are leaving the mortals to decide their fates themselves."

"Oh, no," Grandfather Shadow replied. "I have an errand for you and yours."

"Remember, I do not aid Morigahnti any longer," Razka said.

The street they walked along grew darker still, as if the smoke from the burning city began to gather directly above them. Grandfather Shadow gripped Razka by the shoulder and spun the Stormseeker to face him. They stood, staring at each other.

"You will aid who I tell you to aid." Grandfather Shadow spoke softly, but his tone carried the hint of danger of a Faerii steel blade reflecting the light of the moon at the dark of midnight. "I have indulged you long enough. You will honor our agreement and bring the Stormseekers back to me, all of them, or I will find one that will. I'm sure at least several of the younger wolves want a chance of revenge against the Kingdom and Kavala."

Razka growled deep in the back of his throat.

Grandfather Shadow merely looked at him and waited.

After a few moments, Razka nodded. In a flash of light and a clap of thunder, the Stormseeker was gone.

Grandfather Shadow licked his lips, clicked his tongue, and sighed. What an interesting gesture. The god gave a short chuckle at how satisfying he found it. He wondered why he'd never done it before the King of Order had imprisoned the Greater Eldar, and he knew he might go on wondering until the end of time, or at least until he and his fellow gods ripped the world apart again.

Of that, Grandfather Shadow had no doubt.

Yrgaeshkil had already named a high priest and set Saents to work in the world. How long would it be until the others of the lesser Eldar took it upon themselves to gather Dominions from the other Greater Eldar still imprisoned? Grandfather Shadow couldn't go around murdering them all. Eventually, they would stop their bickering long enough to oppose him. He was unlikely to survive that confrontation without aid. Grandmother Dream was unlikely to openly confront the lesser Eldar, and Grandfather Shadow would beg the King of Order to make him mortal before he approached the only other Greater Eldar walking free. No, for now Grandfather Shadow would do as he'd told Razka: he would retreat to his realm and pay close attention to the Well of Knowledge.

SIXTEEN

A chaotic sea of people swarmed Johki's docks. The rest of the town had been quiet as Julianna and her Morigahnti had passed through. Now they knew why. All of the people were to trying to escape by ship, or according to the Stormcrows, were fleeing from the gates. Unfortunately, there weren't enough riverboats and barges for even a third of the people, but that didn't stop them from trying to get aboard. Crews were forced to beat people away as their captains shouted the orders to cast off. One unlucky barge burned in the water, still tied in its berth.

With citizens fleeing, they had managed to locate horses as they moved to the docks. Julianna rode with the Fist captains and Gianni. The Morigahnti surrounded them all, forcing their way through the panicking crowds. Several times people tried to push through the circle of Morigahnti. Each time, the veiled warriors pushed them back. Fortunately, they had to draw blood only once.

"Your Highness," Julianna leaned toward Sandré and shouted over the din. "Which is ours?"

"That one," Sandré gestured to the far end of the dock. "The *Stormrider.*"

At the end of the docks, Julianna saw a riverboat that dwarfed all the others, one that was almost free of unwanted boarders. A line of sailors creating a barrier with boat hooks and oars stood three quarters of the way up the dock and kept the masses from getting too near the *Stormrider.*

As the Morigahnti cleared a path down the docks, Julianna took in the vessel that would carry them away from Johki and toward potentially greater danger in Koma City. The craft had two full stories above the water, three masts, and a full complement of oars stretched out from holes a few arm's lengths above the water. Its gray denim sails alone declared the captain was either a successful businessman or that Sandré Collaen supplemented the captain's business. Though canvass was just a bit stronger, denim was lighter and easier to work with, store, and repair. Passing the line of sailors and getting closer to the *Stormrider,* Julianna saw the rigging wasn't hemp, but corded silk. This captain had to be the best in all Koma, either that or Sandré supplemented him out of vanity, especially if Sandré traveled on this vessel on anything resembling a regular basis.

When they reached the gangplank, Julianna noticed the sailor who stood just on the other side of the railing wore a *Galad'fana.*

Sandré called to the sailor, "Prince Sandré Collaen and party request permission to come aboard!"

"Granted," the sailor replied, "but please hurry, Your Highness. Captain Haden wants to cast off soon as possible."

Behind them, people began to beg, plead, and cry out to be taken aboard. Julianna glanced back. The line of sailors now fought a retreating battle toward the *Stormrider*, swinging their boathooks in wide arcs to keep the citizens of Johki from overrunning them. Behind the crowds, Julianna saw smoke from over half the town rising into the sky.

When Faelin helped her down from her horse, he leaned close, and said, "It's not your fault."

"I know," Julianna replied. "For a time, I blamed myself, but no longer. The Kingdom of the Sun is responsible. We will give them one chance to make peace and return our lands to us."

"Peace?" Sandré asked in a sneer of disdain. "We are born to fight and conquer."

"We are also meant to defend the Komati who cannot fight," Julianna said. She swept her arm over the smoke-filled sky behind her. "The Komati are not ready to fight as they once might have been. We must seek to free ourselves peacefully first, giving us time to teach them what it means to be Komati, true children of Grandfather Shadow. If the Kingdom does not leave us to ourselves, then we will make them bleed for all the suffering they have visited upon us. We will have our *kostota*, Prince Sandré, but we will be cautious about it. It will come on our terms, when we are ready, when *all* of us are ready."

Sandré opened his mouth, curled his lips over his teeth, and then closed his mouth.

"You have something to say, Prince Sandré?" Julianna asked.

"A merely philosophical discussion that can wait until we are less pressed for time," Sandré replied.

Julianna nodded.

"Now, may I entreat you to board the *Stormrider* so that we may depart this disaster?" Sandré asked.

Julianna nodded again and turned to the gangway leading to Sandré Collaen's riverboat – the riverboat she'd told herself the previous night that she would *not* board.

She sighed, shrugged, and walked up the gangway. For better or worse, and as much as she hated it, this was the surest way to get to Koma city and the Komati heirs.

KNIVES IN THE NIGHT

I have no doubt that someday an assassin will kill me one day. But any who come for me had better be faster, stronger, more clever, and a much better fighter than me. If he fails at any of those, then all the gods in all the heavens had better stand by him, for that is the only way he will succeed. If not, well then, I will gladly introduce him to Old Uncle Night.
– Saent Kyrian the Cunning.

The old saying goes,
"The head beneath the crown knows no peace nor rest,
and those who wear no crown will never know the anguish of waiting."
There is one who knows worse anguish.
He who wears no crown,
yet should.

And those two shall not be blessed.
Not once, twice, nor thrice.
Not at all.

- The Blind Prophet

ONE

Josephine Adryck took another sip of her wine. Her head swam in the pleasant warmth that came with several glasses of the rich, red vintage from the vineyards of the southern Andres lands. While expensive, it only took a small bit to get to this point, so in the grand scheme of gods and men, it wouldn't cost her too much. Worry for her sons had aggravated the aches in her fingers and wrists.

"Another, Aniya," Josephine said, extending her arm.

"Are you sure, Your Highness?" Aniya asked.

Josephine turned her head just enough to give the young countess a reproachful look out of the corner of her eye. Aniya stood her ground, pitcher of wine untouched on the table next to her. Out of all the young women sent by various noble families to curry favor with Princess Josephine Adryck since Xander Rosha had been raised to the White Draqons, Aniya Dashette of House Kutonen was the only one of them who truly understood what it meant to serve those of royal blood. Sometimes those who served needed to question the commands of those they served, because part of serving sometimes meant saving their masters from themselves.

"I had a dream this afternoon," Josephine said. "*He* was in it again."

"I'm not sure who you mean," Aniya said. "And does it matter? Will you give *him*, whoever *he* is, that much power over your choices?"

"On second consideration," Josephine said, "come take this from me. I don't want it anymore."

"Yes, Your Highness," Aniya said.

As she moved toward Josephine, a sudden breeze blew into the room, ruffling the curtains.

"What?" came a voice from the veranda. "How did—?"

At the sound of the second voice, Josephine leapt out of her seat. Aniya rushed to place herself between Josephine and the veranda. Two fighting dirks had appeared in Aniya's hands, and she stood as if she were a wire coil, ready to spring at any moment.

"Your Highness," Maxian's deep, smooth voice came from the Veranda, "I seem to have found an unexpected, and I imagine uninvited, guest."

Josephine started for the veranda. Aniya moved to bar her passage.

"Step aside," Josephine said. "This is not the time to question me."

"Your Highness." Aniya gave Josephine a perfect court curtsy and fell in behind her. Josephine noticed that Aniya still held the dirks.

When she stepped onto the Veranda, she saw Maxian holding a figure by the throat with one hand, pinning him to the wall. Maxian's other hand was latched onto the intruder's wrist, and they struggled for control of a thin-bladed knife. Josephine pulled her gaze away from the blade that shimmered in the light coming from the sitting room windows. This stranger wore all black and gray, including a familiar dark gray cloth wrapped around his head. A *Galad'fana*.

"What will you have me do with him?" Maxian asked.

Josephine considered the man. She looked at the dagger again.

"Treat him as the Morigahnti treat others. Kill him."

Leaving Maxian to his work, Josephine returned to her sitting room.

The sounds of struggle increased. A man cried in pain, followed by a wet cough. Something heavy hit the stone of the veranda. A moment later, Maxian came in, cleaning a knife on a gray cloth. Josephine hoped it was the man's *Galad'fana*.

"You should increase your guard, Your Highness," Maxian said.

Another gust of wind blew the scent of roses mixed with the tangy aroma of blood through the open door. Josephine closed the glass doors so she wouldn't have to smell the blood. Then she crossed the sitting room to the door leading into the hall. She pulled it open with such force that two guards and a serving girl jumped in surprise.

Josephine faced one of the guards. "There is a body on my veranda. Dispose of it, make arrangements to discover as much as you can about its identity, and make it very public knowledge that I was alone when it tried to kill me."

The guard looked ready to protest but appeared to think better of it. He was lucky that he had. There were only a handful of people that Josephine employed who had the privilege of questioning her. Each of those people knew when to use that privilege and when not to. She had no patience for anyone else in her service who thought they knew her well enough to question her commands.

As the guard hurried to his appointed tasks, Josephine turned to Aniya.

"Young lady, go and speak to your leader. Find out which faction of the Morigahnti dares to attack me in my home."

Aniya did not move, rather she fixed her attention on Maxian.

"He is fine," Josephine said. "Nothing short of a god will harm me while he is here."

"Your Highness." Aniya saluted in the fashion of the Morigahnti and left the sitting room.

Maxian watched her go. "Employing Morigahnti bodyguards now?"

Josephine shrugged. "It's probably what caused him to wait long enough for you to discover him and save my life."

"You didn't need to send the girl off to find out who sent him." Maxian held the knife out to her, hilt first. Her breath began to quicken. Plain wooden handle. Thick, triangular blade. Was it fear or anger she felt?

"Thank you," Josephine said, as she took it.

Maxian released the weapon, and Josephine held it next to her lamp. She blinked at the word etched on each edge of the triangular blade. *Kostota*. She pinched the hilt with two fingers to examine the wood. As she expected, Josephine found a symbol carved into the wood: the symbol of the Collaen family.

Josephine let out a sound somewhere between a hiss and a snarl and buried the tip of the knife several finger's breadth into the sitting table.

Few people in Koma remembered these daggers, developed in perhaps the darkest chapter of Koma's history. Assassinations were not only legal, they were encouraged, so long as the assassination was logged with the appropriate government ministry for anyone to accept the contract and so that the parties in danger could prepare defenses. This was during the centuries after the Greater Gods were imprisoned, the thought being that the strong would survive above the weak, ensuring that Koma's noble lines would remain pure and strong to protect the Komati people. She could see Sandré Collaen wanting to take Koma back to such a combative time.

"Kill him," Josephine spoke in a low and menacing tone that surprised even herself.

"No."

She spun on Maxian. "No?" Her voice changed, growing higher and louder. "If you ever loved me, you will kill him for me."

"No, Josephine," Maxian replied. "I will not remove that problem only to create others. If I do, Julianna will suffer, will not likely survive in the aftermath. The best thing you can do is survive and help your sons, and thereby help Julianna."

"I do not play politics anymore," Josephine said. She turned away from Maxian when she added, "Vincent saw to that."

Maxian was quiet as Josephine choked back her tears. She still missed her husband, his laughter and crazed ideas of what would be possible if the Komati reclaimed the technology they'd been developing before the Kingdom conquered them. His absence from her life was like an icicle sliding into her gut.

"You were one of the best at that game," Maxian said, "and your sons need that expertise. They are both in Koma City, being drawn into Kingdom politics at the highest level. Key players each have plans for both Xander and Damian, and not all of them are mortal. "They need you."

Josephine turned back to Maxian. She opened her mouth, but before she could lay into him with the tongue-lashing of a lifetime, she heard something she'd not heard in over two decades within these chambers.

"Is that a baby?" Josephine asked.

"No," Maxian said.

The fussing out on the veranda continued.

"It sounds like a baby."

"It even looks like a baby," Maxian said. "You of all people should know that something can appear to be one thing, when it is truly something else."

"Then what is it?"

"Potentially the most dangerous creature on the physical plane."

She blinked at him, and then closed her eyes, hoping to clear him from her sight. When she opened her eyes, Maxian was still there.

"Why?" Josephine asked. "Why would you bring it here, then?"

"Because I have a plan to use the creature against the enemies of our children," Maxian replied, "but it's going to require a sacrifice on your part."

"I've already sacrificed so much for my sons, what's one thing more?"

"This is greater than anything you've ever done," Maxian said. "Let me teach you a bit of *fyrmest spaeg geode*."

TWO

Xander Rosha stood at his post outside First Adept Kraetor's suite, doing his best not to pace back and forth across the hall. He'd given up hours ago trying not to fidget, stopping only when he saw one of the other Whites or the few High Blood who walked by, the two times Duchess Portia Salvatore came to see how he was, and the time Duke Octavio came once again to thank Xander for saving his life. After the excitement with the assassins earlier that morning, coupled with the little sleep he'd gotten the night before, just standing at this post, guarding this door that didn't really need guarding, was among the worst posts Xander had been assigned since joining the Reds. He should be more concerned with protecting the High Blood and retuning honor to his name rather than worrying about being caught at his ease when he should be at attention.

Looking out the window, to where the fading light of day illuminated the clouds, Xander's thoughts turned to Damian. Xander had been so close to catching his half-brother, and now the little runt was likely across the sea, on his way to one of the various swordsmanship schools he'd traveled to before…well, before the mess with those firearms. As soon as they'd learned Damian was in Koma City, the Whites should have been out in force, scouring every back ally and checking under every bridge. As he'd stood here for hours on end, doing nothing, Xander had had time to think, and he wondered what angle Kraetor was playing, twisting about.

Footsteps echoed on the floor, coming toward Xander. He stiffened himself, standing perfectly at attention. The footsteps came closer and closer until someone stopped just outside of Xander's field of vision.

"You may stand easy, Prince Rosha," a voice said.

Xander relaxed a bit and looked at who had spoken. It was Count Dante Salvatore.

They stood there for a few minutes. Despite being allowed to stand at his ease, Xander still had to remain fairly still. But Dante just stood looking at him. He didn't say anything. The count just kept regarding Xander as if he were looking at an intriguing work of art and were attempting to discern the artist's intention.

Then Xander sensed more than he heard another approaching, and he assumed the perfect stance of attention.

Out of the corner of his eye, Xander saw Dante cock his head to the side.

"I told you…" Dante started, then quieted as Smiles came around the corner.

Smiles saluted, and said, "Good evening, Your Excellency."

"Good evening Commander," Dante replied. "If you don't mind me saying so, I believe you are allowing Hatchling, here, to go to waste."

"Perhaps," Smiles said. "However, his placement is a matter of First Adept Kraetor's whim." Smiles faced Xander. "Your time is finished today. Return to the fortress. No doubt Black Claw will have some training for you. Return upon your appointed hour tomorrow."

Xander saluted. "Yes, Commander Smiles."

As Xander began his journey back to the White Draqon fortress, Dante fell into step beside him.

"You don't mind if I walk with you, do you, Prince Rosha?" Dante asked.

"Of course not, Excellency," Xander lied.

In truth, he just wanted them all to leave him alone, and by them, he meant the High Blood. Xander needed to think, and he thought best by speaking his thoughts aloud to himself.

"Tell me, Prince Rosha," Dante said, "and I expect a truly honest answer: What do you think of her Grace, the Duchess?"

Xander faltered. He stopped and turned to face Dante.

"The Duchess, Your Excellency?" Xander asked. "I'm not sure I understand the question."

Dante smiled. Actually, it wasn't a smile, more like a mischievous smirk.

"You know exactly what I mean." Dante's eyes bore hard into Xander's. "You saw her this morning when you saved the Duke, and she's been here twice to visit you. So, what do you think of her?"

Xander's mouth hung open, aghast at the Count's insinuation. He drew in a deep breath, met the Count's gaze, and choked back a snarl.

"Your Excellency. As you have commanded me to give an honest answer, I must say that were I privileged enough to stand before you fully a Prince of my House, I would take such offence that I would demand satisfaction at your base accusation. I am disgusted that you would even intimate such a stain on my honor. Forgive my brashness, Count Salvatore, but I believe I will continue alone from this point on. I've sworn to do the High Blood no harm, and it would be best if we not tempt that."

Before Dante Salvatore could respond, Xander saluted and turned with every intention of stomping away. Duke Octavio stood in Xander's way.

"Looks like you were right, brother," Dante said. "I owe you a bottle of Inis O'lean red."

"Truly?" Xander demanded, forgetting all rank and formality. "A test? Didn't I prove myself loyal enough this morning when I saved your life?"

Octavio laughed.

This made Xander even more furious. He gave a gesture that might be somewhat recognizable as a salute and hurried by the Kingdom Governor of Koma.

"Prince Rosha!" Octavio called out. "Your Highness, please let me…Bloody damn it, wait just a moment, Xander."

He wasn't sure if it was the use of his familiar name or Octavio's profanity, but Xander stopped and turned. Octavio and Dante were hurrying to catch up to him. Octavio was still smiling, but he had the decency to look a bit embarrassed. Dante's expression was smooth.

"I apologize," Octavio said. "Please understand that I hold you in the highest regard, and I'm grateful for your bravery and quick action this morning, but a man can be tempted in more than one way. I wanted to see if you had any other weaknesses."

"I am the Sun King's loyal subject," Xander said. "I would thank Your Grace not to forget that or question it again, especially not by arranging such an infantile test as this."

Octavio's smile softened. "If you spoke to some High Blood this way, they would strive to see you stripped of that uniform."

"And if this behavior is something I must submit to meekly as if I were some scrawny child before a school yard bully, all to keep this uniform, then perhaps this uniform is not worth wearing. Are other Whites subjected to this? Tested in these ways?"

"No, they are not," Octavio said. "I would like to say, *You are a special and rare case*, but that would be unjust as well." Octavio bent at his waist, leaning on his back leg enough to show Xander the proper amount of leg as was appropriate if Xander had actually been a High Blood Prince. "Please forgive me."

Taken aback by this show of respect and deference, Xander blinked and nodded. After a few breaths, he recalled how to play at court.

"Of course, Your Grace," Xander said. "I must also beg your forgiveness for my outburst. I sometimes forget that while I am a White, my voice is not my own."

"You must spend more time with the Whites," Dante said. "They never hold back from speaking their opinions, even to the High Blood. Oh, they still follow orders, but they do not hesitate to let a High Blood know when they feel those orders are idiotic, stupid, or asinine."

"I've noticed that they are that way with each other," Xander said. "I didn't know they were like that with the High Blood."

"Oh, yes," Octavio said. "Just the other day, Smiles looked at me as we were planning the guard rotation for the Sun King's visit, and he said, *You're an imbecile, Your Grace. A hatchling still eating its own eggshell could see the holes in your plan.*"

Xander laughed at that. Even having known Smiles less than a day, he could hear the White commander speaking those words.

"Very well," Xander said. "Then I don't apologize. But why the test?"

"Because I need someone I can trust in the palace who isn't actually a White and who isn't High Blood, either," Octavio said. "With the Sun King approaching, I must watch for enemies to His Radiant Majesty from within the High Blood as well as without."

"The Brotherhood of the Night?" Xander asked.

"No," Octavio said. "While they are a threat to the Sun King, and others watch for signs of their movement and presence, they are not a threat to the Kingdom itself. Factions exist within all the Great Houses that would see the natural cycle of the Zenith stop and the Kingdom stagnate under one House."

"I don't know what to say." And Xander truly didn't. To him, along with everyone he'd ever known, the cycle of the Great Houses rising to the Zenith and falling again was as constant as the continuous cycle of the seasons and of day and night.

"Don't say anything about it," Octavio said. "I just want you to keep an eye out for something while you are moving about your posts in the palace." He gestured to Dante. "Show him."

Dante reached into his waistcoat, pulled out a yellow cloth, and showed it to Xander. The center of the cloth had a sun embroidered with black thread. The embroidery wound widdershins in an ever-decreasing spiral. Xander followed the spiral to the center. There, in white, which he hadn't seemed to see until he'd followed the path of the black thread, he saw the symbol of Old Uncle Night.

"What is that?" Xander asked in a low, breathless tone.

"That is the symbol of a secret order we've recently discovered within House Floraen," Octavio said. "They call themselves the Black Friars, and they seek to stop the Cycle of the Zenith. Watch for this symbol. Listen for whispers of them. We're telling you, because they may target First Adept Kraetor, not only for being High Blood of a House other than Floraen, but also the death of any First Adept would send ripples of Chaos throughout any House."

251

"Yes, Your Grace," Xander said. He snapped a sharp salute. Then Xander considered this for a moment. "Your Grace, what exactly does taunting me with your wife have to do with trusting me with these political secrets?"

"A valid question," Octavio replied. "It wasn't the nature of the test, though I was wondering about your fortitude when it came to the advances of women. I believe you also met Larayne when you first arrived at the palace today. In truth, I wished to know what your reaction to these tests would be. I already know you are dedicated to the honor of your House and Name, else you wouldn't be wearing that uniform, but it takes a certain kind of man to stand up for what he believes is right, even when faced with the unraveling of all his plans."

"I think I understand," Xander said, though now that he had begun to think in the manner of games at court, something tickled at the back of his mind, something he felt he did not care for at all. "Thank you for trusting me with this. I will watch and listen. Should I see or hear anything, I will bring it to your attention."

"Excellent," Octavio said. "I won't keep you from the fortress any longer. From what I hear, the Whites are hardest on new human recruits during their first fortnight. Best of luck, Prince Rosha."

And with that, Octavio and Dante Salvatore walked away. As the two High Blood rounded the corner, Dante glanced back at Xander and then leaned in close to whisper something to Octavio. Xander wondered what their scheme was and what part he played in it. Few people at court spoke the whole truth, and all of them schemed.

Realizing that he would drive himself mad trying to determine what exactly was going on between Dante and Octavio and what they wanted from him, Xander shook his head and continued to the stairway down to the White Draqon fortress. He didn't have enough to form even the hint of an idea of what was going on, and as he told Octavio, he would watch and listen, but not just for these Black Friars. Xander had been on the battlefields too long, and now his conflicts would be different. He had to be ready to fight at any moment against threats to the High Blood as well as against his fellow White Draqons. Now he also had to be aware of the webs of schemes upon schemes that the spiders at court wove, trying to trap everyone and everything around them in their bid for power.

Halfway down the stairwell, Xander had to step around a small child dressed in ragged black clothes who was scrubbing the stairs with a large brush with thick bristles. His mind was so thick and spinning with how he was going to keep himself alert to everything, Xander didn't realize the bucket next to the child was dry. Not a drop of moisture had seeped through the seams between the wood, and the stairs were dry – not a bubble of soap or drop of water in sight.

Xander turned to the waif, ready to demand an explanation. The scrubbing had stopped. The brush was still on the stairs, and the child was reaching into the bucket. Xander launched himself to the side when he heard something on the stairs below him: the click of someone's heel on the stone and a swish of cloth. It might not be an attacker, but he couldn't afford to risk it.

A crossbow bolt flew past Xander, grazing the slash of leather on his left sleeve. He leapt down the stairs as far as he dared to and still be able to maintain his footing when he landed.

Something clattered to the steps – most likely a crossbow. Whoever had shot at him would want to close the distance.

Xander landed a little off-balance. To steady himself, he reached out for the wall as he drew his rapier from its sheath. When the weapon was halfway free, a shadow came at him.

Xander released his grip on the rapier and dropped to a crouch.

The attacker thrust a dagger into the space where Xander's chest had been a moment before. Without the target there, the attacker, all in grays and blacks, had overextended his arm.

Reaching up as he stood, Xander caught the attacker's arm. Pinning it with his neck and left shoulder, Xander twisted left, pulling the man off-balance. As he did, Xander brought his right fist up as fast and as hard as he could into the assailant's face. Pain shot through his knuckles and fingers, but the *oomph* of pain and surprise he heard was worth it.

The man pulled free of Xander's grip. His hand closed around the hilt of Xander's half-drawn sword. He stepped back into a guard position and smiled, the expression made that much grimmer by the trickle of blood coming from his nose.

Xander tensed his legs to spring back up the stairs.

His attacker stood holding Xander's rapier at full extension, less than an arm's length from Xander's face. Xander steadied his breath as he watched his enemy's hips. Reading his facial expressions wouldn't do any good with that gray cloth wrapped around his head, hiding everything but his eyes. Damian's voice bubbled up from Xander's memories, *Eyes lie; hips are the center of almost every movement we make.*

"Prince Xander," a high-pitched voice said behind him, followed by a distinct *click*.

A little over a year before, on a rain-soaked battlefield near the once-capital of Heidenmarch, Xander had heard the very same *click*. It had come from right behind him as well. The gods had favored Xander that day, as a second, louder *click* followed, indicating the gun had misfired. Sometimes, Xander still woke in the dead of night with that sound ringing in his ears, his mind's eye filled with the look of that Heidenmarch soldier as he died on Xander's sword.

Xander dropped, bruising his knee, hip, elbow, and ribs on the stairs.

This gun did not misfire and the shot echoed like thunder in the confines of the stairwell. Acrid smoke filled the air and burned Xander's eyes.

He drew his fighting knife as he rolled across the stairs, causing more bruises that he would feel later. When he hit the wall, Xander sprang to his feet, facing outward so that no one could surprise him.

A gaping hole had appeared in the attacker's gray shirt in the center of a dark bloom. Xander's sword clattered to the stone steps as his enemy fell backward. Xander tried not to look, willed himself not to look, but he could not manage to pull his gaze away as the would-be assassin fell back as one might fall back onto a bed after a week of travel.

The man's neck hit the very edge of one of the steps with a popping sound, and his head seemed to unhinge from his shoulders on the impact. Xander's teeth clenched together, his shoulders tightened, and his stomach nearly lost the contents of his meager lunch from a few hours before. The attacker slid down two steps, and his head twisted against the next so that his vacant eyes stared at Xander from beside his shoulder.

Xander had lived through dozens of battles, seen countless injuries, but he could never grow accustomed to the way a man's head flopped around at the end of a broken neck.

Forcing his attention away, Xander looked at the child holding the smoking two-shot pistol, still aimed at the corpse on the steps below them.

"Put the weapon down," Xander said.

She – he realized the child was a girl when she looked at him – smiled. Without a word, she dashed across the steps and pulled herself up to one of the windows. Xander leapt toward her trying to grab an arm or an ankle, but before Xander could stop her, she jumped out.

"No," Xander yelled.

He watched, helpless as she fell into the evening mist of Koma City, taking the pistol with her.

"Damn."

How was he going to explain this? He rubbed his hands across the top of his head and pulled his new braids until his scalp ached. Here he was, next to a corpse with a gunshot wound in the middle of its chest, crossbow nearby, no firearm to be found, and the only other person involved had just killed herself. No one would go look for her body. No one would believe Xander.

"Damn."

He kicked the corpse as if he could punish it more.

Two years in the Reds, two years of fighting against the Kingdom's enemies, and it was all for naught. In the span of a few heartbeats, it had all been destroyed.

"Wait." Xander forced his breath to slow. He licked his lips and shook his head. As much as he hated it, he might have a way out of this. "What would Damian do if he were here?"

Xander surveyed the scene one last time.

"He'd lie his tongue right out of his head, that's what he'd do."

Xander unwrapped the cloth from the flopping head; he hated every instant, but he did it. Once the cloth was free, he used it to keep the blood from the gunshot wound from spilling onto his White uniform. Moving a deadweight body was a challenge, but Xander managed to get it up and out the window by the time he heard footsteps pounding on the stairs above and below him. He picked up the man's crossbow and knife. The crossbow followed the body. Just as Xander was about to toss the knife after, he noticed a symbol on the wooden hilt and a word etched into the blade. The word was *kostota,* and the symbol was the Collaen family symbol. Xander slid the knife deep into his boot and kicked his sword into his hand just before the Whites charged down, nearly colliding with him.

Sword in hand, panting slightly from the effort of disposing of the body, Xander hoped he looked like just another White coming to find out where the gunshot had come from. Smiles began barking orders.

"You, Hatchling," Smiles growled.

Xander spun to face Smiles.

"Sir?" Xander said. *Need to think like Damian, just for a moment.*

"Did you see anything?"

"I heard a gunshot." Not a lie. "I wish I had more of an answer." Also not a lie. He did wish he had an answer for what had happened.

Smiles sniffed and grunted. The smoke likely helped mask any scent of fear or anything else Xander might not be feeling.

"Back to the fortress with you, then," Smiles said. "And tell Black Claw what happened here if he doesn't already know when you get there."

"Sir," Xander saluted, sheathed his sword, and headed down the stairs.

Every other step, the Collaen knife pressed against his leg.

THREE

Only the barest hint of light still hung in the sky. The shadows from the buildings and levels above them stretched over everything. Damian leaned against a wall in this almost darkness, finally alone. Gods and goddesses, he was hungry. He was at the point where his stomach clenched tight, as if by doing so, his body wouldn't have to acknowledge how much it wanted food. The young Vara recruits that he'd been training had dispersed a few moments before, having spent the day whacking each other with practice swords. Colt and Gabryl had, true to their word, kept Damian's identity a secret. By the time the bell rang to end training, all had been complaining of hunger for some time. Now, all the recruits headed to the main hall for food, and as much as Damian wanted to rush off to the meal with them, he wanted a few moments to himself to think.

What game were Adepts Czenzi and Kraetor playing, and why did Damian have this feeling that the game Dyrk was playing wasn't actually that far removed from theirs? Was it the same game? Damian shook his head. That didn't feel right. Different game, but perhaps on the same board, or at least with some of the same players. How did Xander fit into all of this?

Something tugged at his trousers. Damian yelped at the surprise and scrambled away.

The little girl who had given Damian his gun back so he could shoot Tamaz stood smiling up at him. She held out a bowl of stew with a hunk of dark bread on top soaking in the broth and flavor. The smell of it wafting into his nose and then down to his stomach overpowered him. He took the bowl and wooden spoon and began to eat.

The stew itself couldn't properly be called stew, but it wasn't really soup either. A poor, bastardly half-breed of both, but Damian didn't care. His mind knew it was among the least-fine meals he'd ever eaten, but his stomach reveled in it as if he were dining at the First Feast of Heroes. The bread was actually good, full, rich, and warm. He used it to soak up the stew and ate greedily.

After he'd emptied half of the bowl, his stomach decided it would allow him the rest of the meal on his own terms. Damian looked up to thank the girl, but she was gone.

Damian sighed. More mysteries and games. He wanted to be as irritated with the girl as he was with everyone else, but couldn't bring himself to be. She'd brought him food, and that meant he could get just a few more moments alone. Not many, he knew that. Eventually someone would come looking for him, but for now, he was his own man. For now.

"I'm my own man all the time," Damian muttered to himself.

He glanced toward the poor excuse for a wall that surrounded the Vara compound. It would be so easy to slip over that wall and be away. Then the goddess's words came back to him: *If you stay, you could become more influential than Saent Julian the Courageous and Kavala, not just to Koma, but to the entire world.* Damian hated that she knew the exact thing to say to him to keep him from getting out of this compound, getting on a ship, and escaping the bloody continent, screaming *Sod off*, as he watched it fade into the distance from the stern of a ship.

Damn gods and goddesses and their schemes, playing mortals as if they were cards in a game. Damian wondered if Kahddria was involved. If she was, it wasn't like her to remain unseen for so long. Damian laughed at that. He and Faelin had known Kahddria for such a short time, yet it felt like he knew her more intimately than he did his brother and mother. Perhaps that was the way of things with celestial and infernal things: They were so connected with the aspect of the universe to which they were bound, it was easier to know the core of them. To know the wind was to know Kahddria.

Damian did his best to push all these thoughts from his head as he finished his stew. With every spoonful, his mind would wander, and he'd have to snap it back under control. Then it wandered to a pair of steel-colored eyes. His spoon paused halfway between the bowl and his mouth.

He sighed again. Faelin had warned him that the woman who called herself the Lord Morigahn was more trouble than Damian wanted. Damian couldn't help but think she couldn't be more trouble than he was in right now, and even if she was, she was still a beautiful lady, and that would have made the trouble a lot more pleasant.

A soft whine pulled Damian from his daydreams of facing troubles with Faelin's friend.

Glancing around, Faelin saw a puppy of some kind poking its head around the corner of a building. Its near-white eyes shone in the lamplight coming from the barracks around them. The little thing's fur was matted and dirty. Was it some mascot or something, or had it crawled through some breach in the walls? Damian shrugged. It didn't matter. He sopped up as much of the stew as he could into the bread, spooned the last of the vegetables and meat into his mouth, and placed the bowl on the ground. He whistled and clicked softly to the puppy as he stepped away from the bowl.

Animals were so much easier than people. If an animal didn't like someone, that person usually didn't have a doubt, unless the person was even more obtuse than most people so as to not pick up on the blatant clues that animals gave off.

The puppy padded over and started licking from the bowl much faster than Damian had expected. He'd thought he'd have to coax it over. As the puppy came closer, it looked like one of the shepherd breeds the Heidenmarchs had bred from wolf stock. At a second glance, Damian thought it might be a wolf, but he discarded the thought. A wolf wouldn't have survived this far into the city. Likely, it had come on a ship and had been cast off or misplaced somehow.

Damian knelt down and scratched behind the dog's ears. It leaned into his affection as best it could without pulling its head from the bowl.

After a moment, several other puppies came out of the shadows and the darkness to share in the treasure Damian had provided. The first growled a bit.

"None of that," Damian said in a soft tone. "Enough for everyone."

He broke the damp bread into smaller pieces and fed it to the puppies. Seven in all surrounded him, licking at his hands as he fed them. One put its forepaws on Damian's knee so that it stood a bit taller and licked his face.

Damian laughed. He missed having dogs. One more thing taken by the Kingdom's asinine laws. Chewing his lower lip, Damian looked around, examining every shadowy corner around him. Seeing no one spying on him, he dove into the pile of fur, petting, scratching, and tickling. The pups reacted as pups usually do, climbing over him, licking, yipping, barking, and nipping. Hunger still gnawed at his sides, but not that I-want-to-curl-up-and-die hunger, and losing himself in the play helped Damian forget it even more. It had been too long since he'd been able to play like this.

He didn't know how long he romped and frolicked with the pups, but sometime later two of the animals stopped playing, faced the center of the Vara compound, and began to growl. Moments later, the other pups joined them.

Standing, Damian scanned his surroundings. Night had fallen while he had played, and he cursed himself as a fool for his carelessness. Too many people had him as a piece in their game, which meant their opponents would want to eliminate him. He was so tired that he'd forgotten the three new friends he'd met in the privs earlier that day. The pups continued growling and occasionally barking, making it impossible for Damian to listen for anyone who might be sneaking up on him.

He glanced over his shoulder as he backed toward the pile of practice swords. One of those would be better than nothing. He kicked one into his left hand and pulled his knife out with his right. Let whoever or whatever was out there in the darkness ponder that. It might work in Damian's favor, or it might not, but either way, it would likely give anyone who planned on attacking him a few moments pause.

Damian held the practice sword in a reversed grip and out in front of him, waiting for something to happen.

The *twang* and *thrum* of a crossbow being loosed rang out from the shadows to his right. Damian tried to fling himself back to avoid being shot, but if the bowman possessed any level of competence...

For a brief fraction of a moment, pain blossomed in Damian's chest.

A flash of light blinded him for an instant, likely from the pain. In the next heartbeat something small and dark flew across his vision, the pain was gone. One of the pups landed in front of Damian, a crossbow bolt in its jaw.

The pups started barking even louder. Hopefully anyone who came running at the sound wouldn't get here until Damian dealt with the problem and got the practice sword out of his hands.

Damian blinked twice. Then he moved, weaving a zigzagging path toward the shadows where he'd heard the crossbow being loosed. A figure leapt from the shadows, a man, a knife in each hand.

Knives? Damian almost laughed at the man dressed in gray and black, with that idiotic *Morigahnti* head scarf thing wrapped around his head.

Skidding to a stop on the cobblestones, Damian dropped his knife and kicked it at the man running toward him. Despite the fact that the knife would, at worst, scratch him a little, the man flinched, slowing his progress. Even though he'd flinched left instead of right as Damian had pictured, it was enough.

"Thank you, Ragkuzani," Damian muttered, switching the practice sword in his hands as he leapt forward.

Four breaths and four slashes later – first to the right wrist, second to the right side of the head, third to the left wrist, fourth to the right knee – and the attacker was on his knees before Damian.

"Ga—" the man started.

Instinct took over, and Damian slashed across the man's throat as hard as he could. Then, for good measure, he drove the butt of the practice sword into the man's head, just behind his eye. The pommel sunk in half-an-inch, and blood spilled from the wound. The man's eye's rolled into the back of his head. Damian didn't know if the man could actually speak miracles, but he wasn't going to take any chances.

Footsteps approached from out of the darkness. The precise strikes of the practice sword were too obvious for Damian to deny if anyone knew what to look for. Dyrk likely did. Even if that didn't give Damian away, it certainly wouldn't help his case that he wasn't something special. Unless…

"Bloody, goat-faced, whore's son," Damian screamed, as he beat his attacker over and over with wild, overhanded swings.

Damian allowed his rage, fury, and confusion to flow through his arms. He let go of all the training he'd ever received and just beat on the corpse. Soon blood began to soak through the clothes as Damian struck again and again and again. People yelled around him, and some dogs barked. He didn't care. He continued screaming, getting more and more creative with the vulgarities and insults he flung down on the assassin as his repeated blows covered all evidence of his earlier display of skill. After a few moments Damian became less concerned about covering the evidence that might damn him, and pictured a myriad of faces on the corpse as he beat it: Kraetor, Gareth, Dyrk, the three idiots in the priv, White Draqons, every Inquisitor who had ever hunted him, and every bastard who had tried to short him on a gun sale, even Xander and his father. Oh, how it felt good to beat them all through this proxy.

Eventually, several pairs of arms grabbed his arms and wrapped around his chest. As they pulled him away from the body, Damian kicked it – for no other reason than for trying to kill him. And for some strange reason, Damian felt the man should have succeeded.

After struggling for a few moments more, just to keep up the appearances of his act, Damian dropped the sword. He relaxed his struggles as the sword clattered to the ground.

"I'm calm," Damian said. They did not release him, so he repeated himself. "I'm calm."

"What in the name of the godless dead goes on here?" Dyrk bellowed as he pushed through the crowd of Vara surrounding Damian and the corpse.

"Zephyr was murdering that man," someone said.

"Let go of him," Dyrk said. "We're enough to stop him if he tries to flee or do something else equally stupid."

Those holding Damian released him.

"Are you alright, Highness?" someone whispered in his ear.

Damian glanced out of the corner of his eye. Gabryl's face was pale under his hood as he looked Damian up and down. Damian gave a slight, brisk nod before other hands pushed him toward Dyrk. Damian straightened, not quite standing at attention, but at least demonstrating some semblance of respect for the general.

"Zephyr," Dyrk waved toward the body, "explain this."

Before Damian could respond, the pups padded between the Vara and came to sit or lay around Damian. That first one, the largest of them, sat on its haunches between Damian and Dyrk, facing the Vara commander. A wave of whispers rippled through the gathered Vara. Dyrk himself took a half step back and pulled his gray hood back a bit to look at the mangy pup.

"What?" Damian asked, his hands raised in a confused half-shrug.

"They don't normally like people," Dyrk said. "We have them in the yard because they do better about warning about intruders than most of the men standing the night watch." He addressed the gathered crowd. "But that's a concern for later. We have a corpse in our yard," Dyrk faced Damian again, "a corpse you put here. Explain."

"He came after me with a pair of knives," Damian said, "after missing me with a crossbow. I just thank Sister Wind," it was so hard not to snort laughter at calling on Kahddria's name, "that he was as bad with his knives as he was with the crossbow."

"And you killed him?" Paedrik Sardon demanded, coming to stand next to Dyrk.

"Damn and bloody right, I killed him!" Damian retorted. "Can any man here say he'd let someone who tried to kill him live just so the man could try again?"

Not a single one of the Vara argued against this.

"Didn't you think that you might want to know why he wanted to kill you?" Paedrik asked.

"Actually, sir," Damian replied, quickly scanning to see if that cub still had the bolt in its jaw – it didn't – "no. Once something flew past my head and he came out of the shadows, I mostly thought about how much I wanted to survive."

"We can't fault him for that," Dyrk said. "You four." Dyrk pointed at four of the Vara, seemingly at random. "Get rid of that body. Wait until night settles in a little more and drop it in a canal somewhere in the commons. Zephyr, I'll walk you to your bunk. The rest of you, just like any time trouble comes to this side of our walls, we settle it ourselves and keep it to ourselves. Understood?"

A chorus of, "Yes, General," echoed throughout the compound. The gathered Vara began to disperse.

"Sir," Paedrik said, addressing Dryk, but looking at Damian, "might I—?"

"You might not," Dyrk said. "Zephyr might be new to us, but he is one of us, just the same. He doesn't know all the traditions we're founded on yet, especially not here in Koma City, but we know them. We'll protect him just as we would any of our other brothers."

"Yes, General." Paedrik saluted and walked away, shouting orders for someone to get a bucket and some scrub brushes to clean up the mess.

"Shouldn't I clean it up?" Damian asked Dyrk, as the four Vara Dyrk had assigned to remove the body carried it away.

"Not at all," Dyrk replied. He started toward the barracks where Damian had been assigned. Damian hopped to catch up with him "You'll come to understand what we do, how and why, before too long. Mostly we have such a dangerous time of it in the streets that we always bear our burdens together, no matter what those burdens might be. Which is why your pay might be a bit lower than you expect. We have several men who have families that need a bit of extra assistance. If you think to protest, remember that two of those men are making it so that corpse you left in my yard never existed."

"Sounds fair and reasonable to me," Damian replied.

"Good," Dyrk said.

They reached Damian's barracks. Dyrk stood in the way of the door. The general's black eyes bore into Damian's.

"I know you are more than you seem, Zephyr," Dyrk said. "You know more of the sword than you want to admit. Don't argue. I've known enough masters of D'fence to know the difference between someone who knows a few tricks and someone born to use the sword. Paedrik knows, too, and a few others. We will not betray you to those outside these walls. We all come to the Vara having enemies."

Damian wondered if this conversation would be happening if Dyrk knew who Damian really was and what crimes he'd committed in the eyes of the Kingdom.

"Know this: Some men also choose to make enemies on this side of our wall."

"Like those three who slipped and fell in the priv this morning?"

"They were not the most coordinated bunch," Dyrk replied. "We tend not to like it when our fellow Varas keep secrets from us. You are new, and so we grant you some time to get used to the idea of trusting us. However, you are bringing more trouble sooner than we are accustomed with new recruits. While you rest tonight, consider with great care how long you want to keep secrets from your new brothers." Dyrk opened the doors and stepped out of Damian's way. "Sleep well, and may the gods grant you clarity."

As Damian entered the barracks, he got the distinct feeling that Dyrk had almost added a *Your Highness* as Damian walked by him.

The barracks were empty, and Damian thanked the gods and goddesses that he was alone. The door clicked shut behind him, and that seemed to bring exhaustion crashing down on him. He stumbled toward his cot, sore, tired, and still a bit hungry. Sleep, he wanted sleep. Everything else could wait until morning.

When Damian reached his cot, he realized the room wasn't empty. One of the pups lay under his cot, its head sticking out. Damian looked around the barracks. The only other door was closed, as were all of the windows. The pup had something in its mouth. It crawled forward and dropped one of the attacker's knives at Damian's feet. He knelt down and picked up the weapon.

"*Kraestu kraenka yn'goska,*" Damian swore when he saw the Collaen family mark on the traditional assassin's knife of post Ykthae Koma.

He dropped onto his cot. He held the knife above him, turning it over and over, trying to make some semblance of sense from it.

"I hate politics so much," Damian said, and stuffed the knife under his pillow.

He wanted to sleep, but all he could do was curse a goddess who tempted him with promises that she might be lying about. He should leave, but he knew he wasn't going to. *Greater than Julian and Kavala, together.* It wasn't so much the fame that such a thing would likely bring him, but more that Damian would be able to sneer at the entire Kingdom of the Sun from the heavens after he died. The chance to do that was worth all the risk in the world. He just had to survive all these games where people were playing with him as a piece or trying to remove him from the board.

He knew one place he could go, perhaps, for some answers, though it might take him a few days to gain enough trust with the rest of the Vara to be able to venture outside these walls alone.

Damian glanced down beside his cot. The cub was still there.

Laughing at his exhaustion for thinking the pup was a wolf cub, Damian rolled onto his side. He felt better sleeping with the animal there. If anyone else came to kill him, hopefully it would wake him. On the other side of the coin, if someone did come to kill him, Damian wouldn't be so tired and hungry any more.

"Either way," Damian said, reached down, and scratched the pup behind its ears.

He fell into a deep, dreamless sleep with the Stormseeker cub licking the last bit of dried stew from his fingers.

FOUR

Octavio Salvatore walked with his wife, Portia, in their wing of the Governor's Palace.

"It seems like today went well," Portia said, snuggling a little closer to him.

"Even better than I'd hoped," Octavio said. Not only had Xander Rosha killed both assassins, but he had also been the first to see them. By giving Xander his first braids as a White, Octavio set the wheels in motion to bring young Prince Xander Rosha into his play for the Zenith. Every campaign for taking the Throne left a large wake filled with corpses. Once he slaughtered all the heirs to the other Houses and Octavio sat upon the Night Throne, he would need loyal men to fill the void that always followed in the wake of the Brotherhood taking the Zenith. "The foundation has been laid. Now I have to build on it, which means eliminating Xander Rosha's last ties to what he perceives as his duty, and quickly."

"You won't be dining with me and First Adept Kraetor, will you?" Portia asked.

"My love…" Octavio started.

Portia held up her hand. "I will give your apologies and charm the grim old goat so that he doesn't miss you a moment. Though I don't understand what could be more important than having a pleasant meal with your wife, and then maybe having her for dessert?"

"Portia!" Octavio cried in mock outrage. "Do you think of nothing other than your physical desires?"

"I only think of my desire to provide my husband with a son."

"Later tonight," Octavio said. "I will come to your bed. Wait for me there, and I will do my best to satisfy your want to give me an heir."

"As my lord husband commands," Portia said, and then stood on her toes to kiss his cheek.

Octavio watched as she sauntered down the hall in a way that accentuated her luscious hips. Already he was imagining all the ways he would make her moan his name come nightfall. Shaking his lustful thoughts away, Octavio turned and headed for the hidden Temple of Night.

With his wife's distracting presence gone, Octavio's frustration rose. Xander Rosha falling into his proper place seemed to be the only thing going according to plan. Just when Octavio needed the Night Adepts gathered and strong, they kept splintering out and dying. Tamaz should have killed Damian Adryck last night, but somehow Adryck had escaped and no amount of scrying could find him. Now Tamaz was dead, and his connection to the Brotherhood discovered. Hardin had forced Octavio's hand. Hopefully Carmine and Graegyr could work together and finally put an end to this new Lord Morigahn. Octavio felt more than just a little silly thinking of Julianna Taraen as *Lord* Morigahn. Even as that thought came to him, Octavio admonished himself for it. The Taraen girl and those Morigahnti she drew to her proved more dangerous and resourceful than any others in recent memory, not since Octavio had led the attack on the Traejyn family.

A small voice in the back of Octavio's mind urged him to postpone his plans for a better time, but after a moment's consideration, he pushed the thought aside. In all the other lands, the Brotherhood stood ready to strike. On the day the Sun King arrived in Koma City, they *would* strike, and High Blood from every House would die, leaving the throne free for Octavio. Koma was the only land where the Brotherhood was not ready, all because they couldn't kill two people, Damian Adryck and Julianna Taraen. If he stopped now, the last fifteen years of planning would be wasted. He was not going to leave any loose ends dangling.

He turned a corner and saw a servant girl in her late teens wearing red and gold Floraen livery and carrying a tray of dirty dishes. He recognized her because he made a point to know all the pretty servants in the palace. This girl was the image of Heidenmarch beauty: golden blond hair, sapphire blue eyes, flushed rosy skin that looked as though she were constantly blushing just a little bit. She dipped into a curtsy as Octavio came near.

"Rise, Larayne," Octavio said. "I won't have you spilling those dirty dishes everywhere."

"Yes, High Blood," Larayne said, her face flushing just a little more when he used her name.

She turned to continue down the hall when he stepped in her way.

"Larayne, I have something that I need your help with in my private chambers."

"But I have to get these back to the kitchen, High Blood," she said, blushing furiously now. "I'll be missed."

"I'll write a message explaining everything," Octavio said. "You won't get into any trouble. I promise."

"I am your servant, High Blood."

"I know," Octavio said, looking deep into her blue eyes. She glanced away, feigning modesty, but Octavio saw her coy smile. He put his fingers to her chin and lifted her face to look back at him. "And right now, I have a need that only you can serve."

Leading her to his chamber and drugging her was a matter of child's play. The Daemyn was already waiting for her when Octavio got her to the Temple of Night. Octavio had used one of the assassin's corpses for the Daemyn to possess. The Daemyn and Larayne were sequestered in the space behind the Altar of Night, where such joining typically took place. Now, he waited patiently for the Daemyn to conclude its business with the girl and then live up to its part of the bargain.

While waiting, Octavio heard the door to the inner sanctum of the Temple of Night open and close behind him. He didn't bother to turn, but kept his gaze on the prisoner delivered to him in secret in the dark hours of the morning. Only three people in the entirety of the Kingdom of the Sun would dare enter this chamber without his direct invitation: Roma, Dante, and Portia. The soft whisper of slippers gliding across the black marble floor approaching him announced who it was.

"Dinner has concluded already, my love?" Octavio asked. "How was it?"

He still didn't face her. He kept his gaze fixed on the prisoner, letting the quiet parts of his mind work on how best to use this traitorous slime. Plans for him were already in motion, but those plans were only laid out in the short term. After this man served his immediate purpose, Octavio would find many more uses for him.

"Productive," Portia replied. "With the exception of First Adept Kraetor, I have most of the men here at court tripping over themselves trying to gain my favor. For some reason they believe your affections wander far from your marriage bed and that I might be seeking attention outside my bed as well."

"And what do their wives think about this?"

"Those who have wives are finding themselves in quite a bind," Portia said. "The wives know that I am only testing the characters of these men whom you might choose for higher positions within the court. For if a man can't be loyal and faithful to his wife, how can he be loyal and faithful to the governor?"

"A very astute observation," Octavio agreed. "But how is it the noblemen are hearing one thing, and the noble women hearing another?"

"Because I give all the servant girls very pretty presents to spread these rumors to the men, and tell the truth to their wives."

"Ingenious. I'll have to be careful or you might start plotting to take the governorship away from me."

"Never!" Portia gasped, feigning outrage. "I know how many tedious papers you have to read each day, and all the inane disputes you have to settle. I'd never survive the boredom. No thank you, Governor Salvatore. I'm far more content to be your beautiful wife, ruling the court in your name. That way, I have all the fun, attend all the parties, and get all the bribes, while you, my dear husband have a mountain of papers flooding your desk, are the target of assassins, and suffer all the head pains."

Octavio chuckled, partly because her words were funny, but also because her words were true.

"Sometimes I wish I'd been born a woman," Octavio said.

"And then what would I have done for a husband?" Portia asked. "No one else is worthy of me."

"Not even the Sun King?" Octavio asked.

"That *boy*?" Portia shrieked. "Your cousin may sit at Zenith, but he will *never* be a great man, not like you. I gave my heart and body to you, Octavio Salvatore of House Floraen, because I love you. I see the same greatness in you that Old Uncle Night saw in you when he named you his First Adept."

Hearing those words, Octavio turned to his wife and kissed her with all the passion and love she stirred in him. It was the best way he knew to show her how much those words meant to him. It also moved attention away from her comment about Old Uncle Night. Out of all those who worshipped Old Uncle Night, Octavio and Dante were the only ones who knew that the God of Death and Lies hadn't spoken to his followers in centuries. Like all the First Adepts before him, Octavio searched for a way to wake his god, or free him from whatever prison he languished in.

One of the two hidden doors behind the Alter of Night opened, and Octavio broke off his kiss as the Daemyn returned from his sojourn with the servant girl, Larayne. At first, it looked like it might be Octavio's twin, but as it strode across the room, the creature shed its human disguise and revealed a bit of its true nature. The illusionary clothes matching Octavio's faded, and coarse charcoal hair grew out of the Daemyn's skin. Its face grew longer, and its eyes slanted more while taking on a silvery sheen and showing no variation of color. Leathery, bat-like wings sprouted from its shoulder blades. While not completely assuming its true form, there was no chance of mistaking it for anything other than a creature from the Realm of the Godless Dead.

And though Octavio marveled at this amazing creature, he desired none of its power. Like all Daemyns, this creature was bound by the ancient celestial treaty, unable to interact with the physical without first making an agreement with a human. Even with all its otherworldly might, it was still a slave.

"Are you sure you want to use this pathetic specimen?" the Daemyn asked, looking at the prisoner before turning its greedy eyes at Portia. "I could do so much more, if you'd care to renegotiate."

Octavio's gloved hand lashed out and caught the Daemyn by the throat. The attack was so sudden the Daemyn didn't have any time to react before Octavio pushed it back against the Alter of Night. Under most circumstances, any but the weakest Daemyn could best Octavio in a physical confrontation, but his gloves were an equalizer. They were spun from pure golden thread, the color and metal of All Father Sun, one of the few weaknesses shared by all denizens of the Realm of the Godless Dead.

"You dare to bring something like that into this sacred place?" the Daemyn hissed as its neck smoked where Octavio held its throat.

"I am the First Adept of Old Uncle Night," Octavio snarled. "You don't have the imagination to conceive of what I've dared in this chamber. Your masters have paled when they learned the acts I have committed here to further the Uncle's influence in this world. If you value your existence, you will never, *never*, speak or even think about my wife in such terms again."

The Daemyn nodded. Octavio was squeezing his fingers so tightly that the Daemyn couldn't speak.

"It is an honor for you to serve me in any way. Now fulfill your end of the bargain, and then get out of my sight."

Octavio pulled the Daemyn up and thrust the creature at the prisoner. The Daemyn went about bonding lesser Daemyns that served it into the prisoner. Screams echoed through the temple, but Octavio ignored them. Instead, he looked at his wife. Her eyes shot daggers of hatred into the Daemyn's back. When one side of her nose twitched a little, Octavio knew there was only one way for Portia to be appeased.

When the screams had died down, Octavio pulled a gold-bladed dagger from underneath his Adept's mantle. Runes blessed with the power of All Father Sun were drawn across each side of the blade, granting the weapon the ability to kill any but the most powerful of all Daemyns. He grabbed a fistful of hair with the golden glove and pulled the Daemyn's head backward. The Daemyn had only just a moment of surprise before Octavio thrust the dagger into its eye. One clause Octavio always included in any agreement he made when bargaining with Daemyns was that they would not harm him in anyway. He was amazed at how few of them forced that agreement on him. Now that the Daemyn had lain with the girl and the prisoner was altered, the bargain was finished, giving the creature no further protection.

"I'll go attend the girl, my love," Portia said. "I will await you in bed."

Octavio nodded, not looking at her as she left. The last thing he needed right now was a distraction. Having killed their master, Octavio had just freed the four Daemyns bound into the prisoner from any direct command from the Realm of the Godless Dead, at least for a while. He would have to exert dominance over them. Even though their cooperation was implied in the contract, it was up to their master to ensure obedience. Now Octavio would have to enforce his own will upon them.

"I am Duke Octavio Salvatore of House Floraen, First Adept of Old Uncle Night, and soon to change the Zenith and sit as the Night King. Serve me well and I will treat you well and reward you handsomely before you return to the Realm of the Godless Dead. Betray me, and I will end your existence on this realm and in all others."

A mouth and a pair of eyes opened on each of the prisoner's hands and feet. They glanced at Octavio and then to the Daemyn sprawled on the floor, dagger hilt budding from its eye.

"We agree to your terms, First Adept," all four mouths said in unison. "What are your commands?"

"Remain dormant in this body until you find the one called Damian Adryck, known as the *Tsumari'osa*," Octavio said. "When you find him, you may show yourselves and devour his soul."

"Yes, First Adept." With that, all the eyes and mouths closed.

Octavio stepped up to the unconscious prisoner and slapped the man's face with all his might. The prisoner groaned and blinked himself awake. After a moment of regaining his bearings, the prisoner's eyes focused and all color drained out of his face. Octavio could only imagine how it felt to wake up and see a man wearing the Adept's Mantle of Old Uncle Night standing over the corpse of a Daemyn. Octavio slapped him again, to bring him out of the shock.

"Gareth, the fence?"

"Yes," the traitor said, too afraid to lie.

"You are a traitor to the Kingdom of the Sun," Octavio said. "Fortunately for you, every individual who knows this is dead. Well, every individual save for three: you, myself, and Damian Adryck. As Governor, I can pardon you in the Name of the Sun King, but only if you perform one minor task."

"Wha... wha... what?" Gareth asked.

"Kill the only other man who could testify against you should the matter ever be brought to trial."

"You want me to kill Damian?"

"I believe that's what I just said, but if you needed it said in such simple terms, yes, I want you to kill Damian Adryck."

"I'll need help," Gareth said.

"Don't worry," Octavio replied. "When the time comes, you will have more than enough assistance. I've already made the arrangements. In fact, you won't need to do anything other than find Adryck. My servants will know when you do, and then they'll do the work. Are you my man?"

"I do this and I go free?"

"With many rewards as well."

"I'm your man."

"Excellent," Octavio said. "My steward, Roma, will be in presently to free you and arrange for any need you have to be met."

"You're not going to let me down yourself?"

"What? And dirty my hands by touching a water-blood traitor like you? Hardly. You will be free within the hour. After that, you will want for nothing before being about your errand. After you are done, I will assess your performance. Serve me well in this, and we'll see what other errands I might have for you."

FIVE

Josephine didn't feel any different as she cradled the child in her arms on the veranda. It *cooed* and *burbled* up at her, smiling in that joyful, heartbreaking way that babies do. The night breeze still carried the scent of roses and tickled her skin.

"This hardly seems a dangerous creature," Josephine said.

"The same could be said of you," Maxian retorted. "Were I the Sun King, I would have let Xander be and had you share Damian's fate."

"Don't underestimate Xander," Josephine said, gently flicking the baby's lower lip with her finger. The baby smiled even wider. "He's just as dangerous as Damian and I, just in different ways. He's smart and observant. Arranging events to ensure getting him into Kraetor's service took some doing. It won't be long before Xander begins to see the little and large hypocrisies in Kingdom Law."

"You're sure of that?" Maxian asked.

"Oh, definitely," Josephine said. "I know *First Adept*," she spoke those two words with the utmost contempt, "Kraetor better than most within his House. Vincent…" Josephine paused and chewed her upper lip while she considered if she was truly ready to share this, even with Maxian.

"Vincent…?" Maxian asked.

Josephine closed her mouth and forced a half smile. It was a challenge to smile and not cry. Gods and goddesses, she missed her husband. Maxian sighed and rolled his eyes. Josephine's smile widened. She couldn't help but take a little joy in irritating him the way that Vincent used to infuriate her. Maxian certainly deserved it more than just a little. And as she smiled, a single tear welled in her eye. She turned away from Maxian.

"Josephine," Maxian said. "It's not your fault."

"Isn't it?" She turned back. Her sorrow was burned away by the bitterness rising up in her breast, heating her face, ears, and neck. "Everything I've done since Damian was born has been one long game of subtle pushes and pulls throughout all levels of Kingdom politics. I have…"

Her skin prickled across her entire body, as if feeling was returning to a limb that had fallen asleep.

"What?"

"That would be the child's attempt to affect you with divine power," Maxian said. "If you hadn't spoken the words to free yourself from that influence, she would be working right now to destroy some semblance of your life. What, I could not begin to tell you, and that's what makes her so dangerous. While she is a Saent, she is a baby as well, with all the lack of control or focus a baby has. Yrgaeshkil is either a genius or an idiot—"

"Likely both," Josephine interrupted.

Maxian stood with his mouth still open. He hated being interrupted, but instead of putting on his wide-eyed, tight-faced expression of indignation, he laughed.

"I'd not wager against that," Maxian said, as he got himself under control. "Not at all. Whether she be genius or idiot, Yrgaeshkil meant to unleash this creature against Julianna, and potentially Xander and Damian. The Mother of Lies has a scheme that reaches from the Kingdom to the heavens, a scheme that's been going on for centuries, possibly since the battle of Ykthae Wood, and her plan is coming to fruition now."

"How do you know this?" Josephine asked.

"Because she's acting now. She's getting directly involved. Her testing the letter and the spirit of the Ykthae Accord are on the same level as Grandfather Shadow's."

"That's frightening," Josephine said. "She's usually more subtle."

Maxian nodded. "Makes me terrified of what threads she's pulling that we don't know about. Are you prepared to play the game on this level?"

Josephine did not respond. She just looked down at the baby in her arms. Saent Muriel the Destroyer looked up at her, eyes open to the world, taking everything in. Josephine squeezed the baby's thigh several times in rapid succession. Muriel giggled that high-pitched baby giggle that Josephine missed so much.

Human politics had become such an easy game for Princess Josephine Adryck of House Eras. She knew the rules of that game and understood the motivations of the players. Stepping onto the playing field with the celestials and infernals was a different matter entirely. They were not human, and so Josephine could not count on being able to manipulate them by playing upon their desires, for the desires of man might not be the desires of those who stood above the mortal plane, whose plans and schemes could be counted in terms of decades, centuries, and possibly millennia. If Maxian was correct, Josephine might now have centuries to learn to play this game alongside him and Kavala, centuries to subtly push and pull the threads of gods and man to better the world for the Komati people, to ensure their freedom and keep them from being subjugated ever again.

Josephine turned to Maxian. "I am prepared."

"And that?" Maxian waved absently at Muriel.

Josephine glanced down and then looked back to Maxian, giving him a half smile. "Oh, I think Yrgaeshkil will regret ever letting this precious little thing out of her sight."

"Good," Maxian said. "Take care of yourself. Just because the celestials can't affect you with their Words and Dominions doesn't mean they can't harm you. A sword, knife, arrow, or bullet will harm you just as much as anyone else."

"Understood," Josephine said. "I just keep living as I always have, taking care with where I sit, what I eat, and all the rest."

Maxian nodded. "I must go. I'll return as I can."

"I won't be here," Josephine said. "I'm going to Koma City. If things are as you claim, with the Sun King coming to Koma—"

"The King is coming here?" Maxian's mouth hung open in surprise.

"Yes. You pay too much attention to the gods and not enough to man. The King is coming to Koma. Kraetor is already here, as well as Xander and Damian. Add that to Grandfather Shadow walking the world again having named a Lord Morigahn and to Yrgaeshkil making her hand known, something is going to happen. Something soon. Something big. My sons will need me."

"And what of—?" Maxian started.

Josephine held up her hand, and fixed Maxian with a scathing look. "We do not speak of such things in this house. Ever."

"Apologies."

"Go," Josephine said. "Be about your business. I'll be about mine."

The wind picked up briefly as Josephine walked across the veranda. When she reached the wide glass door and glanced back, Maxian was gone.

Josephine walked across the room and opened the door.

Aniya stood watch. She saluted when the door opened. Then she looked down at the baby and frowned in confusion.

"I'll explain later," Josephine said. "For now, get the rest of your Fist and someone from the kitchens. Someone unassuming, boy or girl, I don't care."

"Eight, Your Highness?" Aniya asked. "Not even?"

"Again, I'll explain later," Josephine said. "Just know that I'm going to require you all to do something you likely never imagined possible. It's for the greater good of the future of Koma, the Lord Morigahn, *aen Tsumari'osa*, and *aen Keisari*."

"What is it?" Aniya asked.

"I'd rather not repeat myself," Josephine said. "But I plan to teach you a bit of *fyrmest spaeg geode*, and by doing so, give you the ability to protect the future leaders of Koma like no other Fist has been able to do, ever."

Aniya saluted again and hurried off.

Josephine might not know all the motivations the celestials and infernals might have, but she did know they had many more players on the board than she did. In politics, the player with the most pieces in the game usually won, and against Yrgaeshkil, Josephine knew that she was woefully outmatched in pawns and experience. Catching up meant taking drastic measures, measures that not even Maxian might expect her to take.

She cradled Muriel in one arm while she examined the knife with the Collaen symbol on it. The last time she'd spoken to Sandré, they'd come to an arrangement. It seems he didn't feel the arrangement was mutually beneficial any longer. With the proper whisper at court, Prince Sandré Collaen would be even less of a concern to her than celestial and infernal powers. Once she set the Kingdom Inquisitors after him, Josephine could focus on this new game Maxian had drawn her into.

The Stormrider

It seems that the White Prophet was more than a raving mad man. She has been born and has called Grandfather Shadow forth into the world. Though it is not usually our way, we must act in haste to ensure the noble Houses of Koma never unite as they did before we assisted their fall to the Kingdom. It is time for us to reap those seeds of animosity we planted so many years ago. – A note received from an unknown source to Taekuri Grandmaster Vaelidos Lyn.

> *Brothers race toward each other.*
> *The air hangs with cries of hatred and spite.*
> *Their blood billows behind them,*
> *rose petals on the wind.*
>
> *My brother laughed at me*
> *when I asked for peace.*
> *"Peace comes from conquering.*
> *That is our way."*
>
> *"Remember when we sat on the docks,*
> *toes drawing patterns in the water?"*
> *"No."*
> *Time flows on, and those patterns are long faded,*
> *swallowed by the river.*
>
> *Brothers stumble past each other.*
> *The air hangs with cries of sorrow and pain.*
> *Their blood spills to the ground,*
> *swallowing all.*
> - Archer

ONE

The day after the *Stormrider* had departed Johki, Sandré Collaen did his best to pace back and forth in the tiny cabin. Three steps in either direction was not nearly enough space to properly fume and think. Captain Haden had given his cabin to Julianna, as would have been fitting were she actually the Lord Morigahn, and Sandré was relegated to the first mate's cabin. Worse, Sandré had to share the cabin with Haden. Luckily, with tension on the *Stormrider* high and with the divided loyalties between the Morigahnti, Haden spent most of his time on deck.

Tired of trying to make pacing work for him, Sandré stopped and stared out of the cabin's single tiny window. He watched the shore pass by, wondering what he was going to do about this Julianna Taraen.

Damn that girl and her delusional pride.

Once news that the Brotherhood of the Night had killed Khellan Dubhan had reached Sandré, he'd begun considering who he'd place as the next Lord Morigahn. Then this girl had come along, supported by the Stormcrows, claiming to be marked by Grandfather Shadow himself. Placing the scar on the right side of her face had been a nice touch. With her passion and conviction for Grandfather Shadow and the ways of the Morigahnti, she would have made a fine Fist captain. Sandré might have been proud to help her form her Fist by recommending some of the finest Morigahnti he knew. With that thought, Sandré went through a list of which Morigahnti he would place with her and what assignment he'd give them. She might even be the perfect choice to handle the political maze of Koma City.

Sandré shook his head and turned from the window to resume his pacing. He smacked his lips and punched the wall when the inadequate space for pacing stared back at him. This just wasn't going to do. He needed to think, and to think, he needed to pace. Well, the deck wouldn't do – too many distractions up there. He sent a silent prayer to Grandfather Shadow that the hallway would be relatively clear at this point between the crew's shift rotations.

When he opened the door, Sandré found two men, one standing behind the other, looking back at him. Out of the corner of his eye, Sandré saw his guard lying face down a short way down the hallway.

In all his years as a Prince and First Seat of House Aesin, Sandré had become almost blasé about people trying to murder him, so he wasn't really surprised when he saw two people looking back at him. Each had a *Galad'fana* wrapped around his head, and the one in front held a Komati assassination dagger in his right hand. Sandré couldn't tell if the other did or not, because the first was blocking Sandré's view. They both blinked and leaned back, as men did when taken by an unexpected twist in their plans.

Sandré grabbed the first man's wrist before he could recover, kicked him in the shin to put him off-balance, and pulled him into the room. The canvas hammock tripped up his legs, and he fell forward, crashing into the small table and chest.

As the first assassin worked to untangle himself, Sandré slammed the door. It caught the second man's forearm. Sandré smiled at the sound of cracking bones and the gasp of pain. Fingers opened, and the knife clattered to the floor. Sandré slammed the door again. Again the door cracked bones, and he heard a cry, bordering on a scream, of pain. The third time he slammed the door, it closed shut. Sandré pulled the latch down.

Sandré crouched down and picked up the assassin's knife. Standing, he glanced at the handle long enough to recognize the Adryck family symbol.

"Josephine," Sandré snarled.

Two steps took Sandré to where the other assassin was still trying to untangle himself from the hammock. Sandré wasn't a large man, considered slight and even scrawny by some, but when he jumped over the hammock and landed on the man's torso, air *whooshed* out of lungs and ribs snapped. Sandré took his time sliding the knife under the assassin's chin and into his brain.

While the corpse twitched, Sandré picked up the other knife and looked at the blade. He saw the word *kostota* etching in the blade, and the Taraen family symbol stared back at him from the wooden hilt, mocking him for his foolishness. This wasn't the first time a member of the Taraen family had made a fool of Sandré Collaen. His memory pulled a warm breeze from decades before to kiss his skin, and the dust of the Dosahan savannah dried his nose and throat.

Letting his fury go, Sandré leapt up and hurried out to the hall. The second assassin was gone. This did not surprise Sandré Collaen.

"Run as you wish," Sandré muttered as he pulled the body of his guard into the cabin.

The guard was dead, strangled, which also didn't surprise Sandré.

Standing in the room with two corpses and two ancient assassin's knives meant for him, Sandré closed his eyes, and breathing slowly in and out, he calculated a strategy. He'd deal with this pretender Julianna Taraen now, before she poisoned the minds of any more of his Morigahnti and Captain Haden's crew. After that, he'd give the Morigahnti she'd turned a single chance to return to the true path. With the coming war, they couldn't afford to waste Morigahnti lives fighting each other. Once he settled all his business on the *Stormrider*, Sandré Collaen would turn his attention to Josephine Adryck and her two sons. Luckily, he could eliminate them without costing too many Morigahnti lives.

TWO

Wynd crouched in an alcove of crates with Aurell and Korrin. They had arranged this spot in the darkest part of the riverboat's hold the first day on the ship. Above them, Raze lay on a stack of crates in his human form, keeping watch for any of the crew. His bare feet hung over the side, toes dangling temptingly within reach. Normally, Wynd would have reached up to tickle them by now, but the matter at hand was too important to get distracted by anything. It was the second day since they'd set out from Johki, and they'd arranged to meet here to compare observations and to plan.

"Then we agree?" Wynd asked. "At least half the crew are Morigahnti, and Sandré and Captain Haden are keeping this from the Lord Morigahn."

"Yes," Aurell answered. "I recognize Haden and his Fist from when we all attended Saent Khellan's trials with Allifar. It wasn't that long ago. I also met some of the others, but I don't know whose Fist they're in."

"Has Parsh said anything?" Wynd asked.

Both Aurell and Korrin shook their heads.

"It's like he's forgotten there are other Morigahnti in the world ever since Prince Sandré rode into Bastian's Inn," Korrin said. "He just follows on the prince's heels like a faithful hound."

"How is Viscountess Charise reacting?" Wynd asked.

"I think she's out of her depth," Aurell said. "She's lost the Fist she worked so hard to lead and doesn't have the spine to stand up to either Prince Sandré or Parsh, even though he's only a baron and she holds precedence above him."

"Aurell's right," Korrin agreed. "But the important question is, does the viscountess stand with the Lord Morigahn or with Sandré?"

Aurell replied, "I think that when it matters most, she'll stand with the Lord Morigahn."

"But can we be sure of that?" Korrin asked. "And of Parsh? Has he thrown himself in with Sandré to the point of turning on the Lord Morigahn?"

A cold silence followed.

Wynd wanted so much for Parsh's loyalty to the Lord Morigahn to outweigh his loyalty to his House's prince. Unfortunately, she couldn't answer.

At last she said, "We have to accept that Baron Parsh may be motivated by his ambition more than by his faith in Grandfather Shadow."

"Wait," Aurell snapped. "We don't *know* that Parsh will betray the Lord Morigahn."

"We don't *know* that he won't," Korrin countered.

"We don't know any of this for certain," Wynd said. "We might be jumping at shadows because the other Morigahnti on board haven't spoken to us yet."

"It's not that they haven't spoken to us," Korrin said. "It's because they seem to be actively avoiding us, to the point they're pretending to not be Morigahnti. How many of Grandfather Shadow's laws are they breaking with this behavior?"

"The fifth law at least," Wynd answered. "Perhaps more if we decided to look at them closer."

"I refuse to believe that this many Morigahnti would willingly plot against the Lord Morigahn," Aurell said.

"But Prince Sandré doesn't really believe that she is the Lord Morigahn," Wynd reminded her. "We all know that Parsh has two weaknesses, his love of young women and his ambition. He will follow who he believes can provide him with the greatest leap in status. Right now, I think that would be Prince Sandré."

"If that is true," Korrin said, "is Alerick in danger?"

"Why?" Aurell asked.

"You can't be that dense." Korrin rolled his eyes. "As Allifar's only child, he's the only thing standing in the way of Parsh rising from being a baron to a count."

"So Alerick is with us whether he knows it or not," Wynd said. "Charise still remains a mystery. We think she'll side with the Lord Morigahn, but we don't know it for certain."

"Somebody's coming," Raze whispered from above.

Wynd pulled two of her throwing knives from the brace on her sleeve, Aurell drew a fighting knife in each hand, and Korrin cocked both hammers on his two-shot pistol.

"It's Charise and Alerick," Raze whispered. There was a moment of silence, and he followed with, "Oh, damn."

"What?"

"There's a murder of Stormcrows with them."

"This could be trouble," Aurell groaned.

"A lot of trouble," Wynd said.

"How many are there?" Korrin asked.

"I think all the other Stormcrows on board."

"Damn," Wynd muttered.

"You three might as well come out," Charise said. "We know you're down here."

At that moment, Korrin stiffened. He fell back against the crates, his eyes rolling into the back of his head. He spoke in that strange tongue, and writing in that strange script flowed from his mouth into the air above him. Of all the bloody inopportune times to have a foretelling.

"I heard someone back there," Alerick said.

Korrin kept speaking, words spouting in the air from his mouth, as footsteps approached their little alcove.

THREE

Gianni D'Mario sat cross-legged with a stonewood bowl nestled in his lap. The water had finally stilled, and the wreath of holly, mistletoe, and mountain thistle had finally stopped spinning. Getting to this point had been no easy feat aboard the *Stormrider* as it cut its way down the river. This level of stillness was next to impossible onboard ship. Luckily, Gianni had achieved mastery of his mind over his body in only a few short years as an Adept, making jealous many who had studied twice or thrice as long.

Finally the water in the bowl shimmered, and then it rose from the bowl, shaping itself into a head. Gianni recognized his grandfather's image in the water only because he'd seen it this way so many times before. Faces were hard to make out when they were partially translucent and the water softened their features. The twin pairs of war braids hanging down both sides of his head, and the four braids hanging from his chin made Gianni's grandfather easier to recognize than most. Gianni didn't want to think of what the water did to his own features.

"It took you long enough to settle down," Grandfather's gruff voice softened a bit as it bubbled from the water.

"I'm on a boat, Grandfather," Gianni replied.

"I cannot wait to hear the no-doubt breathtaking tale of how you came to be on a boat."

"There's no time for that," Gianni said. "I will try to summarize the important parts of the last few days. Please don't interrupt." Luckily, Gianni had spent most of the time steadying the bowl considering what he was actually going to say to his grandfather. "Carmine D'Mario is an Adept of Old Uncle Night. Sabina, Lancyl, and Kahtleen are dead. Sabina decided to attack three Fists of Morigahnti after they had killed a Daemyn. The Lord Morigahn was with these Morigahnti, and it's a woman. Now I'm on a riverboat heading toward Koma City, surrounded by Morigahnti, to save the heirs to the Komati Throne. Oh, and Carmine has discovered a way to control Red Dragons even when they know he's a Night Adept."

"A woman you say?' Grandfather asked, and then said, "A woman. Do you think it might be her?"

"I can't imagine her not being. She killed a Daemyn. Grandfather Shadow spoke through her. Well, I'm assuming it was Grandfather Shadow. I can't imagine one of the other gods channeling a miracle through her using Grandfather Shadow's divine language."

"And Sabina decided that she was going to fight her?"

"I think she just meant to take the Lord Morigahn captive and return with her to the Hold of Earth, but I never got the chance to speak with her before she became a risk to our mission."

"You had a hand in Sabina's death, didn't you?" Grandfather's voice grew stern.

"I did what needed to be done," Gianni said. "If I hadn't, I'd be dead, too, and we'd not have anyone else in a position to get close to her."

"Is she beautiful?"

"Even with her scar, I cannot think of a single woman lovelier. Her eyes—"

"Never you mind her eyes," Grandfather snapped. "I arranged for you to be there because I thought you the best suited for the task. Do not dare begin to follow her like some love-sapped fool from a Swaenmarch mummer's tragedy. The fate of the Kingdom depends on that woman Lord Morigahn, if she truly is the Daughter of Wolves. I know you're as full of life as any full-blooded Adept of our House, but you must control yourself. Do not let your passions control you in this. Do you understand?"

"Yes, Grandfather," Gianni said. "I won't disappoint."

"Good. Now, turn on that charm of yours, use that smile I find so irritating that the lasses seem to love, and make her your friend. We need her."

With that, the water forming the bust of Grandfather's head sloshed back into the bowl, part of it spilling over onto Gianni's clothes.

Gianni stood and stretched, doing his best to work the stiffness out of this shoulders, neck, and legs.

Make her your friend. As if it were going to be that easy. Still, what lady didn't like to be called on for tea with a handsome man and a winning smile? Oh, and flowers. He couldn't forget flowers. Gianni drew on the Dominion of Life as he fished a few seeds out of a small leather bag tied around his neck.

Friends would be good, perhaps more. If Grandfather and the other elders were correct, the Lord Morigahn, Duchess Julianna Taraen, might make an advantageous political marriage. Gianni did not fool himself into believing that he'd come to love her already. He might never actually love her, but she was beautiful, and that was more than could be said for many political marriages.

FOUR

Julianna sat in the cabin sipping at her tea with Faelin across the table. Her body ached. The simple action of sipping tea helped soothe her. It was the afternoon after they had set off for Koma City, and the first time she and

Faelin had had an opportunity to speak. The moment she'd been alone in the cabin, she'd fallen into the complete and dreamless sleep that came with exhaustion.

Upon boarding the *Stormrider*, Captain Haden had escorted Julianna to his Cabin. Sandré now shared the first mate's cabin with Captain Haden, one door to the left of Julianna, while Adept Gianni was in the quartermaster's cabin, just to the right. Faelin, Korrin, Wynd, and Aurell were housed in the midshipmen's quarters. She wondered why Sandré hadn't taken the captain's cabin for himself. In fact, the Prince had argued with Captain Haden about cabin arrangements, as well as their destination. Remembering that heated discussion, Julianna put her teacup down and let out a soft laugh.

"What is it?" Faelin asked.

"I was just remembering Haden's expression when Sandré said," she made her voice quiet and raspy like the old prince's, "'If you won't take my vessel where I want it to go, perhaps I'll replace you with someone who will.'"

Faelin nearly sprayed his tea but managed to choke it down before bursting into laughter.

Julianna smiled. It was good to have this moment. With everything she'd survived, and with all the people who had not, in the short time that she had been the Lord Morigahn, Julianna needed to remember that there was joy in life. If she didn't laugh and smile in the few times she could, she would go mad…or worse.

And as much as she wished she could hold onto this pleasant moment, Faelin owed her some answers. She put her cup down and looked Faelin in the eye.

"I'm ready for some explanations," Julianna said, "Where do you want to start?"

"Which question do you want answered first?"

"You," Julianna replied. "Tell me how you did those amazing things. Your speed. And how you healed Wynd and Korrin."

"I am Saent Faelin the Sentinel. My purpose as a Saent is to protect the Lord Morigahn."

"So you're dead?"

"No," Faelin said. "A Saent is saved from true death by one of the Greater Gods an instant before death and infused with a small part of that god's divinity. That's what keeps the Saent from passing back into the cycle of Life, Death, and Rebirth."

"Why didn't you tell me you were a Saent?"

"I didn't know. The Daemyn put the idea in my head by mentioning the Ykthae Accord. He said I was breaking it by affecting the physical realm. The only way for that to happen was if some god had raised me to Saenthood. After I figured it out, Grandfather Shadow was able to tell me the rest."

"Are you breaking this accord? Will you be punished?"

"The Ykthae Accord is a document written in an ancient language that is thousands of pages long. The Taekuri have translated about half of it. Some translations are good. Some are terrible. From what I've read, Grandfather Shadow is playing a dangerous game by breaking the spirit but not the letter of the Accord."

"That sounds like him. How and why?"

Faelin chuckled at that. "Why? Likely because it's in his nature. Ever since the very first accounts of Grandfather Shadow's appearance in legends and religious texts, he's been tricky and has pushed limits and tested boundaries.

"As for how he's skirting the line between the spirit and the letter of the Ykthae Accord, well that takes some explaining of the Accord itself, at least what I know of it. Under the Accord, the only celestial beings who can affect the physical realm with impunity are the lesser Eldar, that is, the lesser gods. Aengyls, Daemyns, and spirits can affect the physical realm, but only if a mortal asks them to do so, and these beings must take some form of payment in return for this service. If they don't, they violate the terms of the Accord and are subject to punishment by the Lords of Judgment."

Julianna's face tightened into a grimace at the memory of those three cloaked beings altering her very nature.

"Julianna," Faelin said, "leave them be."

"What?"

"I know that look," Faelin replied. "You cannot gain *kostota* against the Lords of Judgment."

Julianna shrugged. "Please continue. Why are you not actually violating the terms of this Ykthae Accord?"

"Once a person becomes a Saent, they are a divine being, which means that they usually also become a celestial because their god brings them into his realm upon raising them. I am different. Grandfather Shadow did not raise me out of the physical realm, so where I *am* a divine being, I am *not* a celestial, and therefore my presence here does *not* break the Ykthae Accord."

"Because the Accord only limits celestial beings from getting involved, not divine ones."

Faelin nodded. "Correct."

"And Grandfather Shadow made you a Saent to protect me.

"Yes."

Has any other Lord Morigahn had a Saent for a protector?" Julianna asked.

"Not that I've seen from any record," Faelin replied, "nor heard of in any story."

"What makes me so special?"

Faelin opened his mouth and stopped. He closed his mouth and looked around the room. His gaze traveled slowly, stopping when it fell upon the corners or underneath the furniture. He cocked his head to the side as if trying to hear some faint or far away sound.

"What are...?" Julianna started to ask, but Faelin waved her to silence. She ground her teeth together to keep from pestering him with questions.

Suddenly, he moved with the same preternatural speed he'd had when fighting the Daemyn. In two heartbeats he had crossed the room and opened one of the windows at the back of the cabin. His hand snapped into the air outside the riverboat, and when it came back, Faelin held a small animal.

"What is that?" she asked, straining to see the creature struggling against his grip.

"A Nightbat," Faelin answered. "The Brotherhood equivalent of a Stormcrow, although with different abilities and advantages. This creature is why the Brotherhood seemed to be one step ahead of us at every turn."

"Carmine." Julianna snarled. Saying the name left a bitter taste on her tongue. "Kill it."

"Gladly."

Faelin tightened his fingers. The Nightbat's struggling increased as it bit Faelin's hand. Then came a chorus of popping and snapping bones, and the creature went limp. Faelin tossed the corpse out the porthole.

He turned back to Julianna, opened his mouth, closed his mouth, and looked around the cabin again. She watched as his gaze drifted toward the ceiling and his eyes lost focus. Her breath caught in her throat as she waited for his response.

"Julianna," Faelin's voice was flat, "get the *Galad'parma*."

At hearing that tone, she knew better than to argue. Whatever the reason, it was important, so she stood and went to her baggage. She opened her largest pack and withdrew the tome. Even though it had been packed away for only a few hours, seeing it was like seeing an old friend after several months of absence.

"Call on the Dominions of Knowledge and Secrets," Faelin said, "and speak these words: *Vask aen Valbhoja ulos kana ja kiskata hinan nimeta var mina.*"

Closing her eyes, Julianna took a deep breath and reached out with her growing faith toward the divine energy contained in the Tome of Shadows. When the two intermingled, she pulled power from the book into herself and spoke the miracle that would stop anyone trying to spy on her from afar and would name anyone watching.

The cabin grew dark, as if dusk had arrived suddenly. Then there came the sound of water boiling over and drenching a fire, followed by a cry of surprise and pain. Silence followed a moment later. The room grew darker still, and every shadow whispered at the same time, "Duke, Don Octavio Salvatore, Royal Governor of Koma, and First Adept of Old Uncle Night."

Julianna and Faelin looked at each other. She didn't know what to think of this confirmation that the governor was not only a member of the Brotherhood of the Night, but he was their leader. What plans did he have for Koma? She was not so naïve as to think that a man like that would come so far from the heart of the Kingdom without some major agenda.

Just then, someone knocked on the cabin's door. Faelin walked over and opened it. Karstyn Agostan gave a formal bow, offering enough of his leg as befitting a duchess. He did not salute.

"Lord Morigahn." Even still, speaking her title seemed effort for Lord Karstyn. "Adept Don Gianni D'Mario wishes to take tea with you."

Julianna glanced to Faelin.

"Best not offend your guest," Faelin said.

"Truly?" Julianna asked.

Faelin shrugged. "I was thinking it was more like an opportunity to gauge him and his motives. He's a talkative fellow. Perhaps he'll let something slip. Besides, it's a few days to Koma City at the very least; we'll have plenty of time to continue our discussion."

"Lord Karstyn," Julianna said. "Please invite the Adept to join us."

Even though she had many more questions for Faelin, Julianna could not help the curiosity she found surrounding this brash young man of mixed blood. She wanted to get to know him better, and most people put their guard down when sitting at tea. That's where Julianna had always learned her friends' best secrets.

"The Adept is already here," Gianni said, pushing his way past Lord Karstyn. Three steps into the room, Gianni gave Julianna a deep, formal bow and offered her an arrangement of roses. Where did he get roses aboard this ship? "Thank you for accepting my request, Lord Morigahn. My cabin is a tiny thing. Stifling is too kind a word."

Julianna smiled. Such a simple gesture as flowers made her feel like a normal girl, even if only for a moment. She'd never expected a man to give her flowers again, and while she knew it truly meant nothing, the gesture was touching.

"Please sit down, Adept Gianni," Julianna said. "Faelin and I were just discussing the finer points of religious dogma. I could use a respite from such a discussion, as it grows tedious. Perhaps you would regale me with the story of how a man who is obviously of House Floraen becomes an Adept of House Aernacht."

Gianni sat and handed her the flowers. Faelin moved to take them, but Julianna waved him off. She took the flowers herself and set them on the table next to her tea. She couldn't help but smile and shake her head when she counted seven roses.

Julianna looked back at Gianni. He blinked at her, face smooth.

"Oh," Gianni said after a few moments. "You want to hear that story?"

"If you would be so kind."

"That tale is as tumultuous as a ship on a choppy sea. My throat is thirsty from all the praying I have done to speed us on our way to Koma City. Perhaps once I have sampled some of your fine tea and we have a few moments alone, I will indeed recount the story of my youth when my close family drew lines over small distinctions, nearly coming to blows now and then over perceived slights when they should have banded together. However, I would that this telling take place before a private audience." He glanced at Lord Karstyn.

"Would you excuse us, Lord Karstyn?" Julianna asked. Before he could protest, Julianna raised her hand. "From what I've seen, Adept Gianni possesses enough sense of self-preservation to stay his hand, even if murdering me is part of his agenda. I doubt that, even were he to succeed, he would leave this boat alive."

"Indeed," Gianni said.

Karstyn shook his head and left the room, grumbling under his breath. Both Julianna and Gianni possessed the grace not to notice.

The moment the door clicked closed, something tapped at the large back window. Gianni leapt from his chair. Faelin was already heading to the window. When he opened it, a Stormcrow flew in. It landed in the seat Gianni had just occupied and shifted into human form.

Raze shook his head, and looked at Gianni. "Greetings heart brother. Do you remember?"

Gianni gave Raze a slight bow. "We remember."

"What is this about, Raze?" Julianna asked.

Raze turned and saluted Julianna.

"Lord Morigahn, we have a problem."

FIVE

Sylvie glanced frantically from the Draqons to the Daemyns as she cradled Carmine's head in her lap. He had suddenly cried out, clutched his head, and pitched sideways out of his saddle.

She needed him to wake up. She still had so many things to learn from him, and she had no way to control any of Carmine's servants. The Draqons didn't worry her so much. When Carmine had fallen, the three had formed a triangle around him, facing outwards. However, the Daemyns were another matter entirely. The creatures looked between Sylvie and the commoner girl, Tarshiva, with a mix of hunger and lust. One of the creatures licked its lips as its gaze wandered slowly over her body.

"Please wake up darling," she pleaded.

One of the Daemyns walked toward her.

"Keep away from me," Sylvie snarled.

"I take orders from the Adept, not you," the creature said.

Sylvie stood, planted her fists on her hips, and faced the Daemyn without blinking. "I am the first Adept of the Mother of Daemyns."

"Then it is only fitting you mother the child of a Daemyn yourself." One of the other Daemyns moved to Sylvie's side.

Behind them, the other Daemyn stalked Tar. Kaenyth and Rayce stepped in front of her. They put up a brave front, but their valiant effort would last only a few moments at best before the Daemyn tore the cousins to shreds.

"Now, let's speak of how you two ladies are going to please my brothers and me."

SIX

Grimacing mostly from anger rather than pain, Octavio wiped the cooling water off his face. The pain was mostly an annoyance, and while he suspected he'd suffer at least some blistering, a quick detour to the Temple of Earth would remedy that. One of the Aernacht Adepts could heal these wounds in a matter of moments. Octavio could easily blame this on a clumsy servant, or better yet, say that he had tripped a servant causing them to spill some hot soup on his face. Yes, then the fault would be his, and he wouldn't need to produce the servant for punishment.

What upset him most was that Faelin vara'Traejyn had caught him. Octavio knew he should have ended the scrying after the bastard had discovered and killed the Nightbat. But then, Faelin wasn't a boy anymore; he was a Saent sent by Grandfather Shadow to protect Julianna. This knowledge was disheartening enough, but more than that, the Lord Morigahn was bringing this Saent with her to Koma City. Octavio wondered if Roma's knives could hurt a Saent – no, that was a lie; he wondered if Roma's knives could kill a Saent. Perhaps, but Octavio wasn't about to leave that to chance. He wouldn't allow some upstart heathens to ruin all his well-made plans. New measures had to be taken to ensure the Sun King's death when he arrived in Koma City.

Octavio left the inner sanctum of the Temple of Night – it could be cleaned up later – and found Portia and Roma waiting for him in the temple proper. Upon seeing her husband's face, Portia gasped and rushed over to him. His face must look worse than he thought to cause such a reaction.

"It is nothing, my love," Octavio said, hoping his smile reassured her. "I will have it dealt with presently. We do however have a new dilemma that we must prepare for immediately."

He told them everything he'd learned through his scrying. At first both Portia and Roma looked ready to panic in finding out that vara'Traejyn was now a Saent, but Octavio calmed them with a short explanation of his plan. Both approved, and agreed that it was a masterful stratagem.

"While Portia and I will fill the palace with Daemyns," Octavio said to Roma, "you must find Damian Adryck."

"I assure you, Master, the Whites, the Vara, that man Gareth, and the last remnants of the Wraiths are still searching for Adryck," Roma said. "Of them all, only Black Claw does not make excuses, though he does believe the traitor fled the city."

"As long as Adryck is still alive, I cannot make Xander Rosha completely mine." Octavio was close to raving at this point, and he knew it. He didn't care. He had no secrets from his wife, and few from Roma. They both knew all the details of his plans. "I need Xander free from any other paths destiny might choose for him, and all those other paths lead out from his brother. I have not rotted in this gods-forsaken land these past years only to have my ambition crushed by someone who should have been executed even before I became Governor here." He stopped, faced Roma, and said in his coldest tone, "End him, Roma."

"Yes, you're Darkness," Roma bowed and left.

"Now, my husband," Portia said. "Let us see to your face. Those blisters simply will not do for my upcoming birthday celebration."

SEVEN

Carmine heard Sylvie screaming his name. Despite his throbbing head, his eyes snapped open. He rolled onto his side and saw one of his Daemyns holding Sylvie to the ground while a second was busy loosening the drawstrings of its trousers. Beyond them, the other one was circling the Komati Vara *recruited* in Johki. Jorgen and Brynn stood off to the side, very pointedly not getting involved. Doing so would have been death. It was only a miracle that the Daemyn circling Tar had not ripped the Komati boys to shreds.

"Let her go," Carmine groaned. The Daemyn released its hold on Sylvie, and she scrambled away. "You, stop as well." The one circling Tar stopped moving. And now he would gain some favor from Sylvie and the Komati. "Now all of you drop to your knees and beg the ladies for forgiveness. Do not stop until both have given it."

He closed his eyes again and tuned out the Daemyns' groveling babble. Hopefully this would please Sylvie and further endear the Komati to him, but that wasn't the true motive behind Carmine's command. He needed time to be able to recover from losing his Nightbat. It wouldn't take too long; an hour should do. But he didn't want to worry about the Daemyns molesting Sylvie any further.

A few moments later, someone shook him.

"Leave me be," Carmine snarled. "I'm in pain."

"The First Adept does not care about your pain at this moment, Adept Carmine," whispered a hauntingly familiar voice right above him. Carmine opened his eyes to see Roma crouching over him. "The First Adept is concerned about this bargain you have made for the lives of the Komati heir and his brother."

Carmine pushed past the pain and focused on the moment. When he started to sit up, Roma moved out of the way and helped Carmine to his feet.

"Why is this a problem?" Carmine asked.

"Because the First Adept has plans for the heir. If that young man were to die, the First Adept's plans may come crashing down. The First Adept holds you in high regard, Adept D'Mario. Do not make him your enemy."

Carmine rubbed his face and combed his fingers through his hair. Sitting up, he drew in a breath to steady himself. "That is the furthest from my wishes."

The truth was, at this point, he didn't care overly much if he made Octavio Salvatore his enemy. He did care that Roma was here and had the power to end Carmine here and now, just as he had killed Hardin back in Johki. Carmine stood and faced Sylvie.

"My love," Carmine said, "Would you forgive these wretched creatures? I need to ask them a few questions."

"You are forgiven," Sylvie said in a tone that indicated she did not mean it at all.

The Daemyns continued their pleading and groveling. Carmine blinked a moment before understanding. He glanced to the Komati girl, the innkeeper's daughter. She looked to be enjoying herself.

"Please forgive them," Carmine asked.

Tarshiva seemed unwilling for a moment, and then let out a sigh.

"Fine," Tarshiva said. "You are forgiven."

The Daemyns stood and came over to Carmine.

"What do you command, Adept?" they asked as one.

"Can any of you defeat a Saent?" Carmine asked. "Answer honestly."

"No," all three Daemyns answered in unison.

"Can your master, Nae'Toran? Answer honestly."

"Yes. He has done so before."

"Excellent." Carmine turned back to Roma. "I have the situation well in hand."

"Good," Roma said. "The First Adept does wish you to turn your attention toward finding and destroying the heir's younger brother. His name is Damian Adryck. He was last seen two nights ago in Koma City."

EIGHT

An air of uncertainty hung over the *Stormrider* as it traveled east along the River Aesin. Julianna considered the three factions of Morigahnti as she sat in the dark corner of the cargo hold: those loyal to her, those loyal to Sandré Collaen, and those who wished to remain neutral. These lines had been easy to see as she'd wandered unseen about the ship, as Morigahnti eyed and a-voided each other. Julianna wanted to reach out and try to bring even a small few of those neutral Morigahnti into her camp, but she could not do so without potentially sparking off the conflict before she was ready. Those neutral Morigahnti would either come to her aid or not, she would just have to leave it in Grandfather Shadow's hands.

A small oil lamp and two hooded candles provided light in the *Stormrider's* dank belly. Less than an arm's length away, Korrin, Aurell, and Raze huddled over a crate, playing cards. They each held a hand of cards, and cards covered the crate between them. They played the game without end. The only variation was when Faelin or Wynd came down to join them, which was infrequent.

Julianna supposed she could have joined them if she'd wished. She knew the game. Her cousin Marcus had always dominated the table when he played. Julianna had liked watching him and his friends play. She liked trying to guess what cards they held in reserve and who would aid someone or just hold back, biding their time while their opponents slaughtered each other.

Raze tossed a card onto the strong buildup Korrin had made. The card depicted a figure in red armor astride a red horse on a white background. Korrin blinked several times as if Raze's Red Knight might disappear if he did it enough times.

"He'll lead my two Red Cavalries and White Cavalry against your Gray Infantry and Archery," Raze said.

"I will flank with my two White Dragoons," Aurell said. "And support with my White Archers, of course," she added, sliding a third card into the mix.

"Of course," Korrin snarled, and tossed both Gray Infantry and Cavalry into the graveyard pile. "Damn you both."

In his last two turns, Korrin had effectively cut off Aurell from acting against him while at the same time he built up a force to attack Raze. It was a sound strategy. After watching them play so much, Julianna learned that Aurell was the worst at Conquer, but that meant she was usually the last person knocked out of the game. Korrin had manipulated the game so that Aurell had no choice but to attack Raze, situating Korrin to Conquer the weakened Stormcrow with ease and then turn his attention to Aurell with a doubled force. To stay in the game, Raze had changed his normal strategy, placing his White Cavalry at the beginning of the round and holding the Red Knight to lead the challenge.

"You shouldn't have been so obvious," Julianna said. She still hadn't grown used to her voice sounding like Wynd's. "If you had waited another turn or two, she wouldn't have seen your plan until it was too late."

Korrin craned his neck to glare at Julianna. "If you see it all so well, why don't you join us?'

Julianna pursed her lips. Silence hung about the table as Aurell and Raze quickly turned to examine the crates next to them as if discovering the wooden boxes were the most interesting things in the world.

Korrin's face went slack when he seemed to recall who he was speaking to. "Please forgive me?" he stammered.

"There is nothing to forgive," Julianna replied, again speaking with Wynd's voice. "This waiting is making us all a little frantic. Your go, Aurell."

Aurell drew from the deck centered between them. She looked at the card and grinned. She didn't do well at Conquer because she couldn't contain her emotions. Anyone playing against her knew when she had a good or bad draw.

"White King," Aurell said, placing the card down beside her Gray King. "My White King will summon all his armies."

Raze and Korrin groaned as Aurell lay down even more cards. Three Peasants, an Infantry, and two Dragoons, all of White, followed the King onto the crate.

That play almost certainly gave Aurell the game.

"Shades!" Korrin swore.

"This is proof that she has the Grandfather's blessing," Raze said. "He'll even let Aurell win once in a great while."

"Couldn't it be because I'm learning from playing with you for so long?" Aurell asked. "I might be getting better."

"Maybe," Korrin said. "But I think *Galad'Ysoysa* had his hand in it as well. Isn't it my turn?"

"Yes," Aurell said. "And you better make it a good one, because I'm taking your army on my next turn."

A little girl, slightly shorter than Raze, came around a pile of crates. She had the same wild dark hair as Raze and the other Stormcrows when they were in their human form. This Stormcrow, Kysh, was bound to Anaya Thoros, one of the Morigahnti serving on the *Stormrider*. Anaya and Kysh had told the Morigahnti loyal to Julianna about Sandré's plot.

"Save that thought," Kysh said. "It's happening now."

"*Nusia minan ita*," Aurell muttered under her breath and reached for her rapier.

Raze's jaw dropped, and Julianna didn't blame him. It was a rather colorful use of *Galad'laman*.

"At last," Korrin said. "This waiting's been torture."

Julianna stood and wrapped her *Galad'fana* around her head. The other two Morigahnti followed suit.

"Strength of my sword," Korrin said, belting on his rapier.

"Strength of my sword," Aurell echoed.

They left the cards on the crate.

NINE

Faelin leaned on the railing of the *Stormrider's* aft deck watching the sun sink into the western sky. He had placed himself in this vulnerable position in hopes of provoking some of Sandré's Morigahnti into harassing him. When he heard footsteps approaching him, Faelin smiled and turned around. Parsh and two other Morigahnti came toward him. Parsh carried a two-shot pistol and the other two – Morigahnti from the *Stormrider's* crew that Faelin didn't know – had one-shots.

Faelin's smile dropped. "So it happens now?"

"It does," Parsh replied. "A shame, too. I was starting to like you, despite being a bastard."

"So you side with Sandré." It wasn't a question.

"He is the true leader of the Morigahnti," Parsh replied. "He has been ever since Maxian fled."

"You could be loyal to Julianna."

"I am being loyal to the Morigahnti. That girl will lead us all to destruction. Better to stay hidden and survive, not boast of our presence like she did in Johki and bring the Kingdom down on our heads."

As Parsh spoke, others gathered behind him. This was the moment Faelin would learn who in the crew sided with Julianna and who sided with Sandré.

"If only Allifar could hear your words."

Parsh's face tightened, and red blossomed from his cheeks and covered his face and ears. His nostrils flared as he sucked in a deep breath.

"Allifar is dead for the same reason Julianna will die. He couldn't keep his faith a secret. His pride killed him, just like Julianna's will kill her. Now, let's be done with this."

"At least let me turn around?" Faelin asked. "I don't want to see it coming."

Parsh nodded.

Faelin turned back to face the setting sun. Gunshots *boomed* behind him.

TEN

Gianni knelt in his cabin. This meditation was the only thing that held his temper at bay. All his life he'd heard that he had inherited his father's charisma and wit. However, the gods had given him twice his mother's temper as a balance. Now that temper threatened to have him send this whole rotting boat to the bottom of this river.

Even before he'd stepped aboard, Gianni knew he was a dead man if he ever let his guard down. Everyone on board, save for Julianna's entourage, gave Prince Sandré Collaen complete deference. If he had to guess when they first arrived, Gianni would have wagered the Lord Morigahn hadn't noticed. Having spoken with her after the Stormcrow boy shared the news from the other Stormcrows, Gianni reassessed his opinion of her. She was a capable leader, if a bit inexperienced. Should she survive, she would become a formidable force of power with these Morigahnti behind her.

The door of Gianni's cabin rattled as someone tried to open it.

Gianni smiled. His grandfather had not raised a fool, and so Gianni had barred the door – with the bed. It had been like that for the last few hours, ever since he'd returned from taking tea with the Lord Morigahn.

"Adept," someone called. "I have a message for you from the captain."

"Liar," Gianni muttered under his breath. "I think it more likely that your message comes from a disgruntled prince."

Closing his eyes, he stilled his anger. It would return in a moment, but for now his heart was calm and his mind free from distraction. Gianni reached out with his gift for sensing living creatures. His grandfather had told Gianni that he'd received the talent from Mother Earth herself. He felt four heartbeats on the other side of the door.

Only four? Gianni's indignation grew.

On a whim, he extended his life sense into the next cabin. He felt two heartbeats there, presumably Julianna and someone else. Likely one of the Morigahnti loyal to her, or perhaps that young lady with all the knives. Over a dozen heartbeats waited outside the Lord Morigahn's cabin, most of them beating faster than a man's normally should, as if they were all excited or anxious.

She got a dozen, and he got four?

A trio of gunshots sounded above decks. Well, it had started. Only the gods knew how this was going to play out.

He looked down at his broad-bladed short sword and gnarled cudgel, and suppressed a snarl. Now that things had started, there was no reason to keep his rage in check.

Reaching up to hold the metal torc – his focus for Mother Earth's domain of Life – Gianni sent his faith into the weapon and spoke, "*Ar oscaelt.*"

The bed barring the door rose, floating upward, just above the top of the door. It was a small miracle, tiring him only a little, but it might make a difference, either as a surprise attack or to keep reinforcements from coming.

"Enter," he said.

The door opened. Four sailors came in. He noticed none of them wore a *Galad'fana*. That meant they were low ranking Morigahnti, or worse, just sailors. One more stain on his honor. Each one carried a long knife and a work hatchet. They continued to insult him. They should have come with sword and guns. How did they expect to take him with those toys?

For a moment, he considered tossing his weapons aside and fighting them with the rocks in his sleeves the way nursing mothers and young children did among the Aernacht. Then he pushed that thought aside. He needed to end this quickly.

"Welcome, gentlemen," he said. "I've been expecting you."

They paused. Another fatal error giving him time to talk.

Gianni drew on Life again through his cudgel, and spoke, "*Duin.*"

As the wooden door slammed shut, Gianni released the miracle holding the bed aloft.

The bed crashed down on two of the four sailors. They would be the lucky ones.

Gianni leapt to his feet, sword and cudgel in hand.

Growing up at his grandfather's estates, Gianni spent much of his time learning to submerge his temper and studying the gifts from of his Aernacht blood. His success at both was all that allowed Gianni to become an Adept. And even though he'd learned to control it, he sometimes still suffered from bursts of anger. These "temper tantrums," as his grandfather called them, were few, but woe to anyone who fueled the fires of his fury. Rushing at the sailor, Gianni released his pent up wrath.

ELEVEN

Faelin ducked underneath a cut to his head and nearly tripped over Parsh's corpse. Faelin could feel those dead eyes staring up at him. Why couldn't he have stayed loyal to Julianna? Distracted by these thoughts and the more than just a little guilt at his hand in Parsh's death, Faelin ducked into a kick that snapped his head back and sent flashes of light across his vision.

Faelin rolled to his left, away from Parsh. The direction had been clear a moment before, and Faelin prayed it remained clear.

Vision clearing as he came to his feet, Faelin made a wild slash with his sword to keep anyone from closing. The first sailor scrambled back, colliding with another that followed too close behind him. They collapsed into a heap on the deck, and one of their swords went skittering overboard.

Scanning the deck quickly, Faelin wrenched the sandglass from its housing. He smashed it down on both sailors' heads as they struggled to untangle themselves. The second man took three blows before he slumped to the deck. Faelin hoped he hadn't hurt the man beyond recovery.

Taking this momentary respite from fighting, Faelin scanned the deck to take stock of the situation. At first he couldn't make any sense of the chaos. It seemed as if men fought whoever was closest to them. Then Faelin noticed the strips of cloth some of the fighters wore, gray, black, and gold – Collaen colors. At the center of a group of men wearing those strips of cloth, Lord Karstyn Agostan barked orders. No one had stepped forward to lead those who followed Julianna. Knowing the Morigahnti as he did, Faelin knew they wouldn't follow him, but that didn't mean he couldn't disrupt the enemy's command until Julianna or Alerick got up here.

A head appeared at the ladder leading up to the aft deck. It was one of the few women serving aboard the Stormrider. Faelin didn't hesitate before kicking her in the face, sending her flying back into a few others waiting to get up the ladder.

Before anyone else could climb up, Faelin judged the distance, cocked his arm back, took two steps, and launched the sandglass with all his strength. As the sandglass sailed through the air above the fighting sailors and Morigahnti, Faelin kicked one of the dropped weapons into his hand.

When the sandglass struck Karstyn in the shoulder, the Morigahnti spun around, looking for the source of the attack. When he faced the aft deck, Faelin saluted and threw the sword at Karstyn.

Swords were not made to be used at range, and Karstyn blocked the attack easily, sending the weapon sailing into the river. Faelin smiled and saluted again. Even at this distance, Faelin could see Karstyn's face contort with fury. The lord snapped some orders, pointing at Faelin. Four of the men surrounding Karstyn broke off and fought their way through the fray toward the aft deck.

A gunshot went off, and Faelin felt something speed by his head. He ducked down and prepared to meet the first wave of attackers. He prayed he lasted long enough for Julianna to get out here and turn the tide of battle.

TWELVE

Sandré Collaen watched with satisfaction as his men smashed the cabin door inward. A woman cried out from inside the cabin. Sandré smiled. Now, trapped away from those idiots who supported her, she had no power. Soon this charade would be over. Soon, he would change Julianna's cry of surprise into screams and cries for mercy. She wouldn't receive his mercy, though, just like Josephine Adryck wouldn't receive his mercy either.

"What is the meaning of this?" Julianna's voice demanded as Sandré's men rushed into the cabin.

He disliked her long before they met, mostly for her bloodline. After they had met, his irritation at her pretending to be the Lord Morigahn grown in the fertile soil of her arrogance and insolence. How dare that wretched child duchess question him, assault him, and embarrass him in front of his Fist? With the exception of Khellan, no one since Maxian had been named Lord Morigahn without Sandré's approval. Khellan had been bad enough, an incompetent idiot, but this Taraen girl had conspired with Josephine to kill him.

"Surrender yourself, and renounce your position as Lord Morigahn," Sandré called. "Do that, and I will spare your life and that of your servants."

"In betraying me, you betray *Galad'Ysoysa*," Julianna said. "Is this insurrection worth your soul?"

"Indeed?" Sandré chuckled. "And how do you propose to take my soul when nearly everyone aboard follows my commands?"

"We have her, Your Highness," one of his men called from inside the cabin. "She's no threat."

"Excellent," Sandré said to himself.

He entered the captain's cabin that Julianna had appropriated. This room was his by right of rank. She was only a duchess and had no right to claim these quarters before him.

Julianna had her back to the door and was looking out the large window. He felt the power radiating from her *Galad'fana*, the one only the Lord Morigahn was permitted to wear, lost ever since Maxian Taraen had betrayed and fled the Morigahnti. That this *woman* wore it was an affront to centuries of Morigahnti tradition; that she claimed Grandfather Shadow had returned to mark her was just twisting the knife.

Four of his men stood just out of arms reach of her, two trained pistols on her while the other two had scatterguns at the ready. Their orders were to fire if she said even a single word of *Galad'laman*. By the time any of those Morigahnti loyal to Julianna managed to discern what was going on, it would be too late for them to help her. More men waited in the hallway outside.

"Swear yourself to me," Sandré said, "and I will be merciful."

"And why should I swear to you?" Julianna asked, still not facing him. "I have you outnumbered and outgunned."

"You're insane."

"No. I just have a better understanding of the Morigahnti aboard this ship."

Julianna turned around. Only, it wasn't Julianna. It was Wynd wearing Julianna's dress and the Lord Morigahn's *Galad'fana*. How dare she? Sandré had been prepared to offer all those who followed Julianna the chance to redeem themselves once this was over. This girl's blasphemy killed any chance of her redemption. She would hang, and that only after much suffering.

Wynd opened her mouth, and when she spoke, it was with Julianna's voice. "I suggest *you* surrender and consider what words you'll use to beg forgiveness from the Lord Morigahn."

"What are you waiting for?" Sandré demanded from his men. "Kill her."

"No," half of them said. Each one who had spoken was carrying a firearm, and now, instead of pointing the guns at Wynd, those Morigahnti now took aim on him. The sashes they wore to declare their allegiance to Sandré lay on the floor at their feet. He heard fighting start up in the hall outside.

The wardrobe opened, and Alerick Thaedus came out, his Stormcrow perched on his shoulder. Seeing that bird made everything come together.

"The thing is, Your Highness," Alerick said, "those of us bound to Stormcrows know that Julianna Taraen is the true Lord Morigahn, marked by Grandfather Shadow, himself. And none of us are willing to betray her, or our god who raised her."

This wasn't happening. Sandré's plan was so careful. He wanted to do this without bloodshed, well, without any save for Julianna's and now Wynd's. The Morigahnti were few enough as it was. Now many of them were going to die in this pointless squabble, all because Julianna had somehow ensorcelled the Stormcrows. She had to be in league with Daemyns. There was no other explanation.

"*Armahta turva ja kostota,*" Sandré whispered, releasing two of the miracles bound into his *Galad'fana*.

The Dominions of Shadow and Balance flared from his *Galad'fana* as all the shadows in the room surrounded him and solidified, forming a barrier between him and his attackers.

As the shadows moved, Julianna's traitorous Morigahnti fired. Guns were fast, but nothing in the world moved faster than a miracle once spoken. The cylinder of shadow warded him from the bullets, but that was not the intended purpose of the protective barrier.

A moment after the shadows rose to protect him, the Dominions of Storms and Vengeance filled the room with hurricane force winds that flung sleet and hail stones the size of walnuts. Of course, he was safe behind the solid shadows while everyone else in the room was pummeled and beaten by the prepared miracle.

As far as Sandré knew, few Morigahnti knew the trick of preparing miracles and storing them in the *Galad'fanati* until needed. That knowledge had saved his life more than a few times. He had many complex miracles stored in the veil he wore around his shoulders.

The storm receded, and the shadows went back to their natural places. He stayed ready to speak again, in case his miracle hadn't incapacitated everyone.

He need not have feared. Everyone was either unconscious or in so much pain that they had no attention to spare him. That his own men were among them could not be avoided, and though his miracle hurt them as well, they would live. Their injuries served the greater good.

This would be the perfect time to rid himself of these unworthy excuses of Morigahnti. But should he take the time to dispatch them when he needed to warn Parsh and Captain Haden that Julianna and her followers were prepared for them? After a moment's consideration, Sandré decided he needed to kill them.

He went over to Wynd. As he drew the assassin's knife that bore the Adryck family symbol and leaned over her, a grinding sound came from the wall to his left. Sandré looked up to see boards prying themselves apart.

Adept Gianni stepped through the opening. He held a broad-bladed short sword in one hand, and an oaken cudgel in the other. Blood splattered him from head to foot, and two mangled bodies lay on the floor behind him.

Gianni locked eyes with Sandré. Those were not the eyes of a man, but rather of some primal beast walking in a man's skin.

Screaming, the Aernacht Adept charged.

THIRTEEN

Gianni tested Sandré Collaen as they wove between the unconscious bodies, and Gianni had to admit that Sandré was fairly impressive for his age. The years had not cost the aged Morigahnti any of his speed or skill with the sword, or if it had, Gianni thanked Mother Earth that he didn't have to face Prince Sandré while the man was in his prime. Gianni had to do something to cut this fight short, or he might not survive it.

Gianni swung his short sword, slicing at Sandré's head, hoping he'd not heralded the attack enough to arouse the prince's suspicions. Sandré ducked and danced back, just as Gianni had hoped. Rather than follow the Morigahnti and close the gap where his shorter weapons would be more effective, Gianni also stepped back and brought his sword and cudgel into a guarding stance.

Seemingly on instinct, Sandré took advantage of the space between them and retaliated with a long lunge at Gianni. How long had it been since Sandré faced anyone other than an incompetent Nightbrother or someone armed with a rapier? Barking a victorious laugh, Gianni twisted and parried his enemy's thin-bladed sword with his thick, sturdy short sword. Before Sandré recovered from his failed attack, Gianni brought his cudgel down on the rapier. The flimsy blade snapped about two-thirds of the way down the blade. Sandré Collaen now held a weapon only slightly longer than Gianni's short sword.

Sandré scrambled back, raised his finger, and pointed at Gianni's head.

Gianni scrambled backward, sucked in a quick breath, and pulled on the Dominion of Protection through his cudgel. He didn't know exactly what was coming at him, but he knew it wasn't going to be pleasant.

"*Tuska!*" Sandré cried.

"*Cosain mis,*" Gianni cried.

He used the cudgel like a hurley bat, striking the bolt of dark energy that flew from Sandré's outstretched finger.

When the divine focus struck the bolt, the missile exploded into a thousand shards that looked like shattered stained glass. Most of those shards dissipated after a moment, but a few struck a Morigahnti lying on the floor. Where the dark energy hit, his flesh erupted in a fountain of blood. The unfortunate victim woke, screaming in agony.

Having no desire to battle miracles with the maniacal prince, Gianni rushed at Sandré, hoping to close before he could speak again. Sandré parried with his ruined sword, dodged with a nimbleness befitting a man half his age, and it seemed as if their fight concerned him no more than a court dance.

As he pranced around the room, deftly stepping over bodies and avoiding Gianni's sword and cudgel, Sandré spoke, "*Galad aen mina anta na vartalo.*"

Hearing more words in Grandfather Shadow's divine language, Gianni leapt to the right, drew on Protection, shouted, "*Dean balla ce acu diobháel fe'adfadhu ni teaigh thar,*" and threw his cudgel to the floor.

A shimmering wall of divine power expanded out of the cudgel focus, forming a barrier between Gianni and Sandré. Gianni dropped to his knees. That miracle was the most powerful use of the Dominion of Protection he knew, and it drained most of his energy every time he spoke it. He ground his teeth and snarled when he realized Sandré's miracle wasn't meant for him.

Sandré stood on the other side of the wall of power, though he had transformed into a shadow.

Whispered hisses came from Sandré. Gianni assumed that it was more miracles, though he couldn't even make out the language, much less predict the result.

A blast of lightning surged outward from Sandré's outstretched arms. Gianni allowed himself a smug smile as the lightning struck his wall. Threads of shimmering blue-white sizzled along the barrier to the floor. Smoke wafted up from where those threads hit the wood.

Trusting his miracle to hold, Gianni scanned the Morigahnti who lay on his side of the barrier. He recognized the girl who had traded places with the

Lord Morigahn, Wynd if he remembered. She seemed spirited enough, ready to volunteer to dance with Uncle Night and laugh in his face when he tried to take her. Gianni went over to Wynd and placed his hands on her forehead. Closing his eyes, he drew on the Dominion of Life bound within the torc he wore around his neck, and spoke, "*Lig uile sin diobhaeil tu cad e ata leigheas.*"

Wynd gasped as her eyes snapped open.

Gianni forced himself to appear nonplussed. "Prince Sandré is being a nuisance. Choose one other for me to heal. Then we must depart with all haste."

"Why?" Wynd asked as she rolled to her knees.

"Because that won't last forever."

He waved absently at his barrier.

Sandré had reverted to solid form. He spoke a word. Another of those black bolts hit the barrier. The bloody man was as quick of mind as he was of foot. The nature of the barrier held off larger blows more easily. If Sandré could manage to hit the same spot repeatedly and swiftly enough, he could punch through. Another bolt followed the first, and a then a third, all striking within a finger's breadth of the same spot. Cracks formed with the fourth hit.

"Right," Wynd said. She quickly looked around and pointed to Alerick Thaedus. "Heal him."

Gianni had met the young lord at court twice. It had surprised him to learn Alerick was a Morigahnti. Both he and his father had seemed like loyal Kingdom men. Ah, well. Even Gianni had his secrets from many of the Aernacht Adepts. He could not fault Alerick for the deception. Gianni went to Alerick and repeated the healing miracle. Soon, the only thing that would keep him conscious was the propriety of his Floraen blood and his unrelenting Aernacht pride.

Alerick groaned and opened his eyes.

"We have to go," Gianni said, helping Alerick to his feet. "Out the window and we swim for it."

"But the Lord Morigahn needs us," Wynd said. "I have her *Galad'fana.*"

"And she will have to get along without it," Gianni replied. "Or do you think the three of us will survive long enough to aid her? My endurance for speaking miracles is waning. How are you?"

Wynd looked ready to argue when Alerick cut her off.

"He's right," Alerick said. "We can't match Sandré. We can't allow him to gain the Lord Morigahn's *Glad'fana.*"

Wynd nodded, but her eyes showed that she hated the choice.

"You are *Kavala Toinen*," she snarled at Sandré, the words like a curse.

As if given more power by Wynd's insult, one of Sandré's black bolts punched through Gianni's barrier. The bolt flew within inches of her head and struck the far wall. Wood exploded in a shower of splinters.

"Go," Gianni said.

"What about you?" Alerick asked.

A lightning bolt increased the size of the hole, and the captain's wardrobe erupted in fire and shards of wood. One of those shards stuck out of Wynd's shoulder.

"Go. I'll be right behind, but I'm not leaving without my cudgel."

The two Morigahnti nodded. It was no secret which items the Adepts from the Great Houses used as foci to channel their god's Dominions.

Gianni moved to his cudgel as Alerick and Wynd leapt out the window. Sandré leaned against the barrier and started chanting in Grandfather Shadow's language. The other Morigahnti had risen on the other side of the room and joined in the chanting in unison. Gianni snatched up his club. The moment the focus left the floor, the shimmering wall vanished.

When the wall vanished, Sandré stumbled forward.

Gianni swing the cudgel up to meet Sandré's chin. The blow snapped Sandré's head back and slammed his teeth together with a satisfying *crack*. Unfortunately, Gianni had given too much of his strength to speaking miracles. Had he put all his strength behind his cudgel, he might have snapped Sandré's neck.

Cutting back and forth across the cabin, Gianni made for the window.

Gunshots went off behind him. Bullets chewed into the floor around him, kicking up splinters.

He was only three paces from the window when one bullet hit his leg, just below the knee. Even as he stumbled, Gianni laughed. The gods smiled on him today. Though hit, his speed carried him across the remaining distance and into open air.

Falling, Gianni drew on the power within his cudgel. He might have told the Morigahnti that he had no more miracles in him, but he lied. One of the many benefits of being an Adept of Mother Earth over an Adept of All Father Sun.

The river rushed up at him. He hit the water as the last word passed his lips. He felt the miracle suck even more strength from him, but the shock of freezing water helped revitalize him.

Breaking the surface, he tread water, and spoke, "*Lig uile sin diobhaeil tu cad e ata leigheas.*"

The wound in his leg healed. Making it to shore would be a lot easier without the injury. Gianni took a deep breath and swam, heading for the southern shore as they had planned. It was a gamble heading to that side of the river. He knew this whole thing was a gamble, joining with these Morigahnti, but he never imagined the splintered factions between them. This bloody mess was so much worse than he could have ever imagined. Kingdom intelligence, or at least Aernacht intelligence, was woefully inadequate.

Well, Gianni knew he was not a master of all things, unlike many Adepts he knew. However, he was clever and adaptable. The swim to shore gave him time to plan his contingencies. If he was lucky, he might have enough strength to speak between three and four more miracles once he reached land, if those miracles weren't too powerful. After that, he had to trust Mother Earth to protect him. Hopefully, Wynd and Alerick would remember that he saved their lives and would repay their *kostota* by not killing him and keeping the other Morigahnti from killing him too.

FOURTEEN

Even when she heard the first gunshots fired above deck, Julianna forced herself to maintain her steady pace through the bowels of the *Stormrider*. As much as she hated it, she'd known that Morigahnti were going to die. She blamed Sandré Collaen for this bloodshed. His arrogance and ignorance had brought them to this moment. If Wynd and Alerick failed to deal with him, Julianna swore that she would. He, and all the Morigahnti who followed him, would learn the price of betrayal.

Julianna and her small group of followers, Charise, Korrin, Aurell, and Raze, stood at the door leading to the mid-deck. The sounds of steel ringing on steel came from the other side, punctuated by screams, yelled commands, and the occasional gunshot.

"It sounds ugly out there," Aurell said.

"You should be right at home," Korrin muttered.

Aurell drove her elbow into his ribs. He gasped and clutched his side.

"Sorry," he said between ragged breaths.

"We'll settle it later," Aurell replied. "What are your orders, Lord Morigahn?"

There was no way to know which Morigahnti were with them and which were against them. The Morigahnti themselves might not truly know. Some might only be fighting because chaos had erupted across the *Stormrider*.

"Send Raze out," she said. "Have him call the warning."

Raze shifted from human form to bird form. Korrin opened the door leading to the deck. The sounds of fighting grew louder, and the smells of gunpowder and freshly spilled blood flooded through the door.

Raze flew out into the battle zone. The Stormcrow cried out as Korrin closed the door.

Julianna sat down, opened the *Galad'parma*, and flipped through the pages. She felt stupid flipping through the tome while Morigahnti fought and died around her.

"You!" a voice cried from down the hall.

Julianna looked up. Sandré had come out of her cabin, *Galad'fana* wrapped around his head. What had happened to Wynd?

Korrin, Aurell, and Charise stepped between Sandré and Julianna, weapons raised.

"We can end this fighting," Sandré said. "No more Morigahnti need die this day."

Julianna wanted to believe him. "What are your terms?"

"Stand down," Sandré called back. "Give up this foolish game you are playing. They only fight because they want to believe you. They want to believe that Grandfather Shadow has returned."

"He has returned," Korrin snapped. "Raze has—"

"Your Stormcrow lies," Sandré shouted back. "They all lie."

Turning her attention back to the great book in her lap, Julianna hurried her search for the miracle Faelin had guided her to. He hadn't been able to show her himself, for this particular *Galad'parma* had pages only the Lord Morigahn could find.

A Morigahnti wearing a *Galad'fana* rushed up behind Sandré, followed by three sailors. They were all armed with weapons that dripped blood. Each of them saluted Sandré Collaen and moved in front of him.

Seemingly bolstered by these reinforcements, Sandré shrieked down the hall like a spoiled child. "Order your people to stand down!"

Julianna wondered how men could follow such a worthless creature as that. Then she found the page she needed, and scanned the words, making sure her pronunciation would be precise.

"Charge them!" Sandré bellowed.

Placing her hands on the pages of the book, Julianna cleared her mind.

"Strength of my sword!" Korrin and Aurell yelled together.

Julianna sent her will toward the book.

"Honor above all!" Charise called out her family's battle cry.

Taking a deep breath, Julianna drew all seven of Grandfather Shadow's Dominions: Shadows, Balance, Storms, Secrets, Knowledge, Illusion, and Vengeance, and spoke, "*Galad'Ysoysa, mina naena karkota kaki sank-arina. Poista sinan vaealtos ulos their Galad'fanati ja suoda se var nin ken mina voida palate se var hina ken todista arvoinen.*"

In the span of two heartbeats, her awareness expanded first to the Morigahnti who wore a *Galad'fana* on the *Stormrider*. Her mind seemed to explode outward, encompassing everyone throughout the world who wore a *Galad'fana*. She never imagined that so many people in Koma and beyond paid homage to Grandfather Shadow. Had the Morigahnti scattered themselves so far and wide across the world?

In that moment, they were all bound by the power of Julianna's miracle, first spoken by Saent Raethian the Sly after the Ilsaen Morigahnti fled Koma to help found the Kingdom. Everyone who wore a *Galad'fana* was bound by the power of Grandfather Shadow's seven Dominions.

"I am the *Morigahn'uljas*," Julianna announced to them all. "I apologize to those of you who have no quarrel with me; however, I cannot risk anyone using the power of *Galad'Ysoysa* against me. If you prove worthy, I will return his power to you."

As she spoke, another presence filled the strange connection as Grandfather Shadow joined his followers. He brought countless more minds with him, none of which were completely human.

"At last," Grandfather Shadow said. "A high priest who acts as a Lord Morigahn should. Well done. Their power is yours, Julianna."

With those words, Julianna felt her god sever the connection, but not before taking the power held within those divine foci and placing it into the *Galad'parma*.

Her eyes opened, and she blinked in surprise. She had expected to collapse, exhausted from speaking such a powerful and draining miracle. Instead she felt refreshed and invigorated. In her lap, the *Galad'parma* hummed with power. The essence of all seven Dominions swirled in the book, awaiting her.

She looked up. All the Morigahnti who wore a *Galad'fana* stood still, staring into space. They looked to be in the midst of ecstasy, which in some ways they might be. Grandfather Shadow had just spoken to them. The voice of their god had sounded in their heads. For the first time in over a thousand years, Grandfather Shadow addressed the Morigahnti and let them know their faith and service were not in vain.

Julianna stood and looked at the Morigahnti next to Sandré who wore a *Galad'fana*.

She reached out her hand to him. "Join me."

The Morigahnti nodded and walked toward Julianna.

"No!" Sandré cried. "It is a trick between her and those Stormcrows."

Sandré drew a dagger and leapt toward the Morigahnti.

Julianna tightened her grip around the book.

"*Galad rus y seina*," Julianna said, pulling on the Dominions of Shadows and Balance.

Every shadow in the hallway sprang to life. The larger shadows stretched along the walls and then spanned across the hall. The smaller shadows actually moved from where they lay on the floor and walls and crawled to where the larger ones met. The big shadows touched their edges together, while the smaller elongated and thinned, becoming like thread, then sewed the larger ones together. Once that work was done, they all solidified, forming a wall between Julianna and her enemies.

"Are we cut off from Grandfather Shadow's blessing?" Korrin asked.

Julianna noted the trace of sorrow in his tone.

"No," she said. "Your faith keeps his blessing upon you. Now, we must go quickly. It's likely that most of the Morigahnti without a *Galad'fana* follow Sandré."

"We will do whatever is needed," Korrin said.

They moved to the door leading onto the mid-deck. Julianna reached to open it, but Korrin stepped in front of her.

"No, Lord Morigahn. We will all die before you."

He unlatched the lock and yanked the door opened.

Three Morigahnti stood a few feet away, two with pistols trained on the door, and one with a rapier in each hand. None of them wore a *Galad'fana*. Even though they stood ready, it appeared Korrin's forceful opening had startled them. They blinked in surprise for a moment, but that was a moment too long.

Aurell thrust her right arm, which still held a two-shot, over Korrin's shoulder and well past his head, and fired. The frontmost man's face erupted in a spray of blood. His gun clattered to the deck

Even before the smoke from the shot cleared, Korrin lunged forward with his sword, catching the second gunman in the inner thigh and twisting. The man's mouth opened in a lopsided gasp of surprise, and he blinked in rapid succession.

Blood ran down the man's leg like a dark river. Korrin grabbed the two-shot pistol from the man's loosening fingers as he dropped.

The last man dropped both his blades and fell to his knees as his companions died.

Korrin placed the tip of his sword at cowering man's throat. Charise and Aurell moved outside as well, stepping to either side of the door. The two women covered the area, Charise with a scattergun and Aurell with twin two-shot pistols.

"Please spare me!" he cried. "Show mercy, Lord Morigahn!"

Julianna stepped up to the threshold and looked beyond the cowering wretch. Morigahnti crowded the deck, and many of them lay bleeding. About a third of those still on their feet – those with *Galad'fanati* – stood like statues with that dazed, faraway expression on their faces. Of the rest, a few stood open-jawed, gaping at the strangeness around them, three moved about the ones like statues, slitting their throats while they stood helpless, and the rest gathered at the far end of the deck, fighting Faelin, the Stormcrows, and three Morigahnti wearing *Galad'fanati*.

"*Galad pita han viela!*" Julianna cried, summoning the Dominions of Shadows and Vengeance from her Tome of Shadows.

Shadows from all over the deck and up in the rigging sprang to life, immediately wrapping around everyone on deck except for Julianna, her immediate companions, and the sniveling whelp begging for his life. Those trapped by the shadows struggled, but after a few moments, resigned themselves to being held.

"*Armahta* Faelin *ja aen Raevota'korpi,* " Julianna said.

The shadows bonds released Faelin and the Stormcrows. Even though they were at the other end of the *Stormrider's* deck, Julianna could see they were all wounded. Those still trapped craned their necks in order to watch Julianna.

She ignored them. Instead, she looked down at the coward lying prostrate before her.

"You have fought against me," Julianna said. "Therefore, I cannot trust you. If I spare you, that means I will have to make you my prisoner."

"Yes, Lord Morigahn," the man whined. "Take me prisoner. I'll do anything."

She sighed. This was another moment that would define her as the Lord Morigahn. It was a hard choice, but like Adept Sabina, some people had to die for the greater good. If only this one had more of a spine, she might have been able to let him live. At least his death would serve as an example for the other Morigahnti.

"Cowards take prisoners," Julianna said. "Morigahnti do not. Killing is not too good for your enemies."

"Please..." the worm pleaded.

Julianna had the attention of everyone on deck. She swept her gaze over all of them. In each pair of eyes she saw the same questions: *What will his fate be? Will I suffer the same?* She would let them decide for themselves once she dealt with this pathetic thing groveling at her feet.

Julianna drew on the Dominions of Shadows and Vengeance and pointed at his head.

"*Tuska!*"

The dark gray bolt of Grandfather Shadow's essence flew from her finger. She ignored the blood and gore that smeared the deck and stepped over the corpse.

"I will not tolerate betrayal within the ranks of the Morigahnti. You must decide whether you can adjust to the changes I bring. If you can, make your way to the gathering where I shall undertake the trials. If you cannot, then depart the ranks of Grandfather Shadow's truest children. Any further treachery will meet the full force of my *kostota.*" She turned to Korrin, Charise, and Aurell. "Secure all exits from below decks."

The three jumped into action as Julianna strode across the deck toward Faelin.

Bodies lay scattered around him; one, she noticed was Parsh. He was face down, several gunfire wounds in his back. He was not breathing. Faelin was also wounded, though none of his injuries appeared immediately fatal, or even serious. Most of the blood covering him was not his own.

She went and touched the shadows that bound the three Morigahnti who fought beside Faelin, and said, "*Armahta.*"

The shadows slithered away. When the Morigahnti were free, she turned back to Faelin.

"Are you alright?" she asked.

"Well enough," Faelin replied, between panting breaths. "Though I will be better once we are free of this bloody boat."

"Then let us take our leave." She called back over her shoulder. "Korrin, Aurell, Charise, prepare two shore boats while I free the loyal Morigahnti."

"How will you know, Lord Morigahn?" one of the Morigahnti asked.

She smiled. "I am the Lord Morigahn, first chosen of the God of Knowledge. I will know."

Julianna went to the first Morigahnti trapped next to Faelin.

She drew on Knowledge and Illusions, and spoke, "*Galad'Ysoysa rus hano keskustelu aen totus sanati aen Morigahnti.*" As the miracle settled on those who were trapped by her shadows, Julianna asked, "Who do you serve?"

Some said, "The Lord Morigahn."

Many more said, "Prince Sandré Collaen."

Julianna went about the deck, freeing those Morigahnti who had declared loyalty to her.

By the time they were all free, the shore boats had been lowered to the water. Morigahnti were climbing down to them.

Someone pounded on the door Julianna and her followers had come through.

Julianna's followers scrambled into the boats. Korrin and Charise led one, mostly filled with the injured, and they were already heading toward the shore. Aurell was helping others into the second shore boat. Julianna went to the railing, but she did not enter. Soon only Faelin stood with her.

"You must go before me," Julianna said, as the door shuddered. "Just trust that I know what I'm doing."

Faelin looked ready to argue, but then he nodded and slid down the rope into the shore boat.

Aurell called to Julianna. "Come in the boat, Lord Morigahn."

"In a moment," Julianna replied.

"But…" Faelin started.

The door gave one last, violent shudder and burst open.

Julianna turned.

Sandré rushed onto the deck with a group of his followers at his back. His eyes locked on Julianna, and he snarled. The noise made him sound like feral dog denied a meal.

Julianna smiled sweetly at him as she drew on all seven of Grandfather Shadow's Dominions out of the *Galad'parma*. Let him deny her claim after this.

She spoke, "*Galad'thanya kuiva aen eva ruth!*" and brought her hands together.

Thunder crashed across the *Stormrider*. Sandré and his Morigahnti were tossed like leaves into the wall behind them. The force of the miracle shred the bonds of shadow holding everyone else. Some of them flew off the deck's far side. Others slid across the wooden planks. Rigging and sails tore and debris rained down. One of the masts split down the middle. Each half tumbled like a fallen tree into the river.

Let them doubt me now, Julianna thought to herself as she turned back to the shore boats.

She leaned over the remnants of the railing. The first boat was already heading for shore. Then she noticed that Korrin and Charise were pulling people out of the water. With those additions, it had become so crowded and sank so low that the river threatened to suck the boat down.

Below her, Julianna dropped the Tome of Shadows into the boat. It landed with a thud between Faelin and Aurell.

Julianna took two steps to the right and jumped over the railing.

Hitting the water was like jumping into liquid ice. She forced her mouth shut until her head broke the surface, even though her lungs screamed to open up in shock. Still, she could suffer a short time of cold misery instead of trying to land safely in the shore boat. Attempting that would be foolhardy for an acrobat under the best circumstances. For Julianna it would have been insanity.

Moments later, strong hands pulled her from the river. Faelin and Aurell lifted her into the shore boat. The chill night air caressed her wet skin, and she began to shake.

"Make for the other boat," Julianna said through chattering teeth. "We need to help lighten their load and then get to shore."

A short time later, the two boats were side by side and the passengers evenly distributed. They were almost ashore, and Julianna sat at the bow of her boat, shivering and muscles aching. She watched sailors scurrying about the *Stormrider*. Slowly, the riverboat turned and headed for the shallows downstream.

"What do you think?" Faelin asked. He sat just behind her.

"We better find a defensible place to meet them," Julianna said, patting one of the scatterguns Raze and the other Stormcrows had hidden in the small craft.

"I agree."

"But Grandfather Shadow told us all that you are the true Lord Morigahn," Charise said. She was at the head of the other boat, only a few arms away. "Why would Sandré still pursue you?"

"Because Sandré does not follow Grandfather Shadow," Alerick said. "Like my dead uncle, he is blinded by his ambition."

"Whatever his reasons," Julianna said, "we need to be ready to fight."

"We also need to consider that more of them can speak miracles than us," Gianni said.

Julianna turned to face him. Dark bags hung under his bloodshot eyes, and his shoulders sagged as if he hadn't slept in days. Though he was the worst, Gianni reflected everyone's condition.

"No," Julianna replied. "None of them can speak miracles."

"What do you mean? I heard them."

"They could at one time, but I have taken that ability from every *Galad'fana* in the world, save for my own."

"What about the masks of Adepts of House Kaesiak?"

"I do not know." Julianna considered it for a moment and shrugged. "Perhaps."

"And you performed this great feat, how?"

Julianna turned and gave him a tight little smile. "I am the Lord Morigahn, the first chosen of *Galad'Ysoysa*. It is my right to grant or deny any access to Grandfather Shadow's blessing."

"What about First Adept Kraetor?" Gianni asked.

"What of him?"

"I thought he was the first chosen of Grandfather Shadow."

"If you ever see him, ask him to show you his scar." Julianna pointed to the wound Grandfather Shadow had sliced into her face. "Then you will see how first chosen he is."

Gianni blinked several times. His mouth opened, closed, and opened again. His jaw hung open. For the first time it appeared as though the Aernacht Adept had nothing to say.

Julianna turned back to the *Stormrider*. "Does anyone have any thoughts on what to do once that crew starts hunting us?"

"I do," Gianni said. "I know a miracle that will help us. Afterward, I'll have to trust you to care for me."

"After the help you've given me and mine, Adept Gianni," Julianna said, "I give you the full hospitality of the Taraen family."

"And just how extensive is this family?"

"I'm the last."

"Excellent," Gianni smiled. "Let us get to shore, and I will deal with that." He waved at the *Stormrider*.

They continued in silence until they reached the riverbank.

When Julianna stepped out of the boat, Wynd held the first *Galad'fana* out to her.

"Thank you for the honor of trusting me with this, Lord Morigahn," Wynd said.

Julianna smiled, took the *Galad'fana*, and wrapped it around her head and shoulders like a shawl. "You do me the greater honor in facing our enemies in my stead." Julianna placed her hands on Wynd's shoulders. "Receive the blessing of *Galad'Ysoysa* my sister of blood and battle."

Wynd beamed a wide smile that lit up her entire face. Julianna nodded to her, and then turned to Adept Gianni.

"The *Stormrider?*" Julianna asked.

"As my lady host commands." Gianni gave a deep bow, drew in a deep lungful of air, and shouted, "*Gyth'Imyrthae damaeste sin baed do caelisa!*"

The *Stormrider* gave a heaving groan, shuddered from stem to stern, and exploded in a shower of splinters.

Gianni's eyes rolled into the back of his head, and he slumped forward. Korrin and another Morigahnti rushed to catch the Aernacht Adept.

"That was impressive," Faelin said.

"Yes," Julianna agreed. "Wynd. Korrin. I want you to care for Adept Gianni."

"Yes, Lord Morigahn."

Julianna stood, and wobbled a bit. Even with channeling through the *Galad'parma*, drawing so much divine power through her soul taxed her. Faelin stepped up to steady her.

"We have a new problem, Julianna," Faelin whispered.

"Only one?" she responded. "Let us discuss this once we have put some distance between ourselves and that wreckage. The Morigahnti have fought their brothers and sisters enough for one day. Perhaps those who were a-board and survive will realize the truth of things and come to follow me."

"Will you be able to trust them?" Faelin asked.

"We will see," Julianna said. "But that is another test for another day. Now we have to beat Carmine to Koma City." Julianna raised her voice. "Morigahnti, we have a hard journey ahead, made harder by the burden of our guest. We'll rotate shifts carrying him." Julianna joined Korrin and beckoned to another Morigahnti, a young man of perhaps twenty-five winters, to help them shoulder the burden. "Let's move."

FIFTEEN

Sandré crawled out of the river. Somehow, he had survived, and now he wasn't sure whom he should thank. Surely not Grandfather Shadow. Why had the god he'd served all his life turned away from him and blessed such an unworthy creature as Julianna Taraen?

Sandré watched the few other survivors swimming toward shore. With Julianna's escape, all the Morigahnti would soon learn of his betrayal. He would be a hunted man, never again knowing peace in his homeland. He wanted to make them pay, to give them *kostota*, but he could never stand against Julianna's power without the ability to speak miracles of his own.

"You are the most pathetic prince I've ever seen," a woman's voice came from behind him.

Sandré spun around, scrambling off his backside to his feet. He saw a woman just a little taller than he, with midnight black hair and pale skin. Her black eyes smiled wickedly. She wore a gown of black silk, embroidered with silver and adorned with pearls.

"Who are you?" Sandré demanded.

"I am Yrgaeshkil," she replied.

Old Uncle Night's wife, the Mother of Falsehoods. Any other time, Sandré might have had some reaction other than complete lack of caring. His god had abandoned him, and he could not bring himself to care about anything.

"I have no use for you, Lying One," Sandré snapped. "Be gone."

"Do not dismiss me so readily, Prince Collaen. I can give you what you most desire."

"And what is that?"

She smiled. "In addition to my powers, I can also grant you the Dominions of my husband."

"I have no desire to follow the Daemyn God," Sandré said. Even though it seemed that Grandfather Shadow had abandoned him, Sandré was not ready to turn away from all his beliefs.

"Not even for your *kostota*?"

"It is not worth my soul," though he desperately wanted revenge.

"You have been listening to Kingdom lies," Yrgaeshkil said, her voice dripping with honey. "There are ways to utilize a god's power without giving yourself to them. And how could you lose your soul if you have the power to overcome death."

"Overcome death?" Sandré asked. "Is such a thing possible?"

"Of course it is, for those who hold command over the Dominion of Death." Yrgaeshkil fixed her deep, black eyes on his. "Think of it, Sandré. You could not only have *kostota* upon those who have wronged you at any moment in your life, but have the time to make their descendants suffer as well. You could even find them after they rejoin the cycle of Life, Death, and Rebirth and make their next life miserable as well. Such things are possible."

Sandré found himself nodding at the thought of making Julianna suffer, lifetime after lifetime, and just before he killed her every time, he would tell her why. Other people would suffer also, but none so much as the daughter of the man he hated more than anyone. And by torturing her spirit through the decades and centuries, Sandré would have *kostota* on Maxian Taraen as well.

"I'm listening," Sandré said.

SIXTEEN

Julianna and her Morigahnti had been traveling downriver, alternating between a quick walk and a jog. She knew they couldn't keep up this pace forever, especially with them trading off carrying Adept Gianni.

"We need to stop, Julianna," Faelin said. "Your Morigahnti are exhausted, hungry, and their spirits are nearly broken from having to fight their friends and family."

Before Julianna could respond, two Stormcrows flew down toward the Morigahnti. As they landed, both shifted into their human forms. One was Raze. The other was a girl with deep brown eyes, the color of polished mahogany, and her hair was neatly trimmed, unlike most other Stormcrows Julianna had seen.

"Lord Morigahn?" Raze said. His head sank down and his shoulders came up a little when he said her title. He couldn't quite manage to meet her gaze.

"Yes, Raze?" Julianna said.

"This is my sister, Rist, and she knows a secret."

Rist cowered when Julianna turned her attention to the Stormcrow girl.

"What's your secret?" Julianna asked.

"We're only about a day from Tyrth," Rist answered, speaking barely above a whisper. "There is an old Morigahnti temple just south of Tyrth, hidden in a dense wood. It has an entrance to the *ajorta*."

"What's the *ajorta*?" Julianna asked.

"It's how we're going to reach Koma City before Carmine," Faelin said. "The *ajorta* are passageways through the world between worlds. They were created during the Second War of the Gods. They can be dangerous but will be faster than traveling by foot."

Julianna turned back to Rist. "I don't suppose the paths in this *ajorta* have sign posts."

"No, Lord Morigahn," Rist said. "But we Stormcrows know the ways. We traveled them long before we served *Galad'Ysoysa*. We will lead you true through the pathways."

Rubbing her hands together, Julianna considered this. Between needing to beat Carmine D'Mario to Koma City and to stay ahead of any of the survivors from the *Stormrider* that might decide to come after them, the *ajorta* sounded like the best possible plan.

"Very well," Julianna said. She raised her voice. "Morigahnti, we will rest here for a few hours. After that, we make for Tyrth."

Several of the Morigahnti dropped right where they stood. Others spread out a little and settled to the ground. Julianna counted her followers. Twenty-one Morigahnti and eight Stormcrows rested next to the river. She did not count herself, Faelin, or Gianni in that number. The number did not surprise her. It was more than what Saent Kaeldyr had when he returned to Koma to fight against the followers of All Father Sun and Old Uncle Night, and less than what Saent Julian had after the Battle of Ykthae Wood, even counting Ilsaen's desertion.

Julianna looked over these twenty-one Morigahnti who had acknowledged her and pledged themselves to her. While none of them had actually bent their knees and spoken an oath directly to Julianna, by taking up arms against Sandré's followers, they had likely declared themselves outcasts to the rest of the Morigahnti. Some others might follow her on blind faith as Allifar had done, but likely most would not accept her until she passed the trials. Twenty-one Morigahnti followed her against the Kingdom, their fellow Komati, and who knew what other enemies, with no sign of allies anywhere.

Smiling, Julianna recalled feeling helpless as she and Faelin had first fled from Carmine and the Brotherhood of the Night, as well as from the Floraen Inquisitors. Then she promised herself she would stop running as she fled her enemies again at Shadybrook. At least now she was running toward something rather than fleeing. True, she had enemies in pursuit, as she would for the rest of her life. However, now she had goals and objectives beyond mere survival, and she had followers. Considering what she had started with, these twenty-one Morigahnti and eight Stormcrows seemed a legion to her. Now, to truly begin forming them into the army they would become.

"Korrin, Charise, and Alerick," Julianna called out. "I would speak to you."

The three Morigahnti stood, walked over to Julianna, and saluted.

"We have enough Morigahnti for three Fists," Julianna said. "I am naming you Fist captains. I will trust you to arrange these Morigahnti into balanced and effective Fists."

"But, Lord Morigahn," Charise said. "This is not the tradition."

Julianna cocked her head to the side and stared at her cousin. Charise swallowed.

"I think we need to give up any ideas of holding onto the traditions that we lived with after Grandfather Shadow was imprisoned," Korrin said. "I wouldn't be surprised if some families have manipulated our traditions to keep themselves in power."

"Collaen," Alerick said.

"Among possibly others," Korrin replied. "It makes no matter. They will either join with us and embrace the changes our new Lord Morigahn brings, or they will fall."

"Or we might," Charise said under her breath.

"Only if Grandfather Shadow wills it so," Julianna replied. "And as of now, he stands firmly with me and those who follow."

"Yes, Lord Morigahn," Charise saluted.

Julianna smiled, letting go of the air of command she affected when speaking as the Lord Morigahn. "I know this is going to be a challenge for you, Charise. You have no idea how much it means that I have your support."

Julianna pulled Charise into a hug. For a moment Charise remained tense. Then, relaxing, she returned the embrace.

"Don't think too highly of it," Charise said when Julianna released her, "considering my choice was between you and Sandré Collaen."

"She has a point," Korrin said. His eyes and mouth smiled that sly, trickster smile of his.

Julianna laughed. Even knowing him such a short time, she'd missed that smile. It was also good that they could find some humor to balance against their grim task.

"I have no argument against that," Julianna said. "Now that we understand, you three are going to be my Fist captains, and we know where our first destination lies, do we have anything else we need to discuss?"

"No, Lord Morigahn," the three of them responded.

"Good. Now go and choose your Fists."

The three of them saluted and moved off to discuss the arrangement of the twenty-one Morigahnti.

"That was well done," Faelin said, as he approached from where Adept Gianni lay.

"Thank you," Julianna said. "How many times do you think we will have to fight Morigahnti before they all accept me?"

"I cannot tell," Faelin replied. "Word has passed among the Stormcrows, but as you've seen, not all Morigahnti trust them. Once you pass through the trials, most will fall into line behind you."

Julianna nodded.

How much easier would this be if she could just get to the trials and pass through them? She could make that choice, and if she did, she would have most of the Morigahnti standing beside her as she went into Koma City searching for *aen Keisari* and *aen Tsumari'osa*. Doing so would give Carmine D'Mario that much more time to find the heirs and kill them. Then how long would the Komati have to wait before the next family in the order of precedence would have two children come of age? No, Julianna's only choice was to find the heirs before Carmine or any other Kingdom agents did.

While her Morigahnti rested, Julianna sat and prayed. She prayed for guidance as a leader, to keep the heirs a secret from the enemies of Koma, and that Grandfather Shadow would not have to choose a Word for Saent Julianna for a very, very long time.

EPILOGUE

Khellan stood in the snow outside the cave, wrapped in a wool cloak and fur mantle. Even as a Saent, the wind and cold bit deep into him. Occasionally the wind died for a few moments, and the heat from the fire inside the cave would linger, warming Khellan a bit. Then, the wind would come again, his teeth would chatter, and violent shivers ran up and down his body. Not for the first time, he glanced into the cave, wishing that he had the courage to stand up to Skaethak and enter the cave against her orders.

Her words still rang in his ears, biting colder than the wind howling around him. *Only the worthy may enter here. Your presence will undermine what* Galad'Ysoysa *has sent me to accomplish.*

Khellan spat at his feet at the thought of the word Grandfather Shadow had given him: *Unworthy*. The spittle froze into a long, thin icicle before sinking into the snow. He watched as the falling snow covered the tiny hole, wishing that he had been cast into the Dark Realm of the Godless Dead rather than have to stomach this demeaning existence for eternity.

"It doesn't have to be this way," a voice said behind him.

Spinning, Khellan reached for his belt to draw a weapon he did not possess.

A woman stood before him, her pale skin nearly the same color as the snow, long hair the color of blood blew about her in the wind. Bat-like wings rose up behind her, and ram's horns curled back from just behind her ears. She wore little in the way of clothing, just enough strips of leather to leave him wondering about the treasures she hid beneath. And Khellan did wonder. Even knowing who this woman was, he wondered and hated himself for wondering. It wasn't so much a desire of lust as it was a desire to be warm, and she looked warm.

He shook his head clear and reached for Grandfather Shadow's Dominions, but could not grasp them. He didn't have a *Galad'fana*, and while other Saents could draw upon the Dominions from the spark of divinity Grandfather Shadow had given them, Khellan supposed that being *the Unworthy* meant he would not be doing that until he did something to earn a new word.

Khellan opened his mouth and turned his head toward the cave to shout a warning to Skaethak. The Mother of Daemyns held up a hand, spoke a few words under her breath, and a heartbeat later, the biting cold was gone.

"Wha—Wha?" Khellan stammered. "What do you want, Yrgaeshkil?"

"I just want a moment to speak to you about injustice," Yrgaeshkil replied.

"And why should I allow you to poison my mind, Mother of *Lies*?"

"Why should I bother with someone who is named *Unworthy?*" she retorted. "Indeed, you have less power than a mortal. Grandfather Shadow doesn't trust you, and you are a joke amongst the other Saents of Shadow. You, Saent Khellan the Unworthy, would make a very poor pawn."

Heat burned in Khellan's cheeks and ears. "Then what do you want?"

"I want to give you the opportunity to become worthy."

Khellan fixed her with a skeptical look.

"Don't be so quick to judge me. We are not so different, you and I."

Khellan laughed. "You expect me to believe that?"

"No," Yrgaeshkil replied. "I don't expect you to believe anything. I am, after all, the Mother of Lies. But, I'd think that you, of all beings, would understand the frustration of an unjust title. I used to be Mother of Daemyns. Oh, people still call me that, but thanks to my husband, I have no command over that Dominion. I've been a lying bitch since the Battle of Ykthae Wood. Since then, I've been waiting for someone who might understand what it's like to be trapped as I have been."

"Why?" Khellan asked.

"So that I could have an ally, a confidant, someone willing to help me tear down and rebuild the celestial and infernal order."

Khellan licked his lips despite himself. Still, the cold wind did not touch him.

"How are you doing that?" he asked.

"Doing what?"

"Keeping me warm."

"You're not actually warm," Yrgaeshkil said. "Your body is still cold, but I'm not allowing you to perceive the cold. Feelings and perceptions always fall somewhere between a Truth and a Lie. Not even the gods can know the complete Truth about anything. It's a simple thing to lie to ourselves about our senses. In fact, lying about our senses is one of the easiest things to do, whether you are mortal or Eldar."

"I'm still wondering why you expect me to trust you," Khellan said, "if lying to me is so easy for you."

Yrgaeshkil shrugged. "Believe me or not. I am just here to deliver a gift that Grandfather Shadow should have bestowed upon you when you died." She stretched out her arm, palm up. Her hand was empty. "Take my hand for the briefest of moments, and receive what is rightfully yours."

Khellan stared at the goddess's hand. His heart and mind warred with each other, as did his loyalty to his god and his anger at being treated as he had been for his loyalty. Khellan had been the Lord Morigahn and de-served everything that went along with it, even after death. He should be the one protecting Julianna, because he had kept her safe during the Brotherhood attack long enough for Grandfather Shadow to finally break free. And what if Yrgaeshkil planned to betray and destroy him? How much worse could it be than spending all eternity as Saent Khellan the Unworthy, with all the celestial and infernal beings knowing that he was the living embodiment of his god's scorn.

Khellan reached out and grasped Yrgaeshkil's hand.

Some power flowed from her hand to his. *The Gray.* That word spread throughout him, filling him, not just his body. His mind and soul sang with that word filled with divine power. With that power, his ability to speak miracles from Grandfather Shadow's Dominions returned and resonated within him.

Yrgaeshkil shifted her grip on Khellan's hand, gripping it as if she were an old friend greeting Khellan after a long absence.

"It is a pleasure to make your acquaintance, Saent Khellan the Gray," Yrgaeshkil said.

"What?" Khellan asked. "How?"

"Words and Dominions are not fixed," the goddess replied. "Both the First and Second War of the Gods were nothing more than we celestial beings bickering for power." She released his hand. "Words and Dominions can be granted," she smiled and glanced at the cave, with its flickering firelight and the ring of metal on metal, "*and taken.*" Khellan looked from Yrgaeshkil to the cave and back again. The Daemyn Goddess gave Khellan a little bow. "I'll leave you to adjust to your new word, Saent Khellan. If you wish to speak again, call my name."

With that, Yrgaeshkil vanished.

The cold returned, but Khellan didn't care. Power filled him, power that seemed as old as the world itself. It was his, and he was worthy. All the ways that Kaeldyr had channeled his word to power and all words that Kaeldyr had spoken into miracles whispered in the back of Khellan's mind, including the final miracle he'd spoken.

Khellan repeated those words, drawing on the power within him. "*Mina suoda, Thanya'taen.*"

The fabled sword, Tears of Rage, the first weapon ever forged of Faerii steel, appeared in Khellan's hand.

He faced the cave and waited for the ringing of metal on metal to stop.

Soon after that, Skaethak walked out of the cave, carrying a crown of woven silver, inlaid with pearls and onyx. The Crown of Seven Shadows had been remade. Khellan felt that crown would make a nice addition to his growing collection.

Skaethak realized that Khellan had a weapon a moment after Khellan moved.

In the next moment, Khellan stopped the wind from blowing and the snow from falling.

The cold did not touch him as he lifted the crown from the snow and placed it on his head.

Thus ends the third volume of

TEARS OF RAGE

The tale continues in:

JUDGE OF DOOMS

About the Author

M Todd Gallowglas has been a professional storyteller at Renaissance Faires and Medieval Festivals for roughly twenty years. After receiving his Bachelor of Arts in Creative Writing from San Francisco State University in 2009, he used his storytelling show as a platform to launch his fiction career through the wonder of the eBook revolution. His *Tears of Rage* books, as well as *Knight of the Living Dead* and *Halloween Jack and the Devil's Gate* sneak onto several Amazon bestseller lists every so often. His short story "The Half-Faced Man" received an honorable mention in the Writers of the Future Contest. He is a regular fiction contributor for the Fantasy Flight Games Inc. With it all, he's still trying to wrap his head around his success and is trying to find the perfect balance between writing, gaming, and airsoft battles (because it's not as messy as paintball) on the weekends.

M Todd Gallowglas is a proud member of the Genre Underground.

Made in the USA
Middletown, DE
29 January 2017